Chloe's Story

Cause and Effect

D.S. Harders

i

Cause and Effect

ISBN 10 0692880690
ISBN 13 978-0692880692

Front Cover by Brandon BHouse
Cover models: Diana Hughes and Scott Harders

Acknowledgements & Dedications

To Michelle
Here's the first of many worlds you threw away.
I was worth fighting for.

For Chloe
Long may you roar.

Finally
Thanks to Diana Terrill Clark for helping me get through this
process and being an enabler. But most importantly, thanks for
putting up with my manic writing style.

About the Author

Born and raised in Arizona, Mr. Harders spends most of his time surviving in the southwest region of Arizona. When not avoiding plants and animals that want to put holes in you, he spends his time writing.

Chapter One

My name is Chloe. Just Chloe. I used to have a last name, but since the Collapse, it doesn't mean shit. The whole world fell apart and it took my world with it. When the global economy collapsed due to massive debt, the riots began, and anarchy rushed in like water through a broken dam. I lost friends, family, everything when the world fell apart into riots and crime. And it all happened virtually overnight, especially in the big cities like Los Angeles.

I can say from experience that trying to survive in an active war zone is damned-near impossible. I've learned that there are no good guys, just the lesser of two evils. Gangs fight each other for control of land and resources, taking what they can with fist and gun. It's times like this when being a woman; especially a healthy, fairly good looking one like me, becomes a curse. The world is ruled by the strong once more, and the strong take what they want.

Unfortunately, I didn't have the skills required to survive in the nightmare L.A. became. Hell, I hadn't really listened when officials or the news said you should have at least two weeks of food and water stocked. Inside a week, practically starving and searching for food, I'd been taken by a small gang of men and turned into their plaything. Rape and humiliation became my daily torment and I lost track of time as each hellish day blended into the next.

I'm sure there were many who might have thought that being an adult entertainment actress would mean that we could not be affected by rape. Let me tell you something, that isn't even remotely fucking true! In the industry there are rules, and we never do something we don't want to. No woman in her right mind wants to be raped, regardless of who she was or what she did in the world before. Rape is not just a sexual act, but one of power and control. Such an act destroys an essential part of a woman, makes her feel less than human. Thank God for my birth control implant, so at least thus far I haven't had to worry about bringing a child into such a fucked-up world.

My new "home" is now a room in what was once a Comfort Inn motel, I think. The few times I've seen the outside of the building, it reminds me of that kind of a place. A brick, two story structure with metal railings, now neglected, with chipped and fading paint. The pool in the courtyard acts as the only source of water, collecting what rain falls.

There is not enough water most weeks to drink, let alone bathe properly. I'm always thirsty and most days hungry as well. I'm pretty sure that I've lost at least ten pounds since the Collapse, maybe more, and I didn't have a lot to lose to begin with. My caramel-brown Latina skin has paled from a lack of sun. My hair is a matted, ragged mess, kept short to keep me humiliated. This has not dulled my looks in my captor's eyes. They like me thin and weak.

These days I'm chained to a bed in one of the better rooms the wreck possesses. The leader of the gang called The Crazy Eight is a bastard known only as Knick. Clearly it's not his real name, but given his love for knives, it's what he goes by. This man is the worst of the lot, ruthless and vile. Lucky me, I'm his favorite.

I've almost gotten away from these assholes twice, and that's why I'm chained up. Now I'm even left naked, just to help quash any thoughts of escape. I've had to adopt acting like I'm cowed while I look for any opportunity. Although as Knick walks in with a smug grin, I realize that today does not appear to be the day, damn it.

The sound of multiple gunshots reach my ears, although they're far away. No big surprise. L.A. is still a war zone. Gazing up through the holes in the boarded window, I see night is coming. That's when the wildlife really slithers out from under their rocks. The soft glow of candlelight gives me something to see by, but I can't be grateful for the light since it's Knick who brought the candles in.

I can feel his eyes on me and involuntarily shudder, clutching the tattered blanket that was my recent reward for pleasing him. Worse, his lieutenant, Knack, is with him. Knick may be an asshole, but Knack is the whole ass. He treats women as brutally as he can get away with; though he got a beating from Knick once for giving me a black eye. He's more careful about leaving marks, now. I like to think he has unresolved mommy issues. Regardless, he loves tormenting women and if he has a "knack" for anything, that's got to be it. I feel sorry for the three other girls.

There used to be five girls, but two of them ultimately got pregnant, and that's a death sentence here. The last thing the gang wants is more mouths to feed. So those girls were taken out into the street, their usefulness at an end and shot in the head. On the worst days, I think they are the lucky ones.

Knick stops an arm's length away, taunting me with a plate of food as he leers down with that smug grin of his. He's decked out like he always is, in grimy blue jeans and a dark vest holding a number of knives and pistols. All topped off with a black leather jacket that looks like it had seen some abuse before the Collapse.

Knick holds up the food. "You going to cooperate today?"

Asshole! As usual, he is going to make me sing for my supper. Already he's unzipping his fly. God, it's amazing what you'll do to survive. You find ways to rationalize the worst that gets thrown at you to live one more day, even if it means giving in to your rapist. I try my best these days to look like they've broken me, but I'm still trying to find a way out. Some way to get free of this nightmare.

"Yes."

"Yes, what?"

Fucking bastard! "Yes sir."

Knick shoots me a triumphant grin. "That's my girl."

Knick hands the plate to his lieutenant and motions for me to come forward. Knack is ogling me greedily, licking his lips like he sees a plate of ribs with all the fixings. His lecherous gaze makes me want to puke.

"Any time, baby," Knick states while presenting himself.

These guys don't even bathe regularly. Every time, every fucking time, I want to gag. But if I want to survive, I have to go through the motions and hide my real feelings. Probably the only bonus to having been a porn actress is that I have the skills to put these guys away fast. While Knick may have caught on, none of the others have.

As I crawl over, Knack continues to watch me with an expression that sends a chill up my spine. I'd rather be forced to have sex with Knick twenty times than be with Knack once. I don't pay much attention to the shadow moving behind the walking douche-bag of a lieutenant. There are eight men in the gang, so I figure there are a couple more waiting their turns. I certainly don't expect what happens next.

When I look up at Knick, I catch the glint of a blade behind his lieutenant. With uncanny swiftness, the blade cuts Knack's throat. Knick continues to grin down at me lecherously, totally unaware that his lieutenant's blood sprays against wall. The bladed shadow pulls the dying man into the darkness of the doorway. I don't know what's going on, but I do see this is my best chance of escape.

With all the pitiful strength I can muster, I punch Knick right in the junk. His face contorts into a combination of pain and anger. Life goes into slow-motion dread as the fucker starts rearing up to backhand me. I ready myself mentally, closing my eyes as if hoping not seeing it will save me some of the pain.

The anticipated abuse never comes. A wet gurgle forces my eyes open and I see a short sword sticking out of my tormentor's neck. All I can do is watch in shock as Knick falls to the ground, revealing a man behind him.

My savior is dressed in bits and pieces of tactical gear and leather, loaded with weapons and accessories. The upper part of his face is covered by a white mask, almost like something out of Phantom of the Opera. Or the Lone Ranger, maybe. A brown beard and mustache dusted with light gray graces the lower half of his face. His nose is strong and straight. His skin is lighter than mine, but we are lit by candles, so it's hard to tell his eye color. He's tall, not overly-muscled, but clearly strong enough to kill my worst abusers. Where has he been all my life?

Sitting there, I silently watch as he spits on Knick. Then he cleans the blade and sheathes it. When his eyes swivel to me—they're blue—my shock turns to horror as he pulls out a sawed off shotgun. I want to say something, plead for my life, but my voice has deserted me as I watch in wide-eyed terror as he pulls back both hammers.

All I can imagine is that he's going to kill me too. I'm shocked when instead he blasts apart the chain keeping me tied to the bed. The roar of the weapon startles me, followed quickly by a flood of relief. Then, as if my day hadn't been full of enough unexpected events, without any explanation, my liberator turns and walks away.

This is a world gone mad. Why did this man kill Knick and Knack? Why bother releasing me? Why not take me as a slave for himself? All my questions go unanswered as this stranger walks out of the room.

I know one thing for damned sure. I'm safer with him. Scrambling to my feet, I shake what's left of the chain free, and rush out the door.

Chapter Two

I race out of the room and into the hallway, which I find is full of dead bodies. Almost all of the Crazy Eight are there, throats cut or bullet holes in their foreheads. I've never been bloodthirsty before, not in my old life. But now? I feel an insane, gleeful joy take over for a moment as I see the bloodied remains of my tormentors lying dead. This is immediately followed by panic and once more I'm struck speechless as the man continues walking away.

Gathering my wits, I shout after him. "Please wait?"

Spinning, he points his rifle right at me. Fortunately, he relaxes before looking at me impassively, head slightly cocked. Clearly he's waiting for me to say something so I force myself to continue.

"Take me with you."

I catch a slight snort of a laugh right before he shakes his head. Then like that he turns and walks away once more. There's no way in Hell I'm going out into the concrete jungle by myself, even with whatever weapons I pull off the dead gang-bangers. So with grim determination, I surge forward, ignoring the stench and sticky blood under my bare feet and grab his shoulder.

With a guttural growl, he pulls away from my grasp as he spins, baring his teeth. It's like he's some kind of feral animal. In fact, given his behavior and his vicious ability to kill, I start thinking of him as The Beast. Still terrified, I raise my hands and speak to him in the most soothing tone I can manage.

"Look, I don't know who you are or why you did this, but I still need help! You know how to kill. I- I need that kind of training so I don't end up like this again. Please?"

The Beast regards me with some unnamed emotion. After a snort of disgust, he moves past me and back into the room that had been my prison, motioning for me to follow. I do so gratefully.

Inside my erstwhile prison once more, he starts by removing Knick's leather jacket. I'm taken aback when he puts it on me and then zips it up, covering some of my nakedness. Then he points to the dead men and makes a motion like putting on pants. The Beast holds up three fingers, taps them against his watch.

"I have three minutes to get dressed?"

The Beast gives me a curt nod and walks to the door. Stopping at the door, he keeps his back to me like he's standing guard. I'm left there with so many questions, but I've been given a time limit, and I'm sure I'll be sorry if I miss it.

My mind wanders as I scavenge clothes from my dead captors. Suddenly

I am thrust into freedom with the kind of man that should not exist in this totally fucked up world. While he is gruff, he's been kind to me in a way that makes me want to weep. Treated me with respect, almost like a lady.

Of the two dead assholes, Knick had the best clothes. A part of me was loath to wear any of it, but I need something. While some of it is bloody, I hope I can wash it later or find something else. What is really great is that Knack's shoe size is real close to mine, so I have a comfortable, though grimy, set of socks and boots. Finally I take Knick's knives so that I have something to defend myself with.

Once dressed, I swiftly kick both bodies. I can't resist. Wish I could have done more, but at least the bastards are dead. Can't think of a better fate for any rapist than to be dead. Unless there's a Hell. I hope there is, for scum like this. The Beast snaps his fingers to get my attention.

Reaching to the small of his back, he pulls out a revolver, checks the cylinder and hands it to me. I tentatively take the weapon. I've never used a gun. Never felt I needed to. Even felt like they were something I shouldn't have, considering I lived in one of the most gun-controlled states in the U.S. Hell, I'd never even held one. I realized a little too late that as a woman, having one was a necessity to keep from being preyed on by those stronger than herself. In hindsight, I probably should have always felt that way. Maybe if I'd had a gun and the training, I wouldn't have been taken to begin with.

My hand grasps the cold grip of the pistol. I'm so fixated on it that the barrel drifts towards The Beast. With a snort of disgust, he pushes the gun away from his direction as he transmits a scowl at me. I have to fight to keep from quailing under his feral gaze. I've been submissive to those jerks too long to lose the habit immediately.

"Never point a gun at someone unless you are going to kill that person." His voice is a growl, reaffirming my beastly name for him.

So it can speak.

With quiet grace, The Beast shifts his stance to stand beside me. Drawing a pistol from a thigh holster, he aims the weapon forward, finger off the trigger and points at that finger with his other hand.

"This is your number one safety. Keep your finger off the trigger until you are ready to shoot. Understood?"

I nod, a little numb over the fact that he can talk. "Y-, Yes sir."

The Beast appears unconvinced. Finally he shakes his head and holsters his pistol, then motions for me to follow. Pulling up his rifle, he heads out first, leaving the motel and picking up a pack as we exit.

Funny, "fresh air" and "Los Angeles" were not two things one said together in the old world. Yet as I walk away from my nightmare prison, it is the sweetest smelling air I've ever drawn into my lungs. I want to savor

6

the moment, but the combination of distant gunshots and my savior still walking away forces me to follow him instead.

It's a good thing I found comfortable boots before we got too far, for The Beast moves like he is incapable of being tired and we spend the rest of the night walking. We cross the 215, heading down University Avenue, all while moving slowly, and more than once he motions for me to keep to the darkest shadows available. Yet never once does he speak.

As the night progresses, my palm aches and is sweaty from gripping the pistol so tightly. I'm still weak, fearful and shaky, though I try to be brave as we wind our way through the city. My fate with the Crazy Eight was horrible, but certain. Now I am lost deep in the unknown with a man I know nothing about.

Before the Collapse, what I'm doing would have been considered insanity. Now it really isn't much of a choice. But the fact is, he saved me. I was willing to trust, to a certain extent anyway, if only because he'd allow me to see Knick and Knack lying dead before me.

We skirt the bulk of University Riverside, slipping through rundown or wrecked apartment buildings, student housing and residential areas. While the sporadic sounds of fighting continue throughout the night, we never encounter anyone. For that I am very thankful.

The moon is only half full, giving us a little light to see by, so I can't make out most street signs. You might think differently if you still live in a lit city, but L.A. is now dark. Scary dark. The latest street we come to is Galaxie Road. Giving a hand motion I can barely see, he moves forward and expects me to follow.

So I keep up, eyes darting from house to house, watching my footing as the road changes from paving to dirt. My feet are aching as we continue. Remember, I've been chained to a bed for a long time. The Beast starts up a hill and I sigh, plodding on at my best speed. Staying low, his rifle at the ready, he stops just short of the crest before a single house and looks around. The paranoia he exudes infects me, and I strain nervously to see anything that might be lurking in the darkness around us.

In what I've learned is his typical MO, he walks on toward the house without a word and clearly expects me to follow. While dark and hard to make out, the house appears up-scale and sits on top of the hill. Reaching the porch, I see another door resting against the wall, slightly blocking the way. I relax slightly when he pulls out a set of keys and unlocks the real door. Motioning once more, he ducks under the fake one and I follow him inside.

The Beast closes the door behind me, so softly I barely hear it until the lock clicks. I'm blinded when he flips a switch and a number of lights turn on. *What? Electricity? How?* I blink my eyes furiously as they adjust, and find myself in a living room.

Heavy black curtains completely cover the windows, probably to keep anyone from seeing the lights. The living room is well appointed with good furniture and, get this, it even smells nice. Sure is a change of pace from the musty, run down motel where I'd been a prisoner. It also serves to make me aware of the stinking clothes I am wearing, the odor of my unwashed body and I feel ashamed.

My savior doesn't seem to notice though, and says nothing. He just walks through the living room and into the kitchen. While I am curious about what he is doing, I am far too exhausted to worry and collapse onto a pale couch with a grateful sigh and work at the laces on my boots, pulling my aching feet free.

As I massage my feet, I hear glasses clinking in the kitchen. A part of me wants to ask what he's doing, but again, I am so tired. Given his choice to be silent, I hold my tongue as I relax into the soft, clean cushions of the couch instead.

He surprises me by handing me a glass of cold water. COLD water, and a plate of food. Okay, it's not room service, but after what I have been through, it's like Heaven came down from the clouds. Then it occurs to me that the last time someone handed me a plate, I was expected to perform a "service" in return. Worried, I look up at him, and he's shocked at my terror. Then I see realization pass over his face, and he backs up a little, palms up. Without speaking he shows me that I am safe here. I gratefully take the glass and plate as tears prick at my eyes and give him a tremulous smile.

The Beast simply nods and walks over to a chair the same color as the couch, plops into it and begins eating. Throughout it all, it seems like he hasn't changed at all. The rifle is still strapped to his chest, and all his gear is in place. Instead of dwelling on it, though, I focus on my food. Even though I'm exhausted and feel like sleep will overtake me, I am starving.

Chapter Three

I wake to darkness. I'm unsure where I am and feel uneasy. Quickly sitting up, I realize I am on the couch and it all comes back. The lights are off and I'm covered in darkness so thick, I feel like I'm choking on it. My breathing spikes as I frantically look around. The chair The Beast was in is empty and I am not ready for the panic I feel when I realize he's gone Has he left me here? Am I alone now? *Please, god, no.*

"Hello?"

My shaky voice is a little too loud, and I don't like the fear I hear in it, but a sense of dread builds. I get no reply in return, stuck in a dark room and utterly alone. As I scan the coffee table, there's just enough light for me to realize that my pistol isn't there—and I'm naked. As I'm trying to figure out where my clothes are, I spot a hint of light in the corner of my eye and look towards it.

An interior door that faces the living room opens and Knick and Knack walk through it. Fear floods through me. I tremble and shake my head, not sure what is real. Did I dream my rescue? While Knack holds the candle, leering at me as lecherously as he always does, Knick holds a plate of food. Wearing that smug grin, he walks forward and unzips his fly.

"You didn't think you could escape us that easily, did you darlin'?"

I whimper as I try to scramble away and fall clumsily over the couch. Desperately trying to get to my feet and run, I realize that I'm cornered. Before I can think of anything else, the two are on top of me, holding me down and laughing as their hands paw at my body.

My scream wakes me and I sit with a start, trying to regain my bearings in a living room that is softly lit. Before I realize it, or can think to be afraid of him, The Beast is holding me as I try to shake the nightmare. The relief of actually having escaped from my tormentors, being in a safe place, and wrapped in a completely non-threatening hug—I lose it. I weep like I have never wept before. The months of abuse, fear and the depredations of those evil men, it all flows out of me in tears and wracking sobs.

I can't even tell how much time passes before I'm finally cried out and even more exhausted than I was before. Without a word, The Beast lays me down on the couch and puts a sheet over me. Then he goes back to his chair and sits, watching the front door.

Lying there wearily, I try to slow my breathing, still deathly afraid to close my swollen and aching eyes. Slowly my gaze slides towards my silent savior and I begin to watch him. Minutes pass as he sits there, completely fixated on the front door like he expects someone to come through it at any moment. But that sight is strangely comforting.

I wake with a start, not realizing that I'd fallen asleep. Sunlight pours through the white curtained window and I let my eyes adjust as I survey the room. With a yawn, I stretch and sit up. A throbbing headache pounds behind my eyes. I push the pain away while I get my bearings. The Beast is nowhere to be seen and, wonder of wonders, breakfast is sitting on the coffee table. The pistol he gave me is next to the plate.

I'm astonished at what sits before me. Pancakes! Honest-to-God pancakes, with blueberries in them! Two tall glasses sit opposite the pistol, one with water and the other with orange juice. Both have a few beads of sweat on the glasses. A smaller plate holds some butter, a shot glass of syrup and a couple strips of bacon. I want to weep. Quickly I grab the first glass and take a sip of the juice.

Cold and delicious! Before I know it, I've downed the entire glass and start in on the pancakes. To say I was hungry would be an understatement. For months I have been slowly starving. The food tastes like ambrosia and a few tears actually escape before I realize I'm crying. I have to laugh at myself. Crying over food. But it's been so long since I had a decent meal and for a moment, I am back in the old world.

It does not take me long to polish off the plate and I sit back with a grateful exhale. I've gone from Hell to Heaven in the blink of an eye. Of course, as reality sets in, I wonder how long it can last.

The sound of an engine trying to turn over catches my attention. Slowly I get up off the couch, grab my pistol and walk towards the door the sound is coming from. While I try to use the same caution The Beast used in getting to the house, I'm pretty sure I suck at it.

As soon as I open the door, The Beast spins and points a handgun at me. I think I raise my hands faster than he spun around. With a snort of disgust, he relaxes and puts the weapon into the holster before going back to work on the engine of a rather large truck. I think it's a Ford, one of the big ones, but I can't say for sure since the decals are missing. The paint is a dark, metallic gray and the bed is enclosed with a camper shell. I walk into the garage in the hopes that I can determine what he's doing.

Getting closer, I realize what part of the problem most likely is. The front quarter panel has three bullet holes in it. A couple more are in the windshield. At some point his vehicle took some damage and now he's trying to fix it.

"What happened?"

He looks at me briefly, and if he weren't wearing a mask, I might think he had an eyebrow lifted at me. After a few seconds, points to the bullet holes. Then he turns his attention back to the vehicle and growls as he works on it. Clearly that's all the explanation I'm going to get. Instead of trying to get him to talk, I head back into the house while shaking my head at my companion's total lack of manners.

It's a nice little home with a commanding view all around. There's a pool in the back, although it's not much unlike what the Crazy Eight had. It barely holds any water, catching whatever rain it can. In other circumstances, it would have been a nice little place to live, away from the crazy traffic and city noise.

Idly I wonder, as I walk through the house, if this is his home. It's strange, but I find it deprived of any pictures that would possibly tell me. In the master bedroom there are a few picture frames on a dresser, but the pictures have been removed. Now they just sit there, blank and devoid of whatever memory they once held.

The closets are full of clothes. One has a man's clothes, mostly shirts and slacks, but also a few jeans. The other closet is full of women's fashion, someone perhaps a little taller than me. Some of it seems like it could fit, so I start examining what's there. I press my nose to the fabrics and catch a faint whiff of some perfume, something expensive. Opium? Chanel? I think I would have liked her, the woman whose clothes I am perusing through. She had a shoe fetish to match what mine used to be. Though now, with the world the way it is, those tottering heels are as useless as a pair of lady's gloves from the turn of the century. Though, the gloves might actually be more useful at this point.

With the Collapse, I lost everything. That includes my cell phone and my watch. I have no way to say for sure how much time passes as I rummage through the closet. The shoes definitely won't fit, even if they were practical, so I'll have to stick with Knack's boots for now. There are a couple blouses and jeans that would fit well enough. That means I can at least lose Knick's clothes, which will make me feel a lot happier. Grabbing a few things that seem to be my size, I make my way into the bathroom.

That's when I realize there is no running water. *Duh, Chloe!* Why would there be? My decadent breakfast put me in that state of mind, I guess.

There is a bucket of clear water sitting next to the sink with a stack of washcloths. Another bucket sits in the tub, next to the toilet. What strikes me as odd is the mirror. It's a jagged spider web. At least there aren't glass shards littering the floor. Compared to how clean and well-kept the rest of the house is, this makes little sense, but few things make sense anymore, so I decide to try on some clothes.

The jeans fit well enough if I roll the cuffs up, so I happily divest myself of the dirty, baggy pair that used to belong to—and still stinks of—one of my rapists. The water is a little cold. It's not a hot shower, but it's good to feel at least a little cleaner. Starting with one washcloth, I scrub the grime from my face. It feels so good to get what seems like years of dirt off my skin. I work my way over my body, realizing as I go that I really have lost weight. While I do get clean, I still feel soiled. I frown and keep scrubbing, uncovering bruises that still ache, and I remember where each one came from. I realize I'm crying again, and sink to the floor to let it out.

It's not as hard or as bad as the one after my nightmare last night, and I do allow myself to wallow a little. But it doesn't last long. I realize that I am safe. The Crazy Eight are dead. I am clean and full of good food and I will be okay. When the brief jag is over, I get a fresh washcloth and wash my face again. I want to wash my hair, short as it is, but I don't know the water situation, so it will have to wait.

It's also wonderful to use a toilet again instead of a reeking pot, even if I have to fill it manually. Clean panties, jeans and a slightly baggy blouse complete my transformation. With that done, I walk back out into the bedroom.

I find The Beast walking in as I make my way out of the bathroom. He stops cold and stares at me. Thanks to his mask, it's hard for me to tell for certain what he's thinking. His stare makes me uncomfortable, and I shift nervously. Maybe I shouldn't have made free with the clothes in the closet. He doesn't saying anything, though, and finally he turns and walks out, motioning for me to follow.

Wondering what he has in store for me this time, I dump Knick's old clothes on the floor and leave the bedroom. Somehow I just know he is going to ruin my buzz as I follow him back out into the garage.

12

Chapter Four

The garage door is closed and a man sized target has been set up against it. A number of cardboard boxes are stacked behind the target. Near the door is a card table and a pistol, along with a can that has a butane tip. The label on the can is black and green stripes, with big black letters that reads, "Green Gas."

The Beast picks up the pistol and racks the slide, inspecting it. Once he's done, he hands it to me. That's when I realize I left the pistol he'd given me in the bathroom. While I wonder if I'll be chastised for that, I take the one he is offering.

It seems light for a handgun, at least lighter than I was expecting, definitely lighter than the one he gave me yesterday. Something isn't quite right either, like it's a toy. Before I can inspect it further, The Beast snaps his fingers. I look up, worried that I'm in trouble. With a shake of his head, he actually speaks to me. His voice is deep and resonating. I like it. Too bad he doesn't use it more.

"Have you used a gun before?"

"No."

The Beast hangs his head and sighs. "Where is the one I gave you?"

"In the bathroom."

"Go get it," he growls.

Putting down the gun, I run to the bathroom, pluck the pistol off the counter top, and then run back. This is a man I don't want to make mad. He'd killed the entire Crazy Eight gang without making a sound. Anyone like that is a person you do not want to be angry with you. And I don't know him well enough to know if his kindness thus far is a fluke. Besides, I really am interested in what he's teaching me.

Once I'm back in the garage, he holds his hand out, so I give him the pistol. Taking the weapon, he pops open the cylinder and unloads it. He then places it down on the card table and gives me a glare that makes me feel six inches tall.

"For someone that wanted to stay out of the situation she was in, you don't seem very keen on staying free."

"I'm sorry." I'm shaking, but I don't want to insult him, so I try to hide it.

His mouth presses into a thin line and he takes a deep breath. "If I give you a weapon, you keep it on you at all times. Understood?"

"Yes, sir."

He picks up the pistol he just unloaded. "This is a revolver." He snaps the cylinder closed. "Holds six shots then you reload, which is slow.

13

Reliability is high."

"All right."

Putting the revolver down, he picks up the other pistol. "Semi-auto. Often holds more shots and much faster to reload. Better chance of jamming. This is what you learn."

Handing the newer pistol back over, I take it with a nod. "What do I do?"

It's funny. I was taught to be afraid of guns. That they were evil. But I've seen more evil than I care to, and none of that had anything to do with guns. I am eager to learn, and The Beast soothes me with his sure, comfortable knowledge.

Drawing his own pistol, he ejects the magazine and clears the chamber. I watch each movement, hungry for the information he's providing. Once done, he uses it to point at the various parts of the weapon.

"You aim by putting the front blade into the rear notch. They should be even across the top with equal light on both sides of the front blade. Some have dots, in which case you line up the dots." He shows me as he explains and, I don't miss a thing.

"Understood."

I watch everything he does. How he moves, how he manipulates the weapon, I pay attention to it all. Picking up the magazine for his pistol, he slides it into the weapon and motions for me to do the same. I notice the one for mine is different. Instead of bullets, it has white colored BB's. Still, I do as instructed and slide it in the correct way. It's harder than I thought, I have to use all the strength in my hands, which are still shaking a little.

The Beast then points to a lever on the side of the gun. When he holds it down, the slide rockets forward. I do the same and get a similar result. It must be loaded and ready, because he simply steps aside and points at the target. Taking a deep breath I raise the gun and take aim at the silhouette.

I'm expecting a loud bang when I pull the trigger. Instead, there's just a pop and the slide lightly kicks back. A small hole punches into the left shoulder and The Beast gives a short growl as he reaches up and moves my trigger finger. He then waves for me to try again.

Evidently talking time is done.

Slowly I work through the mag, pumping BB after BB into the target. With each shot, my aim slowly improves. When I do something wrong, my instructor will grab that part of my body that's not in the right position. While I'd appreciate something other than grunts, growls and hand gestures, my aim does get better.

When the magazine is finished, The Beast motions for me to put the gun down. I place the pistol gently on the table and watch as he walks over to a gun rack and pulls out a short rifle. Pulling out the magazine, he quickly loads it with BBs and then turns it over. Taking the can, he squirts something into it. I can hear what sounds like a hiss of air not unlike when filling the tire on a car.

With that accomplished, he starts showing me the functions of the rifle. First holding up the magazine, which he then inserts into the weapon. Grabbing a tab at the rear with two fingers, he pulls it back and then lets it go. Then he shows me the safety, clicking it from "safe" to "semi". Finally he shows how it should be held, bringing it up to his shoulder and making it appear like it's held in tightly. I nod, telling him that I understand.

The rifle is thrust into my hands and he waves towards the target. Nodding silently once more, figuring that two can play at that game, I take aim. The rifle's sights are slightly different. Given the initial training I had with the pistol, I quickly figure it out and before long I'm on target.

When the magazine is empty, he grabs my hands and runs me through the motion of ejecting the mag, slamming a new one in and then hitting a button which sends the bolt flying forward. With a fresh magazine, he motions for me to go again, but only after putting a third loaded magazine on the table in front of me.

Understanding what I'm supposed to do, I quickly shoot my way through my second mag. My shots punch neat little holes into the chest of my target. When the bolt locks back, I eject as I try to quickly grab the third. I'm a little clumsy getting the third mag in, but I slam it home and push the button and then I'm firing away once more.

Each shot now hits right where I want it to go, and I'm even being bold and aiming for the head. A little more than ten shots hit the head area. While there are holes all over, I've got more hits in the silhouette than outside it. I am elated! I turn to receive my praise from my instructor, only to find that I am alone in the garage.

This man is a buzz kill.

Chapter Five

Putting the rifle on the table, I grab the revolver. One by one I slip the rounds into the cylinder. I can see what he means about a semi-auto being faster to reload. Once it is loaded, I click the cylinder closed and head back into the house, looking for Mister Silent but Deadly.

When I walk into the living room, I find him sitting in the chair, working on a rifle that appears similar to the one I just used in the garage. It is easy to tell that these magazines are loaded with real bullets, bright brass glinting in the light. Evidently my performance was good enough that I'm being promoted up to the big leagues already. Also on the table is a black vest with numerous pockets and pouches attached to it.

I hold my tongue and approach him. Hell, two can play the silent treatment game. As I start to sit down on the couch, he makes a motion to stop me. Standing up, he grabs the vest and helps me into it. It's heavy.

What the Hell is in this thing?

As if reading my mind, he starts showing me what is in each pouch. The magazine holders are obvious, since most of them are clearly seen. One large pouch holds some bandages and first aid supplies. Another has a map of California and a compass. There's a number of miscellaneous items like a wrapped up length of cord, small sewing kit and matches. Finally, he pulls a watch from his pocket and puts it on my wrist.

The watch is beefy and appears to be solar powered. Before I can even ask he starts showing me all the functions like he's a salesman trying to sell it to me. Albeit the quietest salesman I have ever experienced in my life. Still, this watch does it all; altimeter/barometer, compass and even a thermometer setting. Bold lettering states that it's water resistant to two hundred meters and the casing looks like it could take a beating. Idly I notice as he runs me through the watch that he has the same kind.

Once done, he walks to the front door without a word and opens it. Standing there, he clearly expects me to do something, yet says nothing. *Yeah, I can do the silent treatment just as well, mister.* I stand there looking at him questioningly. Finally he appears annoyed and points out the door.

"Where are we going?"

The Beast simply shakes his head. Pointing at me, he then points out the door and at that it dawns on me what he's doing. *He's kicking me out!?* Of all the... I have to formulate my reply, not only quickly, but tactfully. I don't know how far I can push this man before he decides to kill me. At the same time, I know in my gut I'm safer with him than on my own.

"No."

Okay, in hindsight, I could have said more than that, but that was the only word that fell out of my mouth as I stand there defiantly. It is not well received. He growls in response, lip curling up just enough to show some teeth. Angrily he points at me and then out the door once more while giving me a withering gaze.

I want to run and hide as that pair of seething blue eyes bore into me as if they are red hot pokers. Somehow though I stand my ground. Shaking my head, I try to figure out how to plead my case. I am shaking again, and feel as if I am about to be sentenced to death row.

"I can't." I speak softly in the hopes of dousing his anger. "You can't expect me to be a pro after shooting a BB gun a couple of times? I need help, and quite frankly, so do you."

The Beast goes from angry to confused, his head cocked to one side. His grip on the door goes slightly slack as he stands there, staring at me oddly. I feel like I'm getting through to him, so I continue.

"I need way more training and you are trying to fix your truck. I owe you for my freedom and my life. You and I can work together. While you work on the truck, I'll take care of other things like making the meals. I can also help keep watch. You've got to sleep sometime, right?"

With a sigh he closes the door and I think I'm safe for a little while longer, but at what cost? The Beast stands there, head hung low, his masked expression a mystery. I really want to know what he's thinking. Finally he lifts his head up and makes a gesture around the place before walking back into the garage in what might be a manly huff.

I start breathing again, completely unaware I had been holding my breath as I waited for his decision. Since I'm staying, I take the rifle off and lay it on the coffee table. While I'm tempted to take the vest off as well, I realize that I should keep it on. If I'm going to have to wear it on a continual basis, might as well get used to its weight and being able to move in it.

Looking at my new watch, I find it's a little past eleven am. Perhaps making lunch will help cement our deal, so I head into the kitchen to see just what is available. The bonus is that it will give me a chance to finish inspecting the house.

The kitchen is like the rest of the house, simple and quaint. White appliances and cabinets match a white, stone tile floor. A wood table and four chairs dominate the small dining room attached to the space.

The Beast has a good stock of supplies, and I wonder more than once where he got it all. I find a half-eaten loaf of homemade bread in the fridge wrapped in plastic, along with some crudely cut ham and even some lettuce that still looks fresh.

Checking at my watch, I bring up the date. It has been a little more than a year since the Collapse. That means someone has to be growing food, right? How else could he have obtained fresh ingredients? Instead of trying to figure it out, I pull out the bread, ham, and lettuce and go to work making sandwiches.

I am just about finished with both sandwiches and I can still hear The Beast in the garage working on the truck. I swear sometimes he's simply beating it in the hopes that he can fix it with sheer intimidation. The final question needs to be answered though—mayonnaise or Miracle Whip?

Picking up both jars, I make my way out of the kitchen and into the garage to get his answer. I'm pretty sure I know already. I've known enough men to know that they often prefer Miracle Whip. Still, it's best to be sure.

In the garage, I find that a cable is hanging over the front quarter panel of the truck, and part of it looks shredded. I'm betting it got damaged from one of the bullets the poor vehicle had taken. The Beast has his head stuck in the engine compartment and is grunting and muttering curses under his breath as he works.

I clear my throat and he rapidly lifts his head up. Hands and arms are covered in grease and grime, and there is even a smudge on his right cheek. I can see the look in his eyes saying, "Now what does she want?" He ignores me and keeps working, so I clear my throat again. This time he's clearly annoyed.

First I hold up the mayo, then the Miracle Whip. Of course, Mr. Silence would understand what I am doing. With a wrench in hand, he points to the Miracle Whip and then goes back to work without so much as a thank you. Rolling my eyes, I go back to the kitchen.

I quickly finish the sandwiches and put everything away. To have a working refrigerator, along with decent food and clean clothes really puts me in a good mood. It's actually easy to forgive The Beast for his silence. With a smile, I pick up both plates and make my way back into the garage.

Nothing has changed. My savior still has his head in the engine compartment like he's locked in mortal combat with the metal creature. When I walk in, he barely notices me. Sparing a quick glance, he turns immediately back to the engine as I place both plates down on the card table where the BB guns once were.

Pounding twice against the quarter panel, I then pick up my sandwich and start eating. I make a few yummy noises until, with a sigh, he stops and washes his hands thoroughly at a sink using a bucket of water and some degreaser. Once done, he picks up the sandwich and starts eating. I get an almost imperceptible nod for thanks.

We eat in silence, and it drives me crazy. Even when I was held captive by the Crazy Eight, there was always noise of some kind. Men talking, the other girls sometimes crying, and, when the gang was away, chatting with each other through the walls. Hell, there was even the occasional gunshot coming from somewhere. Evidently the cost of my freedom was being locked in a cone of silence with someone who preferred not making any noise at all.

When The Beast is done, he points at me and then clasps his hands together and places them against his head, making the international sign for sleep. He then points towards the house. While I understand what he's telling me, it doesn't make much sense.

"It's just turning noon," I state with a glance at my new watch.

I get a disapproving glare as my first response. Then he walks over to the driver's side of the truck and pulls out a map, bringing it over to the card table. Opening it up, he points to a location that is circled on it. Then he points to me, then himself and then makes a walking motion with two fingers before pointing back at the map.

"Well, let's go."

The Beast shakes his head and points at the light and then makes a hand motion of his palm going down. I give a nod, understanding that he wants to move out after the sun goes down. Guess that means I'd better try and sleep now.

"All right. I'll try to sack out on the couch."

A snap of his fingers gets my attention. He points towards the direction of the master bedroom and then makes the sleeping motion one more. I'm bemused by yet another kind gesture from this man. A little more than an hour ago he was ready to boot me out the door and leave me to the wolves.

"Okay," I reply as I grab the empty plates.

I decide to leave before he changes his mind. It would be nice to sleep in a soft bed for once instead of a dirty floor, though the couch is more than comfortable. Dropping the plates off in the sink, I then make my way into the master bedroom to get ready. After I dispose of Knick's clothes.

A part of me desperately hopes that once I'm rid of as much of that asshole as possible, that I might sleep better. I really doubt it though. Someone who's gone through what I have is bound to have psychological issues. I'm pretty sure I've got PTSD. Oh, what I wouldn't give for a good psychologist—and a bottle of whiskey.

The thought of some alcohol hits me and after I toss the clothes into the waste bin, I head to the kitchen to search for some. On a top shelf in the pantry, I spy a few bottles of liquor. Struggling to reach them, I have to use the lowest shelf as a step and fortunately it supports my weight.

I pull down two different types of rum, a bottle of gin, half a bottle of bourbon and what I hope for, whiskey. I take my prize out with me, grab a tumbler and check to see if there is any ice. I'm so happy that the freezer works and there is some ice, along with a half dozen bottles of vodka. *Jeez. I guess he has a favorite.* Dropping two cubes into the tumbler, I retreat to the bedroom.

Depositing the glass on the bedside table, I unscrew the cap on the bottle. Pouring a quarter of a glass, I put the cap back on and set the bottle on the table. I inhale first, and then take a warming sip, closing my eyes as the potent liquid fills my senses and burns down my throat. With a happy sigh, I slowly sip the rest of the glass, pondering the situation I've found myself in. Just a day ago, I was at a dead end, and it was only a matter of time before Knick lost his temper and I would be history. Or my birth control would finally wear off and I'd get pregnant, which was another death sentence. And here I am now; relaxed, well fed, getting ready to sleep in a comfortable bed for the first time in, well, at least since this horrible nightmare had begun.

While I do take the vest and gear off, the habit of getting undressed kicks in and I decide against it. While The Beast has made no moves on me, I'd like to keep it that way. I'm obviously not interested in having sex in the near future, and maybe not ever again. The thought of my nightmarish past is making me unhappy and so very angry. I quash it and take another sip. Taking my time, I enjoy the ice cubes too. They are another luxury.

Finally, I feel I might be able to get some sleep, so I lay down on the bed. Grabbing the pillow, I try not to dread the thought of closing my eyes. Deep down I know Knick and Knack are waiting for me, ready to violate me all over again. I deny them attention in my waking world, but fear they will appear as soon as I try to sleep. I realize I've clamped my eyes tightly shut, and I know that's not going to help. Once I relax, though, I have to fight to keep the tears away. I breathe deeply and try to find a happy place in my past; a hike in the wilderness or my trip to Paris. My last thought as I finally sink into slumber is the hope I don't dream.

Chapter Six

Waking up screaming is no way to wake up. My nightmare was the same as the last, with those two bastards lurking in my psyche sometime after I closed my eyelids. The quiet room in the suburbs seems like a vacation spot as I sit up in the bed mid-scramble in an effort to escape their grasp. The stench of their B.O. still clogs my nostrils and makes me want to puke.

My thundering pulse slows as I realize where I am, and I find my throat feels scratchy, like I've been screaming too long. *Shit!* The Beast bursts into the room with a pistol at the ready and startles me, sending my pulse racing again. When he sees me alone, his mouth presses into a thin line and he holsters the gun. Walking over, he sits down at the edge of the bed and pulls me to him in a warm hug. It's a silent invitation for me to let it all out, so I do. And it's awful, but feels good too.

You'd think given the deplorable treatment I've had at the hands of bad men over the past year that I wouldn't be able stand being touched. Yet there is something about The Beast that's different. I can't explain it, really. His presence is simply comforting and completely non-threatening.

It takes me a while to get it out of my system. I feel worse physically, but a lot better emotionally. A good cry is solid therapy, I decide. Once I'm ready to be done, I nudge at The Beast to let him know his work here is done for now. I also give him a nod and stupidly tenuous smile that I regret as soon as I try it. Brushing away the few lingering tears, I nod again that I'm better now. As usual, he says nothing. He simply stands up, taps his watch and then flashes ten fingers to let me know I've got ten minutes to get ready. Once I give a thumbs up, he leaves the room, closing the door softly behind him.

I groan as I get up off the bed, then sigh and make sure I'm as put together as I can be in my state. These damn nightmares make it feel like I haven't gotten any sleep. I see he's left some food behind, another sandwich. I practically inhale it as I dress, along with another glass of orange juice. And I thank my lucky stars my protector is feeding me.

Slipping on the vest, I grab and holster my assigned pistol. I check twice to make sure that I've got everything he's given me, and exit the bedroom in record time. I'm pretty sure that "late" is no longer a woman's prerogative I am allowed to possess, not with The Beast in charge.

I find him in the living room, decked out and ready for war. He's got a different rifle, bigger than the last one. On him it looks manlier, and I hold back making a comment about boys and their toys.

Checking the table, I see that my assigned rifle is still there, but something has been added to the barrel—a long, slender black can that's a little over six inches long. I notice a similar one is attached to his rifle. Wondering what it is, I point at it.

"What's that?"

I'm almost startled at the sound of my voice, he follows to where I'm pointing before responding. Raising his rifle, he makes a motion like he's pulling the trigger, and then puts a single finger to his lips. His explanation completed, he finishes what he's doing before jumping up and down. At first I'm confused, but watching him, I realize he's making sure his various gear doesn't make any noise. Hence the cans, they quiet the weapon. *Oh, a silencer. Okay.* And Mr. Silent but Deadly still lives up to his name.

Grabbing my rifle, I slip the sling over my head and make sure I'm ready to go as well. Clearly he rigged my vest properly when he put it together, for when I jump up and down, I hardly hear anything making noise. As I finish up, he snaps his fingers to get my attention.

"Yes?"

From behind, he plucks a pistol off the chair, with a silencer attached to it. Handing it to me, he points to the revolver and makes a motion to give it to him. Doing as I'm told, I pull the revolver out and trade pistols before examining at it.

This one is heavier than the revolver, but not excessively so. The slide has "HK USP .45 Auto" imprinted on the slide. I pop the magazine out and see it has twelve rounds in it. I then slap the magazine back in. It feels as beefy as it looks, as I can barely get my hand around the grip.

"Listen up."

To hear The Beast start talking immediately gets my notice. Apparently he only talks when it's really important or when he can't easily get something across via hand signals. So I give him my undivided attention.

"Magazine has twelve rounds and one is already in the breach."

"All right."

"Your rifle has thirty rounds in each magazine, with one already in the breech. Six more mags in your vest. It only shoots in semi-auto. The suppressor on it works very well. When we leave, you move as I move, do what I do. If we move into a building, let the rifle lay against your chest and draw your pistol."

"Okay."

"The pistol suppressor is not as effective, but certainly not as loud without it. Only use it indoors unless you have no other choice."

"Yes sir." I answer briefly and respectfully. While I want him to be able to count on me, really, I don't know what else to say.

The Beast certainly doesn't appear convinced, but gives me a nod anyway. "I'm turning off the lights. Let your eyes adjust and when they

22

are, tell me and we will go."

This time I simply nod and watch as he walks over and turns the lights off. We are bathed in darkness; I always forget just how dark the world is now. My breathing spikes as memories of my recent nightmares give me unwelcome and ugly visions for a moment. With effort, I force those thoughts away as my eyes adjust to an almost complete lack of light. It gets better when he pulls one set of curtains open, allowing a little moonlight in.

"I'm good."

The only reply I get is a barely perceptible nod and he quietly opens the front door, letting more soft light in. Silently he ducks out, rifle at the ready, as if expecting to get shot at. Doing as I'm told, I manage to do the same thing without tripping over my own feet. Once I'm through the door, he closes it as softly as possible and then locks it.

The muted sound of gunshots can be heard far off in the distance, the usual music of the night these days. I gaze out across the residential area the house commands. Here everything is quiet and peaceful. There are no fires or sounds of fighting somewhere nearby. It's also devoid of the smell of burning tires, human waste and who knows what else. This area appears to be entirely lacking in human habitation. The stars are very bright now, only muted by the brightness of the moon. I don't think I'd noticed the moon in years, but now it is a powerful beacon and I feel almost too exposed.

As we begin our trek, at first I wonder if we are heading back to the motel where he had saved me from. It certainly seems like we are taking the same route, and still avoiding University Riverside. I vaguely recall Knick saying something about a powerful gang having control of that area. The Beast keeping away from it makes me think Knick wasn't full of shit for once.

We take Linden Street instead of going further to University and pick our way through wrecked, burned or clearly looted homes and apartments. Ruined vehicles are scattered obstacles, some abandoned wrecks and others are burned out hulks stripped of anything valuable. We're about to cross the Escondido Freeway, moving through a collection of rundown and burned out apartment complexes when The Beast abruptly stops. When he drops into a crouch, rifle held forward, I do the same. I'm quaking in a combination of adrenaline and terror.

I strain to see or hear anything that can tell me what is going on, but I'm terrible at it. What is he hearing or seeing that I can't detect? I'm trying so hard that I don't realize I'm holding my breath at first. Internal pressure tells me I need to breathe. As I exhale and take in a deep breath, I finally see what he has already spotted—a raiding party.

My hands tremble and I aim as steadily as I can. The hate that rushes through my system helps steady me. Slowly I see The Beast move his non-trigger hand back and motion for me to stay put. I fight to rein in my breathing as I watch what must be at least a dozen men dressed in haphazard armor. Bits of leather, street signs, tires and even auto body parts cobbled together as protection.

What makes me want to pull the trigger are the five people they are herding along, three of whom are women. Clearly they are going to be slaves, and I know damn well what is going to happen to them. But I also recognize that there are too many bandits and try to keep my rage in check. That doesn't stop my angry tears and I hate myself for my impotence. I really, REALLY want to free those slaves.

Once they disappear behind a set of apartment buildings, we wait a little longer before we start moving again. I did not expect him to break out into a sprint, though, and he quickly disappears ahead of me. Silently I curse as I try to catch up, fast yet still being quiet. That's when a lone raider comes around a corner of one building and spots me.

Chapter Seven

I think all the air in my lungs evaporates when the raider stares directly at me. Adrenaline makes time slow as my body tries to decide between fight or flight. There's not a detail about this guy that isn't burned into my memory like a photograph.

The man is clad in a crude mishmash of leather, plastic and metal armor. Dirt and grease smudges his face and a dark colored, open face motorcycle helmet protects his head. A stop sign is bent to fit over his left shoulder. The same has been done to a speed limit sign, which is clad over his right thigh, proclaiming fifty-five MPH in scratched paint and minor dents. The metal bits are strapped to him with thick, brown leather straps. What appears to be a handmade rifle has a meat cleaver attached to the barrel with faded silver duct tape.

From his expression, he's just as shocked as I am. Eyes are wide, mouth agape as he stares like I'm an illusion, a phantom. Slowly his eyes slide down from my face and stops at my rifle, causing his eyes get wider still.

There's a reason I was chained in that motel room. I am a fighter. My body quickly decides what to do. As I start to realize I need to shoot, the raider sucks in a breath to shout a warning. Everything is in slow motion as I try to swing my rifle up to stop him before he can scream his fool head off. If he gets off a warning, that raiding party will be on top of us in no time. There is no way I am going to end up back where I was yesterday.

My rifle isn't even pointed at the raider yet when something happens that neither of us expects. The Beast appears out of the darkness behind the man. Melting out of the shadows, he covers the raider's mouth with one meaty paw, and shoves a knife into the man's throat. I can't watch, so I turn away and look in the direction the raiding party went. There are gross, wet sounds behind me and I repress a shudder. I thought I was ready, but maybe I'm not.

When the raider is dead, The Beast makes a hiss of a noise. I turn to see him dragging the body into the darkness of an alley. Quickly following, and trying not to be squeamish, I watch as he gives the body a once over. He takes a handful of bullets off the corpse and then starts moving in the direction we are heading. I fall back into the pattern we'd used before; following closely on his heels and moving when he moves. The entire time, I try to get the image of the man that just died out of my mind

Linden Street crosses over the Escondido Freeway, both of which are full of wrecked and abandoned cars. Many are missing their tires, most likely pulled off to be used as a source of light and heat. Unfortunately none of them that I can see are like his truck, so I hurry to keep up.

Los Angeles is surreal as a post-apocalyptic environment. A city that once had a population of over ten million is now practically empty. No insane traffic. No mobs of people everywhere you look. No streetlights. For once I can see the stars over the city. If not for the fact that a girl could be killed or raped at any moment, it would be great to just lie on a roof and sky watch.

But not tonight. Though I could use a break, my feet are killing me! We pick our way through at least four miles of potentially hostile city, decked out in full tactical gear. Come to think of it, it's not just my feet that hurt. The loaded vest is weighing me down, my back and shoulders sore. But I try to keep my complaints to myself. The situation I am in now, difficult as it is, is still a thousand times better than my previous one.

What I can't get over is that my silent companion doesn't seem to be winded in the slightest. Before the Collapse, I exercised a lot. I was fit and in shape. I had to be for my job. Hell, even though I had lost weight because of my captivity, I thought I was in good shape. Oh, my lost innocence. Tonight has harshly informed me otherwise.

Keeping in line with the Escondido Freeway, we finally arrive at a business park full of shops catering to the automotive industry. Moving cautiously through a line of trees, we carefully approach the back of the complex.

All the way, through the entire four miles, or however the hell far we've traveled, The Beast moves from cover to cover. When he moves to a car, so do I. When he moves to a building, I do the same. He has quickly taught me that when he is looking one direction, I should be looking the other. So every time we stop, I put my back to his and look for anything hostile. When he moves, I cover him and vice versa. Aside from the one raider, we've encountered no one, and I'm delighted about that. And even though my feet ache and my body is tired, I feel like I'm actually helping. This makes me happy.

Slowly we make our way to a business titled, "California Hard Parts." With hand motions, he tells me to follow while he moves to a smashed-in glass door. As he advances through the entrance, he draws his pistol and a flashlight. I check behind us one last time before following him into the dark building, praying there's no one in it.

When my foot lands on a section of glass, there's a crunching noise that is far too loud to my paranoid ears. Evidently my savior agrees. I can easily spot his scowl with what little light there is. All I can do is give a sheepish smile. *Hey, moving silently is new to me. It's not something I learned in, Bad Girls do Spring Break!*

Once we are deep into the building and can hardly see, to my great relief, The Beast turns on his flashlight. A spear of blue light shoots out.

When I turn mine on, I get the same. It's enough to see by, barely. I want to ask why the blue, but silence is key to us remaining unnoticed so I hold my tongue as he starts a search.

I really wish he'd given me a list so that I could help him find what he needs. Instead, I take up a position at the front counter and watch the entrance. Sweat forms on my hands as I hold my rifle tightly to me. All the while, the only thing I hear is The Beast rummaging through the parts and occasional gunshots from the dark city.

Staying extremely focused, I don't see anything out the front of the building. I keep reminding myself to breathe normally, to relax a little. When he taps me on the shoulder, I damn near jump out of my skin and start to spin my rifle in his direction. He must have known I'd react like that, because he gently stops my shaky attempt to aim at him. I'm just proud that I hold in the scream that is poised on my lips.

The Beast gazes at me impassively, holding a finger to his lips. *No shit.* Pointing towards the front door, he pulls up his rifle and starts to back out. I wonder if he actually had any success as I follow him out into the night.

At first I imagine we are heading back the way we came. Instead we hang a right and head up Russell Street until it empties out onto Main Street. Silently we move into a convenience store on the corner but find nothing of value. Guess I shouldn't be surprised, and The Beast isn't either. Oddly, we still don't double-back.

Leaving the corner store, my savior leads us south down Main Street. Both sides of the road feature auto service shops of all kinds. We stop in a couple and after a sweep, find nothing he can use. Luckily, we find no bandits either.

The Beast continues to lead us down Main Street. We stop at a little red brick building, with a sign in bold green lettering, "Weed Care." I'm surprised or maybe bemused as he walks up to the entrance and I am left on the sidewalk trying to figure out why he's going into a medical marijuana establishment. Then I shrug and close the distance. It's not my business if he wants to imbibe. These are hard times.

Interestingly enough, the building is still intact, even with a few cars smashed against its only slightly damaged brick walls. Bars cover the windows, some misshapen where people tried to bash their way in. The reinforced steel front door is littered with dents, slashes and bullet holes. It has withstood it all, but as The Beast moves up and pulls out a lock pick set, I laugh quietly because the day has come when the door has met its match. I move closer and watch his back as he goes to work.

I feel like I'm getting better at keeping watch, but it makes me nervous being in one place so long. All I can hear is The Beast working away at the lock for what has to be at least a couple of minutes. It feels like an eternity, and even the slightest sound makes me jumpy. Finally he's successful and the door groans far too loudly. Tapping my shoulder, The Beast moves in with pistol at the ready and I quickly follow. Once we are in, he closes the door behind us and locks it.

Turning our flashlights on, blue light illuminates display cases full of various kinds of medical marijuana. I am awestruck by the different variety of weed. The Beast pulls a wadded up pack out of his backpack and then starts filling it.

"Why are you taking this stuff?"

I don't get an answer. He continues the process of going through the stock, identifying which ones are worth taking, and stuffing them in the bag. I shake my head and considering that the front door is locked and practically impregnable, I head into the back of the shop with my pistol at the ready.

I'm not mentally prepared for what I find.

Chapter Eight

Evidently the business was also the proprietor's home. Past another reinforced door, fortunately open, and at the end of a short hallway, I find two doors. There's something in the air that crinkles my nose as I reach for the first one on the left. Of course there are a lot of new and exciting odors in the new world, so I pay it no mind. The door on the left opens into a bathroom. Doing a quick search, I find a tube of toothpaste and stow it into one of the pouches on my vest. Then I move on.

The other door is closed and locked. At first I think about going back and getting The Beast and his handy lock pick skill. Then I decide to handle it myself. Am I getting cocky? Maybe. But I've got a silencer on my gun, so I put a round right where I think the lock should be.

This is something else the movies lie to you about. The noise is louder than I expect it to be, especially in the confined space. I've got a slight ringing in my ears. On the upside, I'm rewarded by the door opening slightly.

Pushing the door open slowly, the blue beam of my flashlight cuts through the darkness as I peer into a bedroom. The stench of something long dead makes me gag, and when I see the two bodies entwined in a bed, I gasp and spin around—right into The Beast. Once more I damn near jump out of my skin as he glares down at me. When he looks past me, his expression changes, lips forming a grim line. Moving me gently aside, he steps into the room to inspect the scene.

Pulling the handkerchief from my vest, I wrap it over my nose. Don't know that it helps much, but I want it anyway. Then I follow him to see the sad and depressing sight that lies before us.

Lying clasped together are two corpses, male and female. The man's dead hand holds a pistol near his head. Both their heads are together and the bullet seems to have passed through them both.

I watch as The Beast lets out a sigh, walks up and drops to one knee. He whispers softly next to the bodies as if in prayer. When he is done, he carefully takes the pistol out of the dead man's hand, cleans it off and makes sure it's on safe before slipping it under his belt. Then he takes a sheet and lays it over the bodies. Once done, he points for me to leave and I'm actually happy to do so.

Leaving the room, he closes the door and levels a baleful gaze at me. *Oh shit, what did I do?*

"Do not waste ammo," he whispers harshly.

"I'm sorry," I reply back in a whisper. "You were busy. I figured I could handle it myself."

The Beast shakes his head and rolls his eyes. Clearly he does not agree with me, and in retrospect, he's probably right. It was a stupid thing to do and I'm surprised I didn't end up shooting myself. As he heads back into the storefront, I follow behind without argument.

Sitting in the middle of the floor is the pack that he had been loading up. When The Beast gets to it, he picks it up and hands it to me. Given my recent faux pas, I don't say anything about the extra weight he hands me and put it on.

As quietly as possible, we make our way back out of the shop and head down Main Street before cutting through a residential area. I'm pretty sure that we are now heading in the direction of home. Well, his home. Sort of mine, too, for as long as he lets me stay. Hopefully we can make it before the sun is up.

Like everything else I've seen up to this point, this neighborhood is no different from the others. Most homes are broken into, some burned and we pass one with a car crashed into it. Christmas decorations are still noticeable through some broken windows. It appears that the orgy of destruction made its way down the street and left, leaving no one behind, save for the tattered remains of a dead body here and there.

We end up taking Third Street and passing under the Riverside Freeway. After we get past the train tracks, we encounter a stretch of road with businesses on one side and houses on the other. Nothing appears to have survived the destruction of this particular stretch of road as we quietly move along the darkened streets.

I can see a high school coming up on the right just as a bullet careens off the asphalt ahead of us, followed quickly by the sound of a gunshot. Once again I freeze an idiot deer staring at oncoming headlights until The Beast body tackles me.

Gritting my teeth as I hit the road hard, his body presses down on mine. Rolling off of me, he comes up smoothly into a kneeling position and fires twice. Then he moves up to a tree for cover. Cursing under my breath, I scramble to my feet and get to cover as well. As I move, I hear the suppressed cracks as my companion provides cover fire for me. Another gunshot comes from the other side and I try not to panic as I hear a lot of shouting. *Shit! There's more than one. We're not surrounded, are we?* It sounds like the voices are closing on us.

The Beast taps my shoulder as a bullet hits the tree he's using for cover. He motions for me to head back the way we came and make a left turn at the end of the nearby building. I move, running for the corner as he fires three more shots before following. While I hear return fire, no bullets hit anywhere near me as I make it to the corner. My heartbeat is hammering in my ears as I try to control my erratic breathing. I try to remember what he taught me thus far as I dash around the building.

Someone was clearly thinking the same thing. I see a raider move into view at the opposite end of the building. For the second time today, I'm faced with having to take the life of another human being. It's not as easy as the movies make it seem. Especially when you are so close you can see the same fear you feel in their eyes. But this is no longer a civilized world. If I don't kill him, he'll kill me, or worse—I end up a plaything-slave again.

Fuck. That!

While I've already got him dead bang, my hesitation gives him that split second to raise his own weapon. We both shoot at almost the same instant. I'm able to pull the trigger twice, right before his bullet hits me.

Thanks to my moment of indecision, I almost end up getting killed. My opponent's bullet misses my chest by a fraction of an inch and rips across my left inner bicep instead. Heat, quickly followed by intense pain, sears through me. My attacker drops in a spray of blood and stops moving.

I stand there in shock, staring at the man I've just killed. I can't dwell on it for long. The Beast runs up behind me and spurs me into running. Snapping out of it, I run with him as fast as I can, which is a challenge. In my estimation, The Beast is a little over six foot tall, while I'm five foot and change. He can quickly cover more ground than I can. Although I find that pain and adrenaline are good motivators.

Before I know it, all while trying to catch my breath through aching lungs and burning leg muscles, The Beast is pushing me through the broken window of an office building. As I'm trying to crawl away, he's diving in himself. Hunkering down beneath the window sill, he draws his pistol and waits.

I glance around to see that we are in a long office, littered with desks, tipped over file cabinets and all kinds of trash. Fortunately, there's nothing or no one else. Gritting my teeth in pain, I grab my bleeding arm as I push myself across the trash-strewn floor and sit up against the wall. Silently he holds out one hand, motioning me to be quiet. After a moment I realize why. Focusing outside my pain for a minute, I hear the sound of running feet and multiple voices. There's a debate before they take off down the street.

The Beast pulls a dental mirror from his vest and uses it to watch outside. All I can do is sit there in a combination of pain and fear, ready to break down over the thought of being someone's slave again. Hell, I don't even care about the raider I killed. He would have taken me back to those men, and I know very well what my life would have been. It takes every ounce of strength I have to keep it together as I wait to see if we're going to be in another shootout. The pain and smell of my own blood reminds me of my mortality. I am shaking and trying to stay chill, but it is really hard.

Relief washes over me when he puts the mirror away, holsters his pistol and moves over to me. Quickly he pulls my hand away from my wound. Plucking the flashlight from my vest, he puts it in my bloodied hand and motions for me to shine it on my arm. As I do so, he sets his rifle down and opens the first aid kit hanging off his vest to start treating me.

"There are fragments of something in your arm," he whispers. "I'll need to pull them out. You need to be quiet. Bite down on this."

Handing me a short stick with leather strips wrapped around it, I nod grimly. Taking the stick, I bite down on it. Mentally I ready myself for the pain as he pulls out some forceps and starts pulling out the pieces still in my arm.

Fuck!

I want to scream. I definitely cry as I screw my eyes shut and try like hell not to make any noise. I can't force myself to look as he works at my arm. I swear he's just digging into it for fun and I wonder if I'll have an arm left by the time he's done! All the while, I try to breathe through the pain, grunting accompanied by an occasional muffled groan.

I'm shaking and weak and soaked in sweat when he's finally finished. Spitting the stick out of my mouth, I take in huge gulping sobs of air as the pain becomes a more tolerable throb. While he says nothing, I swear I can see a hint of pride in his expression as he finishes wrapping a roll of gauze around my arm and tapes it up. I really want a hug, but he merely pats me on the shoulder and picks up his rifle, ready to move out. That will have to do. We need to get out of here.

Evidently there's no rest for the wicked.

My left arm flares up in protest as I push myself cautiously to my feet. I move as quietly as possible and get up to his position. My sweat-damp clothes feel cold in the still night air. It feels like hours have passed, but it is still dark out, so it only felt like eternity. Carefully looking out the window, he apparently sees nothing and points towards the door. I give a nod and we sneak up to it. Just as we are about to leave, my stomach decides right then and there that it wants to empty its contents. The Beast kindly holds my hair up as I vomit into a nearby garbage can.

Fuck, I hate dry heaves.

When I'm done, The Beast says nothing. He simply hands me a canteen and I splash some water on my face before taking a drink to wash the burning out of my throat. Patting me on the shoulder, he cautiously opens the door and peeks out. When he's sure it's clear, we quickly make our escape. The first hint of the sunrise starts to become visible on the horizon, a warning that we need to move fast.

Chapter Nine

With great relief we reach the house at the top of the hill. I've been shaking and weak for the last mile, but have not complained. It wouldn't help, just slow us down. I stumble through the doorway and into the house as The Beast follows me in, closing and locking the door behind us. While I'm exhausted, I still have rifle in hand and I don't relax until the lights turn on and I'm sure we're alone. Even then, my trembling legs betray me.

Finally, knowing we're safe, at least for the moment, I sink onto the couch and close my eyes. Everything hurts, but my arm is on fire! With a Herculean effort, I slip the rifle sling up over my head and lay the weapon next to me. Then I work at getting the vest off and hold it, uncertain. Do I need to keep it with me? Put it away somewhere? My weary mind has no answers.

Oh God, I am so tired.

Jolting me from my reverie, I realize The Beast has approached and is waiting for me to do something. When I open my eyes, I see that he has a bottle of vodka, a washcloth and another bandage. *Oh.* Inspecting my arm, it dawns on me that he wants to change my now-soaked and bloody bandage. With a sigh, I sit up and nod. I hope this won't hurt as much as it did before.

The Beast sits beside me with an air of professionalism. I can only imagine he was some kind of medic in his former life. He is careful as he removes the soiled gauze. I'm not keen at seeing my own blood and whatever else is going on there. Slightly sickened, I look away. My stomach lurches as he opens the bottle of vodka and I know what's coming next, so I grit my teeth.

Bringing over a cushion, he places a towel on it and then rests my forearm on the towel. Lifting my arm, he holds the washcloth under the wound while he pours freezing cold alcohol over it. I don't scream, but I whimper something fierce and stomp my feet as he cleans it.

Once he starts redressing the wound, I catch my breath as the pain subsides. As he finishes, traumatic memories of the day start flashing through my mind. The man that The Beast killed in front of me. The one I shot right before getting hit myself. A wave of emotions swamps me and I can't help it. I start crying. I hate appearing weak in front of such a strong man. It sucks the pride right out of me. But considering the state he has seen me in—my absolute worst—I guess he might not mind terribly if I have a bit of a meltdown.

Given his normal, day-to-day behavior, I would never expect any compassion from The Beast. Yet every time I have a break down, he simply holds me and lets me cry it out. With the roller coaster of emotions life has thrown at me, it is just the medicine I need. As exhausted as I am, I literally cry myself to sleep in his arms.

With a gasp, I open my eyes and realize I'm in the house and all right. At that I relax, trying to purge the memory of the two men that died last night, one at my own hands. I could see both their faces so vividly in my nightmare, chasing me and covered in blood. Shutting my eyes, I fight back the tears that threaten to fall. I really shouldn't cry over two pieces of shit that would have gladly raped me forty times over. I seem to be at a weak place right now, though, so I let them fall and then wipe them away.

Slowly I become aware of the smell of cooking bacon and it brings me to memories of more pleasant days. I fall back to sleep and live in the past for a time before reality slowly intrudes. The sound of The Beast working on the truck tramples through my dreams and forces me to open my eyes. I swear he's trying to beat the poor thing like it's a red-headed stepchild.

I'm in the master bedroom, lying on the soft bed, tucked under the sheets. Looking down, I find that I'm still in my clothes. At some point The Beast carried me from the living room and tucked me into bed. Amazingly, he still hasn't taken advantage of me, something that I still cannot fathom, but for which I am endlessly grateful.

Maybe he's gay?

Actually, I find that hard to believe. Something about him just doesn't strike me as being gay. I've always had really good gaydar. Then there's that mask. I've not seen him with it off so far. Makes me wonder if he even sleeps with it—not that I've seen him sleep.

Wait. Does he sleep? He must! He's a human being, right?

Checking my watch, I find it's two-fifteen in the afternoon. My arm throbs slightly, but it feels better than last night. Throwing off the sheet, I slip out of bed and head into the bathroom for a much needed call of nature in a somewhat working bathroom. What I find when I walk in is a happy surprise.

The pail of water for the sink and toilet are there and full as usual. But what causes my train of thought to derail is that the bathtub is full. Of clean water! A towel and washcloth hang on the rack. Putting a finger in the tub water, I find it's a little warm. I can't even imagine the luxury of a tub full of water, but I certainly do not intend it to go to waste. Such a thoughtful and touching act does not go unnoticed and I make a mental note to

34

somehow thank The Beast when I'm done. Right now I practically rip my clothes off, do my business in the toilet and then, relishing every moment, sink into the tub.

It may not be as hot as I'd like, but it's still heavenly. I dunk my head under the water and let what warmth there is loosen my sore muscles, careful to keep my bandage dry. After a good soaking, I pick up the soap and wash cloth and clean the grime off my tortured body. Don't think me ridiculous if I tell you more tears were shed. I've had a rough year.

Once I'm done, I reluctantly climb out of the now chilly water and dry off as dirty water gurgles down the drain. I grin when I see my fingers are actually pruney. Wrapping the towel around my body, I go to the bedroom closet and choose the other pair of pants that fit well enough. I notice that there's a woman's version of his uniform shirt, so I choose it instead. The heavy black fabric isn't comfortable, but it has a lot more pockets. Now that I'm dressed, I grab my tactical vest and head out of the bedroom to see what the new day holds in store for me.

Breakfast waits for me in the dining room. A plate holds a stack of pancakes while a smaller one has scrambled eggs and a couple slices of fried ham. No orange juice though, just water this time. I guess our luxuries are running out. Still the smell of food makes my stomach growl and I sit down, digging into my breakfast with zeal.

Before I know it, I've finished everything before me and almost wish there was some more. I'm sure I have to play catch up after being in captivity and getting fed mere scraps each day. Washing the remnants of the meal down with the last of the water, I stand up and put my vest on. It's time to see how The Beast is faring with the truck.

I'll be honest. The scene is almost comical. There are even more parts either hanging out of the vehicle or scattered about. He seems to have almost dismantled half the engine. The Beast is practically half way in the truck, grunting and growling as he works on the metal monster.

"How's it going?"

The Beast looks up, and even through his mask I can tell he's annoyed. With a scowl he dips back into the engine compartment and pulls out a part, tossing it onto the concrete floor with a grunt of disgust. It's circular and has a bullet hole in it. Pretty sure it's the alternator.

"How many parts do we need?"

I get two fingers in response.

"So we head out at sundown?"

The Beast stops and stares at me and, I think he's in shock. Yet I swear, just for a second, I catch just a hint of a smile tug at the corner of his lips. Finally he grabs a towel and wipes some of the dirt and grime from his hands before grabbing the map.

Laying it down on the card table, he straightens it out. Pointing to where we are, his finger traces a line down south to a spot near the Escondido Freeway. My rough guess is that it's about the same walking distance as last night. Albeit the university sits practically right in between here and there.

"What about the university?"

The Beast shakes his head and traces what is almost a straight line south from our location before heading west to the target spot. The map shows hardly any streets that direction, so I'm betting on a lot of hiking through brush and hills is in my immediate future. *My poor aching feet.* Instead of issuing any complaints, I simply nod.

"All right. I'll get my things ready."

Once more he gives me another look, similar to the one last night when he bandaged my arm in the office building. It makes me just a little happy that I could surprise him. With a nod, he heads over to the sink and starts washing his hands while I leave the garage in search of my rifle.

Chapter Ten

I was so right about our hike, because that's what it turned out to be. We trek through a lot of hills and brush, although we leave via the back door instead of the front while there is still some daylight. It actually gives me an opportunity to get more of the lay of the land. A few houses are found down the hill to the south and west. Low mountains are to the north and east.

Remembering what I do of the map, the path he traced out is probably following the mountains as they head south. I also remember his rule from last night about walking as he does and follow as we navigate through ravines in between hills.

I am more sore and tired than I was the night before, but somehow feel more ready, if that makes any sense. I mean, I've killed a man now. There's no going back from that, is there? And as exhausted as I was last night, my sleep was fortifying and I've had more food today. This time, though, I grab some energy bars I found in the kitchen to keep in my vest against another total energy failure.

By the time we hook up with a set of railroad tracks, the sun is down and darkness settles over the city. As usual, when the sun goes down, the violence starts in earnest. Sporadic gunshots can be heard everywhere, but fortunately none of them are close to us. I think I've been shot enough, thank you very much.

Following the tracks, we can usually move where there's cover to keep anyone from seeing us. When there isn't, The Beast motions me to move quickly to the next spot of cover while he aims his rifle, ready to shoot anyone that takes a shot at me. Once I'm across, I take aim while he moves. I feel heartened, like I'm beginning to get the hang of this.

Throughout our trek, we're both silent. I have to learn by doing, and as I've discovered, experience is a vile, evil bitch. My arm still hurts, but not as much as last night. Still, every time I raise my rifle, it complains. I mentally complain back at it when it stings. *You don't like that, bitch? Well don't get shot next time, got it?* Hey, I never said I was completely sane. And my internal voice keeps me going.

The path he's chosen is a good one. It stays away from the university and skirts most of the residential housing areas. Part of the way we have trees or dirt berms to use for concealment as we get within sight of our goal—a Ford dealership. I'm actually excited! We might be able to find everything he needs in one go and get the hell out of this cursed city.

The Beast stops and points his rifle at our destination. My heart skips a beat thinking he's spotted someone, but I quickly realize he's just using the scope on the weapon to scan the area. I turn and put my back to his, watching our rear until he's done.

Reaching back, The Beast taps me twice against my side and I can hear him start moving. Turning, I move with him, sticking as close as I can. I try to stay within a couple strides, as I watch for any hostiles. We continue following the tracks as they cross under the freeway.

The tunnel is pitch black and fear spikes in my blood stream. Afraid of the dark? Me? Absolutely! Fortunately The Beast turns on his blue light flashlight, so as soon as I'm well-in, I do the same. The tunnel is damn near choked with trash and debris. Fortunately we don't see anything else as we cautiously wade through some of it and towards the dealership.

Exiting the tunnel, we turn the lights off and move through some brush and up a hill to a fence line. The Beast shrugs his pack off and pulls out a small set of bolt cutters, quickly going to work on the fence. I watch all around us as he snips the chain link. The lot is full of vehicles, some that might be the same model truck that he's working on. Even better, I don't see anyone.

When he's done, he puts the cutters away and slides his pack through the opening. I take a quick moment to see what he's done and notice that he's made an opening just wide enough that one can crawl through. The Beast lies on his back, rifle clutched against his chest and shimmies through the opening. Once he's through, he's up in a kneeling position and motions me to follow before providing cover.

Per instructions, I do as he does. Lying on my back, I push myself through the breech with my legs. Once inside, I'm up with my rifle at the ready. Again I find that I'm feeling more confident, and I don't know why. Is it because of surviving my first firefight? Killing someone? I don't have time to dwell on the reason as The Beast moves low through the parked cars.

Amazingly, a lot of the vehicles still appear to be in good shape. While tires are missing from some, many appear untouched. As we find a likely-looking truck, my companion stops and slips under it before turning his flashlight on. I catch a hint of blue light as he inspects the vehicle. When he growls, I know it doesn't have what we need and we move on.

On the third truck we find one of the parts he's searching for. Once again, anything we find goes into an extra pack he brought along. And that pack ends up on my back. At least I don't have to sing for my supper, so-to-speak, so I should be grateful. I certainly choose not to complain.

As we get ready to move, the sound of voices reach my ears. Adrenaline spikes in my veins as I kick his boot while he's under our fourth truck. Using a car as cover, I peek through the dusty windows just enough to see a group of men heading our way. A couple of them hold makeshift torches.

The Beast moves up, peers through the windows as well and I hear a low growl coming from him. When I look over at him, I notice he's taking the magazine out of his rifle and then reaches into a large pouch that's tied to his left leg. From it he pulls out a large, circular magazine and clips it in.

Oh shit!

"What are you doing?"

As I breathe the question, there's a gunshot. I jump as my nerves wake up, and at first I'm worried we've been spotted. Checking the direction of the gunfire, I see gang members have only shot the lock off a chain and are now opening the gates and strolling in, laughing and talking.

The Beast kneels up, and watches the men that have wandered in. They are all wearing a hodgepodge of clothing that's typical of the gangs and raiders that live in the city. Most of them aren't even armed with much. I see some pistols before catching sight of a hunting rifle and a shotgun. In the end, I count fifteen men in all.

When I feel a light tap on my shoulder, I look towards my savior. The Beast's voice is practically a whisper on the wind as he explains what is about to go down. My heart is thumping in my chest and that hyper-reality feeling is closing in again.

"We're going to wipe them out. I'll take the hunting rifle, you aim for the shotgun. After that, keep shooting 'til they're all dead. Try to be precise. Don't waste ammo. Understood?"

I just nod. I'm too nervous to say anything. My mouth goes dry and my hands start sweating, but I can keep it together. Better than last time, anyway. I think. We watch the group of ruffians make their way into the service center, all the while yelling and laughing.

When The Beast breaks cover and moves, I reluctantly do so as well. I'm doing my best to be as quiet as he is—an impossibility—while staying low and hiding behind the various vehicles. We cautiously reposition for a clear shot, taking our time and finding a large, heavy vehicle that makes a good obstacle. As we come up on it, he points to a spot right behind the front wheel and that's exactly where I plant myself.

At the same time, The Beast lies down under the front bumper and sets up two legs that were folded up under his weapon. We watch as the raiders set a tire on fire, the light illuminating the service bay they are in, with black smoke curling off it. I shake my head. I used to recycle. I drove a hybrid. I was an environmentalist. Now people are setting tires on fire and nobody is left to care.

"You take the first shot," he whispers just loud enough to hear.

Even though he can't see it, I nod in reflex and start lining up my target. Mr. Shotgun is standing there, laughing at a couple of skinny idiots who are trying to take tires off of a tall pile and failing miserably. I want to laugh. As loud as those idiots are, we could be talking normally and they probably wouldn't hear us. They're typical gang members; playing one-up games, bragging about their crimes and inhumanity toward their fellow man.

As tires go bouncing and rolling across the service bay, I take careful aim. The Beast has my rifle fitted with a scope that gives me a small red dot to aim with. It's so easy to use that it's kind of scary. Once more I've been thrust into a position where I'm going to have to take a human life. I try to remind myself that these men aren't human, not in a moral sense of the word. I've seen firsthand what scum like this are capable of. I don't want to kill innocents, so I've been listening to their boasts about their conquests and kills. I'll be damned if I'll be a slave to their like ever again. That's when I have an epiphany of sorts. I realize that I'm armed, somewhat trained and no longer have to be afraid of these assholes.

With the dawning of my revelation, all my nervousness disappears. Resting the red dot right on the center of Mr. Shotgun's chest, I wait for the right moment. When he stops moving and starts to point and laugh—I pull the trigger.

Chapter Eleven

A spray of blood fills the air as I shoot Mr. Shotgun twice in the chest. I can barely hear his strangled cry as he drops. Almost simultaneously, The Beast tags Mr. Hunting Rifle right in the head and his brains splatter all over the back wall.

Some of the raiders have a deer in the headlights moment and that makes me feel a little better about having my reaction yesterday. It does not stop me from aiming and firing at the next man, and then the next. Five more drop as I tag two and The Beast hits another three with short, automatic fire before the rest scatter to the cover of a nearby car.

Those that are left start popping up from cover to shoot one or two shots. Some just poke their gun over the vehicle and fire wildly. None of them are shooting directly at us, which tells me they have no idea where we are.

The Beast taps my ankle before getting into a crouched position. The thought of breaking cover does not appeal to me, but I can't exactly argue while we are in the middle of a firefight. Quickly we reposition, heading closer to them, but at an angle. Stopping at a small truck, he drops to the ground and sets up again. This time he motions for me to do the same

So I lie down, rifle in front of me, and start aiming. It's a little uncomfortable with the gear on the front of the vest pressing into me, but aiming steadily is really easy. As I peer through the scope I start to realize why we are doing this. Some of the bandits hiding behind the car have their feet and/or knees visible from underneath the frame. The Beast taps me on the shoulder and points left while he starts aiming right. I assume he's waiting for my shot, so when the dot is on a foot, I shoot.

I hear the bandit scream before he drops to the tarmac. His buddy does the same, at least until The Beast puts one in his head. I quickly shift aim and try to put a bullet in the head of my target. When his head pops back and he quits moving, I know I'm successful. Adrenaline surges and I pop another round out before I realize it. *Oops.* I glance over at The Beast, but he doesn't notice. Good. I refocus and keep shooting.

One man realizes what we are doing and drops down with his pistol, trying to see us and return fire. The Beast is faster and puts a round in his skull, his body slumping onto the concrete, blood pooling. He would have done better to run.

At this point they know where we are and I guess they figured hiding wasn't really working out for them. Highly possible they were out of ammo as well. Three of the five that are left yell a war cry and scramble over the car they were using for cover, various sized knives in hand.

All I can do is watch in awe as The Beast leaps over the hood of our truck while drawing his sword and pistol. As he closes, he shoots one of the two that are still behind their vehicle. The bullet hits the man in the shoulder and sends him spinning out of sight. I cover my companion by getting the other, and I watch him go down in a spray of blood.

Then The Beast is on top of the three and fighting like a demon. The bandits on him try to hack and stab, only to be blocked at every turn. My savior has flipped his pistol around, using it not only as a club, but also to parry their attacks. At first I swear it's like he is toying with them, because he simply blocks their attacks and doesn't strike back. When he finally does—it's a violent work of art.

Blood flies as he begins cutting into them. A slash across an arm. A stab into a leg. The fight doesn't last more than a couple of minutes before he has cut and stabbed each man at least half a dozen times. Then they are on their knees, blood dripping onto the tarmac, the fight gone from their eyes. Rapidly, The Beast puts a round into the head of each bandit and then spits on them.

I catch movement from the corner of my eye to the left. Spinning with my rifle ready, I see two men making a break for it, one clutching his shoulder. Clearly they've decided this is not a place they want to be. I can hear more than one set of feet running as The Beast stands up and takes aim. Quickly getting to my feet, I hear the suppressed cracks from his pistol and hear one bandit scream.

By this point they are disappearing into the darkness. I see a moving shadow and take aim. My fifth shot connects and the raider stumbles. I follow up with two more and he falls face first onto the road.

The Beast shoots twice more and then ejects the mag and replaces it with a fresh one before holstering the weapon. Rushing over, he grabs his rifle. Tapping me on the shoulder, he starts moving back the way we came. I have so many questions as to why, but I know this isn't even remotely the time for it and follow as quietly as I can.

Making me slip through the cut in the fence first, The Beast quickly follows. Once through, he zip ties the cut closed. I can't even begin to understand why he would do that. I make a mental note to ask later. I need to know why he does some of the things that he does. It's the only way I'm going to get any better. I just hope he will actually talk. Conversation doesn't seem to be his strong suit.

We backtrack the way we came, and as we cross under the freeway, I notice a sign in the moonlight. A WalMart. Alright, I'm sure everyone would laugh at me, but it's just possible there might be some things I can use. You know—of the feminine hygiene persuasion. As such, I grab his shoulder.

Evidently that was not a good idea, because he spins and bares his teeth at me. It's like I just grabbed a tiger by the tail. All that fear I lost in the recent firefight comes back to say hello as I back away, hands up to appear non-threatening.

Quickly he calms down, looks a little abashed, and then cocks his head, an action I learning means he wants to know what I want. I kneel down to make sure I'm not easily seen and he joins me. Pointing the direction I would like to go, I whisper.

"WalMart."

Now he looks at me like I'm crazy and shakes his head. As he stands and turns to continue walking, I narrow my gaze and stamp my foot against the dirt. When he glares at me. I point at the store once more, this time with a determined glare of my own.

He glowers impatiently, taps his watch with his finger, and again shakes his head. I am uncertain, but stand firm, then put my hands together in a pleading motion. Finally his head sags, he shrugs, and motions in the direction of the store. I silently jump up and down, clap my hands with glee, and follow him towards the dark store.

I know it may sound silly, but there's a reason I'm looking for tampons or pads. That bullet that ripped through my arm took my birth control implant with it. That's what The Beast was picking out of my arm last night, though there could have been shrapnel too. Hell, it was painful enough to have been an entire battleship! Given that, I'm trying to plan ahead. No birth control implant means my cycles will begin to come regularly again, and that means I will need some way to handle it.

The one nice thing I always liked about WalMart is that they were almost always laid out the same. To say that this store is a shambles would be an understatement. Various styles of shelves are overturned, baskets lay here and there, racks of clothes are pushed over, the garments scattered all about.

Of course with no electricity the place is beyond dark. We use our flashlights to pick our way through the detritus, all while checking for any hostiles. A stench of death also hangs about the store, and I can only imagine there's a body or twelve somewhere in here. I try not to think about it as I make for the aisle where the feminine hygiene products should be.

I would have thought a place like this would have been completely cleaned out. Oddly, it was not. In fact, some things were still on the actual shelves. Bottles of mousse and hair spray still sit there like they were recently stocked. The Beast even finds a box of bandages which he picks up and slips into a pocket. I can't repress a smug smile before continuing on.

To my despair, this WalMart has apparently been sacked by a horde of female raiders, who took every single last damned tampon and pad that was available! I search twice and come up empty. Standing in the middle of the aisle, I feel like crying.

Fuck!

The Beast taps me on the shoulders. I turn and see that he's smiling at me. It's slight, but apparently he finds my situation amusing. I shoot him a scowl that lets him know I do not find the situation funny in the slightest.

Looking down, he unzips the pouch for his trauma kit and fishes around in it. From it he produces two tampons, still in the wrapping and hands them to me. Then he leaves me standing there, staring at the two objects in my hand like they were the Holy Grail and all the time he had it in his pocket.

Son of a bitch!

I realize that I'm now alone and spin around. The blue light from his flashlight dances about as he heads further back into the store. Quickly I catch up, wondering what he's looking for in the ransacked aisles.

Tonight has given me a lot of questions. Questions that I really need answers to. I'm sure there's a reason behind everything that he does. Some kind of tactical significance. While he doesn't like talking, I still need to know.

"Why the blue light?" I whisper softly.

The Beast sighs. "It's not as easily seen from a distance."

"Okay," I nod. "Why zip tie the fence closed?"

Stopping, he looks at me and I think he's annoyed. "To reduce the possibility of someone tracking us. Wishful thinking is not a survival trait. So never leave an easy trail for the enemy."

Turning around, he heads into the sporting goods section and starts rummaging among the remaining goods. A few things catch his eye that I guess other people didn't think they would need. A few cans of jellied fuel, a couple packages of glow sticks and a sleeping bag that he tosses to me. Having my rifle in hand, I do not catch it fast enough and it drops onto the floor.

The sleeping bag rolls and stops against a shelf and I quickly pick it up. When I do, I notice a small box under the bottom shelf and take a closer look. It's a box of shotgun shells and I smile. This is probably what he was really searching for, so strolling up behind him, I shake it near his ear.

For the first time since I met this man, he actually smiles. It's a full grin that is practically from ear to ear as he tries to take the box. I snatch it away and give him a grin of my own, and he narrows his gaze.

"Should I give this to you? You didn't even want to come in here. But, you did make me a bath today. And gave me a couple of tampons. So, I guess you can have it."

I give him the box which he stuffs into his pack. Then he takes the sleeping bag out of my arms and ties it off under my backpack so that my arms are free. It feels a little odd to have it there, but at least I don't have to carry it. Quickly he stows the other things we found inside my pack and we head back out so that we can get home before sunrise.

Chapter Twelve

The next six months fly by in a blur, but I'm still having nightmares. Thankfully they are less frequent now, but Knick and Knack still lurk in the depth of my psyche, waiting to pounce once I let my guard down in my sleep. Every time I wake up screaming, and I hate myself for my weakness.

Not long after The Beast and I raided the medical marijuana store, I learn the reason why. Weed—Cannabis, to be precise—has been known to help with PTSD, among other things. So The Beast has me take a small amount, either in a tincture or an oil, in an effort to help me before making me talk about the shit I've been through. Since I am having fewer nightmares following his therapy, I think it is helping.

At this point I've killed at least nineteen raiders, three of which I did with my knife. Under the tutelage of The Beast, I've gotten better quickly. I'm not sure how much I attribute to my teacher and how much is sheer determination. Of course, he knows I have a grudge and good reason to hate those fuckers. And while he doesn't say it, I swear every once in a while I catch a proud smile from the corner of my eye. I pretend not to notice. Since I don't get a lot of praise from him, the silent creature he is, I take the smile as my due reward.

Speaking of my instructor, he's still gruff and still keeps me at a distance. Yet he's most definitely not cruel. He does little things that brighten my day, like cooking breakfast and making sure the tub has water. He seems to notice the little things in life that give me joy. Clean water, good food, tampons. And though I am grateful for his kindness and thoughtfulness, I am thankful that through it all, he hasn't made a single move on me.

Because, let's face it, I'm a mess. Being raped constantly for who knows how long will do that to a girl. I simply do not have a libido. At all. In fact, my only drive right now consists of staying alive and killing bandits. For someone who did what I did for a living, I never could have imagined myself being so disinterested in sex, but there we are. I guess it can happen to anyone.

Not that The Beast isn't attractive in his own way. I figure he's in his forties and in good shape—from what I've seen anyway. That long hair and beard certainly give him that rugged look my old self would definitely find sexy. No, he's not overly muscled, but he is strong, damn fast and has the stamina to keep going all day. Sometimes I wonder when he sleeps, if ever. He's up before I am and I'm always asleep before he is. I just wish I could see under that mask.

I don't feel quite as sore or exhausted these mornings. The exercise, treks and combat I've been put through have gotten me into better shape than I ever have been. I find every day that I'm stronger and have more endurance. I've put back on all the pounds I lost while I was in captivity, and have added much more improved muscle tone than I had before the Collapse. We range further out in the same amount of time and I'm able to carry more equipment.

I've also gotten faster. Not just sprinting, but also in a fight. Along with exercises and tactical training, The Beast has taught me hand-to-hand. Both bare fist and with a knife. Given the fact that men can still out-muscle me, he keeps drilling me to use a blade as much as possible.

My stealth skills have improved as well, and two of my knife kills are thanks to that. Being able to sneak up on a raider while he's unaware and then sink my blade into his throat before he knew what was happening, well that was an exhilarating experience.

With a groan, I wake up from another restless night's sleep. My nightmares are less frequent, don't get me wrong, but they're not gone. God, when it isn't Knick and Knack, it's one of the two raiders I first saw die. Usually it's the kid, and I can see his face as clearly as that night. His eyes wide with fear as he starts to yell for backup. Then The Beast is there, stabbing the kid in the neck and spraying blood all over me.

But I don't wake up screaming so much these days. I guess even major traumas like I've been through eventually lose their teeth. Besides, I've got teeth of my own now. Slipping out of bed, I do my morning business, then clean up. The nightmare means I haven't slept well, so I'm tired. What I wouldn't give for a Starbucks right this minute.

I have a mirror in the bathroom now. I didn't want one for a while, because I didn't want to meet my own gaze. Recently I've wanted to see for myself how much I've changed, and I began asking myself what I was afraid of. I've gotten to the point now that when something scares me, I force myself to face it. Crazy, right? Probably. But I'm surviving the apocalypse, so shut up. It's working for me.

Since we take a day off now and then, I've used that time to get better knowledge of the immediate area. Our front yard is littered with trash and debris. Like the extra front door leaning against the entrance, it's to make it appear like the house was already pillaged. In one of the ransacked homes nearby, I snagged a good mirror and leaned it against the broken one. And that's something else I'm getting used to. Walking into other peoples' homes used to freak me out, but now? I figure they don't need their stuff anymore, and I do.

When I gaze into the mirror, I see a faint bruise on my cheek from where I took a punch before I gutted the bastard who hit me. Knick had butchered my hair, keeping it short to shame me, and it is finally getting longer. Brown tresses are starting to show some curl, but it still isn't as long as I like. At the same time, my split ends are getting split ends and really needs some help.

The Beast gives me a couple hours each day for downtime. I've used some of it to lounge at the poolside. It has high walls, so little chance of someone spotting me. Catching some sun has brought my Latin brown skin back to its healthy caramel state.

My left arm is long-healed from the bullet wound I took months ago, but it certainly left an ugly scar. I can't see the point in worrying about it. My days as a film star are long gone now. Besides, now that I'm a woman of action, it's kinda sexy.

We are still one part short for the truck and that's not good. Our supplies are dwindling, even with what we scavenge off the raiders we kill. In fact, a couple missions have been nothing more than finding a gang hideout and wiping them out to take whatever they pillaged to begin with. And while The Beast has been able to reload what brass we keep, we are still starting to run low on ammunition. Even his end-of-the-world supplies have to run out sometime.

Fortunately we found a couple cans of good diesel last night. The Beast hopes that will help as he worries about the quality of the fuel already in the tank. We're still short a good alternator and can't get far without it. He has a backup plan of sorts. We found a couple good batteries and brought them back, so we could limp along short distances if necessary.

There's a part of me that would be fine with staying. I've found I like killing raiders and scumbags. With every one of those assholes I kill, it feels like I've won back a piece of me that had been so brutally taken. Los Angeles certainly seems to have a steady supply of them for me to shoot. If only I had a steady supply of ammunition to shoot with.

Sigh. So many bad guys, so few bullets.

I've just gotten my clothes on when a knock at the bedroom door shocks me back to reality and I pluck my pistol off the counter. Using the door jamb for cover, I aim at the bedroom door and take a deep breath, hoping it's The Beast. I find it hard to believe it wouldn't be, but I've been informed that I should always be prepared and take nothing for granted.

"Enter."

The door opens and The Beast shows both hands before the rest of himself. I relax and put my pistol under my waistband at the small of my back. I notice he has the map in hand, so he must have a new place he wants to try in the hopes of finding the right part.

"Where we heading?"

The Beast spreads the map out and points to a circle with a note written, Walma. I'm happy to see our destination. Walma is one of the few decent havens of civilization within the L.A. cesspool. I've actually made a few friends there. Also, when we go there, I get to see a different side of The Beast, a softer side he doesn't often show.

Walma used to be a huge distribution center for WalMart and a section of it was for another business that handled storage for frozen goods. Someone was smart enough to turn it into a makeshift fortress and with the massive amount of supplies it had, the settlement flourished. Families live there now, crops are grown and it is a stable trading post.

Thanks to solar panels on the roof, they always had power to keep the refrigeration and lights going. The large number of truck trailers that were present were moved and turned over, forming a barrier wall around the entire complex. Raiders have tried attacking a couple of times, but so far have been soundly beaten back.

The Beast acts like the only reason we go there is to find supplies. Having put out a request, he hopes that one of the scavengers might find the right alternator. However, he does not fool me. Every time we get there, he checks in on the Walma-village children and makes sure they are in good health. It's so adorable seeing the squealing children playing with a man I've seen kill with no fear or remorse whatsoever.

"Missing the kids, are we?" I like ribbing him about it.

I get an annoyed shake of the head before he makes a hand motion like turning a key in an ignition. Putting my hands on my hips, I give him a, "I know you better than you think I do," look. He simply rolls his eyes as he takes the map and walks out. With a snigger, I grab my gear and follow him out the door.

The best route to Walma is by dirt trails that go over the mountains north of the house. The first time we went this way I thought I was going to die! It's not so bad now, and before I know it, we're at the top and gazing out across Riverside, Highgrove and Loma Linda. Clear days like this never used to happen in L.A. I can even see parts of Moreno Valley in the southeast. The air tastes cleaner too. Taking a deep breath, I enjoy the warm sun on my skin.

While we normally travel only at night, when we visit Walma, he feels safer making the trek by day. Since it's over the mountain, there's less chance of running into anyone and no real place for someone to set up an ambush. Once we are at the crest, The Beast always takes a few minutes to scope out the area and see what's changed, thus my moment of bliss in the sun. Then, of course, onward, ever onward.

As is his habit, The Beast stares longest at University Riverside. That location is the bane of the whole area. It has the greatest concentration of bandits, and they always appear well-trained and well-fed. My question is, why are they so well-fed? Who's doing all the work?

While he examines the area, I do what any good team mate should do and watch other directions, rifle at the ready. I don't see anyone across the dull brown, rocky ground as I scrutinize every shape and shadow amongst the scrub brush and rocks.

The Beast taps my side to get my attention. As I turn, he hands me the binoculars and points at the university. Taking the field glass, I switch places with him. While he watches my back, I take a closer inspection and don't like what I see. What was once a sports field as now being used to grow crops. It also appears to be run with slave labor. I can make out people being beaten and pushed around by others. Clearly the raiders running the university are smarter than most if they are growing food.

I give back the binoculars and glance seriously at The Beast. "That's not good, is it?"

He shakes his head slow and ominous. Pointing at the university, he puts both hands together and slowly pulls them away from each other. It takes me a minute to get what he's telling me, but I finally put it together.

"They're going to expand?"

He nods and frowns over the subject. I agree. An expanding force of raiders would be bad for everyone. Certainly for us, as we are practically on their doorstep already. It would not be any better for Walma. They are maybe four or five miles away. That's not much buffer zone and if these raiders amass enough power, they could be overrun.

The Beast holds out his hand and helps me to my feet. We soberly march down the dirt trail and towards our destination.

Chapter Thirteen

We approach Walma with our rifles raised above our heads, the sentries aiming their weapons at us. Even though they know us, they don't take any chances. The village leader, Damien, clambers up to the top of one of the trailers, looking down at us with a grin. The Beast—using his particular sign language—asks if we can come in. Damien grins even more and puts a finger to his ear. I want to laugh as the game plays out the way it always does.

"I'm sorry," Damien states while grinning madly. "What was that? I couldn't quite hear you."

Okay, that's it, I do laugh. While the village leader's expression turns from grin to genuine smile, The Beast shoots me a glare. All I can do is shrug my shoulders and smile contritely. My companion growls at me, looks back up and impatiently motions once more.

Damien gives up, laughing. "Oh, fine. I can't stay up here all day. Come on in."

The gate for Walma is a school bus that has been armored on the outside. I swear I saw it in some movie, but I can't place it. When the bus pulls back, we slip in and the gate is closed once more as the village leader meets us.

"It's great to see you two." He shakes his head and adds, "One day I will hear you speak, my friend."

Damien and The Beast shake hands. Then he gives me a hug. Pulling back, the leader looks me up and down and smiles. I try to figure out how much testosterone is behind that smile, but he has never made moves on me, to my great internal relief. He has such an essential Californianess about him. A surfer vibe, with his blonde hair and easy smile. He always reminds me of Tom Petty.

"Chloe, you are more beautiful by the day!" He touches my hair and examines it. "Although your hair needs work."

I laugh in response. "Thank you for noticing, Damien, I'm desperate for a cut. How are the kids?"

"Well," he responds while leading us towards the building. "I'm sure they will be happy to see you both."

Damien, I imagine, is about the same age as The Beast. Before the Collapse, he and his wife Linda owned a salon. When everything fell apart, they and some friends had found this place and stayed. In all the chaos, they had the foresight to see how this could work for them. Now they had a cache of supplies that kept them fed and protected. They are an island of civilization and I was grateful for their presence.

The inside of the massive warehouse does not match the outside. It's been turned into one big village, with smaller wood and metal structures inside. The bottom level are shipping containers, but the structures are stacked on top of one another, with rickety walkways connecting them. Already there are children squealing as they catch sight of us and it makes my heart soar with joy.

A stampede of kids runs right at us and we are mobbed by bright faces and even brighter laughter. In a world gone wrong, this is one of the only bright spots in my life. With the obvious exception of killing bandits, of course.

The Beast does what he does best. This reinforces my thought that he must have some kind of medical background. He examines each child over, making sure they are healthy and fit. When he finds an injury or illness, he treats them the best he can. Half the time, they don't even care that he's doing it, he's so good with them. It's such a juxtaposition, seeing that killing machine of a man dealing so well with children. I wonder if he had kids, too, in the time before. I often wonder at the mystery of his past. Right now, I laugh and leave him to it, because my poor hair needs attention.

Thanks to their good fortune in establishing Walma, Damien and Linda were able to keep a small salon active in the compound. It's situated in one of the smaller containers on the ground floor. They used to use office chairs instead of the typical barber chairs. That was until The Beast and I wrangled a few salon chairs to Walma a few months ago. Various sized mirrors are set against the wall, one in front of each of the three stations.

Linda, younger than her husband, but still of the same generation, is lounging in one of the chairs and reading an old People magazine. Yet another luxury of the old world. She is a tiny and deliciously lovely black woman with a penchant for leopard and hoop earrings, and I adore her. As soon as she sees me, I get a bright smile. She leaps out of the chair to give me a big hug.

"Chloe! It's so good to see you!"

"You too. How are you doing?"

Linda pulls back and smiles. "Doing well. Please tell me you are here to get that hair cut?"

"Yes," I laugh.

Linda gets the station ready as I pull out three rounds of thirty-eight special that appear brand new and gleam like silver. I place the bullets on her shelf before sitting down. At that, she stops what she is doing and looks at them in awe.

"Oh my God! Are those thirty-eights?"

"Yep," I grin. "I pulled those off a scumbag bandit. Knew you could use them in exchange for doing something with my poor hair."

Linda starts chuckling as she pulls out her chrome, snub-nosed revolver. Slipping the rounds into the cylinder, she snaps it shut and puts it back into its holster. Now grinning herself, she picks up a bottle of shampoo.

"Oh Chloe, you are the best. Now I have a nice, full cylinder."

"Here's hoping you don't have to use them."

Turning me around, Linda tilts me back to wash my hair as our conversation continues.

"I don't know, Chloe. There are some days I'd like to go out and kill raiders like you do."

I chuckle as she works the shampoo into my hair. At the same time, I can't help but groan over the simple pleasure of relaxing while someone works on my hair. Strong fingers massaging my scalp. It feels almost sinful. *Oh god how I've missed this.*

"Trust me, it's not that easy. The second day, I got shot. Since then, I've been in more than one situation where I came close to being killed."

"True, but you also get to learn from the deadliest and most feared man in the greater Los Angeles area."

I start laughing. "Trust me, that isn't easy either."

"What!?" Linda exclaims as she starts rinsing my hair. "Granted, I imagine his stubborn silence has got to be annoying."

"Annoying," I laughingly shoot back. "Oh, Linda, you have no idea!"

It's Linda's turn to laugh. "Okay, but surely there are other benefits? Talking isn't important between the sheets. And that man is an animal. At least from what Marilyn says."

My head practically snaps in Linda's direction. "What!?"

Walma is a village that has connections to a few others like it. There are little spots of decent civilization here and there in Los Angeles County. This means trade, at least when goods can make it through the many raider bands. Trade means new people and that means additional sources of income.

That's where Marilyn comes in. I suspect she was a prostitute before the Collapse, now she is more of a Madame. Her brothel has four girls that tend to men's needs, and it isn't just sex. The brothel covers everything from simple companionship, to massage as well as sex. While Marilyn and I do not get along—she wanted me to come work for her when we first met, which did not go over well at all—I have to respect the way she cares for her workers. Even shot a man who was becoming physically abusive with one of the girls. Still, The Beast does not strike me as the kind of man to use her services.

Linda gives a nod as she continues. "Oh yeah. Was a couple of months before he found you. Paid Marilyn to secure Sandy for a whole day."

"A whole day!?"

53

"Oh yes," Linda replies with a laugh. "Wasn't just all sex, way we were told. He basically hired her for the full package. Dinner companion, massage and finally the wild mambo. She says he went more than four hours, and that he was hardly tame. Of course, this was before you, so we didn't call him "The Beast" yet. But from what I hear, the name fits."

I'm stunned. "I- I don't know what to say. I believe you, but—I never imagine him, you know, hiring someone."

"He's a man, Chloe. Men have needs just like we do."

"And your first mistake is thinking he's a man," I quickly retort. "Don't get me wrong, sex is that last thing on my mind. But my direct observation makes me believe he's the same as me: uninterested. Only thing he appears to want to do is kill raiders."

Linda laughs. "I'm sure you know better than I do. Now, tilt your head forward and let me get a look at those split ends."

Chapter Fourteen

Damien walks in as Linda finishes and shows me her work. My hair looks great, not the hot mess that it was before. It's amazing how something as simple as a haircut can make you feel so much better.

"Baby," Damien gushes to his wife. "You do amazing work."

Linda laughs. "Thank you. It helps when you have a lovely subject to work with."

"Oh stop," I exclaim with a grin.

I'm something of a celebrity to them, as they both know who I was before the Collapse. I'm their only "A list" client, so they tend to fuss over me. And they both flirt in their own way. Sometimes their nonsense makes me want to roll my eyes, but I remind myself how nice it is to have friends who care.

Damien sits down in the other chair. "So how are you?"

"Doing well," I say truthfully. "Learning more and more. Killing my fair share of bandits. You know, the usual."

"Good to hear," he replies with a laugh. "I might have a job for you and Mr. Quiet, if you are interested?"

My interest is piqued. "Oh?"

"We've got a gang that is pushing in on our northern wall. They've hit us a couple times, nothing major, but I think they are probing."

"Fucking gangs!"

Damien nods. "Agreed. Anyway, thought you might be interested, given the way you two usually deal with them. I can certainly make it worth your while.

The grin that Damien gives me makes me a little giddy. "What exactly did you have in mind?"

"First off, we'll pay you partly in advance — two unopened boxes of five-five-six and two boxes three-oh-eight."

Are you fucking kidding me? They must be in serious shit to offer pristine ammunition. Bright, shiny brass was today's version of gold bullion. Most people didn't even shoot it unless they really have to and instead save it as cash.

"Now, once you complete the job, we will give you a case of food, two night's stay at the hotel and two haircuts. The last two to be used whenever you want."

"All right."

Damien gives me a nod. "Well just let me know. There's one other thing you should know, just in case."

"Oh?"

"We think they may be cannibals."

Oh shit! There were many groups that had resorted to cannibalism is order to survive. Almost two years into the apocalypse, food supplies were either gone or becoming harder to find. When people started turning to cannibalism that often meant they went from scumbag to completely batshit crazy! It was the closest thing we had to zombies. The apocalypse always has new and interesting ways to be horrifying.

"Is The Beast done with the kids?"

"Yeah," Damien states with a quick nod. "He got some shopping done and now Marilyn is making a pass at him. Can you believe it?"

Linda and I answer in stereo. "What!?"

"Yeah, can't imagine what she is thinking." He looks directly at me. "You know him? The man doesn't even talk, never mind letting anyone in. I mean, he was with Sandy only once in all that time and never once did he even talk to her."

"Maybe she's just hoping to hook a man she feels can keep her and the girls safe?"

While Linda's question makes sense, for some reason I still don't like it. I have a strange, sick feeling and it's an emotion I can't explain as I think about that woman trying to sink her claws into my—into The Beast. I stand, uncomfortably aware that I feel anxious and angry. I want to go home.

"Well, I should get back anyway. I'm sure he'll be ready to leave if he's done with—with whatever."

"You guys should stay sometime," Damien states as he gives me a hug. "Good friends are always welcome in our home."

"I agree with my husband," Linda quips. "And you know how rare that is?"

We all laugh before I respond. "I'll do my best to talk him into it. You two take care. We'll be back if he wants us to take the job."

I head out of the barber shop as fast as I can and go looking for The Beast.

Thanks to the Collapse and my repeated rape over almost a year by a gang of assholes, my attitude towards people has understandably changed. Especially towards women. Thanks to the disappearance of law and order, most women have been thrust straight down to the bottom of the pecking order.

To many of the new world's men, we are simply objects to be used, abused and thrown away when they tire of us. This attitude, I'm sorry to say, is a carryover from the previous world. Objectification of women is nothing new, and many women in the old world liked to say they were "owning" their sexuality. Hell, I said it to myself on occasion. But the truth is, there has been a perception that women are objects to be used by men for a long, long time. Because of that, it's more important now than ever that we ladies stick together. I think it's safe to say that it was petty politics that led our world straight to Hell. Us ladies just can't keep on with that way of thinking anymore if we were going to keep from being slaves.

Regardless of this epiphany, I still don't like Marilyn. I respect the fact that she is protecting girls whose only usable skill is their looks and what they can do with their bodies. I understand that, having once been a part of the sex industry. My real problem with her is that she isn't doing anything to better the girls either. If I can learn to fight and kill, anyone can. Marilyn keeps them the way they are so that she has a profit-making operation. She's not really helping them, she's securing a place for herself. Now she's trying to snare The Beast.

I don't fucking think so!

I find her talking to The Beast and laughing flirtatiously, like they are both having a conversation. I know damn well that conversation is one-sided. It's rare that man speaks to me, let alone to anyone else.

"Beast, we have a job!" I state it loudly enough to interrupt them. Or rather, her.

I get a dirty glare from Marilyn as I walk up. Instead of playing that game, I give her the sunniest smile that I can. The new haircut gives me the added confidence to do so. The Beast looks at me quizzically. I'm sure he's oblivious to Marilyn and what she is trying to do.

"Damien has a job for us," I ignore Marilyn and turn to him, taking control of the conversation. "He's got bandit trouble and has promised to pay handsomely."

The Beast gives a polite bow to Marilyn, and then motions for me to lead the way. I feel smug, but give Marilyn a polite nod as The Beast and I walk away and I begin briefing him on the job.

"There's a gang of bandits north of here that's been harassing Walma of late. Damien will pay us in pristine ammo up front for this job. Food and lodging on the back end."

He glances toward me, an excited look in his eyes. The supplies are great, but the real pay? Getting to kill more bandits. He knows I'm just as eager to end their miserable lives as he is. I don't know his reasoning, though. In the past six months, I've gotten maybe a dozen paragraphs worth of words out of the man, and all of it dealing with combat and tactics. I still don't know his name, who he was or why he needs to keep killing raiders. I haven't even seen his face without that mask. It's not the best human companionship, but we work together so well now. And I still feel I know him better than anyone else I've ever known. It's real, you know what I mean? Not shallow like most relationships in the old world.

"One other thing," I add as we walk towards the barber shop. "This gang appears to be cannibals."

A deep, rumbling growl comes from him and he spits. I feel the same. This mission certainly should give us both some pleasure, and I plot violence as we go tell Damien we will take the mission.

Chapter Fifteen

It only takes us a few hours to track down the cannibal-bandits. They're in a collection of four warehouse buildings littered with semi-tractor trailers and wrecked cars. A number of tire fires are burning, shedding some light about the place, as well as greasy columns of smoke that can be seen even at night.

We're on the roof of a nearby building—to the southwest. The watch The Beast gave me tells me this. Neat, right? I've even gotten better at seeing and understanding the lay of the land wherever we are. I've memorized all of Riverside, Highgrove and some of Moreno Valley. The Beast has made sure I know my directions day or night so that if we are separated, I know where to fall back to.

I've definitely learned my weapons as well. The Beast is armed with what he typically uses, a Heckler Koch G3. It's a big rifle and tricked out with a sniper's stock, high-power scope and bipod. He keeps the suppressor on it. His initial load-out starts with a fifty-round drum before switching to standard, twenty-round mags.

Thanks to my steadily improving performance, I've been promoted. The short AR-15 I'd started with is now a mid-sized version of the same style rifle. He also set me up with a drum for my first magazine, which gives me fifty rounds before I have to change out—an expensive luxury, but I love it! It has a red-dot sight and a magnifier that can be flipped into place when needed, like right now.

This gang is a combination of crazies and a few who have brains. The central yard between the four buildings has a number of gangers roaming around. They show signs of twitching, shivering and in some cases spontaneous yelling. They aren't armed with much more than various club-like implements, and occasionally break into fights—with each other.

On the roofs of the main buildings, however, there are signs of discipline. Well-armed guards patrol the edge. Most are armed with hunting rifles, but I see a couple of semi-automatic long guns in the mix. The nice thing is that at this range, I can take them. It's a nice warm feeling, and I've already lined up one of the men, itching to pull the trigger. I just need The Beast to give the say-so.

He's posted up right beside me with his rifle just as ready. I think he's formulating a plan as he scans from target to target. All the while he's as quiet as a panther, dressed in black and ready to strike. With a slight tap against his weapon, he gets my attention.

With an almost clinical attitude, he points out which target I take and which he will take. We will start with the building on the right and then work our way left until all the guards are down. If that works, we make our way in and take out the rest.

There are two guards on each building, all are walking a lazy perimeter. They keep on roughly the opposite sides of the roof from each other, and do a fairly good job of actually keeping a look out. By my estimation, I'd say they are about three hundred meters away. Using the magnifier, I aim at my first volunteer. *Come to mama...*

I steady my breathing, resting the small red dot right on the man's chest and wait for the perfect moment. I know The Beast is waiting to go on my shot. It's our standard practice these days. When my target stops, I pull the trigger lightly. I'm rewarded by a spray of blood as he drops, disappearing over the edge.

Following right behind my shot, The Beast puts a round in the head of his target. I want to say he's a show off, but in reality he's just that much better than I am. When you aren't as skilled, you just have to go for the easier part of the body. The last thing you want is for someone to live and set off an alarm, or worse, kill you. I've learned quite rudely that if someone is trying to do you harm, you do it to them first. There's no, "why didn't you just shoot him in the leg?" when it comes to survival.

With slow and deadly precision, we take out the sentries from building to building, two at a time. It's far too easy, but then most gangs don't have any real sense of tactics or smarts. They only fight what they can see, and they have a tendency to only believe what's in front of their eyes. Our plan, as always, is to begin by making them blind and deaf.

It works, and in mere minutes, all their sentries are dead. With a hand motion, The Beast slithers silently down the rope. Once he's on the ground, I follow, and may I just mention, this was one of the hardest things to learn. Men have much more upper-body strength than women, so I am proud to have this accomplishment under my belt. Reaching the broken asphalt of the parking lot, we start to move in.

The stink of burning tires fills the air. I pull my bandanna up to cover my mouth and nose. I have a dead raider to thank for my latest choice in fashion—a balaclava scarf that makes my mouth look like a skull. The bonus is that I look like a bad ass! According to Damien, bandits that survive seeing me have dubbed me, "The Angel of Death." I approve.

Silently we make our way over a low wall of tires and pallets and sneak up to the corner of the closest building. Using his trusty dental mirror, The Beast peeks around the corner. When he puts the mirror away, he pulls out a concussion grenade and makes sure I know what is about to happen before pulling the pin.

One of the many weapons that he has is a crate of these handy little buggers. He's gone and made them more lethal by wrapping thin wire around the fiber body. This creates a makeshift hand grenade that at close range is definitely lethal.

Pulling the pin, he lets the spoon fly right as he gives it a soft toss around the corner. I cover my ears as there is a loud thump a few seconds later, quickly followed by screaming and groaning. This is then followed by another, louder explosion that lights up the immediate area.

What the hell was that?

We both carefully peer around the corner and see many of the cannibals lying on the asphalt, some of them burning, along with a nearby car which is now on fire and adding a good amount of light to the scene. This is our cue to stir up the hornet's nest.

Raiders flood out trying to figure out what is going on. The door behind us bursts open and two men rush out, wide-eyed and ready to play. I teach them the error of their ways. With a simple flick of the switch, my rifle is in burst mode. It bucks lightly in my hands as I put three rounds into each man before they process what's happening. They go down with a spray of red mist. That's when the fighting really begins.

The Beast has his back to mine and I hear the harsh, suppressed shots of his rifle. Right before enemy bullets careen off the metal wall near him. His back presses against mine, telling me to move into the building my two volunteers came out of. I pull my pistol and knife out, moving in and ready for war.

Originally The Beast had me using a Glock 19 with a suppressor and glow in the dark sights. I found that the nine millimeter wasn't always cutting it, especially if the target was hopped up on something. So he moved me up to a FN FNX, and oh, is it nice.

Granted, the FNX is a little big in my hand, but it rules! Chambered in forty-five, it has a healthy kick and puts people down even harder. The slide has a red dot sight built in, making it ever-so-easy for me to acquire my targets quickly. Considering the situation we are in, this is a good thing.

The interior of the warehouse is open, with dozens of makeshift beds on the floor. A few barrels of burning trash provide pools of light in a sea of smoky darkness. The Beast quickly ignites a flare, illuminating the entire space in green light right before the gang floods in.

What happens next is a blur. Gang members pour through the doors. Many of them yelling and armed with clubs or knives. The Beast and I fight back to back, gunning down as many as possible before they get within reach.

As I fight them off, a bullet hits my vest, the trauma plate stopping it. I have quickly learned that bullet-proof does not mean pain-proof. A lot of energy still crashes into you and it feels like you've been punched or kicked—hard!

The hit throws me off balance. The Beast pushes against me on the opposite side. We turn and suddenly it's like a dance. Taking the heat off me, his weapon roars into full auto as we turn. At the same time, I take out another coming in from the door we entered.

My magazine runs dry. Spotting an opportunity, a raider tries to brain me with a long piece of pipe. I block his swing with my gun hand and sink my knife into his gut. The blade slides just below the ribs. When I angle the knife up, his grunt turns into a scream and he drops to the floor, clutching a freely-bleeding wound. Unfortunately he takes my knife with him.

Cursing the turn of events, I swiftly holster the pistol and level my rifle. What is left in the drum runs dry right before The Beast nudges me to turn once more. As we spin, the drum drops out, I slap a fresh mag in. Hitting the bolt release, I lay into these assholes.

Pain flares through my lower leg as a bullet rips into it. Gritting my teeth, I scream in pain-tinged rage. I'm cycling my weapon quickly, yet accurately as another round hits my vest. That bastard gets a bullet in the throat for his trouble. He goes down, flopping violently as he tries to breathe while choking on his own blood.

And just as quickly as it started, it's over. A stunning number of raiders lay dead at our feet. In fact, the number of bodies directly near us have practically made a low wall that we could use for soft cover. Catching sight of a couple running away, I fire a wide shot to make sure they keep running. I can't help but smile, knowing the Angel of Death legend will continue to spread.

The flare is dying out, so we turn our flashlights on and start a final sweep to make sure there aren't any more bad guys. After the pasting we gave them, I highly doubt it, as we start searching for any good salvage.

Chapter Sixteen

Walma's hostel is a collection of rickety shacks built in a line against the west outer wall of the warehouse. Each room has a door and some privacy, but they are small. Even seedy motels that I've stayed in, in the old world, were larger than this. But here I sit, enjoying Walma's finest hospitality.

In addition, there's the smell—a smell one might not associate with even a third-word hostel in the old days. Let's face it, bathing is a luxury these days when it's a struggle to even acquire drinking water. So the room has a heady accumulation of body odor from who knows how many guests. The only upside is that Walma launders the bed sheets frequently and cleans and rotates mattresses to prevent the spread of scabies and the like.

When we got back from taking out the raiders, Walma threw a small party for us before we retired to our rooms. The village treated us to a feast of fresh fruits and vegetables, along with a roast pig. Added to that were a number of different kinds of alcohols, and some guitar music played by a couple of residents. Don't get me wrong, while it wasn't a big feast, it was well-meant. The Beast wasn't thrilled with being the center of attention, so after a bite to eat, we excused ourselves to go clean up and focus on the wounds we had taken.

Now The Beast works by the light of an oil lamp as he finishes treating my leg. It wasn't exactly a bullet that ripped into my calf, but a fragment of one. After pulling out a deformed piece of copper colored metal, he stitched me up and now he's dressing it with some clean gauze.

It hurt at first, but the Walma brand vodka is kicking in and I don't feel a thing anymore, except as a blurry annoyance. The pain of my ribs from the shots to my trauma plates is greatly diminished. I'm now comfortably numb as the alcoholic buzz fogs my brain and I watch my tender medic finish his work.

His delicate touch never ceases to surprise me. One minute he's a fearless killing machine, and the next he has an exceptionally gentle hand. Even his bedside manner is a juxtaposition to how he normally is. It's like I'm working with two different men. I wonder blurrily if he's a Gemini, and giggle softly in amusement. My partner glances at me, brow raised critically. He takes the bottle away and then continues his work. I take the bottle back, but don't take another drink. Yet.

Once the gauze is taped up, he stands and gives a bow—his signature way of saying he's leaving. I stagger to my feet—much more wobbly than I think I'll be—and grab his tac vest before he can get out the door. I can see the confusion is his eyes as I push up onto my toes and kiss his cheek. I'm a little shocked when he jerks back as if I just slapped him. I can't quite read the emotion in his eyes.

"You're rather handsome. Do you know that?" It's not like I'm hitting on him, but the words pop out before I can call them back.

I get no response. Instead he grabs me gently by the shoulders, pushes me back to the bed and sits me down. Taking the bottle of vodka from me again, he caps it this time and sets it on the small desk near the bed. Then he lays me down and in an amazingly sweet gesture, tucks me in. Fucking sentimental sweetheart tucks me in. Giving another respectful bow, he grabs the bottle, blows out the lamp and walks out.

As I lay there in the dark, spinning pleasantly on the bed, the soft sound of crickets is in the background as I think about my day. The number of bandits I took out makes me smile. My treatment from The Beast this evening makes me smile even more for some reason. I thought I was well beyond being grateful to him, coming into my life and saving me from hell. But tonight I'm especially moved by his utter kindness, his willingness to train me, his trust in me on the battlefield. I feel like the luckiest woman in the world. Smiling widely, I slowly drift off to sleep.

As I swim slowly out of sleep, I feel something heavy on my leg. My eyes pop open in panic and I realize that I'm naked. Adrenaline surges through my veins as I sit bolt up-right, trying to figure out where I am, though I have a horrible suspicion I know.

The hotel room is dark, with only a few slivers of illumination coming in from outside. My breathing spikes when I realize there's a heavy chain wrapped around my ankle, keeping me tied to the bed. Irrational fear threatens to swamp me. I don't want to be where I know I am.

The door swings open, soft light bleeds in, revealing Knick and Knack. They both wear their trademark grins as they start to enter the room. Knick has a plate of food in one hand while Knack just licks his lips, ready for the meal to come.

No, no, no, no, no!

With a whimper, I scramble backwards against the bed. I look for anything within reach that I can fight with. My hopes die as I can see nothing I can use as a weapon, save maybe a dirty blanket.

Knick laughs at my terror. "You didn't really think you could escape us, did you darlin'? You are mine. Now and always."

I want to cry. I want to scream. All that comes out of my mouth is a low moan of pure anguish as I watch Knick set the plate down and start undoing the fly of his dirty blue denims. Knack sniggers like a damned Hyena, and I wish I could cave his face in.

That's when I spot my dark knight. The Beast appears just over Knack's shoulder. Ducking low, he throws a knife which thunks into the wood wall just to my left. The lieutenant spins and attacks my companion while I try to wrest the blade out of the wood.

Knick curses and falls on me, determined to keep me from being armed. With a scream, I elbow him in the face and finish working the knife free. Before I can turn it on him, he's back on me and trying to get the weapon out of my hands.

"Get off me!"

"Not until I've had my fill, darlin'."

The stench of his B.O. is awful and threatens to smother me. His weight bears down on me, further inhibiting my ability to breathe. It takes more strength to keep it mentally together than to fight Knick physically. When he tries to push me further into the mattress, I bring my knee up and it finds exactly what I was hoping for.

My attacker issues a strangled groan and rolls off of me. I do NOT give him a chance to recover. With a solid backhand to the face, the bastard is sent rolling onto his back. Then I jump on top of him and start stabbing away while screaming like a banshee.

"I. Am. Not. Your. TOY. EVER!"

Knick gapes at me in horror, screaming in pain as I stab him over and over and over again. Blood splatters against the walls, the bed and even my face as I vent every bit of murderous rage against the one that deserves it the most.

As I shove the knife through his chin and into his brain, I sit back and catch my breath, admiring my handwork. It's a masterpiece. Knick lies there, a bloody mess sprawled out on the bed, dead eyes still gawking at me in shocked horror When I hear a gurgled cry, I crane my head backwards.

Knack has folded in against The Beast's hand, the tip of a short sword sticking out his back. I watch as The Beast lifts up the scumbag's chin and spits in his eye. Then he kicks the lieutenant off the sword. The asshole collapses, expiring where he lands.

Lifting my gaze to The Beast, I smile brightly at him, blood still dripping from my naked body. I can't imagine the sight he witnesses. Clearly he doesn't mind though, because, straightening himself, I actually get a smile in return right before he delivers a respectful bow. From just the right side of crazy, a giggle erupts from me and I get off the bed and pull my knife out of Knick. Then I spit on his corpse and leave my prison. As I breathe in the fresh air, I wake up.

My eyes snap open and I look around. The first rays of daylight are filtering through the cracks in the door and walls. All my gear is against the desk and my rifle lays right next to me. I close my eyes for a moment, breathe a sigh of relief and sit up against the edge of the bed.

As I'm gathering my wits and waking up, The Beast bursts into the room without so much as a knock. There's a hint of worry on his face that tells me I must have been screaming during my nightmare. Still, I'm a little incensed over the fact that he didn't knock and rest my fists against my hips as I glower at him.

"Excuse me! You could knock."

Giving me a respectful bow as a reply, he backs out and closes the door, but I swear I catch just a hint of a grin. Rolling my eyes, I stand up and get dressed. A small mirror hangs over the desk in the room and I stare at the woman who stares back at me. How far she has come in such a short span of time. They say it's been almost two years since the Collapse. Now here I am, an ex-porn actress turned killer in a world gone mad. I wonder what the old me would think of how she turned out. I give a snort of a laugh, grab my rifle and head out the door.

The sunlight this morning is much brighter than it should be. Damned vodka. I slip on my Ray Bans and pretend all is well, but my head is not at all pleased. The Beast is standing in the lot, conversing with Damien and Linda. Children are laughing loudly nearby as they chase a couple piglets. Breathing in the fresh air, I get this odd sense of Déjà vu. At the same time, I feel—better somehow.

I shake my head from not being able to put a finger on what feels different and head towards my friends and instructor. My leg is sore, so I move with a little bit of a limp as I walk up. The Beast gives me a respectful bow once more while Damien and Linda smile broadly.

"Can you please translate?" Damien jokes while pointing at The Beast. "I don't understand his sign language."

The Beast growls while the rest of us laugh. "I'll see what I can do. But to be honest, half the time I don't understand him either. Caveman *is* a dead language."

Shooting me a glare from the corner of his eye, he gives Damien and Linda a polite bow and then starts walking towards the front gate. All I get is a hand motion telling me that it's time to move out. I roll my eyes.

"It was great to see you two."

Linda gives me a hug first. "Same here. Don't be strangers. We still owe you some haircuts."

"I have not forgotten," I state with a laugh. "If you need more help, send a runner, all right?"

"You got it." Damien gives me a big hug, and so does Linda once more.

"Now I'd better get moving before he leaves me behind. Take care you two."

With a wave, I jog away and catch up to The Beast as the gate opens. The guards up-top give us a sign to say that all looks clear. I nod to them as we head back in the direction of home. Deep in my gut though, I can't shake the feeling that something bad is about to happen.

Chapter Seventeen

My feeling proves prophetic over the next few months. It seems our reputation has been striking such fear into the small-time gangs and raiders that some were flocking to the University Raiders for protection—as well as a steady food supply. This meant that the University operation was expanding and they're already practically on our doorstep. It is time to move, and fast!

In the past few weeks, we've wiped out five advance teams. We've had to be smart about it, never hitting any one specific direction so as to avoid making it obvious where we are operating from. This has also made us more feared.

More than once we've overheard raiders speaking of us in hushed tones. Mentioning The Angel of Death and her Beast. They make it sound like we are avenging ghosts or demons that can't be killed. It takes quite the effort to not laugh when I hear it while getting into position to strike. The funniest part is that even people who don't know him call him The Beast now.

Unfortunately our efforts have proved fruitless. The raiders have continued getting closer. Their latest safe house is only a couple streets away. Hell, if I posted up with a sniper rifle, I could tag them from our front lawn. While that fun thought has been tempting on more than one occasion, I've refrained because the truck hasn't been ready.

Fortunately our situation has changed, and it could not have come at a better time. One of the scavengers at Walma came across the exact alternator that we need to run the truck properly. Damien has also offered us safe haven in return for us helping defend the village. He even sweetened the deal by throwing in some armor plating we have used to "upgrade" the vehicle. While neither of us were entirely sure about Damien's offer, we took it anyway. At the very least, it gives us a chance to regroup and plan what to do next.

Can't say I complain about the armor either. They have a bunch or rusty, steel plates that came from a business just across the street. A team brought the plates and a welder and went to work armoring the vehicle I have taken to calling "Truck." I feel like it deserves a proper name, and "Beast" is already taken. Plates now cover the sides, radiator grill and back. The windshield is covered, with slits cut to see out of. The doors are armored, but the hinged plates that cover the windows can be dropped when not needed.

While The Beast finishes fixing Truck, I pack everything into the back. In more ways than one this did not come soon enough. Our food stores would have only lasted perhaps a month or two. Water supplies weren't much better and we'd even gone as far as to reduce our flushing of the toilet. If being able to bathe once in a while meant putting up with a little extra stink, I was all for it.

Aside from the pieces we are carrying, all the weapons he has are stowed away. *All* the weapons. I have no idea where he picked up so many firearms, but given the SWAT emblems on some of the tactical gear, I think a lot of it might have come from a police station. For all I know, some of it is even military.

As I'm stowing our things, he's installing the alternator and trying to turn the engine over. So far no luck. While I am moving and loading gear, he's going back and forth between engine and cab, and it still won't start.

We need to move already! With those raiders damn near on our doorstep, it won't be much longer before they want to move in. Hell, they might hear the truck trying to start. That means a heavy firefight with ammunition that we don't have in abundance. Unfortunately, The Beast still can't get the truck to work and we need to go!

I am about finished stowing all of our useful gear when my companion literally has a temper tantrum. The man starts banging on the truck with his wrench and even kicking the front side panel as he roars like an angry bear. Dropping to wrench onto the concrete floor, it clatters as he storms towards a punching bag and starts beating it to death.

Oh, for fucks sake!

I stride over to the engine compartment and do an inspection. For such a skilled killer and medic, The Beast is a terrible mechanic. Sad thing is that the issue he's dealing with isn't really all that difficult a problem.

It's a 7.3 power-stroke diesel, and there are only so many things that can cause starting issues on these bad-boys. Sure enough, it's the first thing I check. When I find the injector pressure regulator valve, I can see that one of the wires going into it is damaged. I quickly splice the wire, doing a damn good repair job if I say so myself and then try starting the truck again.

While The Beast is still beating the shit out of the punching bag, I turn the truck over at it starts up with a roar. Through the cut-out slits in the armor plate that cover the window, I can see The Beast stop and stare at the vehicle incredulously. Stepping out, I give him the smuggest grin in my arsenal.

I can see the question in his eyes, so I answer. "What, you think I'm just a pretty face and don't have any useful skills? The injector pressure regulator wire got damaged somehow. That was causing your problem."

I dust my hands off on my ass and slam the door. Yes, I am being a saucy bitch. But you would think he could have asked me, just once, in all these months, if I knew anything about repairing a truck.

69

As he narrows his eyes, his expression changes and he draws his pistol. I am shocked, standing there with my grin fading when he yells, "DUCK!"

I drop to the ground fast as he guns down someone who entered the garage from the house. The rather loud bark of two forty-five rounds send the bandit sprawling across the floor—and a deafening ringing in my ears.

Shit! They've found us!

With a growl I can barely hear, The Beast grabs the box of tools and tosses it behind the driver's seat. Grabbing my hand, he yanks me to the back of the truck and helps me into the cab. Actually, he practically tosses me in, giving me no time to argue. It certainly is not the most comfortable choice of seating, however, as my ass is plopped right on top of numerous weapons. If I'd known I'd be back here, I might have arranged things a bit differently.

I'm about to give him a piece of my mind when he hands me the only true machine gun he has —an M249. He quickly shows me how to load it and then points to an ammo can that holds an extra belt. Then he disappears, leaving the back hatch open. *Oh baby. Come to mama.*

Over the rumble of the engine, I can't hear much, but I barely pick up multiple voices shouting. This is quickly followed by the obvious thunder of three-oh-eight rounds going off. Multiple different calibers bark back, a few which rip through the garage door but do not hit the truck. The Beast is engaging the enemy, I think from the front door.

Great, he sticks me in here and then goes out to have fun. What does he think I am, the little woman?

I'm about to get out of the truck when there is an explosion which fiercely rattles the garage door. The Beast comes running, jumps into the truck and puts it in gear. The tires squeal and I barely have time to close the hatch before we launch out of the garage. The door wraps against the rear in the process. I think we hit some of the raiders too, which satisfies my bloodthirsty heart.

When we clear the driveway, The Beast performs a nearly perfect bootlegger turn which sends the garage door flying off, along with two bandits. Now that I can see, I spot a half-dozen more men who were starting to enter the house, but are currently gaping at us in shock. Grinning madly, I pull the trigger.

Fuck. Yes!

The machine gun bucks in my grip as I spray the front door of the house. Red lines of tracers help me to stay on target as I turn the seven bandits into Swiss cheese. All the while, I can't help but laugh manically at them. Damien was right, it's easy to be a hero when you have a fully automatic weapon. One thing's for sure, I love it!

I know he can't hear me, but I holler, "This—is my favorite gun!"

Tires peel out and we rocket down the street as fast as the truck will carry us. I can hear the occasional gunshot, so I'm watching for more volunteers. We speed through the residential section, and when I see a bandit, I treat them to a short burst or two. I don't think I hit any of them, but it sure keeps their heads down. Of course I am still laughing like a maniac. This is a glorious day!

I remember the route he had chosen on the map. We were going to head east over Box Springs Mountain and then loop up north and then west to get to Walma. While it would require a bit of fuel, it would be a good ruse in making anyone think we were fleeing east. We don't want to bring unwanted attention to the village.

At some point, though, I really wish he would stop to let me ride shotgun. The dirt road is rough. Really rough. It's not fun anymore! I close the hatch to keep a cloud of dust from choking me to death, and do my best to clear a section on the truck bed floor for me to sit more comfortably as the vehicle rocks, bumps and jostles about. It certainly has killed the thrill of shooting a machine gun.

When we get to Walma, I just may kill him.

Chapter Eighteen

The Beast and I set up in our new quarters at Walma. Damien has given us a small shack at the top of the heap, not far from where he and Linda live. It's not very big, but is a roof over our heads and a safe place for our gear. However, we've kept the bulk of the weapons and ammo in Truck. Let's be honest. If we tried to fit all of it into our shack, there would be little space left for The Beast and I.

While small, our new home is also cozy, and I don't mean that in a past-world realtor kind of way because I like it. There is a single main room divided into sections with furniture. The "living room" is a small area with a mangy love-seat, a rough-looking chair and a scratched up but usable coffee table. Like most of the upper homes, the walls are made out of whatever they could scavenge. Pallets, lumber and corrugated metal being the bulk of what they could find. The whole right wall, however, is a billboard for IHOP.

Light bulbs hang from the ceiling on makeshift wiring, their naked, unsteady light illuminating the room. I make a note to myself to see if I can find a shade or Japanese lantern. The stark lights feel jarring to me and I can't imagine the havoc it will wreak with our night vision.

A small section to the right of the living room is what you might call a kitchen, if you are kind. There is a refrigerator next to a short counter for preparing food. The fridge doesn't run, mind you. It is simply is there to act as a pantry—and as a bitter reminder of what I used to have. Right along with the IHOP advertisement.

Another thing I will miss from the house is semi-functional toilets. Now we have a closet with a pale wood toilet seat sitting over a tall bucket. The sink is a basin with a small shelf underneath holding a few washcloths and a towel rack. Oh, civilization, how I miss your hot and cold running water.

Finally there are two beds inside, both against the wall opposite the only door that leaves the shack. If I didn't know any better, I'd say this is an attempt by Damien and Linda to force The Beast and I together. Sneaky, but they don't know him like I do. He has shown no sign in all this time of thinking of me at all in "that way." And they also don't know me. I have no interest in such goings-on since Knick and Knack. I decide we will be fine, like siblings. Of course, I don't remember Marsha and Greg taking out bullies at four hundred meters.

But as I place my things next to the bed on the right, I glance over at my companion. My heart twists a little as I see him standing in the middle of room. He looks like a caged animal with no way out. Suddenly this seems like less of a good idea, but we really have no other option at the moment.

Do we? My heart melts for him, but I know he's strong. He'll get through this. We'll get through this.

"Why don't you stow your gear?" I keep my tone light, professional. "Then we can see if there is anything Damien needs."

I am trying to lift him from wherever the pit of his thoughts seem to have taken him to. I don't know if it's helping. At first he stares at me like I'm speaking in some unknown language. After a long moment, though, he nods and drops his personal gear on his bed. Taking his rifle, he slips the sling over his head and joins me.

Everyone we pass smiles, some give a greeting and sometimes a wave. I imagine they are very happy to have us here. Our reputation is such that our presence alone boosts their morale. At the same time, I can feel The Beast bristling at their attention and at all this "civilization," such as it is. I'm pretty damn sure that he's not going to tolerate this well. I think we'll have enough to do, so I can get him out of here on a regular basis and out killing some bandits. I'm trying not to worry.

Come to think of it, I need to sit down with him and have a discussion. The truck is so very important to him, and there has to be a reason for it. Surely he does not plan to use it for inner-city travel? It's too loud, and even with the armor plate, chances are it will end up getting damaged and need to be repaired all over again. No, he's got a plan for it, I know he does. And he needs to tell me what it is. I am certain that he needs me as much as I ever needed him at this point. I don't want to find he's gone haring off on some mission or other, without me.

We find Damien on the ground floor talking with the village quartermaster, Tom. Tom is quite a character. Standing six foot four, he towers over The Beast and makes me feel like an ant. He comes across as fairly buff, but he has the remainder of a gut. Before the Collapse, he was a used car dealer. Ran his own business, and as a mechanic, did more than his fair share of work on the cars as well. Dirty overalls are faded from too much wear, and at least a size too big—a reminder that he used to be fatter—hell, we all used to be fatter. Faded blonde hair is slowly receding and makes his forehead seem larger than normal. His size alone might be enough, but his attitude is what makes him such a character. He's a class clown through and through.

"There they are! The lady and gentleman of the hour," Tom states with a huge grin.

"Hey Tom." I smile back. "How are you?"

"Feeling much safer now that you two are here."

I can't help but laugh. "Don't go relying on us too much. We aren't perfect."

"Are you kidding me? The Angel of Death and her Beast aren't the

73

perfect warriors? Please! As soon as news gets out that you two are living in Walma, the bandits won't come within a mile of here. Maybe ten."

The voice that responds is almost a whisper on the wind, yet ominous. "Reputation is a beautiful weapon, for it often spills less blood. Yet for the psychotic it is an invitation, a chance to make a name."

I spin in surprise. That's The Beast's voice. Damien and Tom are staring at my partner in shock as he walks away. Apparently this was far too much civilized conversation for him. I must admit though, he certainly knows how to silence a room.

"First time I finally hear him speak," Damien remarks. "And he makes me feel like someone just walked over my grave."

"You and me both, brother," Tom adds, shaking his head, all humor gone from his voice.

I watch The Beast as he strides to the exit. "Yeah, he's good at that." I focus my attention on Damien. "Is there anything you need us to do?"

The Beast's statement has rattled him. He looks at me nervously. "Uh, no. At least not yet. Y-you can pull guard duty if you like?"

"No," I reply with a shake of my head. "We'll range out this evening, search for supplies and kill any raiders or gangs that we come across. It's what we do best."

The wickedness in my smile sets Damien on edge, and Tom is looking a little sick. I think for the first time they don't see me as simply a beautiful woman. They realize I'm the living embodiment of my new moniker; the Angel of Death. I ponder on the thought that Damien is wondering if he made the right choice, inviting us in. I know that's what I'm thinking. Giving a tight smile at both men, I nod and jog off to catch up with The Beast.

I find him inspecting Truck. The hood is open and he is giving the engine a once over, probably to make sure it wasn't damaged earlier. Given how terrible a mechanic he is, he's probably trying to find something to do so he doesn't have to deal with people.

Sigh. And I thought this was going to work. It might not. Then where will we go?

"Maybe you should let someone who knows what they are doing take a look at Truck." I say it with a smile, not a smirk, so he knows I'm not just being mean.

At first I get a dirty look. I'm surprised he doesn't growl at me as well. Then he surprises me by sticking his tongue out and goes back to his inspection. I chuckle and stick my head under the hood with him.

"You don't think staying here is a good idea, do you?"

The Beast responds with a shake of his head.

I didn't think so. "Then what do we do?"

He pats the truck a couple times and then points east.

"Head east? Where to?"

Making a "V" with his hands, he puts them over his head. Then he presses both hands together and puts them under his head, like he's sleeping. It takes me a minute to figure out what he's trying to say.

Fuck, I wish he would talk to me.

"Home? You want to go home?"

Giving me a nod, he points to the sun and motions it going down. Then he points to his watch, showing me the number eight. Pointing to me, then to himself, and makes a motion like holding up a rifle and then us walking south.

South? Why south? That's where the house was. I barely refrain from asking him if little Timmy has fallen in the well and instead try to focus.

"Why that way?"

The Beast taps the side of his nose, telling me that it's a secret. I sigh at him and he ignores me. Closing the hood, he walks to the back and unlocks the hatch. Quickly he starts pulling out weapons and equipment. With a hand motion, he asks for my rifle and I give it to him.

Quickly unloading and clearing the weapon, he pulls out a totally different rifle. With this one, the magazine actually fits behind the pistol grip instead of in front. Attaching a bulky scope onto it, he also slides on a laser sight on the left side rail and a flashlight on the other. By the time he's done, the weapon is totally tricked out and placed in my hands.

I quickly get a feel for my new gun and I like it. It's shorter than the AR and I feel like I can maneuver easier with it. Instead of a three point sling, he tosses a one point on it. Given the compact size, it works well enough. I read the lettering on the weapon and it says, IMI Tavor. Well, I think Mr. Tavor and I are going to get along just fine.

Chapter Nineteen

By the time twenty hundred hours rolls around, we're both more than ready to go. Thanks to Linda, we had a good dinner of stuffed bell peppers and ham chased down with clean water. The company was great and I was able to keep The Beast at the table for the entire meal, which was a miracle in itself. He sat with his back in a corner, which I think it made him more comfortable.

Now we're decked out in full tac gear, which for me now includes two thigh holsters. My primary pistol is the FNX and the secondary is my old Glock, of which only the FN is suppressed. Thanks to the first aid training I've been getting, I now carry a small trauma kit of my own on the front of the vest. All this is topped off with six rifle magazines and my favorite combat knife.

A few weeks back, we found some tiger stripe fatigues that were in my size. I was so excited, I may have squeed a little. I've found the stripes work well in both urban areas and in brush. The dark colors blend in and make me difficult to spot. Thanks to my Hispanic heritage, I also don't have glowing white skin to easily give me away, like The Beast. Or a white face mask for that matter. I still use some black face paint to break up the pattern. Four dark, jagged stripes cut across my face, slanting downward at irregular intervals.

I turn and see that The Beast is almost ready, and what a sight he is. As usual, his tactical vest is completely loaded. Instead of the G3, he's running his short barrel FAL which is tricked out similar to my rifle. His Kimber .45 race gun sits in a thigh holster, but that's not his only pistol. Attached to the side of his vest is another holster carrying a Steyr GB. Finally he has the Webley revolver in a vertical holster at the small of his back. And if all that isn't enough, he's also got a combat knife and a short sword.

He's clad in black fatigues that have seen a bit of action. Long brown hair, streaked with gray is tied up into a pony tail. His beard is also peppered with similar gray, but he keeps it trimmed so that it's not overgrown. Finally there's his white mask, covering his face from his forehead to the upper part of his cheeks.

As I stand there watching him jump up and down, making sure all his gear is tied down tight, it dawns on me that I actually find him sexy, as my drunk self noted not too long ago. I don't think it's his actual appearance, though. It's because I know him so well, it's not like I see that so much as I see *him*, who he is. It's in his manner, his actions, the way he carries himself, the way he treats me. Who he is to me is what makes him attractive, if that makes any sense. Sure, he's a stone cold killer, he's gruff and doesn't talk much, but he's always got my back. I will never forget the day he found me, putting the jacket on me to cover my nakedness. That kind of respect, that kind of gentleman, is rare after the Collapse. Bringing his head up, he notices me admiring him and gazes at me quizzically.

"Just admiring the view." I give him a wry smile as I pick up my rifle.

Shooting me a weird look, he shakes his head and walks to the door. Opening it, he lets me walk out before following behind me. *See . . . gentleman.* We walk along the rickety walkway that connects our shack with three others. We are in what is supposedly an elite neighborhood. All of these shacks are for some of the important people within the community.

I don't much care for our location. The walkway creaks and groans like it'll give way at any minute. I've been told it's held up fine so far, and even been through a minor earthquake. I am not convinced. Still, I hold my tongue because the community was kind enough to give us one of the best roofs in the village.

When we leave the warehouse, the sun is nearly set. Once we get to the gate, the guards are already opening it for us to exit. With smiles, they give us an all-clear sign, and at that, we move out.

The Beast isn't playing tonight. As we leave the gate, he's already rifle up and at the ready. Dashing across the street, we move with practiced military precision from building to building, checking and clearing the area around each one as we make our way to the mountain.

Cool night air kisses my face as we get to the base of the mountain and scan the area. I still have no idea what we are doing, but go through the motions. I find that the scope he placed on my rifle is a night vision version. I can see the whole block in green tinted daylight and I don't see anything moving. Meanwhile, he's scanning our way ahead. When he's sure it's clear, he gives me a tap and we move.

As we walk, my mind wanders. My companion is very serious, very focused tonight. Why? I've noticed that he's been different since we escaped to Walma. At first I figured it was just being around too many people. Now, I'm not so sure.

Taking the dirt trail we've used multiple times, we pick our way up to the peak of the mountain which include a fair bit of switchbacks. It's a bit of a steep climb at the end, with the trail opening up into a slightly flat clearing. The moon is almost full, so we have decent light to see by. When we make it to the top, we make sure all looks clear before taking a breather.

The scent of coastal sage is heavy in the air. It reminds me of maple syrup, yet green and fresh, and a hint of Thanksgiving. What? My mom made sage dressing when I was a child. In fact, just the thought has me longing for better days.

Unscrewing the cap on my canteen, I take a drink of cool water as I observe my surroundings. Before the Collapse, this was probably quite the spot. It has such a commanding view of a good part of the L.A. area. If there was still electricity, you could probably see lights for miles. These days it's mostly darkness with pinpricks of firelight instead. Off in the distance I see a blur of a white glow that I bet is the Queen Mary Enclave.

Damien informed me that they'd traded with them a few times. The port that the Queen Mary is tied to was taken over by mostly Longshoremen and immediately turned into a refuge. Initially they raided supplies from the shipping containers nearby, which also made for an impressive defensive wall. Now they do a lot of fishing and farming—both hydroponic and above decks—and some of that ends up in Walma. At least when they can get a trade caravan through.

The other island in the darkness is University Riverside. Bright lights illuminate the sports fields and the school itself. While my scope isn't high powered, I've got enough magnification to see movement on the rooftops. Some of the surrounding buildings now have lights as well. Clearly the University Raiders have been hard at work creating some semblance of civilization. Shame that it's run by a bunch of assholes.

It appears to be so peaceful from up here, like the world has moved on from the violence. But it hasn't. There's a part of me that is so sick of all the savagery. The knowledge that nine times out of ten, if you meet someone on the road, they're going to try to kill you to take your stuff. Or worse, rape you and keep you as their slave.

While I have come to enjoy ridding the world of bad men, I wish there was something we could do to stop this living hell. I know there are good people out there. Decent, hardworking people, like in Walma. People that just want to live quiet, civilized lives. Why is there so much evil and so little good? I sigh and Beast looks a question at me.

"I'm just tired of the death and killing. I want some peace. Why can't we just live in peace?"

The fact that I get a reply shocks me. "Peace is an illusion. The universe is built on conflict. Peace is nothing more than a commercial interruption between hostilities."

The curt delivery of, "The Meaning of Life According to The Beast" has robbed me of my voice. All I can do is watch as he takes his pack off and pulls out a folding shovel. Then he starts walking around, as if he's looking for something. What, I have no clue. When my partner finally stops, he makes a motion, telling me to keep watch before he starts digging.

What the hell is he doing now?

In reality, now is not the time for a debate. Kneeling down, I start scanning the area around us, keeping an eye out for any targets. As I sweep across, I find the house and stop. It's a burned out hulk now, practically gone. As in burned to the ground. There's nothing left. Debris even sits in the pool.

A lump starts to form in my throat as I view the utter destruction. I liked living there. I found myself again while we lived there. As I wonder who would do such an awful thing, I catch movement out of the corner of my eye.

Swinging my rifle, I scan for the source of the movement. It takes a little bit of work, but I finally find it. *Shit!* I spot a pack of raiders moving up the mountain and towards us. From the way they are moving, I don't think they've seen us. They are walking along lazily, not really paying any attention to their surroundings. They are all well-armed though, some with AK's even. I'm itching to pull the trigger, but I refrain and move closer to The Beast instead.

"Tangos moving up on our position," I whisper. "I count a dozen—well-armed, but undisciplined."

At first, the only response I get from him is a low growl as he starts digging faster. Then his shovel hits something solid. Digging frantically, he pulls out something wrapped in some canvas.

Quickly unwrapping it, I see it's an ammo can. With his buried treasure retrieved, he stows his gear, throws his pack on and then grabs the can. Just as we get ready to move, we realize it's too late to escape, because they're here.

Chapter Twenty

The Beast grabs my pack and jerks me backward. We fade into the brush and slip a little way down the west facing slope. At first I'm afraid I might start sliding and fall, but my feet rest on a large rock and I hold my breath. We hear their voices first, then their boots crunching on the rocks until they stop. The dumb-asses take this moment to have an argument, so I listen closely.

"This is bullshit, Jake."

"You gonna tell that to Dean, Bobby?"

"Hell no!"

"Then shut up!"

"Look, I'm just sayin'! The bitch and her dog ran away with their tail between their legs. Everything south a this mountain is ours. So why bother comin' up here?"

The Beast starts growling softly and I elbow him and glare. While I get a glare back, he stops as the raiders conversation continues.

"Because Dean is smarter than you, that's why."

A third voice tosses into the debate. "And word is that they shacked up in Walma."

"Oh come on," Bobby exclaims. "They ran east! Walma is north."

"Doesn't mean they didn't double back," Jake counters. "That don't change the fact that if Dean says we gotta go get a look at Walma, then we go get a look at Walma. If they're there, then that changes the plans for attacking that shit hole."

The third voice interrupts. "Hey, got a hole dug here. Looks recent."

"Really?" Jake sounds exasperated. "Jim, when did you become an expert tracker?"

"Stuff it, Jake. I'm just sayin' that it looks fresh. That's all."

There's a heavy sigh from Jake. "Fine. Everyone spread out and take a look around."

Slowly I draw my knife and edge back up to my side of the brush. From the corner of my eye I can see The Beast moving up with his rifle at the ready. We are both coiled like springs as we wait for the right moment.

That moment comes when one of the bandits sticks his head through the brush. His eyes widen, but I don't give him time to warn his friends. With zero hesitation, I shove my knife into his neck. My aim is perfect as the blade sinks into his throat. He can barely even gurgle as his eyes bulge out and I pull him through the brush and let him slide down the hill. It is a surprisingly quiet death, and he vanishes from view without any fuss at all.

As I make my first kill of the night, it's all the invitation The Beast needs to be unleashed. I can only imagine what it looks like to the raiders as he roars out of the brush, gun blazing. I'm not far behind, and by the time I've gotten through the sage, three men are already down. A few have started running away while the others try to find cover behind various small boulders.

I can hear one of the men yelling as he runs. "Ángel de la muerte! Ángel de la muerte!"

Before they can form an effective resistance, I am laughing maniacally as I drop another two men and wound a third. There are only five left by the time they start shooting back. Bullets fly past me so close that I can hear them zip through the air. It's at that point I begin to realize that we are in a bad position. The Beast is shooting with one hand while carrying the ammo can. Worse, some of the men that bolted could come back with reinforcements.

"Shift left," I yell over the sound of the gunfire.

My response is the sound of suppressed FAL firing in full auto and slowly getting louder as he rains bullets across the area where the raiders are hiding. After running a few feet, I stop and provide covering fire while he moves. Fortunately there are a lot of boulders to use for cover. Unfortunately that means the raiders can find cover as well. We do this until we get far enough to flat out run.

Once we get under the cover of darkness, the raiders are not brave enough to give chase. Instead they fire wildly into the dark and down the hill. I hear bullets impact all around, but it's far too gloomy for me to see just how close any of them are. None of them hit us as we finally bottom out onto the foothills and I stumble over a clump of brush.

"Get after them," I hear Jake yell.

"Shit," I whisper harshly.

Scrambling to my feet, we start running for Walma. What we've just learned is important and Damien needs to know. I'm sure the raiders know this too. I can already hear someone sliding down as we run as fast as we can, often through scrub brush. Just as we get close to the first set of buildings, the shooting starts again.

Bullets punch through neglected walls and previously broken glass as I get to the corner of a two story building. Quickly turning, I provide covering fire while The Beast keeps running for the next edifice across the street. Thanks to my scope, I see the bastards as they make their way down the mountain. I get one perfectly in my sights and fire. I am rewarded when he drops.

"Move," I hear The Beast yell.

You don't need to tell me twice!

I turn and book it across the road. As I move, I catch sight of him using a tree for cover. My partner shoots a single shot at a time. Raiders return fire, but they can't really see us. Bullets just rain everywhere as we move from cover to cover. My legs burn and my lungs ache and my heart pounds in my chest. My pulse sounds like a racehorse in my ears.

Reaching the next building, I finally see Walma ahead. Not too far, maybe a hundred yards or so. I spin, using the building for cover and start shooting. The Beast doesn't even need me to yell and immediately falls back.

We're almost there. We're almost there.

Suddenly a stray bullet strikes The Beast in the back, and another goes through his left leg. The impact sends him stumbling face first onto the ground. Horrified, I freeze, for the first time in forever. I force myself to move—*he can't be dead, he can't be dead.* Then a bandit comes around the corner of the far building, firing in our direction. Instinct and habit kick in and without hesitation, and because I'm so pissed, I open up on his ass while screaming like a banshee.

The lead raider goes down under my hail of fire and the others flee back to cover as I move up to The Beast. Hope rises in my chest when he rolls over and starts shooting, helping keep heads down as I get close. I feel a lump in my throat and that's when I notice my face is wet with tears.

Instead of trying to help him up, I grab the hand hold on the back of his tactical vest and try to drag him while he continues shooting. This is one time I'm glad he's not an over-muscled Alpha male, because while I'm definitely fit, I'm not exceptionally strong.

With a grunt of effort and frustration, I try my damndest to drag him behind the corner of the building. My companion helps by pushing along with his good leg, smart man. While he shoots with his pistol in one hand, he's holding the can against his chest. All the while, incoming enemy fire zips all around us. I keep telling myself, *just a few more feet*, as I strain to get him to some cover.

We are almost there when an enemy round careens off the concrete corner and a piece of shrapnel cuts across my cheek. Pain sears through me. Gritting my teeth, I haul The Beast the rest of the way. Once we are safely behind cover, I yank one of the grenades out of his vest, pull the pin and toss it.

Evidently when we disappeared behind the building, the raiders felt this to be the perfect time to push forward. Now I have never thrown a grenade before. Let's face it, a porn star may have been required to do many things, but oddly, grenade tossing was never part of the skill set.

I feel someone must be watching over me tonight, for my poor toss actually lands in the perfect spot. When the explosive detonates with a solid thump, the raiders were close within its blast radius. I take a quick glance and find all of our remaining harassers on the ground, some not moving and others groaning or screaming. Just the way I like them.

Getting The Beast to his feet, I help him limp his sorry ass through Walma's gate. The guards pulled the gate back when they saw it was us, and a couple men are aiming in the direction we came from, ready to provide covering fire. Never has the village looked so good. I feel bad that we led the raiders here. I hope none of them got away to tell their leader where we are.

As we hit the gate, I get the attention of the guard closest to us. "They're all down. If you're fast enough, you could strip their gear."

"Yes ma'am."

A few whoops and hollers are issued as three of them rush out and head towards the dead and dying raiders. As we approach the warehouse door, we can hear a couple gunshots and then silence. Knowing all those bastards are dead, I get The Beast inside so we can get his wounds treated.

Chapter Twenty-One

It's been a little more than a day now and Walma is in full evacuation mode. Damien is no dummy and took our report seriously. Immediately enacting their evacuation plan, we then got The Beast to the infirmary before my worry spun completely out of control.

Fortunately his trauma plate had stopped the bullet that hit him in the back. I found tears still leaking down my face as we got him out of his tac vest and onto the table. The leg wound was bleeding freely, and Walma's doctor, Amanda went to work on getting it cleaned up and treated.

Shit there's a lot of blood.

My worry reaches a fever pitch as I assist. We strip off the rest of his gear and the bulk of his clothes. For the first time I realize that he has tattoos; one over his left pectoral and one on the inside of each forearm. I've never seen anything like them. They look like a number of golf tees arranged in various patterns. I make a mental note to ask him later.

After cleaning the wound, the doctor reports it is not as bad as I first thought. The bullet went straight through his thigh muscle and missed anything vital. My heart is finally able to stop pounding out of my chest and my breathing slows once I realize he's going to be okay. The tears don't stop, but I manage to help Amanda get him patched up.

Once she is done, I grab a couple of guards and we haul him up to our place and into bed for some much-needed rest. Thanks to whatever Amanda gave The Beast, he's out cold. The adrenaline has worn off, and I know I won't be far behind him.

I unceremoniously dump all our gear on the coffee table, including the suspicious ammo can and walk over to my bed, falling onto it with a sigh. I'm practically asleep as my head hits the pillow.

That night, Knick and Knack do not plague me. Nightmares still do, but this time they are different. This time it's a firefight—a bad one. The Beast and I are trapped in a building, surrounded by raiders. Bullets rip through the walls, we are both wounded and low on ammunition. The Beast is actually using a rifle off a dead bandit, scavenging weapons as we kill these assholes.

We both pop up and start firing again, putting down at least a half dozen of the bastards as they try to rush us. Oddly, as this is happening, I find that I'm not afraid of dying. So long as I take as many of these rapist assholes with me as I can, I feel it will be a good death. The Beast is another issue though.

This man has become such an integral part of me. In the time we've been together—near to a year—we've turned into a well-honed team. He's got my back, and I've got his—even when he makes me so crazy that I want to kill him myself!

When I spare a glance at him, I can only watch in horror as a bullet rips through his neck, sending a gout of blood across the floor. That's where fear I haven't known since Knick and Knack floods through me. I scream in murderous fury as I fire my weapon while rushing over to him.

Blood runs freely from his wound as I kneel next to him, my eyes spilling over. Through what must be incredible pain, he reaches up and caresses my cheek tenderly, giving me a rare smile. I lean down and kiss him, and as our lips touch, he breathes his final breath into my lungs.

I'm kneeling there, shaking his dead body, crying and unable to accept that he's gone. Then I let loose with a primal scream that shakes the foundations. Grabbing his rifle and mine, I rise from cover and start shooting.

Bullet after bullet rips into my enemy as I am eager to get some killing done. All the while, I'm screaming at them like an enraged, avenging angel. Some break cover and run, only to be cut down as I keep firing. When the rifles run dry, I draw my pistols and keep shooting until they finally take me down. When my head hits the concrete, everything goes black.

Waking up with a gasp, I pull my pistol as I take stock of my surroundings. I relax when I realize I'm in our shack at Walma, tangled in sheets and soaked with sweat. Taking a deep, cleansing breath, I glance at my watch and realize that I've slept damn near the entire day away. Rolling out of the bed, I go check on The Beast.

I think this is the first time that I've actually seen him asleep, though right now he doesn't appear peaceful. His face is contorted, like he's angry, and there are beads of sweat on his forehead. Sitting on the edge of the bed, I feel his brow. Instinctively he jerks away but he definitely feels warmer than normal.

Shit! He's got a fever.

Getting up from the bed, I walk over to the bathroom and wash up. In a way they do have running water. Setting up a large tank on the roof, which has to be filled by hand, they have a large pipe that runs down into the village. From there they run a pipe into each home, though they don't want us using a lot of water. It's hard labor filling the tank. So we do our best with a basin and washcloth. I guess it's better than nothing.

Once cleaned up, I feel somewhat better. I grab my gear and head out to find the good doctor and inform her of Beast's current condition. I hope for her sake there is something she can do.

Amanda Belmont is an actual M.D. Before the Collapse, she practiced at Kaiser Permanente in Corona. Fortunately for Walma, she was a general practitioner, and keeps the villagers in decent health. When The Beast would show up, he'd focus on the kids. Partly because they like him, but also because I get the feeling he has previous experience where Amanda did not. I don't think she minded having a bit of help now and then anyway.

Like the rest of us, she also has her demons. She doesn't talk about it, but we've heard she lost her husband when the chaos erupted in the city. They were trying to get out when their car was struck by a semi, impacting the side her husband was on. He was killed instantly and she limped away from the wreck in a daze.

Were it not for Damien and Linda, she could have ended up like me. There may be a haunted look in her eyes, but raiders don't care about that. She is still attractive. Auburn hair is cut short and the good doctor keeps herself in shape. Before everything went to shit, she was vehemently anti-gun. Now she carries a handgun on her at all times.

Amanda is all business when I come in. She's like The Beast in one way: she rarely smiles—or shows any emotion at all, for that matter. Her bedside manner suffers, in my opinion. She bristles with impersonal efficiency whereas at least Beast exudes a calm that makes a person feel better as he treats you.

"Chloe. What can I do for you?"

"The Beast has a fever. You need to give him something."

The first response is a frown. I know she's calculating whether it's worth giving him something from their meager stores. If we run out of antibiotics, it's not like we can order another shipment to replace it. So do you try to save a forty-plus year old man or keep it to save an eight year old child somewhere down the line? Damned if you do, damned if you don't.

Making her decision, she goes to the fridge that holds the perishable drugs and pulls out a syringe in a wrapper. Grabbing a fresh needle, she walks out the door without any argument. I laugh to myself, thinking that in some ways she *is* just like Beast.

I follow closely behind as we make our way up the creaking stairs and walkways. The smell of too many people living in an enclosed space makes my nose wrinkle. Once more I miss the house we were in and curse the raiders silently.

The Beast's condition hasn't changed and he's still not awake. To say that I'm worried would be an understatement. Amanda gives him a quick check, frowning at the results. Hooking up the syringe, she uncovers his shoulder and gives him the injection before I can stop her.

Now he wakes up, and with a roar no less. One hand grasps the poor doctor around the throat and the needle nearly rips out of his arm. I immediately jump onto the bed, straddling his chest and fight to release his hold on her.

"Beast," I yell at him. "It's me, Chloe. You're safe. Let go of the doctor!"

The look in his eye is feral and he bares his teeth. Slowly his face changes as he recognizes me and his grip slackens. Letting go of Amanda's throat, he lays his head back and starts to breathe normally again, while the poor doctor is coughing violently. I squeeze his shoulder reassuringly, to let him know everything is going to be all right.

A sigh escapes me as I get off the bed to help Amanda, making sure she's okay. She's a little worse for wear, and gives Beast a dirty look as I help her out the door and onto the walkway. Once we are outside, I close it softly so that The Beast can rest.

"That man should be put in a cage," Amanda states bitterly.

Okay, I know she's just emotional from nearly being choked to death. I think any of us would be. Still, that's my Beast she's disrespecting and I don't appreciate her tone. I quickly transmit my disapproval with a dangerous glare before responding.

"Careful," I state in a low, venomous tone. "That's my partner you are talking about. He was hit while trying to protect you and everyone else here at Walma."

Wide, fearful eyes stare at me and I see the moment she realizes who she's angering: Ángel de la Muerte. An apology starts to stammer out of her mouth as she tries to make amends as fast as she can. Before she can saying something coherent, I stop her.

"Now what happened should be my fault," I state calmly. "So if you are going to blame anyone, blame me. I've known him long enough that I should have realized that getting stabbed in the arm would provoke a reaction and I should have been ready. So I apologize for my lack of foresight."

Amanda is struck mute by my tactful apology. In part, I don't want to ruin our relationship with the only doctor we know. Also, my apology is truthful. I should have known better and been ready for his reaction. As it was, I allowed my emotions to get the better of me instead of thinking things through.

"I'm sorry," she finally states, looking a little ashamed. "I shouldn't have said that. It was wrong of me."

I shrug. "We both made mistakes. It's all good, doc. Will he be okay?"

"Maybe. Normally I'd give someone a healthy regimen of antibiotics, but we just don't have a huge supply. I'm hoping a second shot will help his immune system to do the rest."

"What can I do?"

"Keep him warm and dry. Try to keep him hydrated and I'd recommend soup to keep his strength up. In fact, I'll have a couple cans sent up. I've been having Tom keep them off to the side for situations just like this."

I give her a nod and a genuine smile. "Thanks doc."

When I actually get a smile back, I musingly wonder if it hurt her to do so. As she walks off, I slip back inside to make sure my partner is all right. I see him moving slightly, so I move over quietly and check on him.

Blue eyes slide towards me slowly and he regards me through an obvious mask of fatigue. Slowly he makes a motion like he's taking a drink. Quickly I grab a canteen from our pile of gear and help him sit up. Ever so slowly he drinks and I'm glad for that. I've already lost too much to lose him as well. When he's done, I help him lay back down.

"Sleep," I tell him softly. "You need to rest and regain your strength. Don't worry, I have your back until then."

The Beast nods slightly and as his head lolls to one side, his eyes closing. Just like that he's out and breathing slowly. Again, I watch him sleep, his face at peace. My hands starts to reach for his mask as I have this urge to see what he looks like without it. Just as I'm about to, I pull back.

No. If I'm to see his face, it needs to be his decision. I have no right.

Looking towards the "living room" I focus on the ammo can he was so keen on retrieving. Rust spots are evident in places where the green paint has been chipped off. Faded lettering is almost illegible, but I read a yellow "5.56" on one line well enough.

Yeah, I think that I have a right to look at you.

Chapter Twenty-Two

Sitting down on the couch, I pull the can over and pop the lid. Okay, I fight to open the lid. The damn thing is stuck and I have to use all the brute force I can muster—which we've already established is not a lot—to get the latch to finally pop free.

Pulling the lid up, the sides scrape like it's on too tightly. Inside I spy a bunch of things in plastic bags. I pull out the first object and it's a leather bound book, wrapped in leather strips to keep it closed. Faded gold letters say "diary" on the cover.

Setting that aside, I pull out the next bag which is a collection of maps. I open the bag to take a look. There are maps of California, Arizona, Utah, New Mexico and Colorado. On many there are copious notes written, with routes marked out in various colors. The Colorado map is almost devoid of any markings at all though. The only thing written on it is a six digit number.

Is this what he means about going home?

Stowing the maps back in the plastic bag, I see what else is in the can. The air leaves my lungs when I notice what's in the next bag. On top of a number of items, I find a picture of a family. A daughter and mother, both smiling brightly. The father is in a Navy uniform, but the face has been torn out. The daughter has Beast's blue eyes.

Oh my god. He did have a family. So much for the theory that he's gay.

I can't even imagine what happened to them, but I know in my gut that this is what made him who he is today. The world took his family from him, so now he vents his anger right back, taking it out on the filth and scum that plagues it.

Tears prick at my eyes as I fixate on the image of a little girl who can't be more than eight. Blonde tresses with curls in them frame a bright smiling face with his eyes.

There are other things with the photo. A gold band. A child's hand-drawn picture in crayon. A small stack of folded papers. A little sticky note that says, "I love you" on it. This is far too personal and I quickly set it off to the side, trying to remove the image of his family from my mind. It's fucking breaking my heart.

At the bottom of the can is something that surprises me even more. Eight small gray balls sit at the bottom. Pressed into each one is what appears to be a digital kitchen timer. It takes me a minute to figure out what they are, and when I do, I almost drop the one I'm holding.

Where did he get serious explosives?

I carefully put the one I took out back in the can. Then I place everything back in with equal care, afraid it might go off if mistreated. I shudder as I recall how roughly we treated it on our way back from the hilltop. Closing the lid, which requires some effort, I put the can down on the floor and then check on Beast.

Gently touching his forehead, he feels slightly cooler and that makes me breathe a little easier. Still, he's warm all over. I rinse out the cloth with cooler water and place it gently back on his forehead. He stirs slightly and mumbles a little before settling back down into a fitful sleep.

With a sigh, I sit down on the bedside and squeeze his shoulder. "You need to fight this. I can't do this alone. I don't even know the destination you have in mind. So you need to get better and then talk to me, damn it. You can't keep leaving your partner in the dark."

Beast mumbles something I can't make out. I frown and squeeze his shoulder once more, hoping he knows that I'm here. Getting up, I walk over and search through our assorted collection of food which consists of a combination fresh grown fruits and veggies, as well as some canned goods.

I choose a can of "gourmet ravioli" and chuckle at it, wondering if there are any gourmets left in L.A.. With the Collapse came certain sacrifices. One was that you couldn't be picky about what you ate when you were lucky to have any food at all. Hell, if all you have is a can of dog food, you eat it and move on. I do take the fresh grapes off a platter as well, just to give myself something healthier for my meal.

Since the back of the couch faces the beds, I sit in the chair so that I can keep an eye on Beast. I open the can and dig in. I'm starving and before I know it I've completely polished off my "gourmet" meal. As hungry as I was, I'm surprised the can is still in one piece.

Sitting back, I relax into the chair as my stomach gurgles happily at me. After taking a drink of water, I roll my head to one side and see Beast is sleeping peacefully. I feel like that's where I should be.

I force myself to get up. Falling asleep in the chair is a bad idea when the bed is right there. In the bathroom, I divest myself of my tactical gear and outer garments. Taking stock of myself, I search for any injuries. Everything I've been through since the Collapse has increased my pain tolerance. More than once I've only realized I took a cut somewhere only after I find an obvious blood stain.

Upon inspection, I find a couple of bruises and scrapes, but nothing serious. I try to clean up in the basin, but it's difficult. The washcloth is quickly covered with grime, sweat and dirt. I rinse and keep trying. It's still better than nothing. When I glance over, I see Beast is still passed out, so I go ahead and pull off my t-shirt and panties.

A thought makes me chuckle. Beast is such a rough and tough individual. Yet when it comes to me being naked, he always disappears to give me privacy. Full-time killer, part-time gentleman. In a way I find it adorable because I am totally not body-shy. Still, as I rinse the washcloth again and finish cleaning up, I almost wish he did find me interesting. I shake my head at the thought. He has no interest in that either. I'm betting he still misses his family.

God, I miss my bathtub.

Once I'm done, I gather up my things and head over to my bed. My rifle leans against the headboard and I slide my pistol under my pillow. Pulling a suitcase out from under the bed, I find a fresh t-shirt and panties. Kicking the case lightly back under, I check on Beast once more.

Still asleep and still too warm. I sigh and worry about him. Changing his washcloth once more, I hope the shot Amanda gave him does the trick. I just know I cannot handle him dying on me. Finally I walk back to my bed and lay down. As soon as I close my eyes, I'm out.

When I wake a few hours later, my head is in a fog, trying to figure out what woke me. There's not much light, so I figure it must still be night. My watch verifies my suspicion when I look at it, the green backlight a little harsh to my eyes. That's when I hear the screaming.

Sitting up, I turn on the lights and launch out of bed. Beast is thrashing, in sleep or in delirium, eyes screwed tightly shut as he shouts in anguish. The pain in his voice wrenches at my heart as I try to help him snap out of his nightmare.

"Beast," I yell, shaking his shoulders. "Wake up!"

The heat coming off of him is oppressive and I worry that the infection is getting worse. I shake his shoulders furiously, and it takes some effort to finally get him to snap out of it. When he does, his eyes are wide and full of fear. Then he does something that I would not have expected.

"Anna," he exclaims as he pulls me down on top of him. "Oh baby, I'm so sorry! I'm so sorry."

My Beast starts crying as he crushes me against his sweat soaked body. I'm shocked and stunned and don't know what to do as he continues to apologize over and over. I can only assume that he's delirious and thinks I'm his wife, and it breaks my heart to see him like this.

"It's okay," I croon, trying to soothe him. "I forgive you."

"Oh baby!" I can hear his voice crack. "I tried. I swear I did. I did everything I could to save you and Katie."

Fuck!

"Shhhhhhh, I know you did. I forgive you. We forgive you. It's all right. Go back to sleep. You need to rest."

91

With a tearful nod, he lets go of me, gives a shuddering sigh and relaxes back into sleep. God, he is so warm. I grab a canteen and a fresh washcloth and put the wet compress high on his forehead, just above the mask. I use a shirt to fan air over him. Slowly his talking changes to mumbling and he's moving less. By the time he's relaxed and sleeping solidly again, my arms feel like rubber.

I sit down beside him and hold his hand. At my touch he shifts slightly in the bed, mumbles something and then calms down. This is what petty politics, selfishness and greed have done—created a broken world full of broken people. Beast and I are alike, not to say that the rest of the world is much different.

Yet in this world of broken people, this man saved me from one of the darkest hells that anyone could possibly experience. He did it without expecting a reward or demanding anything from me in return. He always treats me with respect. This Beast, a stone cold killer ready to rip throats out and bathe in people's blood, found me and, instead of using me, treated *me* with respect.

Sure, he's a pain in the ass. He doesn't talk much. He always expects me to do just as I'm told, no questions asked. But at the same time, I know it's what I signed up for. I asked him to teach me, to show me how to be like him. Never once did he force me to do something that was degrading to me as a woman. Everything he has had me do was with purpose, to teach me and open my eyes. To increase my chances of surviving in this hell hole.

My thoughts are making me uncomfortable. Grabbing my fatigue blouse, I throw it on and step outside onto the walkway. I leave the door open as I stand next to the railing and listen. There's more activity than normal right now as the villagers continue with their evacuation plan.

Damien and Linda may be hairdressers, but they are also canny negotiators. They have had a long standing agreement with an enclave in Moreno Valley that if shit hit the fan, they could fall back and become a welcome addition to that community, or vice-versa.

The children were to go first, and have been sent off this very night. I check my watch again. 02:43. By now the kids are there and the convoy is headed back. Once the convoy rolls in, they'll load up the first shipment of critical supplies and rush them out before dawn. The convoy will then switch drivers and start the process all over again.

We hope that moving the critical stuff at night will prevent anyone from noticing until it's too late. After that, daytime movement isn't as much of an issue. Besides, someone is bound to see the convoy tonight and know we are up to something. Any more night movement by vehicle after tonight is just asking for trouble. Chances are they won't be able to mobilize any serious threat until morning anyway. At least that's the hope.

The shacks below block any view of the warehouse floor, so I close my eyes and listen carefully. From what I can hear, everything sounds okay. They're getting ready for the convoy that's just pulling up. No shooting or yelling, no war-like sounds.

Since everything is under control, I head back in. I really need more rest. The last couple of days have been an emotional roller-coaster and I feel tired way beyond my years. It's the kind of tired that you feel all the way down to your bones. Resting my head against the pillow, I close my eyes and drift off to sleep.

Chapter Twenty-Three

I wake a little after eight in the morning, feeling good, rested and recharged. A little stiff from all that sleep in the past day, but other than that, great. I slip out of bed and check on Beast. He's still out, but he doesn't feel as warm. At least I hope that's the case. He certainly seems more peaceful and that alone lifts my spirits.

While I don't want to leave him, I need to check in with Damien and see how everything is progressing. Slipping into a clean set of clothes, I throw on my tactical gear and grab my rifle. I check on Beast one more time before I go. Giving him a soft kiss on the cheek, I then head out the door.

Walma is a flurry of motion on the ground floor, while the upper floors are almost devoid of people. Boxes are being packed and moved to a staging area. People run back and forth, some yelling orders, directions and or inaudible things. Damien and Tom stand in the middle of the chaos, issuing orders as villagers move. I assume Linda is still in charge of loading. She must be some kind of Tetris master with the way they rely on her skills.

Funny thing about being the Angel of Death is that everyone gives you a wide berth. As I cross the chaotic yard, I feel like Moses parting the Red Sea. It's almost amusing, but I'm not one to ruin my terrifying reputation by laughing, as much as I want to. The only two that don't look at me fearfully are Damien and Tom. Yet even they can't hide a certain wariness in their eyes. I try not to care, but I admit to myself it kind of hurts my feelings. So I tell myself to toughen up, buttercup and swagger as I take the last few steps to meet them.

"Chloe," Damien shoots me a smile as he nods. "How's The Beast?"

"Still out, but I think his fever's broken." I state with far more worry in my voice than intended.

"Toughest son of a bitch I know," Damien replies with a reassuring grin. "He'll pull through."

"I hope so. How's the evacuation going?"

"First day-run just left," he replies while pointing to the north warehouse door. "The north gate is our evac route, so you should pull your truck to that side."

I give a curt nod. "All right. Any activity?"

"We've spotted lookouts, but so far they haven't made a move."

I frown. "How close?"

"We've seen a couple darting from building to building, about seven to eight hundred meters away to the west."

"I think they've set up a forward base in the old FedEx building," Tom adds.

I give both men a predatory smile. "If that's true, let me see if I can do something about it."

Quickly walking away, I climb the stairs back up to the shack and check on Beast. Still sleeping soundly and his breathing seems a little smoother. Now I'm sure his fever has broken since he doesn't feel near as warm. I'll never be happier to see him awake and his old, grumpy self again. I pluck the keys off the dresser just inside the door and head back out.

Per Damien's instructions, I move Truck to the north gate and park it. Locking the door after I get out, I then open the back. Climbing part way in, I sift through weapons, searching for the one I need.

Most weapons he's just got laying loose on a packing blanket on the floor of the truck bed. We've camouflaged them with another blanket and various other things. Nobody needs to know what all we have. There are a special few that are in rifle cases however. One such weapon is an SVD sniper rifle. This weapon is a beast in itself and frankly, it fits him. Grabbing the loops of the soft-sided case, I heft it out of the truck and then grab two boxes of ammunition from an ammo can. Once the truck hatch is closed and locked, I make my way back into the warehouse.

Aside from the shacks for the most important people in Walma, the top-most walkway has one more thing, a ladder leading up to a roof hatch. Before I climb up, I pull my skull bandanna out of one of the smaller pockets on my tac vest and put it on, then I climb up.

Sunlight floods through the hatch as I clamber out onto the roof. Nearby are solar panels large enough to keep any raiders from seeing me, unless they've got spotters on the mountain. Planters with healthy plants also help conceal me. Since my prey is not on the mountain, I've decided not to worry about it. My target is in a building not too far away. One of the men walking guard duty notices me, and I motion him to come up to my position.

"Ma'am."

"Do me a favor," I whisper. "Walk your patrol and tell the other guards to ignore me. It's imperative that no one pays me any attention and gives me away."

"Yes ma'am."

I have to give the man credit. He walks away like we did not have a conversation. When he stops to talk to someone, it looks like they are just having a normal conversation, then he moves on to the next. As he does his job, I do mine.

Moving into the shadows beneath the solar panels, I crawl to the edge of the building. The villagers of Walma erected steel plates at the edge of the building to give the guards on top some protection. There are a few feet of space between each plate, and it's in one of those gaps where I set up.

Beast taught me to stay under cover as much as possible, especially when sniping. If you have to load, clear a jam or setup, lie on your side at the edge of the cover you are using and then lay down when you are ready to shoot. Lying on my side with the edge of the steel plate protecting me, I open the rifle case. Pulling the SVD out, I then get the scope from its protective pocket. The scope slides easily onto the mounting rails and I pull out the mags from the side pockets. I start loading rounds into them while continuing to stay out of sight.

I don't know if the old me would have thought so, but I find the ammo Beast has for the SVD is pretty. The casings and bullets are a burnished copper color that catches the light and look like they should be jewelry. Once I've loaded up four, ten round magazines, I slap the first one in. Taking the safety off, I rack the bolt and then pull the rubber cover off the front of the scope. There's a sliding can that I move out so that it shrouds the glass of the scope and keeps light from reflecting off, thus giving me away. With all that accomplished, I roll into position and peer through the scope.

It's only recently that Beast has started teaching me long-range shooting. In some ways it is more relaxing, and in other ways more frustrating. When you are looking at an unsuspecting target hundreds of meters away, you've got time to line up the shot. Even if you miss, they are stuck trying to figure out where the shot came from. The frustrating part is that the flight time is not instantaneous. Your target can move before the bullet gets there. That means understanding how fast the bullet moves, how much it drops over distance, how windy is it and so on. It is far more difficult than the movies make it look.

Today is going to be easier than my last attempt. I'm shooting slightly downhill, there's no wind and it's a clear day. I start scanning the FedEx building and find a couple guys on the roof. One man is lying there, watching the village through a pair of binoculars. The other is kneeling right beside and armed with a hunting rifle.

Mr. Hunting Rifle is the more important target and I start by putting him in my sights. According to the range finder, I'm just under a thousand meters away. It's a long shot, but easy with this rifle. In fact, the scope is meant to be used out to a thousand before needing to adjust. When I'm ready, I take a deep breath and slowly let out half, then hold it and pull the trigger.

The SVD is Oh-My-God-loud! It's also got a healthy kick, so you need to make sure it's tight against your shoulder. The rifle bucks in my grasp as I "send the round downrange," as Beast once called it. My aim is slightly off, but my bullet still connects and rips through the side of his chest. I watch him drop in a spray of blood, to no little satisfaction.

Mr. Binoculars panics and scrambles to his feet, running toward the roof hatch. I don't plan on letting him get away that easily and take aim. The rifle rocks me as I shoot once, twice and then a third time. On that third shot, the bullet is a little lower than I expected, and it lances right through his leg. He was close to the open hatch when he gets hit and falls face first into it. I can only imagine he's either dead at the bottom or lying there with a broken body.

I smile grimly as I roll away and then move to another spot further down the roof. I low crawl the entire distance to avoid being seen. I then set back up and scan the area. The raider with the hunting rifle is trying to crawl towards the hatch. At first I think about pulling the trigger, but refrain. It's not worth a round that isn't easily replaced. As far as I'm concerned, he can suffer bleeding out.

As I lay there scanning for any additional bastards I can shoot, I wish Beast was here. I'm so elated by how well I did and wish he was here to see it. I know he'd be proud, even though he'd pretend otherwise. Since I don't see anyone else, I pack up and head back inside to check up on him.

Chapter Twenty-Four

It's hard to feel cute when you wake up in a pool of your own blood.

A friend of mine in the old world told me that and it stays with me in moments like this. Cramps that register about magnitude eight on the Richter scale start up in the middle of the night and it's like the elevator scene right out of the damn Shining! Waking with a groan, I get out of my new, now blood soaked bed and stagger to the bathroom.

One thing is for sure, if I'd known massive national and global debt would have led to the collapse of society, I would have voted differently. Tampons and pads are one of the greatest luxuries ever invented: next to toilet paper, food, water and ammunition. Actually, at times like this, I'd rather have a handful of tampons and go hungry.

I clean up the blood that coats my nether regions and find one of the few tampons I have and put it to its intended use. *God, I feel like shit.* With that wonderful task done, and soiled clothing and bed linens soaking, I wander over and check on Beast to see how he's doing.

By the time evening rolled around, I found his fever had indeed broken and he was starting to get better. He was really weak, though, and needed help eating and drinking. After that—and a bathroom break—he fell back into a deep sleep. He wasn't delirious anymore, and the doc said he should be back to normal in a few days.

The evacuation went well for the rest of the day. Amanda had the infirmary packed, and almost all of it was shipped to Moreno, with her along to keep it under her watchful eye. Most of the armory and food stores were gone, along with some of the families and all of the children. Damien figures the entire village will be evacuated within a day or two.

Checking my watch, I find it's a little after midnight. I can really use the escape of sleep now that Midol is a thing of the past, so I turn the mattress over and grab my second set of sheets. Then I flop onto the bed and try to get back to sleep while my uterus tries to claw its way out of my stomach like something out of a science fiction movie.

I'm just about the drop into deep sleep when I hear gunfire. Gritting my teeth, I roll out of bed and slip into my pants as fast as I can while the sounds of fighting increases rapidly. I then grab my tactical vest and rifle and sprint out the door.

In hindsight, leaving without my boots was probably not the best idea. I carefully run across the rough wooden walkway, trying to make sure I don't pick up any splinters as I traverse down to the ground floor and out the door.

Pandemonium is the best way to describe combat that involves a large number of people. Villagers are running every which way, some armed and others just running scared. Me, I'm one of the crazy-ass people that runs *toward* the sound of fighting.

As I get to the top of the defensive wall, I find raiders are pressing an attack on Walma from the south and west—in force. Mr. Tavor and I immediately start trying to help the guards repulse the assault.

I definitely love this gun. The bullpup design makes for a compact weapon that I can maneuver easily. Seems to me that it is also quicker to reload since the magazine is right there at my chest. One thing is for certain, I start ripping through raider after raider as they try pushing up and returning fire.

Bullets zip pass me, while others career off the low metal wall in front of me. And let me tell you right now, the sound of a bullet zipping by your ear is a very—shall I say, invigorating?—sound.

The raiders are yelling war cries as they continue to charge the gate and wall. Most of the guards on my side are trying to stick to cover more than shoot back. A couple have already been shot and are dead or dying. Me, death would be a reward compared to this hell. My goal is simply to take as many of those bastards with me that I can.

In just a handful of minutes, I think I've killed more men than Rambo. They should have checked my calendar, because a woman on the rag really would rather kill you than look at you. Believe it. The drum mag runs dry and I duck behind cover, pull the drum and slap in a fresh magazine. There's no such thing as being wasteful in post-apocalyptia, so I stuff the drum into the dump pouch on my vest before standing back up to start shooting again.

I'm not sure who's more surprised, the raider or myself when I pop up over the barricade to find the man nearly cresting the top of a ladder. Wide eyes stare right at me as my barrel points directly at his sternum. These are the kills that stick with you—the ones so close you can look them in the eyes. This does not stop my rifle from stating my disapproval of his lifestyle and very existence. Two rounds sends him flying off the ladder. Pushing the ladder away, I shoot the men below with no remorse. If they didn't want me to be a cold-blooded bitch, they shouldn't have made me that way.

As I drop to change mags once more, I make a quick scan of the wall. So far we are keeping them at bay, and while I see a few guards down, I do not see any raiders on the inside of the compound. Rising to engage more of the enemy, that's when everything goes straight to Hell!

I can only stand there like a newb as a globe of fire comes streaming toward the wall. It hits the section I'm standing on, smashing into the trailer with enough force to tip it over. Flames rise around me and I feel oppressive heat on my face right before I am sent flying backwards.

The air is driven from my lungs as I hit the broken asphalt hard, back first. My head rebounds off the concrete and I see stars. Struggling to get to my feet—I feel like I'm underwater. My vision is watery and sounds are muffled.

I vaguely hear someone yell, "Breach! Breach!"

Looking at the section of wall I had been standing on, I see it's dislodged enough for raiders to funnel through. It's a struggle to aim, as my head feels full of molasses. When I pull the trigger, I hear dull, muffled shots from my Tavor. A couple raiders drop from my renewed assault and it buys my people time to regroup.

The residents of Walma had enough foresight to set up smaller defensive emplacements inside the wall. The guards have now posted up in them and start shooting back. I breathe a sigh of relief and fallback through the door and into the warehouse in an attempt to clear my head.

Staggering in, I shake my head and take a few deep breaths, trying to get the damn cobwebs cleared out of my skull. When Tom runs up, he grabs one of my shoulders and shakes me gently. Looking up, I have trouble focusing as he talks to me like he's underwater.

"Are you all right?"

At first I shake my head, then nod. "I hit my head."

Even my voice doesn't sound right. Tom pats me on the shoulder and says something. I think it's "concussion," but it's hard to tell with my altered hearing and the sounds of combat drowning everything out.

"Fall back," Tom shouts and points towards the north door, where some people are setting up a barricade.

With a nod, I start for it as I shake my head again, trying desperately to clear it. I think I see Damien behind the barricade, motioning me towards him. Suddenly the warehouse is filled with reddish light before I hear the sound of rending metal. Once more I'm sent flying when something strikes me in the back.

Twice in one day. How lucky can a girl get? Funny how when you've been thrown off a wall and then across a warehouse floor, you still get to feel the cramps that are rending you in half. Fuck. Me.

Pushing up off the floor with a groan, I look back. A section of the warehouse wall has been torn open and a flaming catapult ball rests near the evidence of its destruction. Part of the wall is on my legs and I struggle to get it off.

As I free myself, raiders rush through the breach and bullets fly over my head in both directions. Frantically I reach for my rifle only to find it isn't on me. Looking around, I catch sight of it about twenty feet away, at the foot of the barricade I was heading for. While the initial push of bandits is cut down, there are still a handful left. Damien and the few trying to hold the line are forced to fall back as a flurry of bullets rain around them.

When I glance back, I find myself all alone in the warehouse, with five raiders walking up to me and grinning wildly.

Well, shit!

Chapter Twenty-Five

My wits have begun to come back and my vision is a little better as I watch a raider stride up. Dressed, as they all seem to be, in various bits of leather, he's got a stop sign for a chest piece with plenty of dents and scratches. Speed limits signs have been molded to protect his shoulders, and sections of car tires cover his thighs. A mound of curly brown hair makes me think he's got a head full of pubic hair.

"Well, well," he grins lecherously. "Look what we got here, boys? The Angel of Death herself. Doesn't seem so tough to me."

"There are at least three dozen of your friends today that would disagree with you," I spit back at him.

One of the other men let's out with a whoop. "This one has some fire, Travis."

I glare at him as the other men snigger and laugh. Slowly I'm moving my hand towards my pistol. My first and only thought is to gun these bastards down. The one called Travis points his rifle at me when he realizes what I'm doing.

"Now, now. Let's not go doing anything stupid. The Dean is really looking forward to meeting you."

"Fuck you!"

Travis grins lecherously. "Oh trust me, little lady, that's going to be on the menu. Dean is going to make you his prime attraction. He's got a whole theme park planned for you. And when he gets tired of you, then you'll get to meet us."

There's a part of me that I've tried to bury deep inside, ever since the day Beast saved me. That is the useless woman I was when Knick had me enslaved. The stinking corpse of every raider that I've killed is piled on top of that woman in an attempt to never think of her again. These assholes stare me down, threatening me with slavery once more, and I can feel her trying to crawl out of that grave like some vengeful zombie.

Fuck. That. Shit!

Summoning up every ounce of anger I have, I stare him down. "I'll fucking kill Dean, bathe in his blood and then you'll be next."

It's easy to see the fear well-up in Travis' eyes as the venom in my words runs through his veins. My reputation is solid and a couple of men take an involuntary step back. Others clutch their weapons tighter, like a child holding onto their favorite doll or blanket, hoping it will keep the monster at bay.

As Travis opens his mouth to respond, his eyes suddenly bulge as the tip of a sword blade juts out of his chest. We are all in shock. Hell, I've got a concussion and I'm trying to figure out if I'm really seeing this.

Staggering forward, he drops his rifle and tries to speak while clutching at the wound. All that comes out are some strangled gasps as he looks at me like he wants me to help him. Like I'm going to save him if he repents.

Yeah, right. You'll have a better chance trying to find ice water in hell, fucker!

When he drops, I can barely make out Beast on the walkway behind us and that's when I burst into action. I kick Travis in the face, hard, as the men turn to see where the sword came from. Then everything goes into slow motion as my pistol clears the holster and I take aim.

The fuzziness from my concussion makes it difficult to focus, forcing me to repeat a mantra in my head. *Pull the trigger, pull the trigger, pull the trigger, PULL THE TRIGGER!*

Between The Beast and I, all four men are gunned down before they can get a straight shot off. I'm breathing hard as I stagger to my feet and spit on Travis' corpse. Mentally, I tell that bitch to crawl back into her grave and stay there before pulling Beast's sword out. There's a wet sound as it slides free and I look at him with a smile.

My vision is still a little blurred, so I can't make out his facial expression. But he gives a wave and then tosses some stuff over the walkway. The sounds of fighting are continuing, so I rush over, grab my rifle and then check to see what it was he tossed over.

I find my boots, suit case and his duffle bag lying on the floor. I sling my rifle this time, cursing myself for being so stupid before, jump into my boots and then grab the bags and rush for the truck as fast as I can in unlaced footwear.

As I reach the door, I intercept The Beast as he's heading the same direction. He looks like shit, his color far too pale for my liking. After taking the sword when I hand it over, he bends down and places a gray ball on the main support beam and then motions for me to move.

Oh shit!

It's hard to focus when you have a concussion. I try to run, but the best I can do is a jog without potentially killing myself by falling flat on my face. As I get close to Truck, I hear the locks unlock. Yanking the passenger side door open, I pile both bags into the back of the cab and then climb in.

"Retreat," I hear Damien yell and look that direction.

Beast isn't far behind him, motioning people back as a group of raiders come sprinting around the corner opposite our truck. I fumble for my rifle, watching in horror as Damien and another guard are cut down. Beast, Linda, myself and two others fill the assholes with lead.

I'm out of the truck and running as fast as I can as Beast kneels down to help Damien. It doesn't look good and I can hear Linda screaming as someone holds her back. He's been hit four times, three of them in the chest. He coughs up blood as he looks at Beast.

"I need you to promise me, get Linda out of here." Damien grabs Beast's shoulder in a death grip. "P-promise me!" Drops of blood land on Beast's face and mask as our friend struggles to spit out the words.

Beast closes his eyes and then nods, the words falling from his lips in a harsh whisper. "I promise, my friend."

Damien gives a bright smile. "First time we have a real conversation and you say just want I want to hear. Keep my Linda sa…"

Fuck!

All we can do is watch helplessly as Damien shudders and gasps one final breath before going limp in Beast's arms. Linda wails and I can't blame her. My eyes are wet with tears, making it even more difficult to see clearly. Without another word, Beast grunts as he picks Damien up and hefts him into the truck Linda and two others are in. Then he pounds the side of the vehicle twice, telling the driver to move.

While he's still sick and weak, I know he's pissed. Furiously motioning me to Truck, he falls back as well. Any raider that's foolish enough to come around the corner is gunned down without mercy.

Once he hits the truck, I take over. I have the passenger side door open and shoot until he's in and starting the engine. Leaving the window armor down, I close the door and keep shooting as we peel out.

Clearing the gate, I catch sight of two guards that missed their ride and tell Beast to stop. He hits the brakes and we both gladly provide covering fire, shooting at any raiders while the two men rush to our vehicle and clamber in. The one on my side is wounded, his arm bleeding profusely.

Once they're on board, we're driving away from Walma as fast as we can. We're about a block down when the explosives go off. An enormous fireball rises in the rear-view mirror.

Yeah! Fuck you, assholes!

My fervent hope is that most of the raiders were in the warehouse, celebrating over their ill-gotten gains when the bomb went off. I shake my murderous thoughts away and keep a sharp eye out, rifle at the ready in case anyone tries to ambush us. Once we are the tail end of the convoy, I relax a little and take time to check the wounded man.

The young man is Hispanic, with short, curly dark hair. He's already looking a pale, probably from a combination of blood loss and shock. I grab a bandage and—with a grudging sigh—a tampon from my trauma kit and go to work. He grits his teeth and yells when I shove the tampon into the gushing bullet hole, catching his breath when I start wrapping gauze around it.

"You'll be okay," I tell him over the growl of the diesel engine. "The doc will get you patched up and you'll be back to normal in no time. Trust me, I know. I've been hit in the arm before myself."

I get a relieved smile back and the young man rests his head against the head rest and closes his eyes. Turning around, I sit back down, grab my rifle and help keep an eye out. They all see a calm woman, doing her job. Inside? I'm seething with fury and wondering how to get back at these bastards.

Chapter Twenty-Six

It's been two days since the fall of Walma and I'm standing in a field with the rest of the survivors as we pay tribute to our fallen dead. I hold Linda tightly to me as she weeps. Beast is just behind us, probably ready to catch her if she passes out. Tom is to her right, his arm still in a sling from a bad blow.

My head is a bit better. The headache is almost gone and I've only had a couple dizzy spells. It could have been far worse. I'm glad I didn't end up like Natasha Richardson—an actor's wife who died because of a seemingly minor concussion and brain bleed. Beast has been very watchful, and it's been surprisingly endearing. It freaked me out at first because he took it so seriously. Living in a world after the Collapse means that certain wounds can't be treated so easily. Now even a simple concussion can be fatal.

We gaze numbly as the funeral pyres are lit. A near silent group of battered and bloodied people watching columns of fire rise into the air. The flames consume the bodies of the honored dead and a fire of vengeance rages within me. I lost good friends, a fine and decent group of people have had to flee their home, and I crave revenge.

I squeeze Linda's shoulder gently. "Come on. Let's head back."

We slowly return to the Moreno Enclave, heads low. Our spirits are downcast, and the weather agrees. Dark clouds cover the sky and the drizzle has been unceasing. The ground is wet and muddy, squelching under our boots. It's a nice change compared to the early Santa Anas that have been making the days miserably hot and dry.

Linda's tears and shuddering sobs continue. I keep an arm around her and help in navigating the soft terrain. She is a strong woman, but Damien was her soul-mate, her partner. I shudder to imagine myself without Beast and thank the powers that be once more that he is still alive. I can't even imagine her pain, but I can guess as I glance at Beast briefly.

My partner is looking better today. The color has returned to his face and his strength is back, although he's walking with a limp. At least any signs of infection are gone and he's had no more fever. Even his leg wound is better and less red.

The Moreno Enclave encompasses most of a city block. At first they settled into the high school and middle school on Eucalyptus Avenue. From there they expanded out their defensive perimeter and absorbed a housing development, park and another school. It was the city hall building that gave them additional weapons to help defend themselves.

Everything within roughly five hundred meters has been torn down or torched to create an effective kill zone, all thanks to construction equipment found behind city hall. After stripping the area of anything remotely useful, they used the bulldozers to rip everything left into rubble. With the debris, they built a combination dirt berm with a wood and metal wall on top.

Fortunately they have enough room to easily absorb the Walma refugees and they are quickly integrated. The Moreno leader, Kathy, seems happy with the arrangement, even though it means there is one fewer village to trade with. Now she has more guards and weapons to keep raiders at bay. She's even gained a qualified doctor and extra seeds for planting. It's a win-win for everyone except Beast and I. This kind of arrangement is not going to work for him. Too many people, too closed in.

Kathy is not keen on keeping anyone in the Enclave who isn't willing to stay and do their part. It's not like we have nothing to offer, but Kathy's a hard woman who will brook no argument to whatever she decides is best. She's in her forties, with a gravelly ex-smoker's voice. She's a rough and tough Filipino woman, and takes no shit from anyone. Stringy black hair is often worn loose and she has tactical gear that is tricked out to go along with an M1 carbine.

Of course, our reputation is not to be argued with either. Beast and I are both wounded, and yet I plainly see she is afraid of us. Everyone is. We told her that we would do as she asks while we heal up and got ready to leave. Beast also placated her with a box of .30 carbine rounds, a gift that put a twinkle in her eyes.

That's been enough to keep her off our backs and we've been left alone, given a wide berth even. Only the Walma veterans smile and talk to us. That's fine as far as I'm concerned. I have more important matters on my mind right now—revenge.

Walking back into the enclave, we head to the house Linda has been assigned to. Tom also has a room there. I get the feeling his presence helps to keep her spirits up as she struggles to cope with the immeasurable loss of Damien.

We sit at the kitchen table in silent contemplation. All but Beast, that is. He paces like a—well, like a caged animal. I swear he thinks he can walk the bullet wound off like in some video game. I'm worried he's going to reopen his wound and get it infected all over again.

Okay, seriously? That is one pace too many!

"Beast!" I yell, easily getting his attention. "Sit down, damn it!"

At first he glares, but I'm far too pissed off and don't back down. Instead I point at the open chair to my left and glare right back. I even bare my teeth at him and let my eyes flash. I swear I see amusement flash across his face, but we're scarring the others. Linda and Tom watch with wide eyes as two titans stare each other down. Finally Beast relents and sits down with a pained grunt.

I cool off and place a hand gently on his forearm. "Thank you," I say to him with honest sincerity.

He closes his eyes, takes a deep breath and then bows his head to me respectfully. Both Linda and Tom exhale in unison, as if they had been holding their breath throughout our entire exchange.

"What will you guys do now?" There's a tone of defeat in Tom's question.

"Right now?" I respond with a snort of a laugh. "Heal up. Beast has been shot and I have a concussion."

The poor man grins sheepishly. "I kinda meant after that."

I smile at him warmly. "We'll take stock of our supplies, figure out what we lost and need to replace and then look at getting on the road as originally planned."

"You could stay," Linda states in a pleading voice.

I can only imagine that the poor woman is not keen on loosing anyone else, though she knows we had already planned to move on. Too much change in too short a time. She clings to what she sees as safety. Her face and bearing have aged in the past week, carrying the sorrow and despair from Damien's death on her shoulders. But I can't help but think that, given a chance to heal and rest, she will rise and fight again.

"Part of me wants to say yes, but no. Beast wants to go home, and I think I'd like to see something other than this God forsaken rotting corpse of a city anymore."

"Can't say as I blame you," Tom states bitterly.

"Agreed," Linda concurs. "It sounds like a great idea, actually. But for the moment, we're just happy that Kathy took us in. Some of the Walma folks aren't so sure about staying. Kathy's, well, she's strong, but maybe she's too hard. There is no other place for us to go, so I don't know. I just don't know about much of anything anymore."

Oh, Linda.

Tears prick in my eyes. I grab her hand gently and give it a reassuring squeeze. "Hey, he wants you to go on. Damien made Beast promise to get you to safety."

Linda sniffles, trying to hold back the tears. I scoot over and hold her as she starts to cry again. "It's not fair," she sobs on my shoulder. "We didn't do anything to them. Why couldn't they just leave us alone?

"I know it's not," I reply softly as I hold her tightly.

Deep down I know she's right. The University Raiders did not have to do this. Walma wasn't attacking them. The university already had everything they needed; food, electricity and solid roofs over their heads. There was no reason to attack Walma, except to be assholes and wreck other people's lives.

No more, damnit. No fucking more!

"I promise you this," I state as I tilt Linda's head up so she can see my resolve. "I'll make them pay. Every single one of those motherfuckers is going to pay!"

Chapter Twenty-Seven

It's a cool night as Beast and I ghost our way to the edge of University Riverside and scan the area carefully. We picked our way through the trails and hills east and south of the campus before finally arriving here. Between Beast's injury and moving slowly to make sure we aren't discovered, it takes us all night to get to this point.

We had to slip past a few patrols. Evidently the raiders were learning, though they really didn't know what they were doing. Patrols were lazy and undisciplined, and often they talked so much that we could hear them long before we saw them. Half the time I could smell them before I laid eyes on them. I wanted to kill them, but Beast told me no. I frowned at him, but he actually spoke, so I had to take him seriously. He said that killing a patrol could tip our hand. I had to agree with his deduction, damn it.

It doesn't help that we are loaded for bear. My vest has extra mag pouches on it, including a couple I have on the back to hold four of his. Along with my Tavor, he's also hooked me up with a dual shoulder rig sporting a P-90 on each side. My left pistol holster has been replaced with a drop leg mag holder giving me two more P-90 mags. My only pistol is the FNX, with one extra magazine. Finally I've got my combat knife at the small of my back.

Always carry a knife in case there's cake—or you run into some asshole who needs to be stabbed. So far, I have found no cake.

Beast isn't slouching, and that makes me frown a little. To begin with, he's rocking the G3. As a full size rifle, it's rather heavy. That's not all. He also carries a SPAS-12 shotgun with a shoulder sling full of shells. All this is topped off with his three pistols, sword, knife, extra magazines for everything and finally the remaining explosives he'd had in the secret ammo can.

We've stopped at the top of a hill that overlooks the campus and set up camp. Beast has deployed a camouflage tarp that blends in well with the terrain. Unless someone gets close, we will look like the scrub and rock of the hill.

We are settled down and have set up a spotting scope to watch how the raiders operate. I make sure all my weapons are ready. Fully loaded, one in the breach and suppressors set on the ones that have them.

As I start to zoom in on the campus, Beast taps my shoulder. I look at him and he makes a hand sign for sleeping and then points at me. I really don't feel like it, but given my recent injury, I probably should. Offering no argument, I nod and move to my bed roll. Lying down, rifle beside me,

I close my eyes.

The next thing I know is the sensation that I'm floating, then a feeling like I'm lying on something hard and lumpy. Rolling over with a groan, the ground shifts under my weight. At that, my eyes snap open. That's when I realize that I'm lying on a pile of skulls.

With a gasp, I scramble to my feet and look around. This isn't right. I'm dressed in tight leather armor, and my boobs are—holstered is my first thought—for they are in a fitted breastplate. My posture has never been this good. It's not uncomfortable, exactly, but I'm not at ease, either. There's a sword on my hip. No, I take that back, Beast's sword is on my hip.

As I draw the weapon, I look around once more, trying to figure out where I am. The ground is littered with raider bodies, all lying on a surface of bleached white skulls. The sky is the bluest that I've ever seen, as white, fluffy clouds drift along lazily. Scanning my surroundings, sword still held high, I think I see something a short distance away and head for it.

There's no way to gauge how much time passes as I walk. Eventually the field of skulls gives way to parched, cracked earth and the heat becomes oppressive. Coming over a rise, my steady lope slows and I'm struck dumb at what I encounter.

Knick and Knack are strung up on posts, not unlike a crucifixion, but those are not crosses, rather, "X's." Their hands and feet are staked down, blood running from the wounds. They appear dehydrated, like they've been out in the sun too long. Behind them is a lake of blood, a small tide frothing as it hits the shoreline. While this may be a dream, I can't help but smile at the righteousness of their fate.

As I enjoy the sight before me, Knick's eyes flutter open. Upon recognizing me, they widen in a combination of shock and horror. At first he tries to talk, but his throat is too dry and all I hear is a frog-like creak.

"Chloe, is that you?"

"Hello Knick. Didn't expect to see you—hanging around these parts."

The barb in my statement stings him well and he closes his eyes briefly. Our conversation has roused Knack, and now he regards me in silent horror. I think he wants to run, because he tries to move and moans in pain when he pulls against the stakes impaling his body.

"Chloe, baby," Knick speaks softly. "I'm sorry for what I did. Please help me? Get me out of here."

Are you fucking kidding me?

I start laughing. "Oh, Knick. I like you just the way you are."

I'm savoring every moment of the sorrow that shows in his eyes. Perhaps it's not the Christian thing to do, but I can't help it. This piece of shit tormented me, tortured me, *raped* me over and over and over again. I was never a human being in his eyes. I was a piece of ass for his use, an animal made for one reason only—an object to use and discard at his will. There was NEVER an ounce of remorse in his eyes the entire time he used me as his plaything.

Oh no, honey, you reap what you sow.

Our conversation is interrupted by the roar of a lion from behind me. Knick and Knack both shrink in terror as they look over my head. I spin, sword clearing its sheath and ready for a fight when I am struck dumb yet again.

A woman approaches from the field of skulls, and she is the most beautiful woman I have ever seen. This is coming from someone who worked in an industry full of gorgeous ladies. This woman's perfection blows them all away. It's as if she is the essence of beauty itself.

Dressed in a pristine and glowingly white gown cut like a toga, she looks amazing. The dress is cut to reveal athletic, toned arms. Clasped around her waist is a silver belt studded with lapis lazuli. Blonde hair is cut short, framing a fine face containing eyes of the same color of lapis as her belt. Sandals adorn her feet, with thin straps wrapping up around muscular calves.

It's hard to take my eyes off of her, but my wariness of the lions makes me finally look away. One beast strides along each side and they are damn near pony sized. Long golden manes flow down their bodies. They are the most frightening, yet most majestic creatures that I have ever seen in my life.

"Hello Chloe."

How do I describe that voice? It sounds like a combination of your mother's kind and loving voice mixed with that of a lover whispering in your ear as they make love to you, stealing your breath and your heart.

"Uh, I—hello." *Smooth, Chloe. Smooth.*

"Do you like my handiwork?" She points to Knick and Knack.

I glance at them, shocked at the question, then look back at her and grin. "Oh yeah. I just wish they got more like what they gave me and the other women they kept as slaves."

"That can be arranged."

"What?"

I can hear Knick and Knack pleading and moaning behind me, asking me for mercy, for forgiveness. *Yeah, I'm fresh out of forgiveness, boys. Perhaps you shouldn't have treated me the way you did and things would have been different.*

The woman smiles. "I can see to it that their punishment is more fitting to their crimes."

"No Chloe," Knick screams in terror. "Don't do it. Please forgive us?"

The woman's countenance changes from pleasant to vicious in a heartbeat. With a wave of her hand, Knick writhes in pain, screaming at the top of his lungs. All I can do is watch as the one who was once my tormentor now gets what he deserves. When he calms down, I look back at her.

"What's the catch?" While I ask, I'm ready to sign on the dotted line.

I get a warm smile, the kind your mother would give you when you made her proud. "Thanks to idiots like them, the world is broken and needs fixing. You will serve me. The soul of every bad man you kill will come to me for proper—treatment. In return, you will not only receive my blessing, but I will see to it that these two receive more than just punishment. I will see to it that the demons of the underworld—violate them in ways they never thought possible. Is there really any better punishment for a rapist?"

There's a little voice in my head that shouts a warning that I might be making a deal with the devil. Yet at the same time, how can I possibly say no? How can you ever expect a woman to forgive the men that raped her? These two stole my life. That Chloe is gone, murdered as if they pulled a trigger and put a bullet in her brain. All that's left is the Angel of Death, and she thirsts for vengeance.

"I agree." My voice is firm.

The woman laughs joyously and claps her hands. At the same time, Knick and Knack are lamenting and moaning at their fate. The sound from both her and the men who were once my tormentors, makes me happy.

"Please step closer, child."

Sheathing the sword, I step up, wary of the lions, yet I feel assured that they will not attack. When I get close, she places one palm just over my left breast and smiles warmly. There's a tingling sensation in her touch.

"Take a deep breath, child. This is going to hurt."

I barely have time to register what she's said before physical pain like I've never experienced lances through me as quick as a bullet. It's like I'm on fire while being stabbed at the same time. I can't help but scream as I'm held immobile.

And then it's done. I stagger back, catching my breath as sweat drips into my eyes. With effort I pull the breastplate back a bit and open my shirt. Looking down to see a pattern on my skin. It appears like a number of sticks or golf tees arranged in a specific way and it has a charred appearance, and it strikes my dream self as somehow familiar. Yet as I look at the odd tattoo I've received, it begins to fade until it completely disappears.

"You are now my envoy," she states in a reverent tone. "You will walk upon the earth and deliver love to those who deserve it, or war to those who earn it. You will truly be my Angel of Death."

I bow to her. "Thank you, my lady. I still don't know your name."

"Goddess will do," she states with a smile. "Now it is time for me to deliver my down payment to you as promised."

With a clap of her hands, an inhuman howling fills the air and mingles with the screams of Knick and Knack. I turn to see that both men are writhing on their racks, eyes wide in abject terror as they desperately try to get free.

From the cracks in the ground, black shapes rise up and the sight fills my heart with dread. Whatever they are, they're humanoid in shape, with arms that are far longer than normal. Hands that are possessed of equally long fingers end with sharp looking talons for nails. When their mouths open, I am horrified by needle-like teeth. They wear no clothes and have nothing to denote their sex, with skin that is ash gray and a smattering of coarse black hairs. They resemble nothing more than a nightmare, feral killing machines.

"Chloe," Knick screams over the howling. "Please!? Don't let them take us!"

Knack is just as insistent in his pleas as the monsters—demons?—climb the poles toward their offered prey. I watch in silent resolve while the two men are plucked off their stakes. Talons sink into their skin as both men shriek in pain, blood streaming, snot and spittle spraying.

Their fear does not move me. I've been that afraid, and with no hope as they did worse to me, to my body, spirit, to my mind. I stare with a cold heart, though I am surprised to find a single tear sliding down my cheek. Is it pity? I don't know, maybe. But they should have considered the afterlife while they were making my life a living hell. I don't object as the demons carry both men below the earth. Once they are gone, silence descends once more. I take a deep breath, happy in the knowledge that the men who raped me are being well-cared for in Hell.

"Satisfied?"

I turn to the Goddess and smile sadly. "Yes, goddess, though I wish..."

"Wish what?"

"I wish it weren't necessary. I wish they never did what they did. But... but I don't know how to change the past, is what I am saying, I guess."

"If you change the world, my child, their crimes will no longer be the rule, but the exception."

Reaching out, she brushes the tear from my cheek with a single finger and sucks it into her mouth. Giving me a lovely, yet fierce smile, she hugs me. I get the oddest, sweetest feeling from the hug. As if I'm finally home and my mother is holding me tightly and nothing bad can ever happen again. Then she steps back and stands tall, and I feel proud and happy, simply to be in her presence. I feel healed and whole. I feel... I've never felt this way, but I like it.

"Do well for me, my avenging angel," the goddess states proudly. "I expect to see great things from you. But for now, wake up."

Chapter Twenty-Eight

"Wake up," Beast growls in a harsh whisper as he shakes me.

My eyes snap open and I see Beast hovering over me, concern etched plainly on his face. Quickly I sit up and try to figure out where I am, my head in a fog. The sun is high in the sky, it's hot and we are sitting on the top of a hill overlooking the university campus.

"I'm up," I say softly to him. "I'm okay." I find I am gently rubbing a sore spot on my chest, right above my heart.

Sitting back, he looks relieved. I try to remember the dream I was having. It's like trying to hold on to water as the memory of it slips through my fingers and down the drain. I am left with a feeling of peace, and nothing more. Finally I give up, take a deep breath, and crawl up to where the spotter scope has been stationed.

Next to the scope is a pencil and notepad. On reading the notes, he's been denoting movement on the various buildings, when they appear to change shifts and anything else of interest. For example, I learn they are setting up a scissor lift at one end of the track field, on the opposite side of the campus from us.

When I glance back, Beast is already lying on his bedroll and trying to sleep. I smile and start my shift on watch. When it comes to being "on the clock" we have developed a rhythm that doesn't require much talking. Granted, that's the way he likes it, but it also keeps our prey from hearing us. And that's the way *we* like it.

As I watch the university through the scope, I rub at the sore area on the skin above my breast, a burning sensation that finally fades. As it does, I begin to realize that I feel better. My head doesn't hurt anymore. I feel refreshed and well rested. And, strangely, I feel no after effects of the concussion bogging me down. I guess sometimes a good sleep does do wonders after all. With a grin, I go back to watching.

Just so you know, lying on a hillside, watching men come and go is not very interesting. In fact, it's boring as hell. More than once, I see a raider mistreating a slave and I want to grab Beast's G3 and put a bullet in the bastard! Then I remind myself that as soon as night falls, we will sweep down and kill them all. That thought calms me and I go back to watching.

In time, the sun starts to set, so I lightly nudge the bottom of Beast's closest boot. He wakes up with a start and I give him a hand sign, letting him know were all clear. With a nod, he crawls up to me to see how things are going.

"Not much to report," I whisper softly. "Watched a team of six head east two hours ago. Twice that headed west a little more than an hour ago.

Otherwise nothing but normal guard movement. Although at the running track, it seems like they are setting up for a party."

With silent care, he pulls up his rifle and looks through the scope, glassing the entire area. Once he's satisfied, he sets the weapon down and lays out the plan. We will start by taking out any guards on the building right below us. We'll sweep through and kill anyone inside it before moving on.

At last!

I push myself back and gear up. Aside from weapons and ammo, we didn't bring much. Left almost all the food back with Truck and carried only one canteen. We have a cold meal before the sunlight disappears completely. I drain my canteen so I'm well hydrated and it doesn't make any sloshing noise. The beef jerky and canned pears went down well and I feel ready.

Beast and I are set as darkness descends. Lights at the university come on, creating pools of illumination within the sea of black. In some ways our attack will be perfect. There are clouds overhead, blocking any moonlight that could help them to see us. We will have the spill over from their lights to see by, while they will be light blind.

Setting up the bipod on his rifle, Beast points at the two guards on the roof closest to us. He's going to take the left while I take the right. When I take my shot, he'll take his. I give him a quick nod and start aiming.

The night vision on my rifle makes it easy to see my target. Through the green tint of the scope, I line up on my assigned volunteer as he walks along the edge of the roof. The man is carrying an AK, which I realize is a staple for them. I wonder where they got them all as I release half a breath and hold it.

Stroking the trigger sends a sixty-five grain bullet at my first scalp of the night. Since I'm uphill, it's an easy shot. Actually, I overcompensate on my aim slightly. I watch as the bullet hits him right in the neck and sends him off the edge of the roof and into the darkness. Beast's target drops right after mine.

We stay perfectly still, watching through our scopes while we listen intently. Everything looks clear. I don't see anyone rush out of the building, nor do I hear anyone yelling out an alarm. After a few minutes, we slowly start down the hill, leapfrogging as we cover one another until we reach the parking lot.

There are a few stripped out cars in the lot, and we use them for cover as we scan the area and make sure we are clear. I don't see anyone, and I give Beast the "all clear" hand sign. With a nod, he motions me to move up to the door of the building while he covers.

Excitement floods through me as I rush forward, rifle up and ready while sticking to shadows as much as possible. When I reach the door, I kneel and aim at the center of the doorway, then motion Beast with my off hand.

My partner silently comes to a stop on the other side of the door, lets his rifle lay against his chest and then draws his forty-five and sword. With a wicked smile, I do the same and then move up and carefully open the door. Fortunately it swings open quietly as I pull it just enough to peek in. Through the opening, I don't see anyone and open it wider before slipping inside.

Of the many skills Beast has taught me, stealth has been one of the most important. Tonight I am at the top of my game as I move into the building like a whisper on the wind. I think this was probably some kind of office, but now it's a barracks for some of the raiders. In the center of the space are eight mattresses, five of them occupied and we hear sounds from the bathroom.

Beast moves towards the bathroom door and doesn't have to tell me my part. The Angel of Death sweeps into the room and starts slitting throats. Normally, I would agree that it's not the best way to die, but scum like this simply don't deserve a good death.

I've killed my third raider when I hear a grunt from the bathroom. Beast is getting rid of that man, but the noise causes one of the men in the room to stir. I don't play around. I put a suppressed bullet in his skull. The last man sits up startled and I launch myself at him. Viciously, I stab him in the throat multiple times. He stares at me with wide, shocked eyes as he chokes on his own blood.

Getting to my feet, I smile as Beast approaches, wiping blood off his sword. When his eyes fall on me, he stops, tips his head to the side, and gives me one of his rare smiles. That damn mask makes it difficult for me to read his emotions, but I swear there's something else in that smile. What I don't understand is what it is.

"What?" I ask softly in case there are any enemy about.

Holding up one finger for me to wait, he steps up, gently takes my knife and then stabs it into one of the dead bodies. He then flicks blood off the blade, turning me into splatter paint art project. As he flings blood at me, he stops long enough to regard the pattern and then does it again, acting like he's creating a masterpiece.

I am giggling, silently of course, but I whisper, "Arts and crafts? Now? Really?"

When he's done, he pulls a hand mirror from his top pouch and hands it to me. Gazing at the reflection, I see his masterpiece. Splatter lines of red, cross my face in various directions, along with little drops of crimson. I look like an avenging angel that's walked straight out of Hell.

Handing the mirror back, I smile. "I like it. Thank you. Now let's go get the rest of the bad guys."

Giving me a respectful bow, he grabs an AK off the floor and starts towards the door. I don't know why he feels he needs another weapon, but I follow as we head to the building next door and start the process all over again. I know this is going to be dirty work, but I'm comfortable with it. As I've said before, if they didn't want me to be a cold-blooded bitch, they shouldn't have turned me into one.

Chapter Twenty-Nine

It takes less time than I thought to sweep through the university grounds. Most buildings are empty and it seems like the bulk of the raiders have taken to living in student housing north of the track field. That's where some type of celebration is in full swing. It does explain why we've seen so few of them as well.

Keeping to the west edge of the campus, Beast and I snipe out those that are on guard duty and then quickly hide the bodies before moving on. In some cases we find good ammo and take it before continuing.

In time, we move into a building not far from the track that says "Amy S. Harrison Field" in bold white letters against a faded blue background. A baseball field sprawls in front of it, with rows of corn planted in the diamond. Slipping silently into the building, we clear it before posting up in an office. I take up a position next to a busted out window. We are just in time to see the scissor lift rise with a single man standing on it. I listen intently as Beast and I top off all our magazines.

"Listen to me, my brothers," the man calls out with a bullhorn. "The past few days we have needed to lick our wounds, but we have been victorious!"

The crowd at his feet cheers wildly and I'm beginning to believe that the bastard talking is Dean himself. Rage rises in my chest as I slip the drum mag into my rifle and want to pop up and riddle him with bullets. Beast must read my mind, because he touches my shoulder and squeezes it gently as the speech continues.

"The so called Angel of Death and her Beast are dead!"

Excuse me?

"Yes. See the proof! See what we pulled from the rubble of Walma."

As the crowd goes wild, I peek up just enough to see that he's holding out my skull rag. It looks torn and tattered. I'd lost it at some point in the fighting at Walma, probably when I'd been thrown from the wall.

"With them gone and Walma out of the way, Riverside is ours to control. We will grow, we will prosper and in time we will take all of Los Angeles." A cheer punctuates his statement. "So tonight is our victory celebration. You will all have food, drink and most importantly—women!"

The crowd roars like some hungry, lustful monster that has crawled out of its cave after a long hibernation. Suddenly my purpose for being here is twofold. Not just for revenge, but also to free the slaves that are trapped here.

"You deserve it. Now have fun—that's an order."

Loud hoots and howls of laughter can be heard as the scissor lift starts

120

down. I'm getting ready to shoot when Beast stops me once more. Looking at him, he points to Dean, then makes a motion like he's pulling out a knife and stabbing himself. He wants to make an example of the leader and so we watch intently to see where he goes.

Slipping out from our location, we slowly we stalk the man and his two bodyguards as they make their way to the Highlander Student Union building. Between foliage, buildings, and remains of vehicles, it's easy to follow without being spotted. Two guards are posted at the door to the building, and they come to attention when Dean approaches. I'm getting the feeling that this man is not just a raider, but might be ex-military.

Tapping my shoulder, Beast leads me back towards the baseball field where we slip silently back into the building. The party is in full swing as we post up the spot we were before. I'm trying to figure out why we came back when Beast drops his pack and pulls out some clothing he had to have taken from a raider.

Turning his back to me, I watch as he slowly transforms into one of the gang. Slapping on a welder mask, bits of street signs and car tires. Setting down his G3, he picks up the AK and just like that, he's one of them. All without ever letting me see his face. Then he pulls the last thing from the pack—improvised grenades.

These are not the concussion version of which I have two of in pouches on my own belt. No, he took a good portion of the plastic explosive that was left and placed them in various cans and jars that have screw top lids. The inside of each he lined with window putty and then pressed various ball bearings, BB's and even nails into them. The result, an instant and devastating shotgun blast that would go in all directions.

That's when I realize his plan. He's going to go out into the lion's den and place his explosives within the crowd. If it works, we can take out a great number of these bastards in one attack. If he gets caught, he'll be surrounded by the enemy, more than he can fight off alone. I don't like it.

"No," I tell him softly.

His head rears back and he looks at me with surprise. Clearly he was not expecting me to object. Finally he shakes his head, points at me, then to his eyes behind the welders mask—always a mask, damn it—and finally points at the party outside.

"If you seriously think I'm going to sit here and watch you commit suicide? You are out of your mind."

Beast glowers at me as I think he tries to think of a way he can retort with hand signals. Finally, he gives up on that and speaks. "This is the only way," his voice an echoing growl, low and harsh, reverberating behind the impenetrable black plastic. "We can kill or maim damn near all of them at once. Cover me in case something goes wrong."

Without letting me reply, he turns and walks right out the door. *Ohhh, he frustrates the hell out of me!* I may have a lot to learn, but I am not some damsel in distress to be locked away in the tallest tower of the castle—even if I am armed with a sniper rifle! Though I grudgingly have to admit I could not be camouflaged as he is and hope to get away with it. But I certainly don't want to lose my partner to a stupid idea. Cursing softly, I get into position. Shrouded in shadow as I aim out the window, I watch and wait.

Beast strolls into the crowd like he's one of them. I am surprised at how easily he melts into the group, but I don't take my eyes from him. Some clap him on the back and offer him a drink. In some cases he actually takes one before moving on. When he finally disappears into the crowd, my anxiety kicks up at least three notches. The only thing keeping me from losing my shit is that the party continues like nothing is wrong.

Now that I can't see him, my eyes slide to his white mask, sitting on the top of his pack. As long as the party continues with Beast being out among the enemy, I have no choice but to wait for him to either come back or for everything to go to shit. *I hate waiting.*

I glance quickly at my watch. Again. A little over twenty-two minutes has passed and the party is still going strong. Each minute has crawled by, but so far no alarms have gone up. My anxiety level, however, is through the roof as I keep aim on the crowd, itching to pull the trigger. I am beyond tense, not knowing if that is Beast in my sights or some random asshole.

Scanning the mob, I desperately look for his welder's mask amongst the many faces. Just to see him would make me feel better. Yet, so far I've had no luck. All I see is a bunch of idiot raiders that I want to kill. Granted, given the way he talked to me before he left, I'm damn near tempted to shoot him too!

The sound of a door slamming open and a woman's scream forces me to turn my attention from the crowd. Ducking further into the dark, I gently lay down my rifle and pull out both pistol and knife. A woman whimpers and cries as a man laughs gruffly.

"Just give in to it, baby," he states smugly. "You'll enjoy it a lot better if you do."

"Please. Leave me alone," she screams back.

There's a a brutal slap and then her tearful cry, making my blood boil. Slipping out of the room, I sneak down the shadowed hallway. Not all the light bulbs are working, so there are pockets of darkness for me to hide in

122

as I move over to the locker room where I hear their voices.

When I dart a quick peek through the doorway, I find an asshole has got the girl on the floor and against the wall. She's naked and holding her cheek as she cries softly. The raider looms over her, blocking her escape while slowly undressing, prolonging her torture. This man doesn't even resemble him, but so reminds me of Knack. I want him to suffer. Holstering my pistol, I inch silently forward.

"Don't worry, bitch," he states confidently as he drops his pants. "I won you in the lottery, fair and square. So long as you don't fight it, I'll treat you well." In his mind, it's a completed transaction. She's not a human being to him, she's his property.

"No, please don't..." she cries in despair.

I catch the tone in her voice that she's resigned to her fate. I know because I've been there. Well not today, you fucking bastard. Today the Angel of Death comes calling, and she's got a one way ticket for your soul—destination, Hell.

Thanks to his talking and laughing, he can't hear me as I approach from behind. The girl is so focused and so lost in her horrific life, she doesn't even notice me. With one hand, he fondles his junk to torment her more, and that's when I make my move.

My form is perfect. Right hand clamps over his mouth as the left hand plunges my knife into his throat. The sharpened blade dives easily into his flesh as a muffled, gurgled scream tries to escape from between my fingers. Then I push the blade forward, ripping his throat out and letting him drop to the floor.

Okay, I really didn't have to do that last part, but it felt so good to do. The girl's wide eyes move from the dying raider to me. I have splattered her with some of his blood and she sits there shaking, as if waiting for her death too. I put a finger to my lips. Nodding fearfully, she huddles there while I drag the dead man into the dark.

This poor girl can't be over seventeen, and probably isn't even that. How old was she when the Collapse happened? Fourteen? Younger? Curly black hair is matted and looks neglected. Pasty white skin covers a frame that is a little too thin. Clearly they don't feed slaves well, and that just makes me angrier. The poor child is sporting a number of bruises, some old and some new.

With the body hidden, I offer my hand to her. She trembles as she takes it. I lead her back to my sniper position and point to her and then to a dark corner. With a nod, she goes over to it and kneels down, still looking terrified. When I glance her direction, I put a finger to my lips and then hand her Beast's fatigue blouse. She nods once more and dresses herself as I pick up my rifle and go back to watching.

Shit! Beast has me doing hand signals instead of talking now.

Shaking my head, I focus on the party again, hoping I haven't missed anything important. So far all seems normal with the men drinking, laughing and having a good time. Funny, I never seem to see any female raiders. Yeah. Funny. Right. There's nothing to give me any indication that an alarm has gone off. That's when I finally see him.

Beast just walks out of the crowd like it's a normal day. I'm pretty sure it's him. While I've seen a few other welder masks, no one has his exact clothing. It looks like he's laughing and gives a wave before walking towards what was probably once a soccer field. Now it too has been turned into a section of crops that might be tomatoes. He calmly strides along until I can't see him any longer.

I duck under the window and put my back to the wall. I'm pretty sure he's just working his way around, but since he's left the crowd, I need to focus on securing this building anyway. If one raider came in looking for some privacy, so could another.

None do, however, and after another twenty minutes or so, Beast is done. Coming in, he waves a hand before finally stepping through the office doorway, keeping his head low. When he spots my new friend, he shoots me a confused expression, requiring me to explain.

"Raider brought her in to rape her," I whisper. "His body is in the dark corner of the locker room."

Beast nods and I swear I see a quick smile, but with such little light, I can't be sure. Walking over, he divests himself of the raider parts of his clothing and back into his own, minus his blouse. With camo paint, he quickly puts black, uneven stripes on his arms to help cut down on the white of his skin. I notice he never covers over his tattoos though. Once he's ready, he grabs his rifle and starts out the door.

I move over to the girl and whisper softly. "You stay here, in the dark and don't make a sound. No matter what you hear. Got me?"

"Yes... ma'am."

"Good. I will come and get you once they are all dead."

There's a slight gasp from her. I reach out, give her shoulder a gentle squeeze to let her know she's all right and follow Beast out of the office. Once we get to the exit, we make sure it's all clear before heading towards the student union building, looking for a man with an expiration date on his forehead.

Chapter Thirty

It appears that practically everyone is at the party, so making our way back to the student union is a cinch. We encounter no one on the way, sneaking into a building called Costo Hall. Looks like it was meant to be offices and classrooms, and seems like people are living here too. That familiar stench of unwashed bodies is heavy in this building.

Making our way to the back of the building, we stick to the dark corners of sparsely-lit hallways and search out our targets as we approach the rear of the hall. Peeking out glass doors streaked with dirt, we spot a set of stairs leading to the second floor of the student union and there's still two guards at the doors. All the windows on the ground floor are boarded up, and some on the second floor as well.

"Take the right one," he whispers.

"On it."

I wait as he cautiously opens the glass door. Then we both aim through it. Our suppressed shots drop both men, splatters of gore appearing on the wall behind them. Beast closes the door silently and we wait to see and hear if anyone raises an alarm.

All is quiet, so Beast opens the door once more and we slip out, heading for the stairs. As we reach the landing, we check both men and verify they are dead. One has an AR-15, so I grab his spare mags and stuff them into various pockets. Beast pulls out a radio, turns it on with a wicked grin and pushes the talk button.

A number of explosions go off at the same time and I see a fireball rise in the distance. Windows rattle and I can feel the ground shudder ever-so-slightly. This is our declaration of war, so we move through the doors with no need to play it quiet any more.

It's like an action movie as we sweep into the hallway, catching the raiders completely by surprise. Men come out in staggered waves, many hardly even dressed, with weapons in hand as they try to figure out what is going on. We splatter them against the walls while moving forward, guns blazing. My aim is perfect, trigger pull spot on as I put round after round into each man that presents himself as my target.

Moving up to a doorway, I see a raider on the floor and screaming in pain. When his eyes fall on me, they go wide with fear because even without my bandanna he knows who I am. Raising his hands, he asks me for mercy.

How many women asked you for mercy, asshole?

The closest I can bring myself to being merciful is that I put a bullet right in his head. Brains and blood splatter all over the floor. When I look at Beast, he shoots me a grim smile before we both continue moving forward and shooting those foolish enough to try and engage instead of running.

We move through hallways, death incarnate, and Beast doesn't even bother to reload at times. When he lets go of the G3 and pulls out the SPAS-12. Damn thing sounds like the end of the world has arrived, which, in a way, it has. At least for these assholes. The weapon fits him perfectly. It roars with every shot, spraying buckshot into everyone in our way.

Beast and I are unstoppable, but not perfect. The remaining enemy wise up and begin shooting back before we drop them. Fortunately the few hits we take are stopped by our body armor and I am too amped to really feel the bruising pain. I'm high on adrenaline and rage when we close in on a door reading "Dean's Office" in bright gold letters.

I hope you're ready to die, 'cause I'm coming for you Dean.

Beast slides up to one side of the door and I take the other. I check to make sure my weapon is ready, and give him a nod. This is the moment we have been working towards since Walma was attacked. Very soon, Damien will be avenged.

Everything goes straight to Hell when we bust through the door and find Dean and his cronies are waiting for us. Deployed riot shields stop our bullets cold as the roar of multiple shotguns greets my ears.

A beanbag hits me square in the chest with the force of a speeding car. I hit the floor hard, trying to find the air that has been driven from my lungs, and trying to gather my wits. When I look to my partner, I see Beast in a similar state.

Dean's men are on top of us, dragging us roughly into the room and taking away our weapons. Their leader watches and slow claps, wearing a smug smile. I long to wipe it off his face. With bullets. Or my knife. Either way would be fine.

"Well done," he states while still clapping. "Well done. I am impressed!"

"Fuck you," I groan as our weapons are deposited in a pile between him and us.

Dean shakes his head. "No, I'm serious. You two wiped out my competition, drove the rest to me and now you've probably removed a good number of them. I've now got fewer mouths to feed, which means my team eats better. You've done me and my men a great service. I should probably reward you for that."

"Great," I exclaim, my breath returning. "Shoot yourself in the head and we'll call it even."

Beast chuckles at my comment and one of the men cuffs him across the back of the head. In return, he gives the raider a low, deep growl that tells me he's going to kill that man in a deeply personal way.

Dean sighs and shakes his head. "Actually, I was thinking of something else. You two come to work for me. I'm sure we can come to a mutually beneficial agreement. Together we can carve out a kingdom that will be unstoppable. As for you, Chloe. I was a big admirer of your work before the Collapse. I'm an even bigger admirer of your work now. In fact, be my queen and I'll make you very happy."

Are you fucking kidding me?

I give Dean an expression that makes him think I'm considering it. Then I cast a glance at the two men holding me down, and back to him like I'm clearly expecting better treatment right this minute. With a wave, the men let go of me and I stand up. With a regal air, I dust myself off and then walk up to him with a sensual smile. I know it works, because sensual is easy for me to do and it disarms men quite well.

"So what about the slaves?" I ask as I run a finger down his vest.

"What about them? It is the sheep's purpose to be shorn."

"And Beast?"

Dean shakes his head and looks to my partner briefly. "I don't know about him. Do you think he can be kept on a leash? Seems a little too feral to me."

I can't help but laugh, but I make it a playful one. Like I'm enjoying a joke that he's just told. The smile I get in return tells me he believes he's got me hooked on his proposition. In this world, maybe some women would be. A world like this, where every day is a violent struggle just to eat and survive? Many, if not most, might give up their bodies willingly just to live in relative comfort and security.

"I can keep him controlled," I say seductively as my fingers run down his vest before touch the hilt of Dean's knife. "Do you believe me?"

Snaking a hand around my waist, he chuckles. "Oh, I'm sure you can. So is that part of the deal then? The Beast gets to live so long as you will be my queen? Any other conditions I need to be aware of before I take you into my bedroom to consummate our... partnership?"

It's easy for me to tell that he's excited. Not only can I see it in his eyes, but I can feel it against my hip. Like any man, their base needs are always the same, and the promise of sex typically dulls their wits. Like him, I'm more than ready, but it's not sex on my mind. Dean doesn't feel my hand tightening around his knife. He is lost in the sensual promise of my lips and eyes, taken in by my seeming willingness.

"There *is* just one other thing," I say with a sexy grin, and lick my lips as my free hand travels softly to his erection.

Dean shudders when I touch him. "What's that, baby?"

The agonizing howl that comes from his mouth is like sweet music to my ears as my grip crushes his balls like a vise. Pulling his knife, I begin stabbing and don't want to stop. The memory of my dream where I stabbed Knick surfaces as I scream at him.

"You can bring back our friend, Damien!"

Dean collapses onto the desk, gasping in pain and clutching at his wounds, I draw his pistol and spin. The bloody knife leaves my hand, heading for one of the raiders holding Beast, while I gun down one of the shocked men that had been restraining me.

Chloe's skill with knife throwing? Zero. The blade tumbles end over end and the back of the hilt rebounds off the man's head. The man who had hit Beast. He staggers back with a yelp as I shoot the other man that was restraining my companion.

Beast quickly stands up and catches the knife. It's beautiful and graceful to behold as he falls upon the idiot that dared to hit him. The violence my partner unleashes in nothing short of savage. *Yep, it's personal.* As Beast fillets the man, the fourth guard raises his hands and drops to his knees.

Once the carnage is done, I toss the pistol to Beast, pluck my knife off the floor and then turn my attention back to Dean. Laying on the desk, I can hear his rasping breath as he tries to breathe through perforated lungs. Climbing up, I straddle his body in some parody of a sexual position.

It's easy to see the questions in his eyes, the fear and the lack of understanding. Why did I do this? After all, he was offering me everything. What he doesn't know is that my motives are not what he expects. I will never be another man's plaything—ever again! He and his ilk just can't understand that women. Aren't. Things. Especially not this woman. Give us some skill and motivation and we will show you what we mean by that.

"You see, Dean. What you fail to understand is that bastards like you made me this way. I've been turned into a monster because assholes like you treated me poorly. Treated me like nothing other than property to be abused. Then you have to go and order an attack on Walma and murder our friends. But now?" I chuckle throatily and continue. "You are mine and I consign your soul to Hell."

I'm sure Dean wants to say something, his mouth opening in an attempt to plead for his life. The only thing that comes out is a wet gurgle before I plunge my blade into his heart. He gasps, blood spilling from his mouth, then shudders and expires. I take a deep breath and pray that Damien's soul rests easy as I slip off the desk and turn around.

"And what am I to do with you?"

The only survivor looks up at me with wide eyes, full of fear. As I truly scrutinize him, I realize he's not a man, he's little more than a boy. I doubt he's even eighteen as he looks up at me with blue eyes, wet with tears. A part of me thinks he's probably committed as many crimes as Dean, yet there's another voice in my head. It's a voice that counsels mercy.

If I kill this unarmed boy, do I cross some invisible line? Do I start down a path that will ultimately corrupt me? Thanks to the Collapse, not to mention Knick and Knack, the girl I once was is practically gone. If I cross this line, do I murder the last piece of her just like everyone else has been doing?

No, I have to be able to show mercy. I can't be like Dean or Knick.

"What's your name?"

The boy swallows hard. He knows who he's facing. "Steve, ma'am."

"Well Steve. This is your lucky day. I am going to allow you to live, but you will pay a penance. Are we understood?"

Steve nods his head rapidly, still terrified. "Y-yes ma'am."

I glance over at Beast and he's looking at me like I'm someone else. Finally his mouth presses into a line and nods. Grabbing Steve gently by the shoulder, he helps the boy to his feet and ushers him out the door. As they leave, I turn and cut Dean's head off. It's grisly work, but I hope it scares off any raiders that are left.

Chapter Thirty-One

It's been three weeks since we hit University Riverside and cleaned house. Beast's homemade bombs did a good job of annihilating the University Raiders. Bodies, body parts and a blood soaked track field was proof of that. Those few that survived saw Beast and I and fled for their lives. Only a couple looked like they wanted to fight, but when they saw me carrying Dean's still-dripping head, they decided otherwise.

The girl, Diane, was still in the office, right where I left her. She was as scared of me as the raiders were. To be honest, our reputation did much of the work for us. It certainly kept Steve in line as we gathered up a few things and left for Moreno.

I tasked Steve with protecting Diane, with his life if need be. Because if he didn't, he would have to answer to me. That boy stuck to her and kept her protected all the way back, practically waiting on her hand and foot. Diane seemed happy with this turn of events. If I didn't know any better, I might imagine she thought Steve was cute. I doubted she'd be ready for a relationship any time soon, but it looked like there might be hope for her eventual recovery. It certainly helped that she hadn't been raped yet. While she had her traumas, hopefully she'd recover.

We came back to a hero's welcome. Kathy was delighted to see us and we found out that she sent scouts out to track our progress. Knowing if we succeeded or failed was important information for her. She had a whole community to look after, of course. I got that. Of course, I also think she could have helped us, but she didn't want to risk any of her people on what she saw as an impossible task. I am very glad to have proved her wrong.

I delivered Dean's head to Linda, which laid some ghosts to rest, in her mind anyway. By the next day she was already looking a bit better and less depressed. Tom certainly thought so and thanked us for avenging his friend.

The best news was that we had a new home for the survivors of Walma, and a good one at that. Electricity, greenhouses and plenty of housing. I was almost surprised that Kathy agreed, but another piece of civilization in the area would have made it worth the help they gave. Both villages are close enough that they can keep one another supplied and rely on each other for protection.

Within a week, we had them moved and Beast was helping set up a proper defense. They did not have strength in numbers, so walls were even more crucial. This kept everyone busy, and the Moreno Valley folks were kind enough to loan some of their construction equipment.

Initially it was an inner wall that would protect the core of the village, but in time it was hoped that if they grew and prospered, so too would the defensive walls. At least that was the plan Beast laid out for them.

In two weeks there were still some gaps and a lot of work to be done with so much area to cover, but I got the feeling they wouldn't have any issues for quite some time. The growing legend of the Angel of Death and her Beast have driven any nearby raiders far, far away.

The fact that we were able to send runners to the Queen Mary Enclave and back confirmed our assessment. At no point did they encounter any gangs and there were no attacks against them. A few days later, a trading caravan arrived and they also reported no signs of raider activity.

During that time I was doing more than just hard labor, because I had picked up two stalkers. Though maybe *stalkers* is too harsh. Acolytes? Followers? Minions? Regardless, Diane and Steve stuck to me like glue. Part of it had to be because Diane only felt safe when I was nearby. More than once Beast ribbed me about having picked up a girl not unlike myself. Perhaps that's true, but, as I have snidely pointed out to him, at least I talk to her.

My other stalker was Steve, in part because he continued to watch over Diane. I think he was afraid that I would kill him at the first moment he failed to perform well in my eyes. Oh, I definitely put that boy to work. Surprisingly, he has worked hard and without complaint.

I also found time to take Diane aside and start teaching her how to defend herself. I wasn't going to do what Beast did and adopt her, but she needed to start learning. I made sure Linda and Tom knew so they could make sure other people kept training the girl after I left. This included any other women we'd found in Dean's fallen empire. They were supportive of the idea and would be glad for more rifles on guard duty.

By the third week, things are shaping up well and Beast has started getting Truck ready to go. That's his way of saying that it's time to leave. Deep down, I think I'm ready too. L.A. has far too many bad memories for me. I hope that being on the road, leaving so many ghosts behind, will help to clear my soul.

There isn't a single villager that wants to see us leave, but they all know it's coming. We've made no secret of the fact that we're moving on. My poor Beast has had to deal with far too much civilization for way too long. I could see it grating on his nerves as each day passed. Getting out of here is not only good for his sanity, but also for their continued existence.

One nice thing about coming back to the university was that Beast and I were able to actually do a decent job of replacing the ammunition we'd expended. Dean's operation had been successful for a long time and they had scavenged from military and police locations. Beast even walked away with a new toy, an FN SCAR, which at least help to keep him happy for a little while longer.

Boys and their toys.

We've been staying in one of the better homes in the Canyon Crest housing section. It's been nice to sleep in a decent bed once more and have a bathroom, even if I have to fill everything by hand. Beast has been sleeping on the floor in the living room. Don't ask me, I don't know why he doesn't like beds.

When I wake up this morning, I find breakfast waiting for me and Beast nowhere to be seen. It's not much, but we work with what we have. On a clean plate is a few slices of pineapple and half a can of fried Spam slices. With all the hard work I've been doing, it looks like a five star hotel meal and I demolish it. I practically lick the plate. Okay, fine, I do lick the plate. Once I'm done, I clean my dishes with some water from a nearby pail and place them in the dish rack. Then I grab my gear and go find Beast.

I get this odd feeling of Déjà Vu when I walk into the garage and find that the hood for Truck is open and Beast is working on the poor thing. This is a sight I actually find worrisome. He really is the worst auto mechanic I've ever met.

"Please tell me you aren't breaking my poor Truck?"

He shoots his head up so fast and glares at me that I laugh. That makes him frown. Pointing at the truck, he then points to himself before going back to work. I'm not letting him off that easy, partly because I'm trying to save the poor vehicle from his attention.

"I don't think so," I state imperiously. "I fixed it. I got it running. That makes it, my truck."

Beast raises his head up slowly this time, his blue eyes fixed on me. I think I may have pushed the joke too far when he stands up, watching me impassively and stalks in my direction. I don't know what to think, so I brace myself for—well, I don't know what for.

I'm shocked when he drops to one knee and holds up the socket wrench like he's a knight offering me a sword. This catches me off guard and takes me a moment before I giggle, roll my eyes, and take the tool from his hands with an elaborate curtsy. Then I go check on poor Truck to make sure he hasn't made things worse.

While I inspect the engine, he does the job of loading everything. This is a division of labor I can get behind. All the extra gear goes into the back while he puts out tac vests and a cooler with some food and water in the back seat. Instead of the Tavor, he puts both P-90's on the floor of the passenger side after showing me. Then he takes his new toy, folds the stock and puts it on the driver's side.

By the time everything is packed, I'm done inspecting the engine and it looks good. Granted, I'm no master mechanic, but I have more skill than he does for damn certain. All the hoses and belts are in good shape and nothing looks shoddy. Some things are a little banged up, but it all appears to be in working order.

I find he's standing next to the driver's side, patiently waiting for me. Shooting him a smile, I walk over and nearly invade his personal space, looking up into his blue eyes. His pupils dilate at my proximity. I keep my voice low and calm in hopes it does the same for him.

"While it's clear you want to go, I need to say goodbye to some people, okay?"

Putting his hand over his heart, Beast gives a respectful bow.

"You could come with me? I'm sure they'd like to say goodbye to you as well."

His mouth presses into a tight line and shakes his head slowly. Goodbyes are a sore spot with him, I guess. Actually, I'm not surprised given what I've learned about him. I'm certainly not going to press. I understand far too well what it means to have issues.

"All right. Why don't you make sure we are ready to go and I'll be back quickly?"

Beast nods his head and as I leave, he opens the garage door to pull Truck out. I sigh heavily as I head into the university to say farewell to my friends. Friends that I will probably never see again.

Chapter Thirty-Two

Everyone, save those on guard duty, has congregated in the circular end of the student union. Bright light streams through the many windows that are still intact, rays of sunlight illuminating the room.

Just about every eye in the place is wet, but Linda and Diane are especially teary. Neither of them want to see us go, Diane most of all. I guess I've become something of a big sister to her, and I tell myself I am not abandoning her. I remind myself I've put her in a much better position for survival.

After three weeks of recovery, she looks much better. Having good food on a regular basis is the least of it. The haunted expression in her eyes is almost gone, and that is the healing I was most worried about.

"I don't want you to go," she cries, throwing her arms around me.

"I know, D, but it's time. I've done a lot of good and now I need to see what else is out there. Maybe someday, you will too. You're going to be an amazing fighter one day, you know that, right? And nobody will ever push you around again, you got me?"

Diane nods as tears roll down her cheeks. "Yes ma'am."

I can tell she's not convinced. Somehow I can see her softening up to Steve, who has continued to stick by her day and night. In time maybe they'll be together and raise a family—living, fighting and dying on this patch of land. Through it all, I pray she is granted such a good life that it obliterates all the bad memories.

"Now you promise me," I state seriously as I lift her eyes up to mine. "Whatever you do, be happy. Find someone, find something, and be happy in your life. Alright?"

"Yes ma'am," she croaks.

She recently informed me that Steve has a martial arts background, and he has offered to teach her. This is good news. The doctor, Amanda, has also expressed interest in having her as a nurse. She will be busy, and that's also good.

I smile brightly. "Good girl. Now remember; stay low, shoot straight and conserve ammo."

Giving her a big hug, I approach Linda, who might be crying harder than Diane. I must say, every day since I brought her Dean's head, she's looked a little better, happier. It warms my heart to know I helped, though that may be why she is so sad right now.

"You know you could both have a life here, Chloe?"

"I know," I reply sadly. "But I have too many bad memories here, and I suspect it's the same for Beast as well. He wants to go home, and I think

I'd like to see it. Besides, we're out of bad guys here, you know? I have a feeling there are plenty more out there to deal with out there."

Linda chuckles at my joke and nods sadly. "I guess I can understand that. You just take care, okay? And watch out for that stubborn old war horse too."

I can't help but laugh at her comment about Beast. He certainly is that! Wrapping her up into a hug, I fight to keep the tears at bay. I don't know how, but I succeed while Linda cries into my shoulder. I will miss her.

We are just about done when I hear the growl of the diesel engine on Truck. Beast has driven across the walkways and lawns, coming to a stop next to the windowed wall of the student union. I can't help but roll my eyes.

"Insistent, isn't he?" Tom hits the nail right on the head.

"Yes he is. Let's all go outside, so you can wish him goodbye." And I mutter to Linda, "Watch his face, wait for it..."

With a cheer, we all head outside to the truck. Linda and I laugh at the look of horror on Beast's face as we approach. Linda and Tom walk right up to the driver's side and wish him well, much to his chagrin. I want to laugh out loud, but do my best to hold in as I give Diane one last hug.

Quickly I pull Steve aside, putting on my serious face. "You listen to me and you listen well."

"Yes ma'am."

"Just because I'm leaving, it doesn't mean your job is over. Got me?"

Steve nods solemnly, eyes as wide as the night he met me. I probably shouldn't frighten the poor boy, but I want him to turn into a good man. If fear of me keeps him on the straight and narrow, so be it.

"Now, Diane is still your responsibility." He nods and I add, "I've also learned that you are a martial artist, black belt. That's awesome, but only if you use it for the right purpose. To me, the reason you are still alive and on this earth is to help Diane. So you are going to teach her, and others that need teaching. But especially her. You watch over her and protect her, and I'll tell you a secret as to why. I think she likes you."

The young man's mouth goes slack jawed, then he glances at her for a brief second before looking back at me. "Really?"

"Really. But understand, she's been through some shit. She is not anyone's toy, so you let her decide. And if it's not you she wants, so be it. You can't force her. She'll let you know if and when. And then, should you be so lucky, you treat her like a goddess. You worship her, protect her and make life so good for her she forgets what she's been through. Got all that?"

The fear is gone and now he looks more like a man. A man with a mission. "Yes ma'am."

135

"Good. You take care."

Pulling him into a hug, I shock the hell out of him, because he doesn't hug back and feels as rigid as a steel pole. Letting him go, I quickly walk to Truck. I'm ready to leave before I start crying. As I climb in, there is a cacophony of goodbyes that can be heard over the engine. Beast drives the truck over the lawn and away, and I watch in the rear view mirror as the villagers wave at us.

This awful feeling creeps into my gut that I will never see any of them again. Chances are I will never know how they did, how they lived and how they died. Who had children and lived to see them grow up. The sting is assuaged by this thought from out of nowhere, the strongest feeling that they will be all right. I have no idea how, but I just feel that they will be okay.

Beast pulls onto the freeway, and I can't hold it in anymore and start crying. We get maybe a mile or so when he stops the truck and pulls me into his arms, helping me let it out. It's a cathartic kind of cry that, as a woman, you just have to get out of your system. Beast just holds me like he does every time I've woken up from a nightmare.

It takes me a handful of minutes, but once I'm done, I catch my breath and look at him. I smile and give a nod that I'm better now. My partner doesn't appear convinced, but gives a nod back, puts the truck in drive and we start moving again.

Putting my belt on, I curl up in the seat and stare out the window in a melancholy state as we head up the 215. There are surprisingly few abandoned vehicles on the freeway. By the time shit really hit the fan, martial law was in full swing and most of the freeways were shut down.

Still, Beast drives slow, I think more because he's being alert for an ambush. We aren't exactly silent or inconspicuous in a huge, growling silver-gray truck with rusted steel plates tacked all over it. Besides, I'm pretty sure there aren't many working vehicles on the road these days.

At thirty-five miles per hour, the city doesn't look so bad. Things go by fast enough that you can't easily focus on any one thing before it's gone. Still, every once in a while I see a wrecked car, a burned out house, the tattered remains of a body in the street. Through it all, I see very little sign of habitation. What was once a densely populated metropolis is now a giant graveyard. In my melancholy mood, tears slip gently down my face like rain, and I grieve for what is lost.

All this because we couldn't live peacefully, go our own way and mind our own business. No, we had to meddle, force other people to think the way we wanted them to think, spend money we didn't have or hoard money we didn't need. Human nature is a weapon of mass destruction.

Chapter Thirty-Three

It takes us two days to navigate from the 215 to I-10. And you thought rush hour traffic was bad. We encounter some sections completely blocked off by what's left of military or police vehicles. This forces us to find an off-ramp and pick our way across surface streets, which slows us down even more because they are choked with debris and obstacles.

Of course we are constantly on the lookout for ambushes. We are knee deep in the unknown now, with no clue as to who or what is out here. I keep one of the P-90's on the seat next to me, just in case.

Our travel plans have gone from moving at night and resting during the day, to moving during the day and resting at night. We have enough food and water to last us a little more than a week, but continue scavenging for supplies as a matter of course. The more supplies we have, the better off we are, no matter what else happens. Amazingly, we've actually found a few things and even a small amount of diesel fuel.

We finally hook up onto I-10 with the goal of heading east. Without warning, Beast immediately pulls off the interstate. Quickly he drives into the parking lot of a Hilton just off the 10, near the 215 interchange. With hand signals, he tells me to stay in the truck and keep an eye out while he grabs his SCAR and the spotting scope and enters the building.

There are days he drives me crazy! Without an explanation, he just disappears into an unknown building. Granted, if anyone hostile was living here, we'd probably know already. But still! What in the hell is wrong with that man? Other than he's a man, of course.

I wait impatiently in the truck for a little over fifteen minutes before he finally comes back out. Calmly putting the spotting scope in the back, he then climbs into the driver's seat without a word, naturally, and starts to get ready to drive off once more.

Oh, hell no!

"Before you even start this truck, you had better tell me what you just did! I don't know why you think I am a fucking mind-reader, but if you can't bring yourself to speak to me, write me a note! Jeez!"

Stopping, he looks at me with eyes wide, and I think he's shocked at the venom behind my statement. I watch as he turns around and reaches into the back seat, rummaging for something. When he sits back down, he hands me two tampons.

Are you fucking serious?

"If that's your idea of a joke, it lacks funny."

Beast rolls his eyes and reaches into the top left pouch on his tac vest, pulling out a digital camera. Turning it on, he pulls up the image menu and then shows me pictures of I-10, as seen through the spotting scope. The road looks amazingly clear, with hardly an abandoned or wrecked car in sight.

"Was that so hard? And yes, while it's nice to know at least the current stretch of the ten is free and clear, you could have told me if it was trouble or something else."

Shooting me a quick frown, he starts the truck up and we roll back out onto the freeway. To be honest, I'm still fuming at him and just gaze out the side window as he kicks up to freeway speed and Redlands flies by.

Why does he have to be so difficult? Some days he makes it really hard for me not to shoot him!

We are a few miles down the road and accelerating when he taps my shoulder. I'm so not in the mood and brush his finger away. When he does it a second time, I slap his hand away with some force. I do not want to talk right now. Frankly if I did, I could not be held responsible for the words that come out of my mouth.

When he grabs my shoulder, that's the final straw. "What?" I yell furiously as I shoot him a murderous glare.

The first response I get is a growl as he bares his teeth at me. Then he forcefully points past me and yells. "Mirror!"

Snapping my gaze to the rear view mirror, I see what he's been trying to get me to pay attention to. Three cars and two cycles tailing us and getting closer. As I look, someone hangs out of the lead vehicle with a rifle and shoots, a bullet destroying the mirror.

"Shit!"

Our attackers are three dune buggy style vehicles with armor plates on them and two motorcycles with single riders. I undo my seat belt and cautiously slither into the backseat, hoping I don't get shot. Quickly I slide open the window that bridges between the back seat and the camper shell. Being five foot and change and slim has its benefits. I'm able to squeeze through and into the truck bed.

A couple of bullets ricochet off the armor plate that's been attached to the tail gate and camper hatch. I'm far too pissed to play and I grab the M249, which already has a fresh belt loaded, thanks in part to Dean's cache of ammunition. I hear the buggy engines getting close and pop the hatch, grinning like the devil.

If there is one thing I have learned from Beast, it's that the man knows how to plan ahead, God bless his paranoid heart. While armored plates were slapped onto the outside of the truck, he also had an extra one added inside the tail gate, with risers one the left and right to use for cover—like right now.

When the hatch rises, I just miss the opportunity to shoot at the cycles as they zip by. I find one buggy damn near on our bumper and smile wickedly as I pull the trigger. While the buggies have steel plates slapped all over them, I still see the driver's face and his wide eyes staring down the barrel of a machine-gun. I lay into the vehicle with a couple of short controlled bursts.

Once again this is something that movies make look effortless. Moving vehicles do not make for easy targets, especially when you are in one of them and the driver is weaving back and forth in an effort to avoid getting the truck shot up. Even with a fully automatic weapon, most of my shots ping off their armor, but I get lucky. I think at least three bullets rip through their right front tire and the buggy lurches right before tumbling, wreckage flying across the freeway.

When I hear the sound of Beast's sawed-off shotgun roar to life, I know he's taking shots at the motorcycles. A cycle and rider go tumbling by and I shake my head. *Damn, even in a moving vehicle his aim is spot on.* What the fuck did he do before everything fell apart?

The truck suddenly jolts, sending me to the floor of the truck bed. I grit my teeth as my arm scrapes across one of the rifles. Pushing myself back up, I see a raider has successfully jumped onto the back bumper and is trying to climb in while holding an axe made of a length of pipe with a gear head that has been pounded down on one end into a crude edge.

Instead of trying to get onto my knees, I fall onto my back and draw my pistol, putting two rounds into his chest. With a cry, he falls off the back of the truck and I struggle to get back up while the truck jostles even more as the other buggies slam into the sides of the truck.

"Hold on," I hear Beast yell.

I barely have time to grab ahold of something before he cuts hard right. Through the slits in the armor plate that cover the camper windows, I see one of the buggies smash into the truck and then collide with the low concrete wall. Bits of gray stone shatters as the car crashes through it before tumbling end over end as it falls. As the buggy plows into the street, a mangled mess, the other one brakes hard as it misses following us down the off-ramp. I hear more than see it as the buggy starts backing up.

Beast drives us down and skirts under the freeway, heading into Redlands and toward the mountains. I holster my pistol and pick the machine-gun back up. My arm stings, but I focus on the road behind, expecting to see the enemy vehicle at any time.

He certainly is not making it easy for me, as he makes hard turn after hard turn. I shoot him a dirty look, hoping he'll see it in the rear view mirror. Instead, I see a map flutter up, like he's fighting with it. Since I've not seen the last car, I reach out to close the hatch.

That's when I discover another bandit hanging on to the bumper. With a yell, he grabs my arm. I shriek in surprise, and that emboldens him to try and climb in while forcibly pushing me back. Yet again I hit the bed of the truck back-first and I'm starting to get seriously pissed off about it.

In the time it takes to struggle back to my feet, the raider has wriggled his way in and pulls out a knife. With a hiss, he leers at me lustfully. *Seriously? In the middle of a fight, this is all you can think of? Asshole!* I shuffle backward, putting my back to the wall of the camper shell and my foot finds Beast's sword.

Ah, yes!

The blade slides easily from the scabbard, and I must admit, it feels good in my grasp. I smile wickedly at him. Suddenly he's confronted with a weapon that's easily twice the length of his own, maybe three times. Glancing down at his little threat, he then looks at mine and drops his blade. Seeing his death in my eyes, he takes the coward's route and dives out of the opening. I can't help but laugh as I watch him tumble along the asphalt. Shaking my head, I close the back hatch.

Chapter Thirty-Four

We've been hiding out in a secluded spot in the mountains for a couple days now. We are in the middle of nowhere and I like it. It's a nice change of pace, actually. I am really enjoying the trees and nature. Being secluded like this, it's easy to forget the world's gone to Hell in a hand basket.

It's a beautiful spot. We're at the top of a small mountain, a rough dirt road led us to a clearing where we've set up camp. From here we have a commanding view, even though there are a number of trees. Still, if anyone tries to come up the road we used, we'd see and hear them long before they could get in range.

Maybe it was because of how peaceful it is, but the first night we were here, I was plagued by nightmares. Not Knick and Knack, but others that I killed back in L.A. continue to haunt me. Then there was the threat of being raped by faceless men all led by Dean. Of course I wake up screaming, and let me tell you, I am sick of this shit.

As always, like some white knight charging in, Beast is right there. Somehow, he drives back the demons as he throws his arms around me and I cry in his protective embrace. I feel guilty for doing this so often. I'm grateful to him, and I think he's been wonderful to me, but how long will he have to nurse me at night, like this? I feel like an infant, and I wish I knew how to make it stop.

Once I've cried it all out, he tells me go back to sleep while he continues guard duty. For a few minutes, I watch him while I lay in my bedroll, standing there in silence. Slowly his head moves, scanning the landscape as he looks for threats, every inch the solitary warrior. I sleep well for the next few hours until it's time for me to stand watch.

The next day, instead of leaving, Beast wants to pound out some of the new dents in the truck's armor. One panel is close to rubbing against the rear wheel from the hit it took. Having a blowout would be awful in more ways than one, and I really do not relish the idea of walking to Colorado.

During this time, he also teaches me how to shoot a bow. It's nowhere near as easy as using a rifle, but it's fun and I pick up the basics quick enough. I learn that once you know how to aim one weapon, it's easier to aim with another. Quickly I find I'm not a bad shot.

Beast has a nice, compound bow with a seventy-five pound draw in what I thought was a rifle in a bag. It takes some effort, but thanks to all the exercise I've been doing, it's not that bad pulling the string back. If anything, it's the work of getting used to something you've never done before and getting new muscle memory built up. As well as trying to keep your forearm from getting beaten up by the bowstring, because that stings!

Now we are down in the trees, hoping to take a deer and give us some additional fresh food. We've seen signs they frequent this area, so it's as good an excuse as any to test my new skills. Beast is behind me with the Mosin, just in case I miss. It's still imperative that I make the shot. Shooting a gun could alert anyone nearby to our presence, and that's something we want to avoid. These days, you fear the living.

Noise off to my right catches my attention and I look. A deer! Nice sized one too. Gotta be a male, because he's got a rack that's way more impressive than mine. Ever so slowly I pivot as I draw the arrow back and take aim while trying to calm my breathing.

This might sound silly, but suddenly I'm thrust back to the feelings I had when I first shot someone. It feels like it's the first time I'm taking a life, except this time I'm not under stress. My reaction is probably because I've always been a champion for animals and treating them humanely. My mouth goes dry and my hands start to tremble as I aim at the unsuspecting deer that's standing there, picking at the forest ground.

After some hesitation, I let go of arrow and string, and the bladed shaft leaps forward, flying through the air. Beast has these little Koosh balls near each end of the bowstring. Because of them, there is no "twang" from the bow. In fact, it's almost completely silent as I watch the arrow fly towards my target.

The deer grunts and drops. My shot is near perfect. With a squeal of glee, I jump up and start clapping. Then I throw myself at Beast and give him a big hug. I'm pretty sure he isn't prepared for that, because he's as rigid as a board. After a few seconds, he grabs my waist gently, picks me up and places me in front of him. Then he pulls his knife and heads for the stricken animal.

As I follow him, I admit to being a bit perplexed that he still keeps me at arm's length. Granted, after being repeatedly raped for the most of a year, my libido had taken up residence somewhere near the South Pole. But in all the time he's known me, Beast still hasn't even made a hint of a move. I guess the vain woman part of me might be a little disappointed by that.

The deer's breathing is labored as Beast stalks up to it and kneels down. Stroking its face softly, he whispers something in its ear. Then he slides his blade into the base of its skull, putting it out of its misery. The creature expires with a single exhale as its eyes loll back into its skull.

"What did you say?" My voice is a whisper, just in case.

Beast looks at me, slightly annoyed that I'm breaking silence, but answers me. "I ask the deer for forgiveness, but also thank it for the sustenance it will give us. I pray for it to be at peace."

"Wow," I exclaim softly. "You show no remorse for the many men you've killed, but when it comes to a deer, you're a real softly."

"My grandfather was Cherokee. I learned how to hunt from him."

Pulling his blade out of the deer, he shakes it and then points to me. Just like that, talking time is over. With a nod, I draw my knife and he proceeds to teach me the grossest part of hunting. While I realize this is important for my survival and pay attention, I quickly learn that gutting and dressing an animal is grisly business. Blood and guts everywhere, up past my elbows. Well, not really, but it feels like it.

Yuck!

Once we are done, he pulls a clean tarp out of his pack, throws it over his head and shoulders, and then hefts the carcass onto his back, his head between the fore and rear legs. Since he is holding it by the legs, I grab his rifle and the bow and we make our way back to the camp for what should be a good meal. At least as long as I can get the image of gutting a deer out of my head.

I wonder if deer tastes like chicken?

Taking pity on me, Beast helps me out by finishing the butchering, cutting up the good parts of the deer. These are then thrown into a cooler to help keep them fresh. Slicing off the tip of the tongue, he throws it into the fire.

Once that is accomplished, Beast takes the rest of the carcass back to where we made the kill, leaving it for any predator that might come along. Hopefully, that will keep those other predators out of our camp, as well. I really don't want to take on a bear, although I can picture Beast having fun with that.

Sitting back, I smile as my stomach gurgles contentedly after our meal. I'm satisfied as I settle back against a log. I had no idea that deer, well venison, could taste so good. Especially the way Beast prepares it.

God, can that man cook.

Our meal was a thick, hearty stew made with chunks of venison, the last of our potatoes and carrots and a can of mushrooms. It was cooked over a fire pit Beast dug into the ground, to help keep the light of the fire from being easily seen. Then he set up a stand and cook pot. A few hours of enticing smells, and voila, dinner!

"That was wonderful," I say the thought out loud.

I catch just a hint of a shy smile and it makes me happy. Happiness is something that has been in short supply, so it is nice to have a taste of it. And I like to see Beast more relaxed. I've learned how hard it is for him to be around people. Some days I think it's hard for him to even tolerate me.

I ponder that for a moment. Should I have left when he told me to that first day, after he'd fed me and taught me basic gun skills? Would he be any happier? I glance at him again, he's poking the fire with a stick. Why do men always like to do that? Is it fun? Should I try it? No, I don't think he'd be happier. And I think by now we might both be dead. Deep down I know I made the right choice, for both of us. With a happy sigh, I let that little twist of tension go.

As he cleans the dishes, I gaze up at the night sky and marvel at the stars. You never saw a sky like this before the Collapse. L.A.'s light pollution made it impossible to see many stars at all—well, aside from the ones in Beverly Hills. Now you can see them all, and it is an awe-inspiring sight.

This will be our last night under this patch of sky. Truck is ready to travel and we've still got a lot of ground left to cover. I wrestled the plan out of him while dinner was cooking. Pulling out his maps, he showed me. Using one finger, he traced a line from where we are through a circuitous route to a spot in Colorado.

Beast had been something of a prepper before everything hit the fan. *Big surprise, right?* He'd bought land and built a bunker in Colorado years ago, long before the world collapsed. It's fully stocked and the land has running water year round. With the seed he's got stored there, we can grow our own food and quit skulking through ruins. But we have to get there first.

Preppers! Used to think they were crazy people and laughed at them. Who's laughing now?

As he folds the maps back up and puts them into their protective bag, I thank him with a smile and nod with understanding of the plan. We have enough fuel to get us to the outskirts of Phoenix, we hope, before needing to scavenge again.

Slowly I stretch backward over the log, letting out a happy, sleepy noise. I'm exhausted, but I am thinking I should take first watch since I flaked out with nightmares the night before. Beast gives me a series of hand signs, telling me to go to sleep. I shake my head at him in disagreement, pulling myself up to stand watch, then spoil it with a huge yawn. He shakes his head and points emphatically to my bedroll. I can't disagree, I'm so tired.

Moving to my bedroll, I pull it open and climb in. The nights have been cold, so I'm grateful for the warm sleeping bag and thick pad I've got. And I'm thankful for how Beast treats me. I probably don't deserve it, but he's just—always there. I don't know how I would get on without his strong, comforting presence. So much for strong womanhood, I laugh to myself.

As I slowly drift off to sleep, I watch Beast as he works. After finishing up with the dishes, he picks up his SCAR and slips the sling over his head.

I call his new toy, Teddy Bear, which makes him frown at me. Yet at the same time, I can still see a hint of a smile tug at the corner of his mouth. It's become something of a quest for me. Every time I get him to smile, I hug myself for getting through his grumpy demeanor. Just the memory of it makes me grin as I drift off.

Chapter Thirty-Five

I wake to find myself resting on a luxurious, gold canopy bed draped in red decor and immediately sit up in shock. The room is expensively decorated, and I mean over the top gorgeous. The interior walls are white marble trimmed with gold. Paintings and rich tapestries are well-placed, and elegant furniture is set tastefully about the room. What stands out is a vanity table with an enormous, oval mirror in a golden frame. When I approach, I see my reflection in the mirror and gasp.

Wow!

Okay, if there's one thing that I know, it's French couture, especially that of the 1600s to 1700s. I've always been enamored of French culture. And now, here I am in an exquisite ball gown of gold brocade that tightly hugs my torso before blooming out into wide panniers—and I don't think I need to tell you, my boobs look great! My hair has been pulled up into a tall and elaborate work of art held together with pins of gold and strands of pearls. An expensive gold necklace holds an enormous teardrop ruby that rests just above my now-fabulous cleavage.

As I stand there in stunned silence, gazing at my reflection, the door is flung open and startles me. A young woman who must be a servant, rushes in and she is clearly agitated and tense. When her gaze falls on me, she lets out a sigh of relief and rushes over to me.

"Mademoiselle, le parti a déjà commencé."

Shit! My French is rusty.

"Uhhh, Oui, je sais. Je suis prêt."

I must do a good job telling her that I'm ready for the party that's already, apparently, started without me, for the young woman looks relieved. Quickly she brings over a white mask with black feathers and gold filigree and helps me put it on, tying in the back without mussing my coiffure. When I gaze once more at the woman in the mirror, I am momentarily mesmerized by her.

I don't have long to stare at my reflection. Taking my hand, the girl practically yanks my arm out of its socket as she drags me out of the chair. *Impatient much? Jeez!* We hurry from the bedroom and through an opulent mansion. Paintings, tapestries and luxurious furniture decorate the halls, each more elegant than the last. Finally we arrive at a ball room full of exquisitely-dressed people in masquerade masks.

"Mademoiselle Chloe," the young woman announces.

Every pair of eyes looks in my direction, and even with this amazing gown on, their stares make me feel naked. Everyone either nods, bows or curtsies, before going back to their revelry. Once their eyes are off me, I begin my exploration of this fantasy world I've found myself enveloped by.

It's a fancy party with a quartet playing in the far corner. A long table near the left hand wall is laid out with a huge variety magnificent foods. Even the air is filled with sweet perfume.

I move to the buffet table to feast my eyes. A platter of fresh strawberries catches my attention and I take one. It's so succulent, juice gushing as my teeth sink into it. It's been so long since I've had a good strawberry.

A new song begins and people move to take dance partners. I bow out, choosing to watch, partly because I'm still stunned by the opulence of it all. Many of the guests pair-off and the dance begins. The floor is suddenly filled with beautiful, colorful butterflies that pirouette their way around the floor.

I know I'm in a dream, but my breath still leaves me when the crowded dance floor parts as Beast strides towards me. He cuts directly through the center of the ballroom as if it were not populated by a throng of dancers. Yet they move skillfully around him as if it's the Red Sea parting for Moses himself.

At first, I hardly recognize him. Dressed in a fine, French-aristocrat style suit with a knee-length coat of blue with gold trim, he commands attention. A waistcoat of the same design and color is underneath, along with breeches to match. A white cravat and white, frilly cuffs provide a dash of different color. Short, white shoes with rounded toes cover his feet. Only three things about him are the same: his hair, beard, and his mask. The long brown and gray streaked hair is worn loose, stopping just below the collar. Beard is well trimmed and his mask is gold instead of white.

Just the sight of him makes my mouth go dry and my heart skips a beat. I don't know how to look at him this way, and am filled with both uncertainty and a strange joy

Blue eyes the same shade as the sky after a summer storm, gaze at me as if I'm the only woman in the room. No, more like the only woman in existence. He has never looked at me this way during our waking hours, and I am both terrified and filled with glee. His face sports a lascivious grin as he saunters towards me, silently telling me of a myriad of erotic things he'd like to do with me. When evil men have looked at me with lust, I have been angered and repelled, but here and now? With that expression on Beast's face? I don't know. I feel... butterflies and anticipation.

"Bonjour, belle ange," he states with a respectful bow. "Tu es tres belle."

Holy shit! He speaks French? Hell. It's my dream. OF COURSE he speaks French.

I try to reply to his beautiful compliment, but I'm stunned into silence.

147

My mouth opens and sounds fail to come out. With a wolfish smile, he steps closer and with two fingers, gently pushes my chin up in order to close my mouth. I feel little arcs of electricity go through me at the feel of his brief touch.

"Danse avec moi?"

At first, all I can do is nod when he asks me to dance. "Oui."

My knees are trembling as he takes my hand in his and leads me onto the dance floor. I will my legs to move and we join the waltz that is in progress. My eyes become locked in his as he leads me around the floor, and the rest of the world just becomes a blur as we twirl around to the beautiful music.

When the music stops, I find the former setting has disappeared, along with the other revelers. Now we are in the bedroom where I began this dream. My heart beats double time as Beast gazes at me in such a way, I feel naked once more. His expression is one of a man dying of thirst and I am the only nourishment he needs. Seeing that look in his eyes, I want to be the one to quench it. With deliberate slowness, he steps around behind and slips one arm about my waist. My breath catches in my throat when he whispers in my ear.

"Voulez-vous coucher avec moi, ce soir?"

I whimper as I melt into his embrace. "Oui, monsieur." *A thousand times, yes.*

At my consent, his lips find my neck and I suck in a breath as electricity jolts through my body. His caress moves up my neck, lips and tongue tease behind my ear before he pulls my earlobe between his lips, and I gasp while clutching his hand at my waist.

Strong hands travel across my body, moving towards my back to undo the laces of my gown. As he helps with my dress, he continues to land soft kisses all about my neck and shoulders until I've finally stepped out of it. I'm left with soft, lacy white lingerie that leaves little to the imagination. *These are not 18th Century under drawers. I love them!*

Without warning he stops and lets me go, leaving me standing there to gather my wits. Walking over to the divan that sits at the foot of the bed, he takes off his knee length coat and places it on the arm. Then he sits down, giving me a carnal, appreciative gaze that heats my blood even more. Again I am reminded of other glances of such a nature and how I loathed them. And now, how I relish his look.

"Danse pour moi."

"Oui monsieur."

I'm so hot, so ready. There is such an erotic look in his eyes, I feel I may burst into flames on the spot. Somehow, though, I start to dance to a tune in my head. My body sways to the beat as he smiles, fixating on me with a dark look as he watches while I'm dressed in nothing but lingerie.

"Dépouiller pour moi."

Strip for you? Gladly.

Taking a page from his book, I do a slow tease with my bra while I continue dancing. When I take the bra off, I spin around so at first all he can see is my back. With a flick of the wrist, I toss my bra and it lands perfectly on his head, one cup flopping over his face.

As I turn, he smiles darkly at me while lifting the bra off his head and laying it gently on top of his coat. The intensity is heightened as his eyes never leave mine. Slowly I dance closer to him, shimmying out of my panties as I do so. Once they are around my ankles, I step one foot out and then lift the other, planting it on the edge of the divan, right between his legs.

With a licentious grin, Beast carefully takes my offered leg and removes the panties, then sets my foot back down. I watch as he takes them, places them to his nose and inhales deeply, closing his eyes briefly before locking them on mine once more. Once done, he places the panties next to my bra.

Sliding off the couch and onto his knees, his strong hands reach out and glide up my thighs. Grabbing my ass, he pulls me closer to him. I am shaking so hard, he strokes my back a little to soothe me. I'm trying to control my breathing as I watch him start planting kisses on my inner thighs, alternating from one to the other as he edges closer and closer to his true goal, with his beard adding tiny, tickling fingers against my skin.

Oh. My. God!

It feels like he's worshiping me. My hands, which are holding his shoulders for stability, move up and fist into his hair as his tongue finds that magical spot and I cry out. I almost try to dance away because of the sensitivity, but he holds me firmly. Throwing my head back, I surrender myself to an expert tongue that swirls, licks and teases me until I explode into a spectacular climax as I scream in absolute ecstasy. I feel my knees go weak and fall against the divan.

Chapter Thirty-Six

I sit up in my bedroll with a gasp and try to figure out what just happened. My wits are scattered and my heart is still pounding as the remains of my orgasm rushes through my body faster than a Lamborghini on the Autobahn.

What the fuck was that?

It's still dark, and I catch Beast watching me with what might be a raised eyebrow behind that damn mask. My cheeks heat and I wonder what he saw or heard. Good lord, I'm not sure how to behave around him right now. I have just experienced something incredible. And yes, all that stuff you see in porn is fake for the most part. It's called acting for a reason. I look away to catch my breath and calm down.

Yeah, calm down, 'cause that's never going to happen. He is still grieving, and I'm not... I'm not ready for this! Am I? What the holy fuck?

I lay back down, looking away from Beast. Catching my breath, I let my heart slow as my mind races. After a few minutes, I check my watch and realize it will soon be time for me to take over watch. Rolling onto my back, I gaze at the stars to find my calm once more. The forest is quiet, with only the crackling of a small fire to be heard, and the occasional crunch of Beast's boots against the ground.

I have not had a wet dream in years, and certainly not since the Collapse. Are my body and mind trying to tell me something? Part of me disagrees with that, and not because I don't think Beast isn't handsome in his own way. It's simply hard to believe he would be of the same mind. He has never looked at me as an object of desire that I could tell. At that thought, I feel a quick lance of pain in my chest.

I need to quit thinking about this.

Getting up, I slip my boots on and lace them up. Then I grab my rifle and walk over to Beast. I know he can hear me coming, yet he acts like he doesn't. Probably doesn't want to waste time on pleasantries. Same reason he doesn't want to talk. The more he limits human interaction, the better he is at keeping his walls intact.

"I'm awake," I state softly. "I'll take over."

Giving me a nod, he goes over to his bedroll and gets ready to sleep while I start a slow walk around the campsite. Out of the corner of my eye, I catch him knelt down in prayer, whispering something that I can't make out. Sometimes I think he's speaking in another language. Latin maybe? I try not to pry—okay, I try to make it look like I'm not prying.

Before long he's fast asleep and looks peaceful. I gaze at Beast briefly before continuing. Yes, I keep my attention on my surroundings, but my thoughts wander. I'm not wondering only about Beast, but also about the friends I left behind. I know it's only been a few days, but I do hope that they are doing all right. Especially poor Diane. I hope she will be able to live a good life, free from any further evil.

I actually find myself praying for them, and that's not something I've done in a long time. In all honesty, I had a falling out with God after I was captured by Knick and Knack. I felt like God had abandoned all of us to a life of misery and torture. But for reasons I can't explain, I don't feel that way anymore. Diane, Linda and all of the Walma veterans are the focus of my prayers. I even put in one for Beast, asking for him to be healed somehow. He deserves real peace, not just the oblivion of sleep.

I can't help but worry about him. We've both been through a lot, but I can't even begin to understand the depth of his demons. If he could bring himself to talk about it, maybe he could start to exorcize them, but we know how well he talks. He would rather hold it all in and suffer, stupid idiot. I have an idea what it is, of course. I know it has something to do with his family. Whatever happened, he clearly blames himself and believes he must suffer.

At that, I begin to realize that perhaps this is why he keeps people at bay. If he doesn't get attached, he can't be hurt with another loss. While it makes a certain amount of sense, it seems like a really lonely way to live.

And I thought women were complicated.

"No," Beast calls in a low voice.

When I glance over, I see he's rolling back and forth in his sleeping bag. He's got to be having a nightmare, and the thought of what is plaguing him causes my heart to constrict in my chest. I quickly rush over to his side.

"Don't touch her,' he mumbles in a pained voice.

"Shhhh," I say softly. "It's alright, my Beast. I'm right here. We're safe."

With the sound of my voice, he calms immediately. His head stops thrashing, the creases in his brow smooth out, and his entire body calms down. I know he's finally out of the woods when his face becomes peaceful once more and his breathing slows.

I kneel over him a little longer, watching over this man who has become an essential part of my life. Normally he looks after me, so it's nice to be able to help him for a change. Once more I'm tempted to try and remove his mask and see the man underneath.

With some effort, I refrain and stand back up. I walk away as quietly as I can so I don't wake him. I did ask him once why he always wore the mask, and I got a hand signal for "explosion," and that was all the explanation I ever got. Somehow I don't believe it. The mirrors back at the house, all of them shattered, make me think it's something else. Something far more psychological or traumatizing. The explosion was something inside of him that detonated. That in part, is why I keep my curiosity at bay. I don't want to send him further down the rabbit hole.

Leaning against Truck, I daydream a little, hoping that life will be better as we head down the road. There's a part of me that longs for a more peaceful life. It's one reason I had to leave with Beast. I'm hoping that "home" will be far away from gangs, raiders and scumbags that require more trigger time. The submissive, rape-victim Chloe has been buried under enough corpses to be considered well gone at this point.

The cynic in me doubts this will be the case, but it's nice to dream, to have hope. Hope is probably one of the most powerful things that keeps us going even when things look to be their darkest. As George Michael said, ya gotta have faith.

Shaking my head at the pop culture reference, I still hum the song and try to pay closer attention to the world around me as I stand my half of the watch.

When the sun starts rising, Beast wakes like clockwork. With his trademark silence, he starts fixing breakfast and I stay on watch. God I wish he would talk to me. It's not only boring without conversation, it's also lonely. Hell, he might as well still be asleep! I can't help it, I'm gonna poke the bear. I start a conversation with myself.

"Good morning, Beast. Did you sleep well?"

I lower my voice to try and sound manly. "Why yes I did, Chloe. I must say, you are looking quite beautiful this morning."

"Why thank you! I'm trying some new blush. It's called Raider Red."

While he's trying to ignore me, I catch just a hint of a laugh as he takes the last of our eggs and starts cracking them. The sound reminds me somewhat of a horse snorting. Pretending to ignore it, I continue.

"Well, Chloe," I state in a low voice. "I must say, it certainly looks good on you. Reminds me of the time we took out the University Raiders."

"Oh yeah. Those were fun times."

"I really liked that hallway fight. You were amazing!"

I giggle playfully. "Awwww, thank you. And let me say, the way you slipped into that celebration party like you were one of them and planted those bombs? That was phenomenally clever and masterfully done! But to tell the truth, I totally wanted to kill you."

"Kill me?" I try to keep my voice extra low. "What? But why?"

"Because what you did was stupid dangerous, duh!"

"It wasn't stupid," I exclaim in my now perfected Beast voice as I shoot him a grin.

He's standing there, cooking and trying to pretend that he isn't listening. *Yeah, buddy, I know better.* With a smile, I continue on.

"It was totally stupid! You could have been killed, with your partner unable to do anything about it. In fact, had it all gone wrong, we both would have been tortured like no other. We were the ultimate prize to them. If you ever pull something like that again, I'll most likely shoot you myself."

I'm staring him directly in the eyes with a half-grin as he stands, turns and walks towards me with a plate. The swagger in his walk is almost exactly like it was in my dream and, at that, my body heats. Once he's close, he hands me the plate and then strolls back to the campfire. I chuckle as I look down to see what he's cooked, and my brain stops. Lying on the plate is an omelet, complete with some tomatoes and chunks of ham.

Wow! He may not be much of a conversationalist, but he sure can cook.

I immediately dig in and it is astonishingly good, for post-Collapse cuisine. The fresh eggs really were great while they lasted. I chase my meal with clean water and before long the plate is empty. With my stomach happy, I clean my plate while Beast finishes his meal.

Out of the corner of my eye, I notice him watching me as I dry my plate and silverware and start packing up camp. I'd really like to know what's going through his mind at this moment. I wonder if I took things too far, although if I did, I'd think I would know it already. He's good at that.

I'm about half way packed when he's done eating and cleans up. It doesn't take us long to finish breaking camp. We've done it often enough that we're like a well-oiled machine, never getting in each other's way and seamlessly putting things where they belong.

With a contented sigh, I unsling my rifle, climb into the passenger seat and start getting comfortable. I hear the back hatch close and not long after, Beast silently climbs in after stowing his Teddy Bear. As he is about to put the key into the ignition, the alarm on his watch goes off.

Odd, he's never set the alarm on it before.

Turning in the seat, he reaches into the back and rummages in his pack for something. All I can do is sit there, watching him curiously. Finally he produces a small box, wrapped in plain brown grocery-bag style paper. Sitting back down, he hands it over to me.

A present? Beast is giving me a present?

I'm so stunned it takes me a moment before I take the box from him. I inspect it and it's not very big, small and slim. Slowly a smile forms on my face as I look at my partner. Beast is fixated on me, and I think he's waiting to see what my reaction will be to what is inside.

Quickly I tear open the brown paper held down with medical tape to find a black, slightly beat up box that probably at one time held a piece of jewelry. I can't wait any longer, so I carefully remove the lid and look down in pleased surprise at what lies inside.

Chapter Thirty-Seven

A sleek, black MP3 player sits in the box, nestled in tissue paper, complete with a set of ear buds and a USB cable to plug it into the dash. It has some wear and is a little scuffed up, but it's perfect! This is so not what I was expecting—not that I knew exactly what to expect—and I fight to hold back the tears that prick at my eyes. Picking it up, I see writing at the bottom of the box.

Happy birthday.

I look at him, confused. "It's not my birthday."

Pointing to his watch, he shows me the date. At first, I'm even more confused. I have to sit for a minute or so, trying to understand what he's telling me. Then at last it hits me. It's been a whole year to the day since he rescued me from Knick and Knack. Beast remembered the day I was given my freedom? Now I do cry, and I have no shame.

Setting my gift carefully on the dash, I throw myself at him in a big, sobbing hug. I know this is not what he was expecting, and I feel his muscles stiffen. For so long he's avoided being a human being so that he could vent his anger on the raiders in L.A.

"Thank you," I say softly, if a bit raggedly, and give him a bright, genuine smile.

Once I let go of him, I sit back down, digging in my pocket for a handkerchief. Giving me one of his signature bows, he starts up Truck. Seemingly unmoved, he starts driving us back down the mountain.

I turn on the player to see what music it has on it and I'm impressed at the selection. Multiple playlists are set up; from classical, to rock, to metal and even rap. The number of artists are all over the spectrum as well. Thanks to Beast, it's almost fully charged. I slip one ear bud on, and then a thought hits me and I laugh. When he shoots me an odd look, I answer him.

"The nice thing is that with you, I can have both ear buds in and not be rude," I state with a sly grin. "I don't need to hear you as you wave your hands about."

At first he frowns, then slowly sticks his tongue out at me before shaking his head and paying attention to the road. Memories of my wet dream flash through my mind and I blush furiously as my insides clench. I quickly look back to the player, deciding on a song that will take my mind off that damned dream.

Starting with one of my favorite bands, Nightwish, I let some symphonic metal serenade me. While the music wails, I pay close attention to the road ahead, watching for ambushes. The P-90 rig is still on the floor, so I grab one and place it on my lap. Given the close confines of the cab, it's a much better choice should I need to start shooting.

I have not heard music in so long that it brings tears to my eyes. Smiling brightly as they roll down my cheeks, I sniffle. This is such a perfect gift, not to mention so thoughtful. I really need to think of something special that I can do for him in return. Then thoughts of my dream, he and I naked and sweaty come unbidden to my mind. I shut that down immediately.

But then, if I'm honest, I finally must admit to myself that I wouldn't mind sex if it was with Beast. Given the kindness and respect with which he has always treated me, I'm certain he'd be a good lover. What I worry about is his reaction to the very idea. I'm afraid he'd run away screaming if I tried to seduce him, so that's out. He doesn't do well when subjected to too much civilization, let alone anything that involves possible feelings. And nothing can screw up a friendship faster than sex.

With a sigh, I start thinking of some other way I can do something for him. He most certainly deserves it. I'm slightly startled by his finger touching my cheek as he wipes away a tear. When I look, he's shooting me a worried expression.

"I'm just happy," I tell him reassuringly. "It's such a beautiful present."

It's really rare that he smiles at all, but this time he does. It's not a hint of one or a slight tug at the corners of his mouth. No, it's a wide grin he flashes before putting his attention back on the road. While he doesn't realize it, he's now given me two amazing presents today, because it's nice to see him smile for once.

Slowly we make our way down and back into Redlands, but take a different route that leads into Yucaipa. I'm sure he wants to make it difficult for anyone to try and ambush us, especially any of that gang that jumped us on the freeway.

The area is desolate and shows no signs of recent habitation. Any vehicles are just shells, stripped of anything and everything that can be used. There's not a single building that does not look run down, abandoned, and in some cases, totally wrecked. Weeds and other plant life are growing out of control. Grass sprouts up through sidewalks and asphalt as Mother Nature works to take back that which is rightfully hers.

We finally hook back up on the ten and are flying down the freeway once more. Well, it feels like flying, though we're crawling along compared to pre-Collapse speeds. I've got my armored hatch down so that I can look at all the windmills, some of which have fallen while others are charred and black. There are quite a few that still turn though, churning away as they provide electricity to a power grid that no longer functions.

I can't help it, and I blame the music, but as Palm Springs begins to fly past, my eyelids begin to get heavy. As I look at Beast, he's glued to the road, and I swear he's just itching for someone to come along so he can shoot them. As I study his face, Delain sings sweetly in my ears and I slowly fall asleep.

Beast nudges me softly and I wake up, stretching happily as I look at him. It nice to see that he isn't angry at me for falling asleep. Pointing ahead, he directs my attention to a barricade up ahead as the truck slows. Adrenaline kicks in with a vengeance and I sit up quickly, readying my P-90.

A number of trucks are blocking the freeway, with tall barricades of steel set up on the beds. Behind those barricades are men with weapons pointed at us. In front of all of that is a single California Highway Patrol car. Both doors are open, and while the passenger has a shotgun pointed at us, the driver is holding a rifle against his hip while he talks through a handset.

"You be kind enough to step out with your hands up, put your weapons on the hood and then walk forward."

I shoot Beast a worried look. As he puts Truck in park, my partner just nods to me calmly and opens the door, doing exactly as ordered. Following along, I leave the P-90 on the seat and put my pistol and knife on the hood while Beast is still disarming. Once he has put half a dozen weapons on Truck's hood, we both step forward.

As I take a closer look, I realize none of these people appear to be a gang or raiders. Just about all of them look like farmers. Jeans and button-up shirts dominate, and most weapons are bolt action rifles or shotguns.

The only man that is different is the one issuing orders from the patrol car. He's decked out in a tactical vest and police uniform. He also has the only military style rifle that I see, a full length AR-15 with a twenty round magazine.

When we are about twenty feet from the patrol car, he motions us to stop. "That's close enough. What's your business here?"

"Passing through." There is an undercurrent of a growl in Beast's response.

"Really," the officer replies, giving my companion a look of scrutiny. "Ain't nothin' but trouble comes from L.A."

Both men are locked in something of a stare down, and I know full well who will be the winner of that contest. The officer is already starting to appear nervous, and that spurs me to speak up in an attempt to prevent bad things from happening.

"Look, we're just trying to escape from that hell hole! Can't we please pass?"

Silence descends upon us as the officer thinks about my plea. While he looks at the both of us, he keeps sizing Beast up. I'm worried these two are going to come to blows, mostly because my companion will instigate it.

"You willing to pay a toll?" The officer looks nervous as he asks.

Beast emits a low growl while leveling a hard stare at the man, and I can see him start to wither while gripping his weapon a little tighter. I nudge my companion in the side with my elbow as I address the officer.

"What do you need?"

The officer swallows hard as his gaze slides to me. "What we need is an army who can take care of the bandits who keep attacking us. However, some ammo would be nice. If you got any we can use, of course."

"What bandits?" The Beast's tone of voice has softened.

Looking curiously at my companion, he replies. "A group coming down from Midland. Keep stealing food and livestock, killed a few of our folks and kidnapped a couple women. Problem is that they are a lot better armed than we are. Hard to put up a fight against automatic weapons when all you got is some shotguns and lever action rifles."

Beast nods. "We kill them; we get food, water and safe passage?"

"Shit," the officer exclaims. "You do that and I'll even spare you some diesel!"

Removing his right glove, my companion holds out his hand. At first the officer seems puzzled, but light dawns, and he grins as they finally shakes hands. It's easy to tell that they give a firm shake that lasts longer than it should, and I think it's because they are testing each other. Men... I swear.

"Bargain struck," Beast finally states. "Will need directions. Could use some sleep."

"You got it," the officer exclaims with relief. "Name's Jack. You two can have dinner at my place and clean up if you want. But please, leave your weapons in your vehicle. People here are a mite nervous these days."

"Understood." Beast gives a nod.

Jack turns and gives a hand motion. Trucks start up and pull away as the group breaks and heads into the town. Beast starts back towards Truck and grabs his weapons off the hood, tossing them into the back of the cab and I do the same. When I climb in, he's already starting the ignition.

"Do you think we can trust them?"

Beast stops for a moment and looks at me. "There are two kinds of people in this world. Good folk who mean what they say, help others when they can and aren't deceptive. Like these people. The others—well, you know them far too well."

As usual, when he speaks, Beast does a good job at silencing the entire room. Those words evoke memories that I want to burn from my skull. It was those experiences that have driven me to kill raider after raider, to enjoy it, to look forward to it. And the thought leads me to ask myself a question: is that what I really want to be? Is that all I am?

While removing vermin that prey on my friends and I is a worthy goal, and saving women like Diane is a very rewarding experience, I've started to realize that I'm heading down the same path as Beast. It is a dark path I do not want to go down, or rather, it's a path to darkness and I don't want that to be my whole life. And I realize my compunctions are the reason I spared Steve at the university. I can't be so cold, not forever. I can't harden myself so much I sacrifice my humanity. I'm going to need to do some soul searching and decide just who this new Chloe is going to be. Right now though, it's time to go into the house of our host.

Chapter Thirty-Eight

Jack's house is simple and may be a little run down, but it also looks like a well-loved home. In fact, all the homes on the street appear to be about the same in this little town of Blythe.

There are very few weeds and no trash in the front yard, and it appears lovingly tended. A white picket fence sets the boundary for the small yard, paint chipping and peeling here and there. I also notice solar panels, the small, efficient ones. Nice. Something that might seem expensive, but sensible in the old world is a godsend in this new one.

Beast parks Truck next to Jack's patrol car along the side of the house and we pile out, joining up with Jack before heading inside. As we make our way in, I notice a windmill in the back yard, and I wonder if it's for additional power or if it's a well-pump. Electricity and running water? Yes please!

We walk into a home that looks like it is full of love. It's smaller than the one Beast had, but it's cozy. To my right, a sofa and chair sit in the living room, looking well-used and comfortable. The coffee table has a number of sadly out-of-date magazines arrayed across it. Against the wall is an entertainment center with DVD and CD racks, all of which are full.

On the left is a dining room with attached kitchen. A round table with four chairs sits in the dining room, with a simple overhead dome light. The kitchen is shaped like a "C," with faded yellow cabinetry and appliances that still go well with the black tile floor.

A woman is working happily in the kitchen, and delicious scents of cooking fill the air. Now I'm certain there is power because country-western music is playing. Dressed in a pale blue blouse and red checkered skirt, her dirty blonde hair is tied into a pony tail that sways as she dances. Jack smiles as he walks up behind the woman and wraps his arms around her. Spinning around in his arms, they share a passionate kiss.

When they come up for air, she spots us. "Well, hello! Who's this?"

"Mel, these two friends say they can take care of our bandit problem."

"No, really?" She asks excitedly. "That would be wonderful. Please, come in! My goofy husband hasn't introduced us, I'm Melissa."

I smile back politely. "Hi Melissa, I'm Chloe and this is my friend, Beast."

Both Jack and Melissa look like I just said something utterly awful before looking at my companion fearfully. I want to laugh so hard, but I hold it back to be polite and try to assuage their fears. It occurs to me we may be legends even this far out of L.A. But that can't be true, can it?

"Don't worry, it's just an affectionate nickname. He's actually a teddy bear."

When I shoot a grin at Beast, he's rolling his eyes and shaking his head. Jack and Melissa don't seem convinced. They still appear frightened as they both nod nervously.

"We're not being proper hosts," Jack states, recovering first. "Please have a seat and take a load off."

Beast and I both take the chairs that face the window, thus keeping our backs to the kitchen, and therefore a solid wall. Jack and Melissa share a quick kiss before he dives into the fridge and I hear bottles rattle. Then a bottle is placed in front of me—a beer bottle.

I point at it in shock. "Is that—a beer?"

"Yes ma'am. We brew it local. Ain't the best, but it's better than none and I think they're getting better."

Picking up the old fashioned bottle, I pop the cap off and swing it away before taking a drink. It's cold and delicious. Sure, it's not pre-Collapse beer, but when you haven't had one in years, it might as well be the most amazing brew ever made.

"Oh! This is divine!"

Beast pushes his bottle away and stands up. Giving a polite bow, he walks out of the house. Through the bay window of the dining room, I see him post up under the front porch like he's standing guard.

"What's his deal?" Jack looks a little offended.

"He's not being impolite," I hope to soothe any hurt feelings. "He's been through a lot. I think this is just a little too much civilization for him. One of the reasons I call him "Beast" is because he doesn't do well in captivity."

Jack nods like he gets it. "Guess I can understand that. Times have been rough. We've heard all sorts of nightmarish rumors about L.A."

"I can tell you from experience that they probably aren't rumors. Beast and I have had to kill a great number of raiders. That's why we left."

Melissa starts setting down full plates. "That's awful." She hovers with one of the plates. "Um… Is your friend hungry?"

"Most likely." I give her a polite smile. "I'll take it to him. He's accustomed to me. Thank you both for this."

Jack waves a hand like it's no big deal. "If you can take care of our bandit problem like he says, it's the least we can do."

Giving our host a reassuring smile, I grab my bottle and both plates and head outside to where Beast is standing. Walking up beside him, I bump into him lightly with my shoulder. When he glances down at me, I grunt before handing over his plate.

"Food," I say in a mocking, caveman voice. "Eat."

Beast glares at me for a moment before finally taking the plate. Now that

161

I have a free hand, I snap my fingers and point to the bench nearby, copying one of his frequently-used hand-signs. He stares at me again, shaking his head and seats himself at the bench. I plop down next to him and we eat in silence as the sun makes for the mountains to the west.

Taking a swig of my beer, I sigh and lean close to him. "You don't have to be a hard-ass all the time. You know that, right?"

Beast doesn't answer me. He just keeps eating while staring off into the distance.

"And you could be a little more communicative with your partner."

That gets his attention and he stops eating to gaze at me, confused at my statement. I take another drink before explaining.

"You did really well today. You said more words than usual, and maybe that's what's got you all grumpy, but I'm just saying. All the time it's, snap your fingers, wave your hands and then 'Hey, Macarena.' You could actually say something once in a while. Strike up a real conversation for once. With the exception of when we are getting shot at, the road has been rather boring so far."

Beast gives me one of his, 'Oh Really?' expressions in response.

"See, you just proved my point. You object, yet you don't say why. If we are going to take out some well-armed bandits, don't you think we should be planning this?"

Now he looks annoyed and I wonder if I've gone too far. I'm relieved when he actually talks to me though.

"You are annoyingly persistent."

"Of course I am," I reply with a smile and a wink. "That's part of my charming personality."

He takes a deep breath, and I think it's to reign in his emotions. This whole talking-to-others thing is well outside his comfort zone. It's "civilized" behavior, and that's something Beast doesn't feel like doing anymore. And then? He speaks!

"We will get some rest tonight. Tomorrow I will gather intel on the location the bandits operate from and then plan the attack. Good enough?"

"That's a good start. Thank you. Now, finish eating."

Beast shakes his head and goes back to his meal. I can't help but smile as I polish off my own plate. Maybe I'm finally making some headway with him. It certainly is nice to hear him talk, even if only for a short time.

The sun is setting when Jack walks out and takes a deep breath. "That's what I love about this place—great sunsets." Turning, he smiles at us. "Shower is ready if you'd like one?"

Did I hear shower?

Excitement blooms in my chest. "Did you say shower?"

"Yes ma'am," he replies with a short laugh. "We have a windmill bringing up well water, but we still have to pump it into an overhead tank by hand. We basically have running water. And our solar still works, so we have power and hot water. There's only so much in the tank though, so we keep a timer in the shower. Please don't run over."

I squeal with unbridled joy and jump up, giving Jack an involuntary hug. "Thank you."

Jack laughs at my reaction. "No problem. Head inside. Melissa will get you set up."

Looking at Beast, I clap my hands excitedly and see his eyes roll as I rush inside. I'm not going to let him derail my joy. It has been a lifetime since I've had a shower, let alone a hot shower. I damn near tackle Melissa and have her lead me to El Dorado.

Chapter Thirty-Nine

Closing the door to the bathroom, I am armed with towel, washcloth and clean clothes. Depositing them all on top of the toilet, I start getting out of clothes I've been in for far too long. Then I step into the shower, trying to contain my excitement.

That excitement is quickly brought under control when I see the timer sitting in a rack that hangs off the shower head. It's one of those old kitchen timers that you dial to the time you want. A big red mark is colored over the seven minute mark. I get ready to set the timer, but quickly decide I won't let this ruin my good mood.

Using just enough water to wet my hair, I lather up with the available shampoo. Yes, they actually have shampoo! Once my hair is well-lathered, I set the timer and let the hot water rain down all over me. Even though I know it won't last as long as I'd like, it is glorious and the shampoo smells like honeysuckle. There is also a choice of citrus body wash or an individually-wrapped motel soap. I take the body wash. I smell so good right now, I am in ecstasy.

I relish every moment of hot water spraying over my body. Humming softly, it feels like the wretched soul that had inhabited my body for so long is washed away. How is this different from my baths in Beast's house? I don't know, but this shower, hot, wonderful, it changes me. Cleanses me; body, mind and spirit. By the time the alarm goes off, I feel refreshed and renewed. It truly is amazing just how healing a hot shower can be.

I thoroughly dry off and take a look at myself in the foggy mirror. Even today, I have a hard time recognizing the woman that looks back at me with brown eyes that show pain survived, torture endured, but also, revenge accomplished. She's rougher, tougher and has been through a hell of a lot more than I ever could have imagined. There are a few scars marring her once-perfect brown skin, and I see deeper scars reflected in her eyes.

Pulling my gaze from the mirror, I slip on fresh panties and a clean pair of jeans. Wrapping my towel around my breasts, I practically skip out of the bathroom and into the guest bedroom where we will sleep. I love the feeling of cleanliness, and I love being in a normal, sane place for the moment.

Like the rest of the house, the bedroom is small, yet cozy. It has that feeling of home, for reasons one can't quite explain. Maybe it's the wood frame bed, with its handmade quilt. Or the rustic wooden furniture with a southwest flair. Dark green curtains cover the high set window. The wood slat floor is covered by a couple of rugs, woven with various southwest patterns, like a cowboy on a bucking bronco.

I smile at the fact that I get to sleep in a real bed tonight. As I walk around and start getting ready, my jeans start to inch their way down my hips. Searching for my belt, I realize that I must have left it in the bathroom. Hitching my pants back up, I head back to the bathroom in search of my wayward belt.

Back in the hallway, I reach for the bathroom door only to have it open before I can put my hand on the knob. Startled, I look up to see Beast, naked from the waist up, mask still on, of course.

All I can do is stare at him. For a man in his forties, he's in great shape, and well-built for not being overly muscular. The hair on his broad chest almost forms a cross, with a smattering of gray hairs amongst the darker ones. With all the walking, fighting and killing that he's done so tirelessly, I'm surprised to see love handles on his hips. Scars of all kinds dot his torso, mostly long lines, some of which are a little jagged. There's also a few white and puckered circular marks that I know are bullet wounds. A few beds of water remain on his skin.

Beast is shocked at my presence, but his eyes leave my face. They travel slowly down my body. For the first time since fate thrust us together, I actually see an appreciative gaze in his expression. Memories from my dream starts to surface as we *see* each other in near carnal appreciation.

"I'm sorry," my voice sounds almost meek, not me at all, but I'm still trying to clear my head. "I forgot my belt."

Respectfully, he steps aside and allows me to walk in. I do a quick search and find my belt is lying on the white tile floor, in between the toilet and sink. Picking it up, I stand and look to see that Beast has left. Sighing painfully, I try to purge certain persistent wayward thoughts from my mind and walk back to the bedroom.

I find him standing near the foot of the bed. He gazes around like he's been thrust into an alien environment and doesn't know what to do. The sight of this makes my heart constrict. We've come so far, and yet he's still lost deep in the woods.

"They only have the one spare room," I state like it's an apology.

Beast turns and looks at me, perplexed at first. Then he nods and grabs a pillow from the bed. Doing a quick search, he finds an extra blanket. I watch, somewhat painfully, as he lays the blanket at the foot of the bed and then lies down. As if he's a guard dog lying at the foot of his master's bed.

"The bed is big enough for the both of us."

Looking up at me, he shakes his head and then lays back down.

With a sigh, I walk over to the bed and get ready. Since he's lying down already, I go ahead and strip out of my pants, drop the towel and throw on one of his t-shirts. As tall as he is, they make great night shirts for me. "Navy" writ large in faded dark blue, faded letters is emblazoned across the gray threads. I lay my pants on the dresser and slip into bed.

My head hits the pillow, and of course my thoughts gravitate towards Beast. Why is he like this? What happened to make him this way? I've been through a lot of shit, yet I still look forward to a comfortable, warm bed. I like being around people, even if I feel like I need more alone time than before. With a sigh, I glance toward the end of the bed. I can't see him, but I know he's there. My poor Beast, lying on the floor like an animal. It breaks my heart.

I wish there was something I could do for him. He looks like a caged lion.

Laying my head back down, I stare at the worn popcorn ceiling and feel a little empty. Leaving L.A. has put us in uncharted territory in more ways than one. We've not just left ghosts and demons behind, we've also left good friends. Beast and I are on our own, and while we have each other's back in combat, I feel like our relationship is moving beyond that. Given all he's been through, it's probably a scarier prospect for him than it is for me.

While I've done a good job of slaying and burying my demons, I know he still fights his on a daily basis. Whatever his issues, he's not past them yet. Could that be why he wants to go home? Maybe he thinks that when he gets there, he can put them to rest. I certainly hope so. He deserves better than this. We all do.

At least I'm getting him to talk to me more. God, the silent treatment was getting old! Maybe that will help as well. Start the process of rebuilding his humanity and get him out of the feral rut he's been caging himself in.

My eyelids begin to get heavy and I close them, ready for a good night's sleep in a comfortable bed. As I relax, the silence—and my calm—is shattered by the gradually building sounds of Jack and Melissa making love. And from the sounds of it, they both like it rough.

Great! While they're getting some, I have to go without. Thanks guys.

With a groan, I pull the pillow over my head in an attempt to drown out the sounds to get some much needed sleep.

Chapter Forty

It's late in the day as Beast and I crawl through the desert brush toward where we are told the bandit's base is. The rush of going into combat has brought up our spirits. Beast actually grinned at me before we left Blythe.

Maybe he is getting better after all.

I keep my assigned rifle off the ground as I low crawl toward our chosen position. I have the SVD, at least for the initial foray. I remember telling Beast about my two kills after the fall of Walma once he'd gotten better. I was rewarded with his smile, high praise from him. Since I'd done such a good job then, I get to use it tonight. *Hot damn!*

Thanks to Beast's hard work, the SVD now has a suppressor. I had to laugh when I first saw it. An oil filter is attached to the front of the barrel, and it's partly held there with duct tape. Duct tape? When I gave him an incredulous look, he simply called it, "the handyman's secret weapon."

Jack and the townsfolk happily colored in the big picture for us. About four months ago, a gang came out of nowhere and settled in to prey on the people of Blythe. Food was stolen, citizens were wounded or killed, and women had been kidnapped. Of course we know what the purpose was in kidnapping the ladies.

The only good rapist is a dead rapist.

We've been told the bandits had taken root in a place called Midland. It was a mining operation back in the seventies but was long defunct. Jack said it recently started back up shortly before the Collapse, but there were oddities, as he put it. The site had been secured with fences and razor wire. There was heavy private security. He was confident it was some kind of military operation. Of course, now it's a bandit stronghold, though whether the military people have been exterminated or joined the bandits is an interesting question.

We stop, and I pull up my binoculars to have a look at the scene. Beast has his G3 and is doing the same through the high-power scope. There are a lot of men, all in the typical post-apocalyptic wear that is all the rage with gangs these days. A few tents litter the area. Worse, they most definitely are heavily armed.

What a lovely looking bunch of guys I wouldn't want to take home to meet my folks. Looks like the Crazy Eight times ten.

As I pay more attention, I realize these guys are looking more and more like Dean's core team. While they have sections of tires or street signs, it's all woven in with tactical vests. Numerous mag pouches can been seen and that worries me.

In the many fights before, Beast and I actually had the advantage. Most gangs were working with scavenged gear, so they had one, maybe two mags for their weapons. That's why they had metal and used tires for armor. Between other gangs, firefights didn't last long before they were trying to kill each other with clubs and knives. That also gave Beast and I an advantage, as we could keep shooting long after they ran dry.

I turn my attention to Beast and whisper. "Well, what do you think, monsieur?"

He shoots me an odd look before responding. "Wait until dark. Snipe their lookouts. Kill the rest."

"You think we can do this?"

"I don't know," he replies dryly while going back to his scope. "Can you?"

I narrow my eyes and shoot him a disapproving glare before going back to watching the raiders. Applying my training, I pay close attention to my prey. How they move, their habits and behavior is all critical to our performance in talking them out.

While I'm confident, I know he's not so sure. Long range shooting is not my strong suit, though I am improving. I just don't have enough trigger time to be a pro like him. Yet. Walma still taught me that I'm not that bad at it either.

Slowly and carefully, I set up the SVD, making sure not to get any dirt in the action. Deploying the bipod, I pull the lens cover off and pull out the shroud before using my scope to glass the targets. While we work, the sun makes its way below the mountains. Soon the Angel of Death and her Beast will make themselves known in Blythe.

Night has fallen and the warmth of the day is rapidly evaporating. I'm glad that I'm decked out in full fatigues and tactical gear. It keeps me insulated as we prepare to start shooting our targets.

Through the scope, I can see that our prey has started a fire in the middle of their camp. Some of their people are already lying down while others head towards the mining camp. We've determined they work long guard shifts, and that's to our advantage. It helps that like most gangs, they are undisciplined and spend more time talking than paying attention to their surroundings.

Turning on the reticule light, the scopes version of crosshairs are illuminated in a soft red. Using the rangefinder, I line up one man and determine the rough range to target. Once I've got that, I whisper to Beast.

"Range: four hundred."

"Agreed."

"I'm zeroed in."

"Calm night," he reports. "No real wind to compensate for."

"Right. Ready op."

Beast continues watching through his scope, deciding how we are going to take them down. Over time I've learned is that he's good at planning a strike on the fly. Yet he also has serious medical skill. Once again I wonder if he was some kind of Special Forces.

"Four men on watch," he states softly. "Lazy, undisciplined. We start left, make our way right. You engage first. I'll spot, follow up if needed."

"Right," I reply while lining up my first volunteer. "Call it."

"Far left man that is drinking. Take him."

I drop the top chevron onto my targets chest, take in a breath and then let it half out and hold. When I pull the trigger, the rifle pushes hard against me, but there is no roar. The report is so well suppressed that I hear more of the rifle's action than the shot. My target drops before I can get the scope back on him.

"Kill shot," Beast reports. "Right through the heart."

"Yes," I exclaim with a harsh whisper and give a fist pump.

Beast growls, harshing my buzz. "Don't get cocky! Next tango. Ten meters right. Heading in your kill's direction. Take him."

Scanning with the scope, I spot the target and start lining up. "Got him."

I pull the trigger and shortly after, Beast reports. "Nice. Right through the neck. Clean kill number two. You're getting better."

Is that a hint of approval? I think I'm going to faint.

Beast shifts slightly. "Tango is up and investigating. Take him as he crosses into the shadows. I'll take the third guard."

"Got it."

I line up my target and shoot right after I hear the suppressed G3 take the shot. I'm pretty sure my guy takes the round square in the back and falls forward into the darkness. Beast's target takes a round right in the head and drops. The noise of bodies dropping causes the last guard to turn around.

"Last guard knows something is wrong. I've got him."

"He's yelling," Beast growls. "I'll take right, you take left, campfire is middle."

"Understood," I whisper before I start shooting.

Mr. Yelling is first, and my bullet rips right through his chest. Beast and I keep shooting as men get up, trying figure out what's happening. Our last target is in front of the fire, and when he sits up, we both shoot him nearly simultaneously.

"Okay, that last one was clearly mine," I state with a grin.

"He was on my side of the fire."

I'm still looking for targets as I respond, sounding like he's crazy. "Excuse me!? He was clearly on my side. I guess if I was your age, I'd forget my left from my right as well."

I finish my sentence by looking at him, wide grin plastered to my face. When he looks up at me, he's got a dark expression that reminds me of my dream. Suppressing an ecstatic shudder that floods my nervous system, I am delighted to see him grin.

Oh, yeah, keep that up and I'll be useless.

"All clear," he states while pulling up onto his knees. "Keep an eye on the camp."

I nod and get back on my scope while Beast activates the radio on his vest. "Jack. Bring the truck up."

We both have radios, so I hear Jack's response through my earpiece. "You got it."

As we wait, I can't help but look forward to what happens next.

Chapter Forty-One

Beast and I walk through the camp, double checking each body and making sure they are dead. The camp now smells like blood, urine and shit. It's a stench that I've never gotten used to. My partner doesn't seem to be affected at all as we do a quick strip of the more useful gear and ammo, then dump it into the back of Jack's truck.

Jack has parked with the grill sitting just inside the edge of the firelight. He's got one man with him, standing behind the cab with a rifle at the ready. They both look at us with a combination of awe and dread. We've taken out ten bandits without them firing a single shot. I really want to glance at Jack with a wicked grin and say, "It's what we do," but I'm afraid I might break his brain.

I look to Beast after checking my last body. "Clear."

"Clear," he responds back with a nod.

Making my way to him, I'm ready for a real fight and hoping to hear the right words from him. "Now what?"

Beast motions me to follow and we head to the back of the truck. Dropping down the tail gate, he starts pulling out some different gear. Clearly it's time to switch up and I watch as he takes the SVD away and pulls out something new.

It's a rifle that appears to be like his, with the exception of the fact that it's much shorter. A squat suppressor sits on it as well, with a vertical grip and laser sight fitted on the fore grip of the weapon. A single point sling is attached to the stock.

"G3 Kurz," Beast states as he hands it to me. "It has more kick than the ARs you've been working with. While you've got the last of my subsonic ammo, keep it in semi-auto. You go to full auto and the suppressor will quickly fail and everyone within a mile will know where you are."

"Understood," I say softly. I'm in awe at the new toy I'm being given, as if he's giving me expensive jewelry.

"Gear up while I top off my mag." He is already clearing the magazine in his rifle.

I grab the already loaded magazines and start stuffing them into the pouches on my vest. I remind myself over and over that each magazine has only twenty rounds. I know why he's doing this. I've graduated again, and this time it's into the major leagues.

Beast has an ammo can open and he's slipping fresh rounds into his drum mag. As we are getting ready, our audience is staring at us like we're crazy. Still, Jack finally speaks up when we're about finished.

"What do you want us to do?"

"Hide the truck," Beast states as he slams the drum into his weapon. "Strip the dead of anything else of value and the guard the area. Be ready in case we need to leave fast. The goal is simply to kill as many of them as we can. It gets too hot, we'll fall back."

"You got it," Jack nods.

Beast's head swivels to me at me and gives a ghost of a smile. "Ready?"

"Ready."

I give Jack and friend a nod and we head off into the darkness while they do their job and finish policing the bodies. We move across open grounds full of scrub brush, low hills and washes as we approach the original mining camp. Quietly we climb up a dirt berm that runs all the way around the perimeter.

Most of the buildings are wrecks, along with a number of concrete foundations being all that remains. We can see some movement around the few buildings that are still intact. We also catch sight of a couple guard patrols. Beyond that is a large hill with a road leading up to a rather impressive looking opening. I'm beginning to think that the theory the military moved in might be on the level.

Giving me a hand motion, Beast slips back down the berm and I follow. "This is going to be different than the fights before," he states seriously. "You are running point. Engage the close targets and I'll focus on the long range ones. Use your ears as well as your eyes."

I nod to let him know that I understand. Oddly, I'm excited for the coming fight. Before it was more grim determination and revenge that fueled me, kept me going. I wonder why, as he starts laying out the plan. Is it because he's really talking to me? Because of the hint of pride in his voice earlier? I can't place it. One thing is for sure—I'd do anything for this man and killing rapists is just the icing on the cake.

"Are you ready?"

"Yes," I reply back a little breathlessly.

"Then together, let us lay the enemy low this night."

The way he says that, I'm suddenly hot and wet in all the right places, trying to control my erratic breathing. As I gather my wits, Beast climbs back up the berm and takes aim, shooting the first patrol. Hearing the suppressed shots forces me to move up.

I barely spot the dark shapes of two bodies lying on the dirt road not far from us. Motioning me to move up, I climb over the crest and start sliding down the other side as Beast fires two more shots. I quickly, yet quietly, make for the closest building, keeping my new weapon up and at the ready. A bandit appears around the corner as I am rushing up, and I pull the trigger.

Holy shit! Beast wasn't kidding when he said this gun kicks!

The Kurz bucks hard in my hands and sounds softer than I expected as I put two rounds into the man's chest. He drops in a huge spray of blood. Of course, I didn't know two of his friends were close behind, and they yell a warning before firing blindly through the wood wall.

Cursing under my breath, I dive into the dirt as a half dozen bullets rip through the corner of the building. Splinters fly as their guns bark out loud reports. The two idiots come running around the corner, looking for a target and don't spot me until it's too late.

Pumping two rounds into the man closest to the corner, I smile when a bullet hole also appears in the forehead of the other. Both men tumble into the dirt and don't move. Quickly scrambling to my feet, the sound of shouting can be heard in the distance. Taking a quick peek around the corner, I don't see anyone near, so I motion for Beast to move up while I cover.

Fighting quickly becomes a blur as Beast and I make our way toward the hillside entrance. It's a hairy fight, and more than once I think I'm going to be killed. My trauma plate takes close to half a dozen hits before we've cleaned out the area. I feel like I've been repeatedly beaten and kicked. Beast isn't much better and, in fact, his left arm is bleeding.

Fuck! I hope that's all of them.

While my companion provides cover, I quickly wrap a bandage around his arm. It looks like a minor flesh wound, having gone through the upper layer of muscle, just below the shoulder. As I tighten the gauze, he growls lightly.

"Save it for the assholes inside, big guy."

In response, I get a wolfish grin that excites me. I've got no time for such wayward thoughts though. We move up to the door and concrete wall that is set in the hillside. Posting up on one side, I change to a fresh magazine while he sets his rifle down and draws both a pistol and short sword.

Oh, things are about to get bloody.

I rack the bolt on my weapon, loading the first round in the magazine. Then I turn the laser on, and a green dot appears on the wall. This is certainly going to make life easier as we move into close quarters. I look at Beast and he gives a nod. At that, we burst through the door.

Chapter Forty-Two

Beast bashes the door and it swings open as he charges in ahead of me. I know what he's doing, acting as a distraction while I slip in behind and fire from around him. Harsh, fluorescent lightning greets us, damn near blinding me. He grunts when a couple shots hit the SAPI plates of his chest armor while I gun the bastards down with quick shots.

I'm sure some would wonder why we would do it this way. Wouldn't it be better to shoot from the door frame? Yes and no. As Beast once told me, the best way to keep the enemy off balance is to keep them on the defensive. If your actions disrupt their thought process, they don't act properly. They'll hesitate, their aim may be off, giving you the opportunity to end the fight.

With a roar, Beast rushes forward as more men try to engage us. They realize a little too late that a demon has walked in. All I can do is stand and watch as he rips through five men in a matter of seconds, short sword tearing into bodies as he pumps pistol shots into others.

God, he's breathtaking in action!

I quickly move up to his side as we fight down a large main hallway. As we pass a door I thought was clear, I'm blindsided by a raider. His knife slashes across my left arm. I scream in a combination of pain and fury as I dance back while bringing my weapon his direction. A face, etched in crazy, continues charging me with knife raised as he howls and gibbers like he's on some kind of drug.

When the green dot rests on his chest, I pull the trigger once, twice and a third time. Each one hundred and sixty-eight grain bullet hammers him back. With each shot, I scream, "Don't. Touch. Me!" The bullets rip through his chest, sending blood sprays out his back. Stopping, he looks down at the three wounds and then back at me like I've just insulted his mother.

Are you fucking kidding me?

Crazy turns to unbridled rage as he somehow manages to charge me again with knife raised. I fall back to gain distance while raising the green dot up a little higher. When I pull the trigger, the back of his head splatters against the wall. His head snaps back and he falls. I take a deep, shuddering breath. When a couple bullets zip past me, I snap out of it and charge forward, catching up with Beast.

We continue down the hallway, gunning down any raider who dares to try and stop us. I take a few more hits, but fortunately the trauma plate holds up. I know my partner certainly has taken a lot of hits. We've become terribly battered by the time we finally reach a door at the far end, a trail of dead bodies behind us.

Checking my weapon, I've got a round in the breach and the mag is dry. Popping the magazine out, I grab a fresh one, only to realize it was hit and has a bullet lodged in it. With a sigh, I toss it to the side and grab the next, slapping it in as I try and catch my breath. My chest feels like it's on fire, and I wonder if I've got broken ribs.

With luck we're almost done. I've only got two mags left.

I'm trying to shake my head clear and gasp when Beast splashes vodka from his flask on my wound. He then wraps a bandage around my bleeding arm. In the heat of the fight I'd totally forgotten about it. It's easy to spot the look of displeasure in his face as he wraps a gauze roll around my arm and ties it off. I know he worries about me and that means he cares, but seriously, given the hits he's taken, he's got no right to say anything.

Once we're ready, we post up at the door, and yet again, Beast is determined to take the lead. I want to tell him that he trusts his armor too much, but since mine probably doesn't look any better, I refrain.

Crashing through the door, he breaks left while I go right. We find ourselves in a large room, with only bedroom furniture. Standing between us and the bed is a man holding a woman hostage, gun pointed to her head. Three other women are on their knees in front, cowering in fear.

"Who the fuck are you people!?" The piece of shit asks while pressing the pistol to the woman's temple.

"I'm the woman who's going to put a bullet in your rapist head!"

As I finish my statement, I've already got the green dot resting right on his mouth. I just need the right moment and I can take him out with the least possibility of endangering the hostage.

"Fuck you, bitch! You do, and this whore here takes a bullet too."

Beast growls his displeasure, rattling the bandit that I'm betting is the leader. I'm stuck in a moment of indecision. Do I take the shot and risk the woman's life? Her only crime is being born a woman in the wrong time. If I let him go, he'll prey on someone else, and that makes me responsible. You can't let such a vile disease run rampant.

"Now," the leader yells. "Let me walk ou—"

I don't let him finish his sentence. The suppressed gunshot flies right through his open mouth and splatters the back of his head across the bed and floor. As his body falls, he twitches just enough that the pistol goes off. The only saving grace is that it wasn't pointed at the woman's head any longer.

The pistol round clips her in the shoulder and I can only stand there in horror as there is a spray of her blood. Dropping to the ground, she screams in pain and the other women start screaming as well, probably thinking they are going to die.

Fuck!

Releasing my weapon, I hold out both hands to let them know we aren't here to harm them. At the same time, Beast rushes in to do the other thing that he does best—patching people up. I calm the other ladies down, letting them know that Jack sent us and that they are safe. But I keep glancing at the woman who almost died because of me while radioing Jack for pick up.

By the time we get back to Blythe, it's nearly dawn. Already, the first rays of light can be seen on the horizon as I sit on Jack's bench on the front porch, staring blankly at the coming of a new day.

My whole body is injured and sore. Upon inspection, I've found that I have a little more than a half dozen dark bruises across my chest, but no broken ribs. Beast has stitched up the cut on my arm. It now has a fresh bandage on it. Right now I really don't feel any pain. I'm far too numb from damn near getting that woman killed.

I'm so wrapped up in my sorrows that I don't even hear Beast walk up until he nudges my shoulder with a cold beer. I glance up to see his worried gaze. Giving him a nod, I take the bottle. As I pop the beer open, Beast sits down beside me. We both drink silently while the sun crests the horizon, bathing Blythe in ruddy-golden rays. Already some of the townsfolk are starting their daily routines, and a couple give us a friendly wave as they walk past.

Breaking character, Beast actually speaks to me. "You did good today."

"Did I?" I'm trying hard to keep from breaking down. "All I keep thinking is that she could have died because of me."

"No. She would have died because of him. You saved her and others from a fate you know far too well. Even if she had died, she would have been far better off than remaining in his clutches."

I take a long, hard drink off of my beer. While I understand what he's telling me, I'm not entirely convinced. The image of that poor woman getting shot in the shoulder just replays over and over again in my mind.

"Is that why you are the way you are? Everything so easily rationalized? No emotion factored in?"

Beast takes a deep breath, then a long pull off of his own bottle. "Bad men like the one you shot, made me the way I am. But sometimes, yes. You have to rationalize some things in order to save whatever sanity you have left."

I don't have the strength to reply, so I just nod. By the time we got back into town, I was exhausted! Now the beer is making me sleepy. With a pained sigh, I lay my head on his shoulder as the sun continues its upward climb. While there's some hesitation, his arm wraps around my shoulders and it's like an invitation to start crying.

It probably sounds stupid, but I never wanted to cry in front of this man. Was I trying to impress him by being tough? Maybe. I'm sure being battered and tired plays a part in my breakdown. But Beast does something I would not expect. Picking me up, he carries me into the house, cradling me in his arms.

All I can do is sob into his chest as he takes me into the guest bedroom. Closing the door softly with his foot, he lays me gently onto the bed. Without a word, he slips behind me and holds me close as I cry myself to sleep.

Chapter Forty-Three

I wake with a start. It takes a moment to realize that I'm in Jack and Melissa's guest room. Beast's warm arms are wrapped around me and he's still asleep, breathing peacefully behind me. Looking back carefully so I don't disturb him, I can see his peaceful demeanor as he lies there, holding me so protectively.

This is the best I've slept in a long time and for the first time in, like, forever, there were no bad dreams. Had Beast's presence keep the demons away? To be honest, I hope so. For once, I find myself with feelings for someone. Deep, real feelings. Nothing like the shallow nonsense of the old world, and in this case, for a man who is worthy of them.

Satisfied with the situation, I crane my head a little further in hopes of getting a better look. He suddenly wakes. Blue eyes gaze at me, and my smile is instantaneous and warm. It's hard to read the emotions behind his eyes, but I do certainly feel a certain something further down that seems to be happy that I'm pressed against him.

"Hi." My smile is still happy to see him.

Beast simply nods and slips out of the bed. He bows, as he does, and leaves the room, closing the door softly behind him. Rolling onto my back, I groan in despair and sigh. And I'd thought we'd had a breakthrough. Then I fling the pillow across the room. Damn it.

And my Beast is back to normal. What the hell happened to him to make him this way?

I head to the bathroom for a call of nature. Since I happen to know Beast was at full attention, I'm sure he's not capable of going just yet. Finding I'm correct, I quickly do my business before washing up.

Then I head out to see where Beast is. I find him outside with Jack and a few of the men. They are looking into the back of Jack's truck, probably going over the part of the haul that we brought back. There's more, but the weapons and ammo we recovered are critical for the town's defense in case we didn't get all of the bandits. Jack seems very happy and claps Beast on the back. I notice my companion flinch, but no one else seems to see it.

He doesn't even like to be touched. Oh my Beast. How could this have happened to you?

"This stuff is incredible," Jack gushes with a broad grin. "You have no idea how much you have helped us. We will set aside food, water and diesel as promised. You want to go over what's here before we head back out for the rest?"

Beast nods somberly, and that takes the wind right out of their sails. I watch as bright smiles start to fade. Probably a good bet that some of them are worried that they might be next on the hit list. After all, my partner and I took out easily three dozen raiders in a single night. As I approach, I try to diffuse the tension.

"We were happy to help."

My smile and presence brings the happiness back to everyone, save Beast who is impassive as always. Jack laughs and shakes my hand while the others look me over a little more than just appreciatively.

"Help doesn't even begin to define what you did." Jack exclaims happily. "But I guess it will suffice. Tonight we'll have a celebration. You will stick around long enough for that, right? Only seems fair, since you two are the reason for it."

Beast is starting to shake his head no when I touch his forearm lightly. His head snaps my direction and he looks at me questioningly. I've been with him long enough to at least have an understanding of how he thinks.

"Please?" I plead softly.

Beast closes his eyes and sighs. Then he stares at me for a moment and finally nods.

I smile brightly and look at Jack. "We will."

"Excellent!"

All the townsfolk give a yell. Then Beast and I go over the haul with Jack. Once we get this sorted out, we can head back and finish cleaning out the raider's stronghold.

The rest of the day is spent hauling and sorting equipment that the bandits had hoarded in their base. It was most definitely some kind of military establishment, but I don't think it had been finished before everything fell apart. Getting it stocked must have been one of their first goals though. Not only did it have a large cache of weapons, ammo and even some body armor, but there was also a huge stock of M.R.E.s.

I guess the bandits didn't much care for them and decided to use the weapons to steal food from Blythe instead. Beast seemed rather happy with the find, though. He made sure Jack understood that we would be taking a few boxes of them. Jack didn't care and said we were welcome to as many as we wanted.

After everything was sorted and stowed, Beast and I finally got a chance to clean up. Being a proper gentleman, he let me go first. Once more I was grateful to have a hot shower. Jack was feeling generous and gave me an extra few minutes as a kind of reward. I didn't argue.

Feeling clean once again, I gaze at myself in the mirror after clearing away the steam. I look an absolute mess—scars, scratches, bruises— yet oddly it doesn't bother me. I've become a woman of action, and the cuts and bruises from combat are my badges of honor. The wound on my arm is a little angry and red, but Beast stitched it up well.

Keeping the towel wrapped around me, I leave the bathroom and head into the guestroom. Since we are attending a party this evening, I decide to pull out my best clothes. A pair of jeans in very good condition and a green blouse are laid out on the bed. I quickly get dressed so I can let Beast know that the bathroom is free.

Once I'm decked out, I find my partner outside the house. He's at the back of Truck with the tail gate down and hatch up. I see that he's fussing over his latest toy, an M-60E3. It's a beefy machine gun firing three-oh-eight instead of five-five-six. I think that find put a bigger smile on his face than the M.R.E.s did.

"Bathroom is free, good sir."

Looking up at me, I think confused at first. Finally he sighs, then nods and sets the weapon in the trunk. Closing everything up and locking it, he gives me a respectful bow. Then he hands me the keys and walks into the house.

There's a large open lot not far from Jack's house where I see people already setting up for the party. A lot of wood is being stacked into a pile, so I guess there will be a bonfire. According to Jack, there will be quite the feast. Chicken, beef, pork, fruits and vegetables, a bit of everything they grow and raise. There will be beer and wine, too. It has the makings of a fun evening.

Then I glance at Jack's house and frown. The problem is that this evening will be a huge dose of civilization, and have no doubt Beast is well past ready to leave. Hopefully I can keep him placated for the night, and we can leave in the morning. Because I need this. I need to keep in touch with what's left of the girl I once was. I need to remember that spark, because that memory feels like it's all the humanity I've got left, and I don't want to end up hollow and sad like my partner.

Jack and Melissa pass me carrying food and drink. Jack has a box filled with several bottles of beer and Melissa carries a pan with racks of ribs in it. When Jack spots me, he motions with his head for me to follow and I gladly catch up.

"I let your friend know we were heading over," he tells me. "We like to set up before it gets too dark."

"Anything I can do to help?"

"That's kind of you, but no. You two are the heroes. All you need to do is kick back and have fun."

I laugh. "Yes sir."

Smiling people are already waving at us as we walk up to the field. Sturdy folding tables are set up for the buffet. Jack tosses me a bottle of beer before putting the rest on a table. I notice a set of bleachers near the bonfire site, and children of various ages are already sitting there goofing off while others run around, playing tag.

Already I feel more relaxed as I pop my bottle open and take a drink. But then, I do relish the company of others and feel in my element in a group. All the same, I find myself constantly looking at Jack's house, anxiously waiting for Beast to join the celebration.

Come on, Beast. Don't you dare disappoint me.

The party is in full swing by the time the sun goes down. A huge column of flame reaches up into the night sky, lending some warmth to us as we celebrate in the cool night air. There are so many things to try. Melissa's ribs are delicious! They don't have a source of molasses, but they do have oranges. So she makes an orange sauce glaze that is to die for. There are also various kinds of chicken, pork and even rattlesnake, which was new to me. The snake was on skewers, with chunks of vegetables and fruits. And it really does taste like chicken.

Beast finally makes an appearance when most of the rest of us are already eating. He chooses a few things from the long buffet, then stands there with his plate for a few moments before he catches sight of me. I've saved a seat at the end of a table for him, but when he sees it, he frowns and walks over to a spot near the bleachers. I think he purposefully does not look at me so I can't even encourage him to come sit with me.

Damn stubborn man, why can't he just loosen up for one minute? I try to relax with the rest of the group, but his presence is like a burr, irritating and difficult to ignore. I am determined, though, to try and appreciate the work and kindness that went into this evening.

After a feast that leaves me feeling joyfully stuffed, the music starts. It's not long before people start dancing. Of course, being an attractive woman means I have damn near every man asking me for a dance. Well, every man except for Beast. As I laugh and smile, I can't help but glance in his direction as I spin around the fire. It's as if he is the true north to my compass. Whatever that means.

My poor, anti-social partner stands not far off, still in the shadows near the bleachers as if he's standing on guard. Every time I glance his direction, I notice him watching me. Hell, if I didn't know any better, I'd say his eyes never leave me as I move from dance partner to dance partner.

181

Clearly he needs cheering up.

When the dancing brings me close to where he is, I ask my dance partner to spin me towards Beast. With a grin, he does so. I only realize I've had a bit too much to drink when my companion catches me. I'm breathlessly grinning as I look up into his blue eyes, the light of the fire dancing in his pupils.

Maybe it's the alcohol, but I can't help myself. Slowly I push up on my toes in an effort to bring my lips to his. I'm close when he realizes what I'm doing. A low growl escapes him and I pull back, looking at him with a sly smile.

"Are you growling at me, Mr. Beast? Cause that's kinda hot."

Leveling a hard stare at me, I think he expects me to back off from it. Oddly I find I don't care. When his fierceness doesn't work, he gently pushes me from him, gives his trademark respectful bow and then turns to walk back to Jack's house. I watch until I see him disappear inside.

Standing there, feeling bereft, all I can do is stare at the house. A lump has formed in my throat and I feel like crying. Yes, again. Silently, I will him to come back out here and kiss me, damn it! But another man grabs my arm and before I know it I'm dancing again. While I'm polite, it's no longer fun. My mind is back in the house with Beast, hoping he will relent and come back to the party. But he never does.

Chapter Forty-Four

I'm definitely tipsy when I stumble into the bedroom, hours later. At first I was sad when Beast jilted me and left the party, and then I was angry. Obviously nothing is wrong with me. All the men in Blythe and some of the women have danced with me tonight. I might have had a few too many beers, and I'm ready to wake him up and yell at him.

When I enter the room, I find my anger deserts me. Sleeping on the floor, at the foot of the bed, Beast is twitching and fidgeting in his tormented sleep. Memories of his nightmare when he was delirious hits me like a speeding car and sobers me up.

My poor Beast.

I quietly slip out of my good clothes and into another one of his t-shirts. This one has a logo that says, "Jakobs. If it took more than one shot, you weren't using a Jakobs." Like most of his shirts, it's long enough to cover me to mid-thigh.

Grabbing a pillow and a sheet, I lie down behind him instead of on the soft bed. I carefully slip my arms around him and his twitching stops almost immediately. As I hold him to me, I can feel his breathing calm and slow. That makes me smile, knowing that I can bring him some peace as he's done for me.

Slowly my breathing matches his and I close my eyes. Memories of the past twenty-four hours flit through my mind. From the combat with the raiders, to the way he took care of me when I had my breakdown and then us staying for the party. Through it all, even as difficult as Beast can be, he still makes me smile, still makes me feel like I'm home. As I fall asleep, the smile is still plastered to my face.

Birdsong greets my ears and the sun is warm on my skin. I roll over in my drowsy state and feel dew from soft grass kiss my cheek. Grass? Dew? I quickly sit up to figure out what is going on.

I'm lying in a grassy area, almost completely surrounded by trees. Looking down, I see that I'm in a plain, brown medieval style dress. A simple leather belt cinches my waist, complete with a pouch and dagger. Simple sandals adorn my feet.

When I gaze around, all I see is grass, trees and a pale blue sky with a tinge of purple. A green slope leads down to a cabin in the distance. It feels like my cabin somehow and my heart is gladdened by the peaceful sight. Birds sing joyously, uncaring of my presence. When I stand I notice I've been lying on a slight incline which leads up to a pool of crystalline clear water. Getting a quick taste, the water is the best I've ever tasted. As I drink, I notice the sounds of nature stop.

The hairs on the back of my neck stand up as I spin to see a man clad in black plate mail at the end of the grove. I'm so caught by surprise that I don't know what to say as the man slides up the visor of his helmet.

I definitely do not recognize him, but I do recognize the smile that slowly forms on his face. It's the same kind of expression Knack always sported when he was about to have his way with me. Looking to his left, he makes a hand motion and my dream starts to turn into a nightmare as three men-at-arms come running. They all smile lecherously.

Oh, hell no!

I draw the only weapon I have, the small dagger at my belt. In response, they all laugh at me. Instead of giving them a response of my own, I slip into a stance and ready myself. The knight's men approach, putting their weapons down as they close. Yeah, they're that confident.

"Now, lass," an older man with a bald head states in British accent. "It be more fun if you was to cooperate."

I glare at him. "That which does not kill you makes you stronger. Except for girls like me." I grin. "Girls like me will fucking kill you!"

All three men are taken aback by the combination of confidence and venom in my voice. But they're stupid and lunge for me—three on one. I am not a fool and dance left, catching the bald man right in the throat with my blade.

As I spin to face the other two, my blade easily rips his throat out, spraying blood all over the emerald green grass. The other two men are pissed and scowl at me as their friend goes down, choking as he dies. They split up, trying to divide my attention and open my guard.

Yeah boys. This isn't my first rodeo.

As they start their rush, I make like I'm going to attack the man on the right and then slash left. The right attacker jerks to a stop, dodging an attack that never comes as I slash his friends head. My next volunteer stumbles away screaming as he clutches his face. I can't be sure, but I think I got one of his eyes.

Oh yeah. This is me cooperating.

The third man tackles me before I can recover and we tumble along the ground as I scream out in shriek defiance.

"You fecking twat! You'll pay for that!"

He tries to wrest the dagger from my hand, but I reach down with my free hand and grab his balls. When I squeeze, he lets go of me while letting out a high pitched squeal. I release my grasp and he rolls off of me while cradling his damaged jewels. I don't give the bastard an opportunity to recover. Leaping onto him, I stab him in the chest multiple times. Blood sprays all over the ground as he expires with a shocked look on his face.

Slowly I stand up and turn to the black knight, smiling at him with a blood splattered face and dress. There's no easy way for me to take this guy, but I'll be damned if I'm just going to roll over and let him have his way with me. The expression on the knight's face says that he plans on doing just that.

Drawing a sword longer than the one Beast uses, he starts closing in on me slowly, a smug grin on his face. I get ready, looking for any obvious spots in his armor where I can slip my blade in and kill him. But my weapon is just not that long. Bastard is covered head to toe in steel so he's not going to go down easy. Still, I know he is going to want to take his soft parts out eventually, so I'm not giving up just yet.

When he gets within range, he starts toying with me, making fake thrusts and pushing me back. There's not much choice but to give ground as I look for an opening. With another thrust I dance back and hiss at him. In return he laughs at me.

Fucker!

When he gives another playful thrust, I slap his blade away and dart in for a thrust of my own. My dagger aims for his face and he's shocked at my ability to attack. My hopes are dashed when he jerks back and just the tip scratches his cheek.

Stopping, he touches the streak of blood and looks at the drops on his gauntlet. "You are a cheeky bit, aren't you?" He smiles again, more menacingly this time. "You poked me with your dagger. Now I poke you with mine."

Grabbing his crotch to make his point clear, he marches forward once more, this time with a serious swing. I have no choice but to fall back, only to have my foot find nothing but air. I can't help the shriek that escapes my mouth as I fall backwards into the pool of water with a huge splash.

The black knight is laughing as I try to free myself from my wet dress, which is clinging and entangling my legs. Stabbing his sword into the soft earth, he moves forward with a leer to pluck me out of the water. I bare my teeth at him and prepare to use my nails and teeth to good effect if nothing else.

Before he puts his hands on me, though, the sound of running feet catches our attention. Joy leaps into my chest as I see Beast approach, drawing both his short sword and a hammer with a spike on the opposite side of the head. Dressed in red leather armor with gold colored buckles, he is the most glorious sight I've ever seen. With a snarl, he strides toward the black knight while I'm still struggling to stand.

Okay, I have no desire to be a damsel in distress, I swear. I want to fight my own battles. But right now? Yes, I am a damsel in this dress.

Grabbing his sword, the black knight meets Beast half way and they clash, both men bellowing. They each have their own advantage. The knight has a longer reach with his sword, but Beast has two weapons. Also, his armor is lighter and more flexible, so he has speed and more visibility, for he's not wearing a full-face helm.

The fighting is fast and furious and they both trade off wounds. The black knight puts a cut across Beast's thigh, eliciting a dark growl. My companion returns it with interest, getting a shot just under the knight's sword arm.

Screeching in pain, the black knight gives ground as Beast roars, smelling blood. Then he begins spinning the hammer around so that he's swinging with the spiked end. Once there's an opening in the knight's guard, Beast swings and connects. That spike pierces the steel plate. The knight grunts and stumbles from the shot to his chest. Beast follows up by putting the spike into the man's head, killing him.

I breathe a sigh of relief and get my soggy ass out of the water so I can rush over to help. Slipping under his arm, I help him to stand. Blood trickles down his leg and he's got a cut on his side I hadn't seen that's leaking as well.

"Oh, thank you, my lord. But, you are wounded. My cabin is not far from here. Let me help you?"

Wait, did I just say that?

Growling in pain, Beast nods. Slowly we make our way down the hill and toward the cabin in the distance.

Chapter Forty-Five

I unlatch the cabin door and help Beast inside. It's a single room with a stone fireplace in the center of the back wall, a kitchen and table on the left, and bed in a curtained alcove in the far right corner. The scent of a beef stew cooking in the pot hanging in the fireplace smells delicious. A hint of lavender is also in the air, along with a mix of herbs that are hanging from the rafters over the kitchen.

Helping Beast over to the bed, he sinks down with a grunt. My clothes are still a wet mess, clinging to me and leaving very little to the imagination. I look like I was in a medieval wet dress contest and probably won first prize.

Somehow I know this place, and so know where everything is and what is available. I don't understand it, but accept it and move over to a satchel near the table, throwing it open. Pulling out bandages, thread, and a packet of needles, I gaze at Beast.

"I'll help you take off your armor, my lord. We need to clean and bandage your wounds."

Why am I talking this way?" I mentally shrug. *"Fuck it, just play along.*

Beast nods and together we remove the red leather armor that covers his body. It's slow going, but he starts with his legs first, uncovering well-muscled calves and thighs. While there's a lot of blood, the cut doesn't look as bad as it could be. Quickly, I clean the wound and ready a needle and thread.

He growls when the needle pierces his skin, yet remains perfectly still. With diligent concentration, I carefully stitch up the cut until it's completely closed. Then I clean off the residual blood, apply herbal salve and bandage it. Next, I inspect his other wound now that he's nearly naked, save for some underwear and his mask. White skin is only marred by a number of scars, along with the same tattoos of symbols I've never recognized that adorn him in my waking world.

"Turn to the side, my lord," I state softly. "So I can see your wound better."

Following my instructions, he turns giving me a better look. This wound isn't nearly as bad as the leg and isn't deep enough to need stitches. Taking up the bandage roll and a poultice, I place the bag against the wound and then wrap the gauze tightly around his chest. All the while, he growls and snarls lightly, but never moves.

Once I'm done, I put everything away and then check on the stew while he catches his breath. Stirring the meaty broth with a wooden spoon, the scent of basil and rosemary waft of to greet my nose, and it makes my mouth water. The stew can wait though. I have another meal I plan on partaking of first and glance over at Beast as he still sits on the bed.

He is my Beast and isn't. I don't know how well this dream Beast will react to my overtures, but if the last dream is any indication, I may well be allowed to kiss and touch to my heart's content. I hope so. It would soothe my aching heart. And I have nothing to lose. It's just a dream after all.

Thanks to the heat of the fire, my dress is a little drier now. I watch his face as I saunter over to him with an inviting smile I know he can't miss. There is hesitancy in his eyes as I approach and place a hand on his shoulder.

"You just lie back, my lord. I will make you feel better. It's the least I can do after you saved me."

Pushing him back, he doesn't resist and falls onto the bed. I pull off his underwear, leaving him gloriously naked. I'm certain he won't let me touch his mask, so I don't even try. Instead, I take his cock in hand and go down on him. I can't believe he is allowing this, but I am so glad he is, it does my heart good.

I hear Beast suck in a breath as I let my mouth and tongue do as it will. His entire body shudders and he's hard in no time at all. I am pleased at his size, once he has become erect. Not huge, mind you, but not small either. Definitely better than average. Swirling my tongue around, he hisses through gritted teeth as he flexes his hips.

I stop before he can climax and make my intentions clear. With some coaxing, I'm able to get Beast to shuffle up onto the bed. Hitching my dress up, I straddle his thighs, trapping him between us. His hungry eyes are locked with mine—oh, how I love that expression! I can't help teasing him by swaying my hips as I slowly pull my dress up. Pleasure spikes through my blood stream as I grind him against me.

Beast growls and his hands grab my hips as I slip my dress up over my head and let it drop behind me onto the floor. And oh, he's working with me now, grinding his hips and pressing his erection against me. I think the tables have been turned and now he's teasing me. I feel control slipping and a hungry whimper escapes me.

I know he feels my wetness against him as we move against each other. His eyes have become dark with desire, and I imagine mine show him how pleased I am already. I find I am breathing in gasps, and when he thrusts his hips up, I cry out as a jolt rockets through me. Oh yes, this is affecting him as well, for a low, guttural growl escapes from him and it sounds so damned sexy.

"Take me, my lord," I plead breathlessly. "Please, take me now."

There are no words, only a low rumble from the wild animal that lays beneath me, ready to ravage me. I lift up, giving him all the space that he needs, positioning his erection right at the entrance of my pussy. He enters slowly, filling me a little at a time, but that's not enough. I want more. I groan and seat myself fully, then rise and look him in the eye. He's still in control and sees what I want.

When he slams into me, I throw my head back and cry out in ecstasy as he fills me. Strong hands on my hips hold me down firmly against him.

Oh fuck! I've so missed this.

Beast moans through gritted teeth and shuddering as we both adjust to the heavenly sensations. I'm just trying to catch my breath when he begins to move, twirling inside me with strong, circular hip movements that take my breath away.

I moan and whimper, trying to plead for him to move, to fuck me. As if sensing my need, he lets my hips go so I can move, setting the pace up and down in a slow, yet steady rhythm. I gasp loudly every time he fills me and it's so deep. With each thrust, I hear his building pleasure in rasping breaths and growls, often displaying clenched teeth. I sense it's been far too long for both of us.

I lay my breasts against his chest and whisper hotly in his ear, "Take me, my lord."

When his eyes snap open, there's a fire of lust behind those blue rings. Quickly he rolls me over, his weight pressing down on me, the hairs on his chest teasing my nipples. As if he truly were some wild beast, he nips and sucks at my neck, all while buried inside me to the hilt. I squirm with desire and my hips grind against his, my strained breathing begging for more. He breathes a growl against my neck and I am covered with gooseflesh. In a good way.

Pushing up onto his arms he starts to move, and not slowly. Fast at first and then faster still as he settles into a brutal rhythm, all the while snarling like some animal in heat. Even fucking he's like a feral beast. It's overwhelming and so, so good. The pleasure builds and I meet him thrust for thrust, the sound of our flesh slapping; harder, faster, mercilessly. One hand slips into my hair and forces my lips to his in a wild frenzy of kissing that travels from my lips, across my face, ears and neck. His growls intensify and my heart feels it's about to pound out of my chest as we reach a fever pitch.

Thrusting into me so hard, he pushes me up to the edge. I'm so close, ecstasy running rampant through my body and stealing away coherent thought. All of me clenches, passion spilling over and through the haze, I feel him harden even further. That thought sends me sailing over the edge.

Holy fucking shit!

I wrap my limbs around Beast like a vine, holding on for dear life as my orgasm rips through my body like a wildfire across a dry prairie. My scream fills the room as he climaxes within me, letting loose with a lion's roar that damn near shakes the bed.

Then I wake up.

Chapter Forty-Six

Beast and I both wake and sit up, gasping at the same time. All I am capable of is simply sitting there, catching my breath and trying to think in a happy, post-orgasmic haze. I hear him breathing just as heavily and that makes me wonder why. I glance at him and see a fine layer of sweat on his forehead.

He is in the same state I'm in. Holy hell...?

"What was that?" I ask querulously.

He shoots me a wide eyed look, but says nothing.

"You were in the forest with me, weren't you?" My voice is disbelieving.

Beast's eyes get even wider.

"You were! How is that possible!?"

Instead of answering me, he's on his feet and out the door without his trademark bow or even closing the door behind him. I'm left sitting there, heart pounding, in an attempt to understand what the fuck just happened. Finally I get my pants, pull them on, and rush out after him.

Exiting the house into the chill morning air, Beast is readying the truck and trying to ignore me. Hell, just like me, he's barefoot and doesn't care about the rough ground under his feet. Given what's just happened though, I want answers and rush up to him.

"How could we both have the same dream? How is that possible?"

Beast shakes his head furiously and continues packing. *You are not going to ignore me!* Storming up, I grab his shoulder to make him to look at me. Pulling away, he bares his teeth with a hiss.

"Don't you growl at me," I shoot right back. "And don't you *dare* give me the silent treatment!"

All I get back is a glower, but I don't care. He no longer scares me. Somehow, deep down, I know he would never hurt me intentionally. Oh sure, he puts up a good act, keeping me at arm's length, but it no longer works and I bare my teeth right back at him.

"You don't scare me. Talk to me, damn it!"

Beast tears his eyes away and storms off, stopping at the edge of the road with his back to me. His head hangs down, shoulders sagging as he looks utterly defeated. The sight makes my heart clench.

Fuck! Did I just make things worse?

With a sigh, I approach Beast slowly, partly because the gravel is hurting my feet. When I get up to him, I touch his shoulder softly. He flinches and looks at me with wild eyes. I don't say anything. Instead, I wrap my arms around him and hug him tightly. I know he's shocked

191

because he's frozen for a moment, but he finally hugs me back and we stand there quietly.

Slowly I let him go and look up at him with a sigh. "I know you don't want to talk about it. I respect that. But I am going to want to talk eventually." His expression softens so I go on. "I'm going to get ready go, and I'm going to leave you out here, trusting you won't panic and take off without me, okay?"

Beast gives me a slow nod. Giving him a smile, I walk back to the house. Wiping my feet off on the welcome mat, I head inside, my aching soles glad to be on a smooth floor. Stepping into the bathroom to do my business, I can't stop thinking about the dream we shared. I'm almost certain that we did after his reaction.

Shaking my head free of erotic daydreams, I clean up and head back to the bedroom to get dressed. In a way it'll be good to be back on the road. Beast seems to do better when he's on the run, away from civilization, or killing bandits. Whatever it is eating away at him, maybe I can get him to talk to me once we're away from people.

Whipping the t-shirt and jeans off, I get into my clean fatigues, all thanks to Jack and Melissa's working washing machine. I certainly have missed the joy of clean clothes, although I'm still missing the added joy of fabric softener. No point in worrying about it now. I grab our things and take them out to the truck.

Most of the town has shown up to wish us farewell. The food, water and diesel Jack promised as payment has been stowed. With the MRE's and weapons, the back of the truck is well-packed, save for a small corridor I can squeeze through if needed. Truck has a full tank and with our reserves, we should have enough to make it to Phoenix easily, maybe even a little further. Although, hopefully, we will find fuel there. We still have a long way to go.

"You know," Jack states with a smile. "You are both welcome to stay after all you've done for us?"

Beast merely shakes his head.

"We know," I reply for the both of us. "We have a destination though. Thank you."

"Well, you are always welcome here. Blythe won't forget you two anytime soon."

I give Jack and Melissa a hug. "That's good to know. By the way, Moreno has an enclave run by a woman named Kathy. There's another group at Riverside University run by Linda and Tom. If you do get in touch, tell them the Angel of Death and her Beast sent you, and I'm sure they will be open to trade. They're good people."

Jack nods, looking a little shocked at the delivery of our nicknames. "All right. Good to know there's decent folk there. Now, up ahead, we've heard of some enclaves in Phoenix, but without proper water, there aren't many. The good folk are said to be on the north end. Mostly gang territory south, so you want to be careful taking the Ten."

Beast taps me on the shoulder. I know he's itching to leave. There are too many people around him and that makes him uneasy. Shooting him a quick smile, I give both Jack and Melissa one more hug. These two were kind enough to let us into their home and deserve some respect.

"There are a lot of good people in Moreno and at the University. They would be glad for your friendship. And thanks for the heads up. You all take care of yourselves now."

Jack gives a nod. "We will."

As I turn to head to Truck, Beast tosses me the keys. In shock, I look at them and then to him. He simply nods and walks around to the passenger seat and gets in. With a chuckle, I slip into the driver's side and start the ignition.

Truck roars to life and I head for I-10 as Beast kicks back and lets me drive. I suspect he wants to keep me busy so I don't pester him with questions just yet, but I've promised to give him time, so I will be patient.

Once more I find myself thinking about new friends that I'm leaving behind. Another potential home behind us. I wonder as I drive if heading all the way to Colorado is worth it. Then I glance at Beast, and something inside me says, emphatically, yes.

Pulling onto the freeway, we cross the bridge that spans the flowing Colorado River and into what used to be the state of Arizona. As I drive, I do want to know why he's given me the privilege of being behind the wheel. Not that I'm complaining, it's just that with Beast, there's usually a reason behind everything he does, and I wonder if I'm right.

"Why am I driving?"

He looks at me confused, but says nothing. Great, I've got the old Beast back. I roll my eyes over his decision to not talk to me. Fortunately the road is empty and we are on a straight stretch, so I shoot him a glare as I ask again.

"Why am I driving?"

Frowning at me, he points to his eyes and then to the road ahead. I roll my eyes again and shake my head. I know I'm drifting a little, but there's no traffic to worry about. Typical overreaction from Mr. Beast.

"I'll look at the road when you answer my question."

Beast narrows his eyes at me and is about to say something when our conversation is rudely interrupted by the sound of a police siren. Quickly glancing at the rear view mirror, I see a highway patrol car behind us with its lights flashing.

You have got to be fucking kidding me?

My first time driving Truck in a post-apocalyptic world with very few working cars and I find the one functioning highway patrol? I don't fucking believe this is happening. When I look to Beast, he's got two pistols out, one pointed towards each door. I go ahead and pull Truck off to the side of the road, especially since there is no way we could outrun a patrol car. Readying my own pistol, we wait.

Through the rear-view mirror, I see two officers get out of the car and start walking toward us. One disappears behind Truck, heading for the passenger side while the other comes right up to my door.

My day just gets weirder as a fully decked out, Arizona Department of Public Safety officer steps up to the open window. A big black mustache sits on his lip, mirror shades and a wide brimmed hat keeps the sun off his brown skin. I think he might be of Mexican descent. The name tag on his uniform says, "Ramathorn".

The other officer is Caucasian and is dressed the same, but lacks the mustache. I can barely see his name tag, which says, "Roto". Neither are behaving aggressively, but both have that hard ass air that you always expect from an officer, or at least, the way you used to. In the old world. Before the fucking apocalypse.

"License and registration."

"Officer, uh, um." I can't even talk, this situation is so weird.

"License and registration, please."

"We don't have any license and registration, officer. It's the apocalypse, after all, and the DMV hasn't been open for what, gosh, two years."

Ignoring my question, he continues. "Do you know how fast you were going?"

Are you kidding me?

"What?"

Officer Roto repeats the question. "How fast you were going."

"Uh, 65?"

"63," Ramathorn states factually.

"Well, isn't the speed limit 65?"

"Yeah," he replies. "It is. Where you folks headed?"

"Colorado."

The officer looks to the road ahead before looking back at me. "Colorado huh. Almost made it. Are you okay?"

What? "Yeah, sure."

194

"Yes sir?"

"Yes sir."

"Now did you say, yes sir?"

The other officer chimes in. "I think she said, yeah sure."

"Well, I said yeah sure, but I meant to say, yes sir."

The fuck is with these guys?

My officer glances at his partner. "You smell something, Rabbit?"

Roto takes a sniff. "Bad ass."

Taking a look inside the cab, it's not difficult to see the weapons that are laid out and ready to go. Beast even has his new toy, the M60, sitting in the back seat with a belt already loaded and ready to rock.

"Well, you were weaving a little in the lane," Officer Ramathorn states seriously. "We'll let you off with a warning this time. Drive safe, folks."

I can only sit there in shock as I watch the officers walk back to their patrol car, get in and drive away, disappearing into the horizon. Once they have completely vanished from sight, I look at Beast.

"What the hell was that? Is this Fuck-with-Chloe day?"

All he does is shrug, as dumbfounded as I am. Finally I shake my head and start Truck again. As I get back on the road, Beast pulls out a map and starts looking at it as we head towards Phoenix.

Chapter Forty-Seven

There wasn't enough daylight to make it to Phoenix before sundown. Driving cautiously means driving slower, means it takes longer than it could have to get to your destination. As far as I was concerned, getting there alive was far more important than trying to get there quickly. Plus, slower means better gas mileage, which we also need.

We did make it to a rest area before it got dark and with practiced precision, cleared both sides of the freeway, making sure there are no hostiles. We're lucky and find no one, and the rest-stop caretaker's house is still in good condition. Another lucky surprise, it has some supplies. It also has working solar power and even better—running water. Evidently, water comes from a still-functional electric well pump in the back yard and is stored in a large tank. Beast has indicated we will be boiling it for drinking, just to be safe.

It is still nice to be able to take another shower, and this time a much longer one. While I luxuriated under the hot water, Beast did the laundry, thanks to a washer and dryer. He also went to work making dinner in an actual kitchen. To be honest, I am excited to see what he can whip up in a real kitchen.

Stepping out of the steamy shower, I dry off and check myself. So far the wound on my arm looks okay. It's red and sore, but it isn't infected and I am happy for that small miracle. The many bruises all over my chest make me look like a beaten housewife though. I think I'd rather have hickeys.

That thought brings back a myriad of memories from last night's dream. My companion still hasn't talked about it. In fact, that episode appears to have pushed him back to his original demeanor. I hopelessly wish I could get through those walls of his. Every time I start to get close, he shuts back down. While I know it has something to do with his family, I don't know enough to truly help. I'm afraid if I push too hard, he'll simply retreat further into his shell. With a shake of my head, I get dressed and then wander to the kitchen to see what culinary delight Beast has cooked up.

Oh. My. God!

Waiting for me is a surprisingly fine meal. The plates that wait for us each has a chicken breast, with a small amount of Melissa's orange sauce on it. Along with that are fresh mashed potatoes and steamed green beans. A bottle of white wine has been opened and a glass has already been poured for me. The MP3 player Beast gave me is playing through a docking station set on the edge of the table, classical music filling the air.

Damn it. Who can keep up with this? One minute he's pissing me off and the next he's warming my heart. The front door opens and I reach for my pistol, but relax when I see Beast walk in, wearing actual civilian clothes. Granted, he's not wearing a three-piece tailored suit, but my mouth goes dry when I see how he's dressed.

A nice pair of black jeans that look almost new hug his legs and show off his butt. In contrast, he's wearing a white, long-sleeved, button up cotton shirt. The sleeves are rolled up just enough that I can see part of the tattoos on his inner forearms. His beard looks recently trimmed and more uniform. Given how long we've been on the move, it had gotten scraggly. That long hair of his is loose, stopping just below the collar and making him look like a bad boy from the wrong part of town—especially with that mask on.

Wow, he cleans up well. Wait. Is this a date? I didn't dress for a date, what the heck? That is totally unfair!

Beast gives me a respectful bow and walks up, pulling the chair out for me. *Such a gentleman* Shooting him a shy smile, I sit and he takes his own seat. Picking up his wine glass, he holds it forward. I am tickled, so I pick mine up and we clink glasses. Taking a sip, I happily sigh and then pick up my fork to taste the meal he's prepared.

It's so good. He really can cook, especially when you give him a proper kitchen to do it in. The chicken is seasoned and goes well with the sauce. The chunky mashed potatoes have just a hint of pepper and a dash of dill along with some actual butter. Finally the green beans are well- buttered and salted. Pure, delicious comfort food. Oh, yes, good food is heavenly, but I wonder if he is trying to distract me from my purpose. I still intend to get answers from him. All the same, while this may not be the heaven I'd like to be in, I can't complain either.

We eat to classical scores and I often catch him watching me when I look up at him. It's so hard for me to read his face, but I'm pretty sure he can read mine. After that damned dream, it feels like my libido has kicked into overdrive and is aimed squarely at him. Especially since hope blooms in my chest that this romantic meal is him making a statement.

The meal satisfies much, the gazing back and forth, the music ... I feel warmed and somehow don't mind the lack of conversation. I watch him, and he never seems to take his eyes off mine. It's very intense, and that intensity warms me thoroughly. Just a few months ago, this would have terrified me, but I feel so much different now.

When the meal is done, I rise to clear the table, but he takes my wrist before I can do anything. I just wish I knew what he was thinking as he stares back at me with those piercing blue eyes.

Rising smoothly from his chair, he stands up next to me and my pulse goes into double time. He is still holding my hand and my heart is racing as he guides me into the living room. Sitting down on the couch, he bids me to sit on the floor where a cushion has been set up. I'm confused, but far too mesmerized at this point even question why, so I sit, nestled between his legs.

Picking up the remote, he hits a button and the DVD player starts up, the TV automatically turning on. The movie, *The Princess Bride,* begins playing. As the opening scene unfolds, Beast begins to massage across my back, neck and shoulders. This is so unexpected, but all I can do is close my eyes and revel at the feeling of his hands working on my sore muscles. I can't help but moan as I melt into his hands.

Damn it. He's good at this, too?

I feel as if my brain is melting as his magical fingers slowly erase a year of tension that had been building up. My attention span has been reduced to just him and the movie becomes mere background noise as my muscles relax. Between the excellent meal, the wine and his skillful hands, I'm relaxing into utter exhaustion. Was this his plan all along, letting me drive, wearing me down? Perhaps, but right now, I just don't care.

Time has no meaning as I find myself nodding off. I remotely realize he has picked me up and is carrying me into the only bedroom. I want to look up into his eyes and silently tell him how much I want him, but I'm enjoying the surrender of laying my head against his chest as he cradles me. As I breathe in, I realize he even smells good, like cherry blossoms from the body wash that was in the bathroom. I nuzzle my nose against his chest and breathe deeply as we enter the room.

He gently lays me down onto the soft, queen sized bed. Throwing the covers over me, he tucks me in. It's such a sweet gesture, though a little condescending, as if he feels I am too young, too naive, too … something for him to take seriously. But it still makes me smile for the comfort it brings, even as I try to stay awake in an effort to pull him into the bed with me. I fail miserably, but I feel his kiss on the top of my head before sleep overwhelms me and I dream of better days.

I wake up to the sound of birds chirping happily away as sunlight streams through the gauzy white curtains. For a moment the sound reminds me of the erotic dream of the night before, but I am much more comfortable in this bed. Rolling onto my back, I stretch languidly and moan. That massage did wonders and I feel so much better. Well, not as better as I would like, but well enough.

Beast is nowhere to be seen, but the scent of bacon fills the air, so I imagine he's cooking breakfast. Slipping out of bed, I make my way to the bathroom where a warm shower is calling my name. Yes, I know I had one last night, so sue me. It's possible I may not have another shower again, ever.

Oh yes! Warm water cascades down my body and those once sore muscles sing their praise. God, I feel like a new woman. While leaving good friends behind has been heart breaking, it's also been good for my soul. L.A. just held way too many bad memories, and leaving has allowed me to begin real healing.

My thoughts wander to last night. While it was heartwarming and romantic, it did not progress as far as I would have liked. Still, perhaps progress is the right word. Beast has been through some terrible shit just as I have, but with him it seems it has to be baby steps. I'm hoping that's what last night was, a small step in the right direction.

I certainly hope so. To be honest, I went from zero libido to raging hormones practically overnight. A bit of good fucking would be just what the doctor ordered about now. Even thinking about it makes me want to remedy the situation with my fingers.

Checking my watch, I realize I'm burning daylight. With a heavy sigh, I quickly clean up and then turn the water off. Unfortunately, necessity dictates I save my sexual pleasure for another time. If I'm really lucky, maybe I can get Beast to help me with that.

Drying off, I lay the towel neatly on the rack and crack the door open. With the bedroom clear, I head out and get dressed into my fatigues. Then I pack everything up and head out the door with suitcase and weapon in hand.

Sure enough, I find breakfast waiting for me. The place is as completely untouched as when we found it. The fridge and freezer still stocked. While pretty much everything in the fridge was bad, there were things in the freezer that were still good. A lot of canned goods were still within best use dates as well.

Beast and I decided to use only what we needed and leave the rest. I know it may sound silly, but think about it. We discovered an oasis within the desert. Running water, electricity, working appliances and a solid roof. This is a blessing, not something you rob and ransack.

My companion is nowhere to be seen. I imagine he's getting us ready to leave. Dropping my things next to the table, I sit down and start eating. Oh, bacon. It's been so long since I've had such a luxury. Thanks to Blythe, we had a few eggs again, and Beast has made some scrambled eggs that are already lightly salted. And to wash it down, clean water and frozen orange juice.

I'm almost done when he comes in, showing his hands first to let me know it's him. Setting my pistol down, I smile his direction before finishing my meal. Giving me a respectful bow, he grabs my things and carries them out.

While it appears I've got the old Beast back, something in my gut says otherwise. Maybe it's my imagination, but there seemed to be more life in his eyes. There was even a slight smile in his expression. As I take a moment to clean my dishes, I'm hopeful.

Suddenly an idea hits me and I walk over to the desk that's in the living room. Finding paper and pen, I write a note. It's not for Beast, it's for whoever finds this place after us. Simply asking that anyone who stays here, to treat it well. There are not many places like this left. Such an oasis needs to be preserved. Please.

Giving it a read through, it seems perfect. I know I am probably being overly sentimental, but I leave it on the floor near the door. Closing it softly behind me, I head for Truck. My heart is full of joy and hope as I look ahead to the future for the first time in a long time. Next stop, Phoenix.

Chapter Forty-Eight

We stand near the outskirts of Phoenix in front of Truck as Beast looks through a pair of binoculars. Given Jack's warning about the south end of the city being controlled by gangs and warlords, we are proceeding with caution.

It's like L.A. all over again.

I watch Beast while he surveys the land ahead. I still haven't gotten him to talk about our mutual wet dream, though I'll never give up hope. If he can get his point across with hand signals, he continues to do so. But if he imagines he can avoid it forever, well, over my cold, dead body.

What he did last night was very sweet and touching, and if I'm honest, a little disheartening. Making me a fine meal and then treating me to a massage before tucking me into bed was very tender, caring, sweet even, but not even remotely what I wanted from him. Of course, I shouldn't complain, either. I woke up well rested and relaxed. Even though he wasn't beside me in the bed, I didn't have any bad dreams, which was a bonus. But I still need him to stop thinking of me as some sort of daughter figure. Why doesn't he see me as the woman I am? The one who is slowly falling for him.

Not once have I seen the face that is under that mask, either. I think he even showers with it on. He must know it's not his looks I have feelings for. It's who he is and the way he treats me that is far more important. In retrospect, that's really what every woman wants, to be treated with love and respect. I've learned from experience that looks don't last, and often it's no indicator of a good person. But the more important thing is that he treats me as an equal. Most of the time, anyway, when he's not refusing to acknowledge the feelings I know he has for me, if our shared dream is any indication.

Beast snaps his fingers, bringing me back to reality. Taking out a map, he unfolds it and smoothes it out over the hood before pointing to it. Truck is not small, so I step up on the bumper and take a look.

"What'cha got?"

He rears his head back, glowering at me. I keep trying to trick him into a normal conversation. So far he hasn't fallen for it, like now. Tapping on the map, he points at a spot telling me where we are and then traces a route that heads south and around the Phoenix sprawl.

"You think that's the best route? Didn't Jack say the gangs were in the south?"

Looking at me, he shrugs.

"That's not very convincing," I shoot back, but can't help my grin.

Beast shoots me a glare. "Then we'll have you to kill anyone who gets in our way, won't we?"

I stare in shock that he just spoke as he gathers up the map. When he gets into the truck, I have to scramble to catch up as the roar of the engine brings me back to reality and I clamber in to the vehicle.

As he starts to roll out, he hands me the map and I fold it up properly. We pull off I-10 and onto State Route 85 heading south. As we drive I keep one of the P-90s on my lap, ready for a possible ambush. So far we see nothing but lots of open, weed choked fields that used to be sprawling farm land.

When we get a few miles down the road, we spot a Shell station and Beast pulls Truck into an empty lot next to it. Getting out slowly, we scan for signs of human life but don't see anything. The fact that we haven't been shot at is a good sign in itself.

Scavenging is a fact of life since the Collapse. No one is making damn near anything. Just having good food and clean water is a blessing in itself. Hell, I'd still kill for a decent cup of coffee. I think fondly of plush hotels with room service. *Oh, I really miss room service.*

Beast pounds on the hood twice, snapping me out of my daydream. Pointing towards the back of the truck, I meet him as he's pulls down the tail gate and starts getting our gear ready.

I know I've said before that Beast plans ahead, and that's no joke. He keeps two different tactical vests for me now. One is set up for the AR platform as a "light and fast" rig. The other is set up for the G3 Kurz as my "heavy" option. Right now he's loading me out for light and fast, which given what we are going into, makes sense.

Of the many weapons we have in our inventory, six of them are ARs. The one that he's tricked out for this rig is the first one he ever gave me. A short barreled rifle with a fore grip, laser sight and red dot sight on top. The way the iron sights are arranged, I can use them through the glass of the red dot to save battery power. In fact, I pop both sights up and keep the red dot off for now. After I've checked the weapon, I look at Beast with a smile.

"Normally I'd hope for flowers or jewelry, but these days, this is what a girl really wants. Thank you, sir."

My companion slowly looks at me impassively. Then he gives a snort before pulling out the rest of his gear. I wonder briefly if I'm wearing him down. Though this is probably not the time anyway. Right now it's time to do some shopping. Charging our weapons, we close and lock Truck and move towards the station. As we leave, Beast activates the alarm on our trusty steed and it makes the typical chirp.

I take point as we move up to the entry door. Beast is not far behind me, armed with his short barreled FAL. Fortunately we're both suppressed so we won't blow our eardrums out if we have to start shooting. Especially if he does, because three-oh-eight is fucking loud! Even with the sound dampening devices, your ears can still end up with a little bit of a ring.

Moving through the entrance, we sweep in and start searching. Weaving through the aisles, I keep my rifle at the ready. So far the gas station appears mostly stripped, with trash littering the floor. There are no hotdogs roasting or drinks chilling in the beverage cases and it smells musty. Beast breaks left while I head straight down the middle.

As I make my way down the aisles in the back, I come to an abrupt halt when I see something I thought I would never see again—an unopened box of tampons. It sits there on the shelf, light gleaming off its plastic wrap like a shining halo. My face breaks into a huge smile and I want to cry tears of joy as I start to reach for it.

I almost have my hand on the box when someone tackles me and I'm on the floor, gasping. A man that is clearly not Beast is trying to pin me. Stringy, greasy, long brown hair frames a weather-beaten face. Brown eyes flash "vacancy" in his pupils as he smiles lecherously at me, reeking breath puffing through the gaps in his teeth. Worse, he stinks like old urine.

As I struggle, I realize that I'm not in a good position, although I'm sure my attacker disagrees. My rifle is trapped under my body and I can't get to it, so I need to get this asshole off of me first. I try to push him off, but he's got a strength and weight advantage on me, so I fight for some leverage.

"Oh my! Been a while since I seen me a pretty one."

"Get off me," I yell as I struggle against him.

The man sniggers. "Only after I'm done with ya."

I don't think so!

Reaching for the small of my back, I'm able to pull my combat knife from its sheath. The man is fast and blocks my attempt to stab him and we end up wrestling across the dirty tile floor. As I'm fighting, I catch sight of Beast as he comes around the corner of an aisle and looks down at the scene, clearly amused.

Why aren't you doing something, damn it?

As if answering my unspoken question, Beast leans against the shelving rack. The bastard crosses his arms over his chest and watches as if he's taking bets on who is going to win the bout. I've got twenty dollars on me, but that's because I plan on slapping the shit out of him when I'm done with this guy!

My fight. Figures. Damn it, old man!

Summoning all my strength, I nearly get a knee into the bastard's crotch. It's close enough that he jerks away and that gives me an opportunity to push him off. I scramble to my feet with my knife at the ready. This idiot still wants to play and pulls a blade of his own as he stands up.

Here's something else that's not like the movies. A fight against a knife has a higher chance of you being injured than gun play. Bullets are small, flying objects trying to intersect the target at just the right time in the right space. As such, if the target is moving, you can easily miss. With knives, not quite the same thing. Your target is closer and you are swinging a blade across a flat plane that covers more area.

This fight is no different, a couple times I'm not quick enough to block or get out of the way. The hits hurt my pride more than my body, especially with Beast just standing there watching. In both cases my reflexes are at least fast enough to only end up with a minor cut and not laid open. At least I'm giving better than I've received, as my opponent is bleeding from five minor wounds that slow him down.

The bandit is getting angry. He thought he had himself a free piece of pussy and here I am, making him work for it. When he is about to lunge, he rears back thinking he'll get extra strength in the stabbing motion. The problem is that he's telegraphing the move and I'm totally ready. When his blade comes in, I block his arm away and then stab him twice in the arm pit. With a gasp, he drops to the floor and I pull my pistol, putting a suppressed shot into his skull.

I spin around, angry and ready to beat Beast to a pulp when I spot another bandit trying to sneak up on him. *Oh shit!* As I point and start to yell, two muffled gunshots reach my ears and the lurker goes down in a spray of blood.

Beast uncrosses his arms with a smug grin and blows the smoke from the barrel before holstering the pistol. Yeah, he's trying to be funny, but I'm far too pissed off! I march right up and slap him—hard. The sound of my hand smacking his cheek echoes off the walls.

"Bastard! Why didn't you help me?"

My partner goes from smug to savage in a heartbeat. Snarling at me, he moves toward me, lip curling up and showing teeth as I backpedal. When I hit the wall, I realize I may be in trouble. By being violent, I've just crossed a line with him and now I'm unsure what he will do. Beast is so angry and feral that he's shaking as a low growl rumbles through him.

A thought hits me and I act on it instinctively. Grabbing his face, I swiftly bring my lips to his. I pour all my sexual frustration and passion into the kiss. I'm hoping like hell that it will diffuse the situation, tame the wild animal I was stupid enough to let out of its cage.

At first it feels like he's starting to reciprocate, but then something worse happens. Breaking my hold, I see fear in his eyes. Fear. Tearing his gaze away from me, he practically runs from the store like a wounded animal. Sorrow pours from my heart and I berate myself.

I've seen this man kill multiple times, even going toe-to-toe with multiple foes without batting an eye. In each and every encounter, I've never seen a single hint of fear like I did just now. With a painful sigh, I pick up the box of tampons and quickly leave the store.

Chapter Forty-Nine

We stand before the wreckage of a bridge that traverses a dry river. Chunks of dirty gray concrete and twisted metal cover the river bed and there is no easy way around. The sides of the road are too thick with trees and brush and the ground is too rough. We can't risk blowing a tire we might not be able to replace.

I note a piece of graffiti that seems familiar somehow. I can't place where I've seen it, but memorize it in case I see it again somewhere. It looks like a "K" with a slash across the lower half so that the bottom of the "K" is an "A". Somewhat similar to an anarchy symbol. Odd.

"No going that way," I say to Beast. "Now what?"

He snorts in disapproval before pulling out the map and laying it out on the hood so that we can figure out where we are going. Our previous pique has been forgotten, or at least deliberately ignored, as we were forced to pay attention to our surroundings. After a pause, he taps on the map and starts laying out a new route.

"Lot of back roads through what looks like farming country. Think anyone is still out there?"

Beast shrugs, points to his eyes and then does a flat palm across the horizon.

"Of course I'm supposed to keep both eyes open."

I get this look of disbelief right before he points the direction we came from.

"Oh, come on! Cut me some slack. Do you know when the last time I saw an unopened box of tampons was?"

Beast chuckles, and then breaks into a full blown laugh.

I gasp. "Oh, my god! It laughs! Has Hell frozen over?" I have to admit to myself that I love the sound of his laugh, but I'm still kind of miffed from the knife fight.

His laughter dies away and he sighs and shoots me glare, points at me, then to Truck.

"Yes sir."

Giving him a mock salute, I clamber back in Truck and get ready to roll. I see Beast shake his head before getting back into the driver's seat. We turn around and retrace our path before locating our new route.

The maps were correct. It looks like nothing but farm country around here. Some plots have some green in them, though most vegetation is dead, or at least as though the desert is reclaiming its own. We definitely don't see anyone as we ramble down the road.

We are heading east down Hazen Road when Beast suddenly slows the truck. I glance at him and see his eyes narrow, like he's spotted someone. Turning my attention ahead, I don't see anything out of the ordinary.

"What's wrong?"

Bringing the truck to a stop, he shakes his head and then makes a throat cutting motion.

"Shit! Are you sure? Do we go back?"

Taking a deep breath, he puts Truck into reverse and pulls off the road. Once we stop, he puts it in park and then looks at me seriously. Last time he looked at me like this, we were about to take out the University Raiders.

Finally, he growls. "Don't ask me how I know, but that's an ambush. I feel it."

"Okay. So now what do we do?"

"We go in on foot, kill anyone there and take what they have. Then continue on. That gas station may have had a lookout. That means they know we are here. It's probable that bridge was taken out to funnel people this direction. Only way out now is through."

I take a deep breath to calm my nerves. I don't think its fear though. It's excitement. Not only is he talking to me again, we also get to take out more bandits. That is something that we definitely do best.

"All right. Let's do this."

"Are you sure? This is different. This fight may be up close and personal. Like Midland."

I can't help but smile, and I think he likes it. "Yes. We've gotten this far, haven't we?"

Beast snorts a laugh and starts getting out of the truck.

"By the way," I state with a grin. "I really like it when you laugh."

He stops and stares at me for a moment but it's hard to read him, as always. Finally he closes the door and heads towards the back. I quickly join him, hoping that I'm wearing him down in a good way.

When he opens the tail gate, he starts gearing us both up. Were going for bear, so he's pulling out the G3 while giving me the Kurz. The bonus is that we will both be using the same magazines and he's already got the fifty round drum in his.

As we finish getting ready, he pulls out a pistol case and has to unlock it. From the case he removes a handgun I've not seen before. Dark wood grips adorn it and as I get a good glimpse, it almost looks like a Beretta 92. Taking my hand, he gives it to me as if putting a ring on my finger.

I smile at him playfully. "Is this your version of an engagement ring?"

Beast's eyes go very wide and I have to quickly placate his fear.

"Oh, calm down, I'm joking. What is this?"

He seems to relax before telling me. "Beretta 93."

"What's this thing in the front?" I ask as I flip down this small metal post ahead of the trigger guard.

"Fore grip. Useful if firing the pistol in burst fire mode."

I look at him in shock. "This fires in bursts?"

"If you set it that way," he states with a nod. "I recommend semi-auto."

"Oooh, I love it! Thank you, sir." I slip the Beretta into my thigh holster in place of the FNX. "Any reason why I always get the girl gun?"

Beast looks at me questioningly. "Are you kidding me?"

"Just wondering."

With a shake of his head, he rolls his eyes. "Just finish getting ready."

"Yes, my lord."

Beast gives me a hard glare before going back to getting ready. I don't know how, but I am certain we had the same dream. No other reason he would react like that. And of course, once again, I find that now is not the time.

Fucking bandits!

Once I'm ready, I make sure everything is secure and do a jump test to make sure it's quiet. I then sling my rifle and get ready to move out. Beast looks ready when he closes up Truck and locks it. Then we move into the brush next to the lot where he thinks the ambush is and sneak in.

We work our way through fields that are abandoned and choked with weeds. Moving low to the ground, we slowly pick our way through until we finally get to the edge of the last field. It appears to be a feed lot or something. Crossing a dirt road that Mother Nature is trying to take back, we drop into a tree and weed covered ditch, getting into position.

While I watch for anyone who might be nearby, Beast is already looking through his scope. When he chuckles, I know he's spotted someone. More importantly, he's been proven right and he's happy about that.

It has to be a guy thing.

"Single target, acting as sniper. Roughly eleven o'clock, you can just see him poking up over the crest of the roof."

Following his finger to where he points, it takes me a minute to finally spot the guy. Thankfully he moved a little, making it easier to catch his position. Since Beast has him dead to rights, I start looking for any other snipers. As I hear the suppressed gunshot, I'm pretty sure there are no other obvious targets.

"Tango down," Beast states coldly.

"I don't see any others," I report.

"Now we move in, kill them all. No remorse."

That statement causes me to take in a deep breath. I get close to Beast and whisper in a sultry voice. "I love it when you say things like that. It really turns me on."

Before I can witness his reaction, or he can even reply, I'm up the ditch and into the lot, heading towards a nearby building. Off in the distance I can hear thunder, telling me a rain storm is coming. The thought of dancing with Beast enters my mind and I smile as a raider comes into view. With a pull of the trigger, the fighting starts.

Chapter Fifty

Our G3s send out lead death to any who dare to stand in our way. Our surge and wait, cover, watch, attack has become a kind of dance. Beast and I move like the well-honed team we are, slipping through buildings, between trailers and over or under derelict vehicles. I get the targets up close, he tags them from further out. Today we are unstoppable and haven't even been touched.

Sweeping through one end of the lot, we head towards the other. I empty the last couple rounds of my second magazine into my latest bandit and swap mags while Beast covers me. A part of me wants to climb onto a roof top and watch my partner work as he cuts a bloody swath through the enemy that rushes to meet us, but he needs me here.

We learn too late that we've wandered into a hornet's nest. It's impossible to count how many run at us from around the next corner, but the magazine I was trying to put into my rifle gets knocked from my hand and I'm forced back. Dropping my weapon, I draw my knife and Glock to press my own attack. I'm able to gun down three of them before the rest are on top of me.

At the same time, some huge bruiser of a man tackles Beast and they get into a fight of their own. While I can hear my companion let out a hiss, I don't have time to pay attention. I've got at least five men trying to take me. What worries me is that they are trying to take me alive.

I get a couple shots off before I realize my pistol is almost better used as a club, though one of my bullets hits a bandit in the leg, slowing him down. After that I'm forced to defend as I parry attack after attack, getting in a slice here and there when the opportunity presents itself.

My enemy is armed with pipes, and they are doing a damn good job of trying to beat me into submission. I take a couple blows to the chest and shoulder, but don't let the pain stop me. I'll be damned if anyone takes me as a slave again. They'll have to kill me because I'll never let them take me alive.

The butt of my pistol catches one man in the jaw as I duck under the swing of another. Getting in under that swing, my blade slashes across his gut and he falls back screaming as his intestines fall out. *Shit, what a mess!*

At that point the remaining three aren't so gung-ho anymore. I may be battered and sore, but I don't let them see it. Borrowing a page from Beast, I hiss and snarl in an attempt to frighten them further. It doesn't quite work, but their hesitation gives me time to flip the pistol around. They realize their mistake too late.

First man takes it right in the chest and falls with hardly a sound. The second gets a bullet in the gut and falls to the ground with a grunt. I can't get my pistol aimed at the third man fast enough. The pipe strikes my gun arm and my pain-numbed hand lets go, the gun falling to the ground.

This one's too fast and my thrust is narrowly avoided. I parry the pipe with my knife and vice versa as we start trading back and forth, trying to get under each other's guard. I wince when the pipe hits my thigh and dance back. *Fuck that hurts!*

To make matters worse, Beast is not having an easy time with the hulk he's dealing with. I can't help but worry, yet I have to be rid of this last asshole before I can help him! I try to center beyond the bodily aches and pains and focus on my task.

Fate deals me a lucky hand. My opponent is getting angry. I mean, how dare a woman be a better fighter than him? With a yell, he rears back with the pipe over his head in an attempt to put more power into his swing. I block his arm and swing it away, creating a perfect opening and my knife finds his armpit twice. Dropping with a gasp, he doesn't get back up.

I pick up my pistol and turn just in time to see Beast take a rather nasty blow to the side with a hammer and he roars in a combination of pain and anger. I watch in shock as he goes altogether savage and rips into the brute like a man possessed. In a matter of seconds, the bruiser is falling back as Beast lays into him with cut after cut, the short sword swinging so fast it's practically a blur.

My companion then gets in a perfect thrust, running the blade right through the man's heart. Beast shakes in furious rage as he hisses into the dying man's eyes. I can't even imagine how terrifying that must be. It's a sight I'm sure that raider will take to his grave and beyond.

When the bandit collapses in a heap, Beast staggers back and drops to one knee while clutching his side. I rush up, worry rising in my chest as I help him get back onto his feet and check him over.

"Are you alright?" My voice is full of concern.

Beast sounds exhausted when he replies. "I'm fine."

"You don't look fine."

"Yes. I'll be..."

Suddenly Beast takes three shots in the chest. The force of the bullets rips him out of my arms and he falls to the ground. I scream in primal rage as I spin and see three men, all with guns pointing at me.

One man, skinny and looks like a weasel with dirty brown hair, points his pistol at me. "Drop it, missy. Our boss, Kane, wants to talk to you."

"Fuck you!"

All three laugh as their spokesperson replies. "Oh, there will be plenty of that after our boss gets first crack at ya."

Like hell, he will. I meant it about them not taking me alive. Fury rages through me and I'm itching to go for my pistol. My hand moves slowly towards the new Beretta that Beast had given me. The only thing going through my mind is the image of me gunning them all down.

"Don't even think about it, chica," the weasel states while waving his pistol at me. "We got you dead bang. Kane said he wants you unharmed, but we ain't above putting some rock salt in ya to quiet you down some."

I notice, even in my fury, a tattoo on the forearm of the weasel. A "K" with the bottom crossed, similar to the graffiti I'd seen earlier. My eyes fly to the other two and they, also, have the tattoo. What *is* that?

"Yeah bitch," a fat man with a shotgun gloats. "Be a good..."

We are all taken by surprise when Beast swiftly sits up, raising his own pistol while drawing the Beretta in my thigh holster. With both guns blazing, he burns two of them down. That distraction is enough for me to pull my Glock to shoot Mr. Weasel. With a yelp he drops and doesn't get back up. He's still alive, though. His breath whistles and blood bubbles out between his lips. I think he's trying to speak, but as I get closer to end him, I realize he's laughing.

"You're dead, lady, you and your boyfriend. You don't know Kane, he won't let this go." More laughter bubbles up with his blood, "You're so fucking dead." His body shakes in pain and amusement and I feel a chill go up my spine. "Kane will never stop 'til he catches you. Never."

I don't like the thought that their leader is so tenacious, and if I wasn't so worried about Beast, I'd make sure we got directions to this Kane's hideout before I killed this fucker. But Beast is down and the Mr. Weasel is bleeding out. Before I can ask anything, he passes out. Frankly the bastard deserves a nice slow death. In a fog of panicked dread, I rush to where Beast fell, bracing myself for the worst.

In an instant, I'm kneeling down next to Beast and looking him over. "Shit! I thought you were dead."

"Vest caught it," he speaks, sounding tired and breathing hard. "I'm fine."

"You're not fine! You've been shot, damn it!"

The storm is getting closer, if the rumble of thunder is any indication. In fact, I see a flash of lightning reflect off the side of the nearby building. The sweet, earthy smell of the coming rain fills my senses. Beast looks up at me with annoyed blue eyes a girl could get lost in. Of course he goes and spoils it by speaking.

"Damn it, woman. Is there any way to shut you up!?"

He did not just ...

Rearing back in shock, I'm absolutely flabbergasted that he would say such a thing. A myriad of responses run through my head, and none of them are kind. I square my jaw, about to give him a piece of my mind when a much better thought hits me.

"Yeah," I state, damn near yelling at him. "There is!"

Grabbing his vest, I pull his lips to mine so hard that our teeth almost clash. Every ounce of anger and passion and ragged frustration is poured into that kiss as the first few raindrops fall. To my amazed and gratified surprise, he reciprocates this time and before long we are locked in a passionate embrace.

Chapter Fifty-One

The rain pelts Truck and the sweet earthy scent of a desert storm fills the air. The occasional rumble of thunder follows us as we take shelter in an abandoned house a few miles from the ambush site. We hide our faithful steed behind the home, tossing some ratty tarps over it and retreat inside before we are totally soaked.

The house has a fireplace, the reason Beast picked it, I think. Thankfully there was some wood in a tarnished brass bin. Before long, he has a warm fire going, our wet fatigues drying in front of it. Now Beast relaxes on the couch not far away. I love seeing him at ease like this, and not looking at me as if have two heads for wanting him. And I do, don't get me wrong. But I want to let him set the pace, now that he's not in complete denial.

With his shirt off, his tats are out in the open as he lays back, eyes closed and resting. His long hair is loose and still damp as his head rests against the back of the couch. I've wrapped a tight bandage around his chest. Between the hammer blow and the bullets, he has a couple of cracked ribs.

I'm not much better off, bruised and battered as I am, but I'm not as bad as he is. So I figure it's my turn to make dinner for the two of us. I'm not much of a cook, but I do the best I can with what we have.

I've heard that MREs are full of calories and not flavor, but they do have a number of useful things in them. One of those things is coffee. It's not the best, but at the end of the world it is a homey comfort and honestly, it smells wonderful. I use one of the cans of jellied fuel to heat up two cups for us.

When I take a sip I find it's not all that bad, especially with some creamer and sugar that was also provided. I grab the cup for Beast and take it over to him, the packet of creamer and sugar in hand since I don't know how he likes it. Chuckling to myself, I realize that we've killed bandits together for over a year, watched each other's back and stayed alive, yet I don't know how he likes his coffee.

"Here you go." I whisper softly.

Beast opens his eyes and looks up, giving me a rare smile. Taking the cup from my hands, he nods and rips both the creamer and sugar packets. Pouring them in, he then drinks at least half the cup in one go.

"Those MREs we found in Blythe are still good. I've had better coffee, but it's not the worst either."

"Thanks," he says with a nod.

I kneel down next to him and caress his cheek. "I like to see you smile."

"From this old, broken face?" He snorts in disgust. "I don't know why."

His pain makes my heart constrict. "Because it's beautiful to me. You, showing signs of life, the smallest piece of joy that makes me happy."

"Beautiful? Give me a break."

He is so aggravating. I swear, he is going to learn something tonight if it kills both of us. "Damn it, I love your face, what I get to see of it. Your eyes, so fiercely blue. The way you hold yourself, your quiet strength. Even when you won't talk to me, I love being near you. Even when you look at me like you're looking at me now, like I'm crazy."

His face is a blank for a moment, but as I speak his head shakes in the negative. Lips are pressed together in denial. I know that stubborn expression, so I take another tack.

"Besides, if there's one thing I learned before the world went to shit, real beauty is rarely on the surface. It's who a person is, how they treat others that makes them beautiful, and you have treated me with more kindness and respect than anyone else ever has in my entire life, outside of my parents."

He sighs and his blue eye gaze at me with weary sadness, so I continue. "Do you know what I did before the world went to hell?"

Beast shakes his head.

"I was a porn actress. An adult film star," I state without a hint of shame. "Nothing to be ashamed of as far as I'm concerned. Pay was good, sex wasn't bad at times and I got to see some of the world. While there were many handsome men, not all of them treated me with the same respect you have."

With a pained sigh, he shakes his head. "I treated you poorly. Was hard on you. Didn't have to be."

"Yes you did," I state with surety and he looks up, surprised. "The world has turned into a hard place. You toughened me up to live in it. To not end up like you found me."

Beast raises a hand and tentatively caresses my cheek. I can't help but let out a small sound at the feel of his touch. It's been a long time coming because I thought my libido had been killed forever, but now? All I want is to be with this amazing, fucked-up man who has been by my side through thick and thin. There's not a doubt in my mind that he has become the most important person in my life.

"You are far too beautiful an angel to be mistreated so."

"Oh, how can I resist you when you say such lovely things?"

I lean in, wanting to kiss him, but wait for him to meet me half way. I don't want to push this on him again. I want him to want me too, or what is the point? Fortunately, he doesn't leave me hanging.

One of his hands slips into my hair and pulls slightly, tipping my head back as his lips move across my jaw and then my neck. Gripping his shoulders, I straddle his thighs in order to give him better access. Taking my offer, he suckles and nips his way up my neck. I let out a gasp when he nibbles on my earlobe.

Heat and urgency envelops us quickly and we become nothing but lips and hands as we kiss while struggling to remove each other's clothes without losing physical contact. When I'm reduced to bra and panties, the entire would has become his voice, his touch. After those dreams, I'm beyond ready for this as my damp hair falls around our faces like a curtain and we kiss and kiss and kiss.

I moan into his mouth as he flexes his hips, his erection pressing against me. He gives me a low growl back and it sends a delicious shiver up my spine. Strong hands grip my ass and he stands up with me clinging to him. We never stop kissing as he carries me into the master bedroom. With each step, anticipation builds while thunder rages outside and rain pelts the roof. *Could we be blessed with a more romantic setting?*

Slowly he lays me onto the bed and I know what he's going to do. Fingers hook under my panties and with teasing slowness, he pulls them down my legs while I unhitch my bra. Then starting with my feet, he lays soft, gentle kisses, licking and sucking as he moves tantalizingly up, and up, and up. My breaths are ragged when he reaches the apex of my thighs and blows gently upon me. *Oh shit!*

I can't help but writhe as he hovers there. Gazing down my body, all I can see are those blue eyes behind a white mask, looking at me like a feast, like a wolf that's found his prey. Heat rushes through my veins and I feel like I will combust at any moment.

"Oh, don't stop now" I cry out, begging for him. "Please, my Beast, please?"

My heart is pounding and my body convulses and the first touch of his tongue. One hand clutches at the sheets, my other fists into his hair, pulling him to me. I cry out, back arching off the bed as his tongue swirls around again and again, giving me such sweet torture. Grabbing my hips, he holds me down and starts rapidly fluttering just the tip of his tongue against my clit. *Oh fuck!*

Mind, I've had a lot of sex. A lot. It was part of my last job-description. But this? This isn't sex, it's making love and it's powerful beyond description. I can't hold back, I know he's going to push me right over that edge into blissful ecstasy and there will be no disappointments with him. And at that, I let go.

My orgasm rips through me as I nearly levitate, my body shuddering, my voice expressing my pleasure. Beast holds me to him, not letting up his assault, but backing off the tiniest bit to prolong it, stretching out what seems a blessed eternity of ecstasy before finally showing me some mercy.

The shudders subside and I find myself molded against him as I come back from the depths. Beast is laying beside me, stroking my back and flanks and watching me. All I can do is smile and reach for him. I have no words for what he's just done to me, but I want more. When I take a quick gaze down, I see he's definitely ready for action and there's a feral look in his eyes that makes my heart skip a beat. *Oh! Yes please!*

"On your knees." His voice is low and it sounds like an order.

Right now, I don't care that it's an order. Besides, I know he would never hurt me. Quickly I roll over, heart racing as he moves in behind me. I moan as his hands caress my ass, slowly getting into position, teasing me once more.

"Fuck me, my Beast," I plead. "Please!"

The only response I get to my begging is a low, guttural growl right before he eases into me. *OH FUCK!* It's been so long. Slowly, inch by blessed inch, he fills me until he's all the way to the hilt. The feeling of fullness takes my breath away as I moan in appreciation.

Once we've both adjusted, he moves slowly at first, his beast-like growls matching my moans. Then he starts to pick up speed, *oh shit!* It isn't long before he's ravaging me in a brutal rhythm that makes me cry out. One hand wraps around my hair and pulls my head up, delivering bites and kisses along my neck as he pounds into me.

Thrusting into me over and over again, my body tightens around him. He never stops while pushing me so close to the edge and I whimper as I hear him let out a harsh growl right next to my ear. As his grip tightens against my waist, I can no longer hold back. I detonate around him as he slams into me one last time and comes. My scream mingles with his roar, our voices filling the air.

Collapsing onto the bed, Beast then collapses onto me, our sweaty bodies pressed together as he pins me against the mattress. Our breathing matches and slows and I wince when he slides out of me. When he slips off of my body, I roll over.

As my sanity finally returns, I realize he's worshiping me again, planting soft kisses all over. Once he sees that I've recovered, he dives in and tortures me once more with that masterful tongue of his. *Holy fuck!* Within just a short time I can already feel my body heading towards another release, my legs beginning to tremble. When his lips close around my clit, I'm gone once more. As I scream out in ecstasy, the world is replaced by stars.

I'm utterly spent; tiny, lovely aftershocks coursing through my veins. I'm so wrung out and exhausted I barely even register when he moves up and gathers me into his warm arms, holding me tightly to him.

We spoon together and for the first time in a long time, I feel whole. The world taught me quite rudely that safety was nothing but an illusion. Yet as his body wraps about me like a cocoon, I feel safe, if only for a time. Smiling in blissful joy, sleep overtakes me.

Chapter Fifty-Two

When I wake a little more than an hour later, the thunder has moved on, and the rain has stopped. Beast is propped up on one elbow behind me, running his fingers softly through my hair. I sigh in contented pleasure. What a wonderful way to wake up.

Without a word, he rolls onto his back and has one arm open. I immediately understand just what he is offering and snuggle into the crook of his arm, my body pressed against his side as I lay my head on his chest. Once more he runs his fingers through my hair, starting my temple and tracing a line over my ear. I reciprocate by running one of my fingers through his chest hair, eliciting a small moan from him in return. I hadn't realized how much I've missed gentle, human touch.

For once I don't mind that we are totally silent. I'm still in bliss from the multiple orgasms he's given me. I only hear the soft lub-lub of his heartbeat as he caresses me. I'm certainly not prepared for the words that tumble from his mouth.

"They killed my wife and daughter. Made me watch." His voice is rough, harsh, and I think he's only able to speak because we are intimate and safe.

I lift my head, appalled. "What?"

"My wife and daughter, Anna and Katie. We were trying to get out of the city. Got ambushed by a gang."

When he closes his eyes to the painful memories, I place a hand on his chest to let him know I'm here. I feel his heartbeat quicken under my palm, but can't tell if it's because of my touch or the nightmare he's reliving. I just hope I'm providing some solace.

"They, uh..." his voice cracks and tears prick my eyes. "They wanted to make me suffer for killing their friends. Gang raped my wife in front of me, then executed her and our daughter. Staked me out in the sun and left me for dead."

With that, the last puzzle piece falls into place. The reason he'd been killing raiders and why he stayed in L.A. had become abundantly clear. Just like me, he was extracting vengeance for the wrongs that had been done to him. A tear rolls down his cheek and I kiss it away.

"How did you survive?"

"I was two days dying, mostly just staring at the bodies of my wife and child. I wanted to die, so didn't even fight it. I don't remember much after that, but I woke up in the care of good folk. Evidently they'd gotten me out of there and nursed me back to health."

Those blue eyes slide to me and he looks serious. "I changed that day.

219

Damn near dumped all my humanity on the gods-forsaken street and became what you see before you—a beast. An unlovable savage."

"You aren't any of that! Do you remember the day you saved me?"

"Of course. Why?"

"When you agreed to take me with you; the first thing you did was take the jacket off Knick and put it on me, then zip it up to hide my nudity. It was kind and respectful. You were giving me back my dignity in the very first moments you knew me. I knew right then that you were more than just a killer—although you are really good at that."

Beast gives a snort. "That came easy. I hunted those bastards down and avenged my family. After that, I just kept looking for assholes to kill. There was no shortage. It wasn't until finding you that continuing on to Colorado came back to mind."

"Why is that?"

"To get you somewhere safe."

"But why? Why was that so important?"

He gazes into my eyes without a hint of guile. "Because after a few weeks of you being with me, I couldn't bear the thought of you ending up the way I found you. I love you."

"You do? But, how? Why? You- you pushed me away, you didn't want me. I had to share a dream with you before you would even begin to show me..."

Those three magical words have finally sunken in. My heart soars, feeling like it's going to fly right out of my chest as I melt into his embrace. Tears of joy leak from my eyes as I caress his bearded face and beam him my brightest smile.

"Chloe, I didn't want you to be with me because you deserve better than me. You are a perfect flower, my angel, and you deserve a man of peace, not a broken old war horse. But you never looked at anyone else, even when they all wanted you, tried to impress you. Your insistence terrified me because I don't deserve you. I knew today I was too tired to fight you anymore when you were all I wanted."

"Oh, my lovely Beast. I love you. I love you!"

Sliding on top of his body, I pepper my words with kisses until we melt together and kiss each other passionately. Then slowly, ever so slowly, we make love again before unraveling in each other's arms once more.

Sunlight streams through a lightly curtained window where it floods my face with brilliance and wakes me. The golden rays of light illuminate the dust in the air. Rolling onto my back, I stretch my limbs, sore from bruises, but also, happily from our recent activity. It was wonderful and the memories brings a smile to my face.

Last night had been incredible. And it's like I went to bed with two different men. I have a hard time deciding which version of Beast I like better. Mr. Ravaging Animal or Mr. Sweet Loving Beast. They both have their perks. No matter which one was loving me, I felt worshiped like a goddess.

Speaking of my companion, he is not in the bed with me. The bed sheets are a tangled mess. The bedside table has both my new pistol and his lying on it. The lingering scent of the recent rain still hangs heavy in the air. There's something else too, I think it's the scent of eggs. As I start to get up, the door opens and Beast walks in with a bed tray.

"Morning, handsome. What's this?"

He rewards me with a smile. "Room service."

How did he know how I adore room service?

I smile brightly and sit up against the headboard as he sits on the bed next to me. A plate of ham and scrambled eggs rests on the tray, along with a steaming cup of coffee and a glass of water. Now how did he manage this from a packet of MREs?

"Not the greatest room service, but the best I could do."

"Oh no," I exclaim with joy. "This is wonderful! How did you know?"

"You talk in your sleep."

I laugh with him and take a bite of the meal that he has prepared for me. I love breakfast in bed. Actually the eggs aren't as bad as I thought they might be. I wash my bite down with some coffee and take a deep, satisfied breath. Then I look at Beast and give him a warm smile.

"Thank you."

"Quite welcome, my lady."

"Though, I must apologize because I was in charge of dinner last night, and all you got to eat was me."

I grin in wicked delight as he cracks a smile and his eyes twinkle. *Be still my heart, but I love that smile.*

Reaching out, I cup his cheek and kiss him before continuing to eat. I'm guessing he's already had breakfast since there's only enough for me. I notice that he's watching me and I can help but watch him back. Blue eyes adore me through that mask of his. My heart flutters again at the unaccustomed, but so very welcome sight.

"Are you ever going to take that mask off?"

"No."

"Why not?"

"Because the man underneath it isn't me anymore. I don't want to see his face ever again."

A lance of sorrow pierces my heart, and it all clicks into place. He blames himself for the death of his wife and daughter. That's why all the mirrors in the house were shattered. The mask keeps him from seeing the face of the man that he blames for their death. I reach out and touch his shoulder softly.

"It wasn't your fault."

"Yes it was," he states softly. "I should have been faster. Should have been paying better attention. I wasn't strong enough."

"Hey… look at me."

Slowly his blue eyes lift up to mine, wet with unshed tears for loved ones he's probably never even mourned properly. God he looks so sad and defeated, not like my Beast at all. I hope that I'm helping.

"Those gang members killed your family. Not you."

He doesn't appear convinced. "I wish I could believe you. I don't know that I will ever be able to accept that."

"Oh, love. It was not your fault any more than Knick and Knack were mine. I will try help as long as I live, so try to believe it," I tell him with a wry grin. "Because you know how persistent I can be?"

Beast glares at me. "Eat your breakfast."

"Yes, sir," I giggle.

He gives me a smile to tell me we're okay as I finish my meal. Frankly, I'm burning daylight and we really should get moving. Traveling at night is far too risky, so wasting daylight means wasting travel time.

Once breakfast is finished, we clean up together. It certainly is nice to have someone wash my back. While a part of me wants to get frisky, the combination of cold water and needing to get on the road quashed that. And, to be honest, I'm sore.

When we're done, we dress, grab our things and leave the house that sheltered us. A part of me wishes we could stay here, because it has sentimental value. But we have a long way to go still. Pulling the wet tarps off, we pile our things into Truck.

After tossing an ammo can into the back, I give Beast a quick kiss. "Last night was wonderful, my lord."

The dark, carnal gaze that he shoots me makes my heart skip a beat. "If you behave, I'll give you a repeat performance."

"When do I not behave?"

"I can think of a few instances that come to mind," he states with a grin.

I can't help but scoff. "Oh, please. I think the one who needs to behave is you."

Giving me a dark smile in response, he playfully slaps me on the ass. "Let's get moving. I want to put as many miles behind us as possible."

"Then let's go."

We clamber into Truck and the engine starts up with its typical growl. Pulling out of the backyard, we get back onto Hazen Road before finally making it onto MC 85, another name for Buckeye Road. Beast hands me the map so that I can continue to navigate as well as keep watch. We are going to head for Fifty-First Avenue.

"What do we do after getting to Fifty-First?"

"We take that south." Beast remarks. "It will turn into Beltline and then into Riggs Road. I hope to take that all the way to Ellsworth on the east side and then work our way to the US 60. With luck, find gas and supplies on the way."

I nod. "Sounds like a solid plan. By the way, thank you."

"For what?"

"Talking to me instead of just pointing and waving your hands like a mad man."

While I grin at him, he shoots me a sidelong, disapproving glare as we continue. With lightning fast reflexes, his arm shoots out and starts tickling me. I screech and thrash and curse as he tortures me. When he stops, we are both laughing as we continue heading down the road.

Chapter Fifty-Three

Our journey across south Phoenix is uneventful at first. My companion is not surprised by this. Beast surmises that without a consistent source of water or electricity, most people would have abandoned the city. That actually made a lot of sense.

I mention the graffiti to him, and to my surprise, he tells me he noticed it too. He did not, however, see the tattoos on Kane's men, and we both think about that for a while. Eventually, we decide old gang signs are now a way to mark territory. Kane has basically peed on his territory, including on his followers. We both try to keep an eye open for the symbol as we drive.

While I know it's possible for us to find another Walma or Blythe, the odds are probably higher that we'll find more of the gang activity that Jack told us about. I really hate the idea of spending more of our dwindling ammunition.

The drive goes just as Beast has planned until we are well-into Chandler. Through it all, we see nothing but desolate remains of buildings and homes choked with weeds. We are approaching Pecos Road, according to the map, when I notice activity ahead.

"Hold up, something's happening up there."

Beast already has his foot on the brake to slow us down, but then things start happening fast. Pecos is a major street. There is a cloverleaf ahead and we can spot movement on several levels. I point to the concrete ahead and the "K" symbol painted on it. *Fuck.*

"It's an ambush."

Beast screeches to a halt, but not before turning the wheel enough to power-slide the truck awkwardly so as to face parallel to the cloverleaf and the nose of the truck facing east. That's when I notice the overpass behind us on Chandler Boulevard is also occupied. I point it out to Beast and he begins a steady stream of curses.

We take a quick look at our situation. Enemy ahead and behind. I glance out the back and see an apartment complex on the west side of the road. And spot a few snipers popping up on the roof. Directly ahead of the truck, over a hillock that is overgrown with weeds and such, is a motel that reminds me immediately of my lodgings with Knick and Knack and the Crazy Eight gang. I shudder in revulsion and take a closer look at the map.

"We have to move." Beast's voice is an angry growl.

"We're surrounded," I exclaim in return.

Now I've spotted snipers on the roof of the motel as well. Though there is a burned out building south of the motel that could give us some cover. I look at the map again and the enemy chooses that moment to begin firing.

"Which direction?!" he roars as bullets ping off our armor.

"Straight ahead, to the right of that burned out building!"

He guns it and Truck bumps off the road and ramps up over the hummock that edges the freeway and back down again, more bullets pinging off Truck's armor plating. I am worried they will hit a tire, because even though we have two spares, we don't really have time to change one right now.

We hear shouting as we leave the freeway and the shooting intensifies. But we don't stop. A moving target is much harder to hit, after all. We come out in what must have once been a warehouse district. I tell him to take the frontage road north, then east past both the motels and the warehouses, even though that is heading toward some shooters because I don't know what is waiting in the warehouse area.

Sure enough, snipers pop up from the roof of the warehouses lining the freeway, but we are already skidding around the corner to head east and away from the ambush. Bullets ping off the back of the camper shell. I instruct Beast to keep east until the road ends at a grocery distribution center.

When we get there, instead of the stable, Walma situation, there are only wrecked trailers and broken down fences. I wonder briefly if it was gangs or just the general population that ravaged the area. Times were tough once people started realizing new supplies would no longer be arriving with food and other things I repress another shudder and instruct Beast to turn north and then cut across an abandoned lot, toward an automotive sales and service area.

We don't slow down, but dodge between buildings and through back alleys until we have put miles between us and the ambush site. Since we have no clue where they might pop up next, we stick to a labyrinthine world of backstreets and side roads. Rather than going to more open land and farm fields, we are forced to go further north to avoid Kane's gang. Every major freeway is a hazard, bridges are down, gangs might be in hiding. It's a nightmare full of fear and paranoia.

We have a few followers, though. Just when we think we're well away, that's when we spot some guys on motorcycles weaving back and forth and searching for us on a main road. Once they see us, they swerve our direction and there are about a dozen of them. *Fuck.*

Without even waiting for instructions I clamber into the back where we have set up the machine-gun. My favorite. I can't imagine they're going to expect this. I am grinning with anticipation, even after Beast swings sharply around a corner and sends me against one side of the narrow passage we had cleared to the back of the truck. Fortunately everything is well tied down, so I don't get crushed.

225

Oh, the expressions on the riders' faces when they see what is coming at them. Once again, I am in charge and make short work of the assholes following us. Those to the side are a different story. There are four bikes left, and they're riding double, the passengers armed with Uzis. Where the fuck did they get those?

"Beast!" I almost shriek the words, "They're armed! Incoming fire!"

"I see them." I hear. "Hang on!"

I do what he instructs and put my head down, hanging on for dear life. The truck goes through some fancy acrobatics now, and I hear shouts and gunfire from outside, and multiple impacts with more than bullets. I realize Beast has sent us into another controlled spin and has taken out all but one of the cycles. Once we come to a stop, everything is still for the moment, so I pop my head up to see furious eyes peering through the hatch.

He's speaks. "Kane's gonna kill you fuckers, be ready for that. He'll never let you go. Depend on it."

"Depend on this, asshole." I draw my pistol and put one between his eyes. Then I realize we still aren't moving. Why aren't we moving?

"Beast?"

I hear a roar from outside the truck. *Fuck, what is going on?* I look wildly through the back and can't see anything, so turn to look out the front. I catch a flash of movement and hear shouting. In a panic, I dive toward the front so I can see what's happening.

As I get to the window adjoining the bed and the extended cab, I spot Beast facing off with the last two raiders. It's like we're suddenly in the Old West or something and they're about to draw up on each other. *Damn it, who does he think he is, Wyatt Earp?*

Tension rises as they stare each other down, but if I know my Beast, he's gazing at them impassively. They all go for their weapons at the same instant. I watch in awe as Beast manages to get two shots off into each of the bandits before they've even had a chance to aim at him. My fucking hero.

As I climb into the front of the truck, I find blood on the driver's side seat. Panic starts to rise as I look to see what he's doing now. Calmly he's walking up and putting a bullet in each raider's head.

"Beast, get in here, I need to see where you're bleeding!" I shout, trying to compose myself.

His voice, calm and composed, comes from the passenger side. "'Tis a scratch. I've had worse."

"Are you quoting Monty Python at me? Let me see that."

He is hit, but it barely grazed his arm. It's bleeding freely and I want to bandage it, but we don't know if there will be more raiders after us. I slap a gauze pad from my trauma kit on his arm and tell him to hold it. I'm driving.

Truck growls as I hit the gas. I take us miles east to a random suburban neighborhood. It is very strange to drive the quiet streets, filthy with two years dirt, weeds, and garbage. Most of the houses look pretty good, though we drive through one section that has completely burned down. Some of the yards are heavily overgrown since they were desert landscaped, but the rest are dead and brown with new desert seedling starting to push through the dry earth.

Finally, I see what I'm looking for, a house with a carport which is half-hidden by overgrown mesquite trees. I pull the truck in, hoping for a few minutes' peace. Then I turn to Beast and see he's already done a pretty good job bandaging himself. I frown at him and insist on checking him over to see if there are any other injuries. He checks me too, but I could have told him I'm fine.

"If I didn't know better, I would think this is an excuse to grope me," I tease and he smiles back at me, sending my heart racing.

"Do or do not, there is no try."

"Now Yoda? You're quoting Yoda?" His hands continue to move over me until he is apparently satisfied that I'm all right.

"I'm testing your pop-culture knowledge."

"What? If I'd known there was going to be a test, I'd have studied."

I'm trying to be cute and funny, but he's moved on, caressing my back and pulling me to him in a kiss. We take our time.

We stay the night in the house in the suburbs. It was once a really nice home. We figure it had been abandoned from the beginning and was quiet and dusty, haunted by the photos on the walls and the personal items we find. It may sound silly, but we use a guest room rather than the master, because it feels like an intrusion, even though these people are probably long dead.

As a bonus, we also find some canned food and other packaged items that are still good, so we take them. I also found a pistol in the master bedroom bedside table. Makes me hope they might have made it after all, if they felt safe enough to leave a weapon behind.

Of course, there's no shower, and the pool has long dried up, but there is still some water in the toilet tanks, which is all sanitary good water that's remained covered and untouched for all this time. We still boil it, of course.

It's a quiet night and we think we've lost our pursuers. How could they

227

ever find us in a random house in the middle of the suburbs? We're not going anywhere until morning, and we light the room with a few glow sticks after blocking the windows. Under the red, yellow and green glow, we take the time to plan out a few routes that don't depend on overpasses or likely ambush sites. It's a circuitous route that will waste precious fuel, but should get us out of the area safely.

Later that evening, we spend some quality time in bed. To say that my Beast pleases me is an understatement. He is as attentive and loving as the night before, if not more so. The tender intimacies cement the love I feel for this man. He is a treasure and doesn't even seem to know how wonderful he is.

At one point, when he has made love to me until I tremble, I find myself weeping in his arms from the sheer amount of emotion I feel, and he is upset once he realizes.

"Chloe, my angel, I'm sorry. Have I hurt you? I'm an idiot. Are you okay?"

"Yes, of course, my sweet Beast, I'm- I'm happy. Women leak emotions from their eyes, it's how we work." He just holds me tighter, stroking my hair in a comforting gesture.

With a final sniffle I add, "Plus, I found some feminine hygiene products in the bathroom," and begin to giggle wildly.

He groans and begins tickling me until I beg for mercy. Still laughing, we snuggle together and I imagine the world when this was the norm. Of course, he had another family back in the old world, and I know he still misses them.

I will take this world with my Beast, as guilty as I feel for that selfish desire.

Finally, we both drift off to sleep in the silent, abandoned house in the city turning back to wilderness where we are the hunted.

Chapter Fifty-Four

Slowly I wake to find Beast has his arms wrapped tightly around me. I can feel his chest rise and fall slowly against my naked back, telling me he's still asleep. The moment fills me with joy and I feel like the luckiest person alive.

While I curse the collapse of civilization and the petty politics that caused it, right now I cannot complain. I am amazingly blessed. The man that walked into my life not only rescued me from a dark, hellish existence. He also healed me, or rather helped me to heal myself. Treating me as an equal, training me how to survive and giving me the vehicle to exact my revenge. All that has helped me to be where I am now—a strong woman partnered with a man worthy of my respect and love.

Of course it doesn't hurt that he's good in bed. Just thinking of what he's done to me with his tongue alone makes me sigh blissfully. If I didn't know any better, I'd think he was a lesbian in a previous life.

The thought makes me giggle and that causes him to stir. I crane my head to stare at his face, hoping to get a look of him sleeping peacefully before he wakes. I'm rewarded with perhaps a minute or two before those blue eyes gaze at me lovingly. *Oh, be still my beating heart!*

"Hi," he murmurs.

"Hello yourself." I beam him a bright smile.

"Ready to get back on the road?"

Sighing wistfully, I turn in his arms. "Oh, I guess so. I was getting so used to this bed though."

I can't help but wiggle my crotch against his. After all, he's rock hard, and an erection is a terrible thing to waste. Oh, the look he gives me makes my heart start beating double time. Licking his lips, he says nothing and instead starts kissing his way down my body.

Oh! Beast!

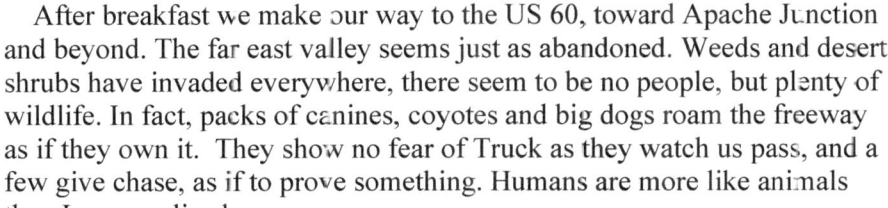

After breakfast we make our way to the US 60, toward Apache Junction and beyond. The far east valley seems just as abandoned. Weeds and desert shrubs have invaded everywhere, there seem to be no people, but plenty of wildlife. In fact, packs of canines, coyotes and big dogs roam the freeway as if they own it. They show no fear of Truck as they watch us pass, and a few give chase, as if to prove something. Humans are more like animals than I ever realized.

When we discover we're not being followed, we stop to check for

229

supplies of any kind. Most of the places we check are completely sacked of vital supplies. Thanks to Blythe, at least we have enough fuel to make it to Globe. We hope to find something along the way, because otherwise it's going to be a really long walk.

We've been traveling along US 60 for a couple hours, and so far we'd seen nothing and no one. I am relieved, though I don't truly relax until the outskirts of Phoenix are well behind us and all I see is desert foliage.

Along our route is a town called Superior that has survived behind a high, makeshift defensive wall with plenty of guards. Guards who are pointing rifles at us and motioning for us to get out. I look at Beast and he nods. I have no reason not to trust his gut up to this point.

Stepping out of Truck, we keep our hands raised while the two men look us over. One is Hispanic and the other Caucasian, although he's clearly a little sunburned. Neither are heavily armed, just hunting rifles.

"What you want, gringo?" Mr. Hispanic asks the question straight to Beast.

"Just passing through. Got any diesel to trade?"

"Yeah," the guard replies. "Circle K. Keep the weapons holstered, unless you wanna get shot."

I smile at them. "Thank you."

We get back into Truck, waiting tensely for them to move the barricade. I keep a wary eye out for an ambush. There's no way to say who is truly peaceful anymore until they prove it. Once the way is clear, we drive in slowly.

I find it ironic that the town is called Superior, because there doesn't appear to be anything superior about it. It's small, maybe the same size as Blythe. Run-down houses and buildings look like they were in an economic depression long before the Collapse hit. Any open land inside the wall has been devoted to growing food and raising livestock. Amazingly, they seem to be doing well, so they must have a steady supply of water.

I look at Beast and ask, "You think this town is okay?"

"Maybe," he replies with a shrug. "Just keep your eyes open and don't get distracted by any wild tampons."

"Not funny."

"Yes it is," he shoots right back, almost as if he knew what I was going to say.

While I try to shoot him a disapproving glare, I fail at it because I can't get the stupid grin off my face. He's in such a good mood that it's infectious. Actually, it's probably the sex. A good round or ten of love making tends to do that to people.

Finding the Circle K is easy. US 60 is their main drag, so it makes sense that the businesses are located on it. One of them is an old-fashioned, corner store with a faded red "Circle K" sign posted out front. Standing under the awning are two guys and a gal, all well-armed. One man and the lady are Hispanic and the other man is black. All three watch us warily when we pull up and get out. Beast quickly grabs something from the backseat before we head in.

Walking into a post-apocalyptic Circle K is a surreal experience. There are almost no processed goods on the shelves. No attractive, colorful packaging to catch the eye. Instead, shelves are full of homegrown and home-made goods like ears of corn, tomatoes, potatoes and even some glassware holding preserves of various kinds.

We cautiously look around, checking out what they have before making a decision. It is a somewhat stressful experience, as we are under the watchful eyes of the proprietor and her guards. Beast and I simply smile as we shop. I grab some fresh foods, thinking they can be used later for making a meal.

Beast finds what we really need, diesel fuel. There are a line of gas cans along the far wall, most labeled as diesel. He pops the caps and does a sniff check before being satisfied. I notice he also picks up a slab of ham. We then step up to the counter to begin the fun and exciting process of bartering.

Yet another thing I miss from before the Collapse is proper money. Everything had a price, you knew what it was and if you could afford it, you bought it. Now paper money isn't worth much of anything except stuffing a mattress or cushion with so it's a little softer to lie on. These days, bullets tend to be the currency of choice, until Beast surprises all of us.

"What ya got in trade?" The woman behind the counter asks while eyeing us suspiciously.

I think she's Native American. While her skin is the same color as mine, and straight black hair, her facial features aren't typical for those of Hispanic descent. She is gaunt with loose skin that shows she's lived through hard times, and she's got a hard edge to her.

Beast pulls a white, plastic holder from his pocket and puts ten silver bullion coins onto the counter. The woman's eyes light up like its Christmas. On top of that, he places ten thirty-eight cartridges onto the counter. We don't have anything that fires them, so when we comes across them, we keep them for barter.

"Deal?" Beast asks impassively and offers to shake her hand.

She gives the handshake and sweeps everything off the counter so fast, it's a blur. "Deal."

Giving his trademark bow, he puts the section of ham under his arm while grabbing the two cans. I gather up everything else, smile and follow Beast out the door while he holds it open for me.

My paranoia is spiking as we put everything into Truck. The guards have followed us back outside and are watching us like hawks. I can't help but think they might attack us. After all, we've shown that we have material wealth. Rolling us would give them what we have and they can resell what was already sold.

As I walk back to the passenger door and get in, I stand up on the runner and look at the guards with a polite smile. Suddenly a thought hits me right out of the blue as I think of a question to ask them.

"Hey, by any chance is there a Mexican food restaurant here?"

They seem to relax, and the girl gives me a nod. "Los Hermanos, ma'am. Just down the street."

"Thank you."

As I sit down and close the door, I look to see that Beast is gazing at me an unspoken question. I'm sure he's curious as to why I asked. The suggestion I'm about to make may not go over well, but I'm going to make it anyway.

"There's a Mexican food restaurant just down the street. Could we stop? I know we're burning daylight, but it would be a nice change of pace."

Beast checks his watch and then appears to be lost in thought. Finally he hits the ignition and Truck starts up. When he looks at me again, he nods and pulls us out of the parking lot. I clap my hands with glee and whoop, and at that, he laughs.

Chapter Fifty-Five

Los Hermanos is more than just a restaurant. A proud sign proclaims that it is also a tortilla factory and lounge. The brown brick exterior has a shape that reminds me of buildings that I've seen in Old West movies, right down to the narrow overhang in the front of the establishment. The parking lot is almost bare, save a couple trucks that I bet run diesel as well.

I walk in with a big smile because for some reason it feels like home. The interior walls are lime green. Various decorations hang on the wall, many sporting a sun motif. There are a few mirrors in various shapes. Christmas lights hang from the edges of the ceiling, dropping down the walls and are actually working, though there are a few dark bulbs. Soft Mexican music plays over scratchy speakers hanging in the corners. I'm betting this is the local watering hole for the town.

An older Hispanic man approaches us with a broad smile. That, and his gray hair and beard remind me of my father, though he is a little portly. He still moves like old age has not caught up with him yet. Jeans and a checkered green shirt are his ensemble.

"Welcome," he says with open arms. "Please, take an open table anywhere."

I return his smile in kind. "Gracias."

Beast doesn't even have to tell me. I guide us to a booth in the corner where he can have his back to the wall. We sit down in old, dark green, vinyl seats, some of which have been repaired with fading silver duct tape. The table is worn but very clean.

Our host brings us menus. "I am Mayor Peralta. I'll be taking care of you today. What can I get you to drink?"

"A beer if it's cold," I reply.

Beast's reply is simple. "Water if it's purified."

"One beer and one water, coming right up."

We sit in silence, gazing at each other instead of the menus. Those blue eyes warm me. All I can think from his expression is that he's already decided what he wants. It's not food, and that he'll take me right here on the table. I'm so breathless at the erotic images that flash through my mind, that I'd probably say yes if he asked. We are interrupted when the Mayor drops our drinks off.

"I'll give you a few minutes to decide."

As the mayor walks off, I'm forced to tear my gaze away from Beast and look at the menu. It's pretty simple, with only eleven choices. They can only serve what they can grow, so it makes sense the choices would be limited.

I give a heavy sigh. "Do you have any idea how long it has been since I had Mexican food?"

"Probably a long time," he replies with a chuckle.

"A lifetime ago."

"Well, that was your old life."

I look at him, confused at the statement. "How do you mean?"

Setting the menu down, he gives me his undivided attention. "When something horrible happens to radically change you, the past becomes your old life and you are now living your new life."

"Is that another way to rationalize the shit that happens to you?"

"In a way. Profound pain changes people. Can you really say that you are the same woman you were before the Collapse?"

That's actually a question that's been on my mind a lot recently. I sometimes think about that Chloe and feel a little sad. Part of me still curses that woman for being so weak. Being so easily captured and then my life of repeated rape by Knick and his band of assholes.

"No," I finally reply in pained a whisper. "I was happy, carefree and enjoying life. Never harmed a fly, let alone another human being."

I get a tender, concerned smile from him. "And there you have it. Happy Birthday and welcome to your new life, and new you."

We clink glasses together and I can't help but giggle. Upon hearing me laugh, his smile brightens as well. Clearly our happiness has a positive effect on each other. Idly I wonder if that's the true definition of love; when someone's happiness is as important to you as your own? It's at that moment I have an epiphany. I already know I love this man, and the thought of spending my life with him, even in such a fucked up world, fills my heart with so much joy. It fills me and I smile brightly at him. How will I ever show him how much I adore him?

I sigh happily and lean forward seductively. "So, what's our next move?"

"Well," he leans in close and whispers conspiratorially. "After a late lunch, we get back on the road and get as far into the mountains as we can. There are a number of campgrounds we can park at. Hopefully they won't be in any kind of hostile territory. Especially since I'm in the mood to hear your singing voice again."

"Oh," I swoon, closing my eyes at his wonderful suggestion. "I would love to sing for you again."

I bite my lower lip and I get a low growl in response. Just that sound makes my insides clench and my heart skips a beat. Letting him have me right here on the table is beginning to sound better and better. I do wonder if the locals would mind too much.

Speaking of the locals, our seduction is interrupted by Mayor Peralta, who walks up to take our order. "So, are you ready to order?"

"I know what I want," I state while looking right into Beast's blue eyes. All he gives me is a sly smile while waiting for me to order. "I'll have the enchilada platter. And can we get some more water?"

"Si, seniorita. And you, sir?"

Beast never takes his eyes off of me. "I'll have the tacos. Hold the chilies and peppers."

"You got it," the Mayor replies with a smile I can't see. "How do you plan on paying?"

Beast is becoming annoyed as he is finally forced to tear his gaze from mine. "What do you need?"

"You got any seven-six-two by thirty-nine? My guards and I all have rifles that use it."

"We do," Beast replies with a nod. "How many?"

"Five each?"

"Deal."

I notice that Beast stands to shake hands one a bargain is reached. Very formal, old-school gentleman, and this is another new thing about him. We still have so much to learn about each other. Hell, in some ways, I still have a lot to learn about the new me.

"I'll be back with your food in a little bit," the Mayor states and walks off.

"Can't handle anything spicy, huh?" The opportunity to rib him cannot be avoided.

His wolfish smile sucks the air from my lungs. "My tongue is very sensitive, and better employed in more important ways, as you found out last night. You are all the spicy I need."

Involuntarily I shudder as I take in a deep breath. Fuck, just the thought of what he can do to me with that tongue damn near sets the booth on fire. Closing my eyes for a moment, I drag myself under control. When I open them again, his eyes tell me he's just won a fight.

Oh, this is so not over. Wait until you see what I can do with my tongue.

After gazing into each other's eyes for what feels like an eternity, I remember I wanted to ask him something. "Why do you shake hands when agreeing on a deal?"

"Honor," he states simply. "It's a way of saying that both sides will honor the deal. When you're shaking someone's hand, look into their eyes, and you will know if they are as honorable as you are. Speaking of, I should go get our payment. Be right back, my lady."

I watch him leave. Well, mostly I watch his ass as he leaves. Even while wearing black fatigues, it's still easy to see that he's got a nice butt. While he's gone, I start to formulate my plan for getting sweet revenge.

Chapter Fifty-Six

I practically lick my plate clean! The food is that damn good. Or maybe it's just the fact that I haven't had decent Mexican cuisine in such a long time. Clearly Beast agrees, for his plate is equally clear. I sit back against the booth and sigh, content and happy.

"That... was so good."

He smiles back at me. "Yes it was."

Mayor Peralta walks up and grins. "I would ask if you enjoyed your meal, but clean plates always say it best."

"It was delicious," I gush with praise.

"Good to hear. Now, as to the agreed upon payment?"

Pulling a handful of rifle bullets from his pocket, Beast hands them to the Mayor with a nod. Mr. Peralta takes them and they are quickly handed off to one of his guards who carries them off in a hurry. I get the feeling they were hard up for that kind of ammo.

"Thank you. If you don't mind me asking, where are you headed? Don't see many working vehicles these days."

I scoff. "Tell us about it. Took us a year to find parts and get out of L.A."

"Ouch! I've heard rumor it's worse than Phoenix."

"Avoided most of Phoenix," I state in agreement. "But what we did encounter leads me to agree. In fact, there is a bad gang in Phoenix, led by someone named Kane. He has a symbol, a 'K' he marks his territory with. Here let me show you." I take a pen and, on the back of a piece of paper I sketch out the graffiti and tattoo we'd seen. "If you see men with this tattoo on them, they are bad news."

The mayor nods seriously and takes the paper. He calls one of the waiter/guards to him and whispers to him for a moment before turning back to us.

"Thank you for the information. And I'm sorry to hear you've encountered problems. The world is in terrible shape, and full of bad people who think they deserve to take that which they did not earn."

I nod. "Truth."

"Where are you headed?"

"Colorado," Beast states in a monotone voice.

"Long drive," the Mayor replies. "Well, Globe is in good shape. We trade with them. I've been told that most tribal lands are friendly, so long as you are respectful."

Beast nods. "Understood."

"Is it safe to travel through the four corners?" There's probably a little too much excitement in my voice, but I don't care.

The Mayor shrugs slightly. "Don't go that far ourselves, but I haven't heard anything bad. Mostly tribal lands."

Our conversation has gone on too long, because I feel Beast's nerves bristling. This has officially become too much civilization for him. I wonder if that will ever change, or if this is simply who he is.

"We should get moving, my lady." He states after checking his watch.

I nod in agreement, and we both stand. Then I look at the Mayor. "Thank you for lunch. I haven't had anything that tasty since my abuelita used to cook for me."

"De nada, señiorita. Safe travels to you. And our cook thought you'd like to take some of the tortillas with you. No charge."

A tiny Hispanic woman shyly comes forward with a bag of warm tortillas. Crinkled brown skin is even more so as she smiles at me. Her silver gray hair is tied up in a bun, reminding me of my nana. I wonder if I remind her of a family member. Tears prick my eyes. Kindness is still alive, and I hug the small woman gratefully.

"Gracias, señora, gracias por su amabilidad." She shakes her head and retreats shyly, still smiling.

Flashing the Mayor a huge smile, I follow Beast out the door where Truck is still waiting diligently for us. Even better is that it does not look like anyone tried to mess with the vehicle. I like this town. Some of the people in it remind me of Walma or Moreno. Slow to trust, gruff but honest and honorable. As we get back onto the highway, I hope we can come back sometime.

We drive through the rest of the town and the road begins to rise as we near the last of the habitable area. Slowly we start our climb up the mountain, coming at last to a stop at a barricade right before we would enter a tunnel. The guards on duty give a wave and open the gate so that we can drive on through. Once we are through the tunnel, I have been thinking, so ask some questions while still keeping an eye out for anything dangerous.

"So, what's in Colorado?"

"Safe house."

"Can you be a little more vague?"

Beast laughs. "I have a bunker there, fully loaded."

Some days it seems like I take one step forward and two steps back with him. He probably thinks that was oodles of information. Unbuckling my seat belt, I shift over to the middle of the seat and put that seat belt on. Then I snuggle up against him in the hopes that will bring him out of his shell. When he sighs and puts an arm around me, I know it's working.

"Go on," I coax while watching the right side of the road.

237

"It's a multi-layer bunker called The Eagle. Twenty-four hundred square feet of complex divided up in six separate sections. Only the first section appears to be the bunker, while access to the other sections is by secret doors."

Taking a deep breath, he continues. "In total, the bunker has four individual living units, each with its own bathroom and living area. It has air filtration, water filtration, large community kitchen, over two years of food for up to twelve people. I added a seed bank and machine shop. It's also got solar power and even entertainment centers. Basically, the works."

"That much space?"

"It wasn't just for us. My wife's family and my own family pitched in to buy the land and build it."

"Do you think anyone else made it there?"

Beast shakes his head. "I don't know. A part of me hopes so."

I snuggle into him a little tighter. "I hope so, too. You've lost enough already."

"We all have, my lady. We all have."

Isn't that just the damned, ugly truth? As far as I know, all my family is dead. I lost all my friends. Beast is all I have in this God forsaken world gone mad. But at least I've had room service again. That thought makes me smile.

"We've only got a few hours of light," I remark after looking at my watch. "Any idea where we will stop?"

"Top of the world," he states with a grin.

I shoot him a disapproving glare. "Are you trying to be vague with me again?"

When he laughs, it makes me smile. "That's the name of the place. RV park and some houses. The Mayor didn't mention it, so there may not be anyone living there. If that's the case, it'll be a good place to park for the night."

"How do you know so much about this place?"

"Over time I traversed every route I marked on the maps. I know where everything is, within reason of course."

"Within reason?"

"Well, I can't keep up-to-date on everything. Businesses change, road construction happens, gangs move in after the Collapse. You know, the usual?"

It's my turn to laugh. "Point taken."

"I do love it when you laugh," he remarks while squeezing me to him a little tighter.

Looking up, I kiss his cheek. "Ditto."

Letting out a contented sigh, I continue snuggling with him as we drive down the highway. While I'm paying attention to my side of the road, I daydream of better days.

Chapter Fifty-Seven

Sitting in the passenger seat, I've got my knees up and the window open. The wind moves through my hair as I watch the terrain fly by. Driving through the mountains of Arizona has been a great experience. Tall green trees line the road, with forests as far as the eye can see. We've even found some thriving towns in the mountains, some more friendly than others.

Globe was the biggest, and the mine there was still pulling out small amounts of copper and lead—and guess what that is useful for? Like any other place, they also grew food for staying alive. While they were typically mistrustful, we were able to do some trading. This included a small amount of diesel which came close to filling up one of our half empty cans.

We spent five days there. In part it was to help the township with a bandit problem of their own. Of course Beast and I were more than happy to say yes. In return for taking care of the problem, we were given room and board, and some local made diesel. Fortunately Truck is a multi-fuel engine, so we shouldn't have issues.

Hunting a target through trees instead of a city took me some time to adjust to. You have to learn new ways to move quietly, adapt to new terrain and so forth. After a couple of days training, we moved out and took care of a group of raiders that had made their home in an old mine.

Removing the bandits took less than a day. Yeah, they weren't all that much of a problem for the likes of us. Beast even spotted their sniper before he saw us. In all, seven assholes dead and very little ammo expended in the effort.

The rest of the time was spent doing the other thing we do best—loving each other. While the days are filled with work; from taking care of Truck, reloading brass and helping the locals. Beast finds ways to drive me crazy with anticipation. When we finally turn in for the night, he worships me and I'm showered with ecstasy.

From there we made our way further into the mountains, passing a couple more small towns in between camping at night. Travel in the new world is nowhere near as easy as it used to be, though. There is no department of transportation looking after the roads anymore, so when a bridge is washed out, it's out permanently. We can't go tooling along down the road because we never know what will be around the next corner.

All the same, the few couple weeks have been wonderful. My Beast has finally opened up and every night is a new adventure in love making. Shit, the man is as insatiable as I am, and inventive, bless him. I've learned something interesting about older men: endurance, knowledge and skill.

Oh yeah, it's pretty great.

I look over to see that Beast is concentrating on driving. I still haven't seen him with his mask off. I don't know if I ever will, but I guess I don't really mind. He is who he is, with or without the mask. Besides, I figure we've had enough change for the moment. One step at a time. Shooting me a quick glance, he smiles.

God, I'd do anything for that smile!

"Just what are you on, my lady?"

"You, my lord."

A deep laugh issues from him. "It looks like you are addicted."

With a seductive smile, I crawl across the bench. Kissing him softly on the cheek, I then whisper hotly in his ear.

"Very."

Laughing once more, he steals a kiss from my lips. "My lady. Please put your seat belt back on."

Shaking my head, I slip back into the passenger seat and put my belt back on. He's still looking out for me, but at least now I know why. It's simple... he loves me. Now he wants to get us safely to Colorado, where he has promised me a surprise when we reach the bunker. The way he said it left me breathless with anticipation. I have no idea what it could be. I make wild guesses that make him laugh. Trapeze? Stripper pole? So far he hasn't given me any hints.

"We should hit Four Corners tomorrow," he tells me, shaking me out of my daydreams. "We'll find a place to camp for the night."

"We're so close, can't we just keep going?"

"No. Headlights would make us easier to spot and very easy for someone to hide."

He's right. The days have been getting shorter, and we don't want anyone who might be watching to see where we stop, another change from the old days. I laugh to myself when I remember how easy it used to be. Ah well.

"Fine, fine. You're right. Camping it is, with a night of love making under the stars. How I suffer for our love..."

"Oh please, there is no suffering involved."

"Well, I suffer until I finally get you in my bed again... Let's hurry."

"I really do like the way you think."

"You should," I reply with a grin. "Wait till you see what I have in store for you this evening."

Eyes glittering, he smiles wickedly. "Oh really? Maybe I'll have a treat for you. I do have more than one pair of handcuffs."

Holy fuck, that sounds hot!

My heart skips a beat, my mouth going dry as I finally respond in fake shock. "My lord! So kinky. I didn't realize you liked that."

"You would be surprised what I like, my lady. But mostly what I like, is making you sing—loudly."

I stretch out against the seat, purring at the thought. "We are definitely going to have to explore that."

As we continue down the road, we both laugh while I pull out a map and start looking for places where we can stop for the night.

Now I stand at the Four Corners monument, walking on the concrete platform that shows the corner of the four states and the point at where they all touch. I've never been to this spot, and neither has Beast. It's actually a little bit off our planned route, but I really wanted to see it and I've learned that my dear Beast has a hard time saying "no" to me. Isn't that adorable? He makes me so happy.

In all honesty, I try not to abuse that. Beast has quickly come to mean everything to me. How could he not? He's saved me in more ways than one. By rescuing me from Knick and the Crazy
Eight, certainly, but also by teaching me how to survive in this totally fucked up world. While he had to be tough on me, he was still respectful as well. Unlike other men, he has never taken advantage of me. While the reasons became obvious over time, it doesn't detract from the fact that he has always treated me right. But that's not why I am in love with him, that's just why I'm grateful to him.

Love is something so much deeper, and I love him for who he is, not just for how he's treated me, how he's respected me. I love him for the depth of his heart, the joy in his laugh, the danger in his eyes. I love him for all the things that make him uniquely him. I like to think I would have fallen for him in any other place and time as well, and I feel like the luckiest woman left on this messed up planet.

With a smile I gaze at my man. Standing a few steps behind me, looking all over the place, vigilant as usual. At first his expression is impassive, typical for him when watching for hostile targets. When he looks at me though, he softens and smiles. Well, that's progress. He's still trying to be a hard ass all the time, but I'm overjoyed to see him connect with me on a deeper level now.

While the sex has been great, I've found we are a match mentally as well. Among other things, he really does know French. Like me, he is a bit rusty though. I figure we will have years to practice on each other.

He walks a few steps away, inspecting the dirt between the monument and Truck. As I watch him contentedly, I realize something is wrong.

"Qu'Est-ce que c'est?"

Beast looks at me, and I think he's trying to formulate the words in French. Finally he gives up while shaking his head.

"Maybe nothing. Maybe I'm being overly cautious, but it seems to me these tracks and wheel marks are fresh."

"We did encounter those helpful natives not far back. Maybe it's just locals?"

It took us longer to get here than first anticipated. The tribes we ran into were difficult at first, and then Beast surprised them. In his bug out bag he still had his identification, which included his Native American identification. That changed their attitudes at once and we were welcomed, spending a few days with the tribe.

Finally he gives me a nod. "Hmm. Probably."

"You worry too much," I rib him with a smile.

"I have an angel at my side. I do not wish to see anything bad happen to her any more. So, yes, I do."

His statement is made without a hint of humor or guile. Such seriousness warms my heart and I bend down, bringing my lips to his in a soft, passionate kiss. When we separate, I give him a smile.

"You sir, are a romantic."

"This is true, my lady. Now get back in the truck before I decide to take you here on the monument."

Oh really? Can we do that?

I stand there, thinking about his delicious threat. It really is hard to decide if I should get back into Truck, or waste daylight with a session of wild, passionate, outdoor sex. As he stands up, my heart starts to race.

"Well?" He's looking amused.

"Hold on," I reply with a grin. "I'm trying to decide which the better choice is. I mean, making love in four states at once is quite the temptation. Certainly that's a first most people have never enjoyed."

In all actuality, I've already made up my mind. Such a lovely offer cannot be turned down. I know just how to goad him into action as well. Deliberately, I bite my bottom lip while gazing at him playfully. Beast growls at me and smacks my ass.

"Truck, wench," he says in a low, sexy voice. "Now."

Laughing at him, I scamper backwards toward the vehicle. "Wench!?"

The next growl that he gives me is long and low and makes my insides tighten in that wonderfully delicious way. As he stalks towards me like a wild animal, my breathing is start to run ragged. *Fuck, I love how he makes me feel.*

"It's really hot when you growl at me," I warn him playfully while slowly backing up. "The monument is sounding better and better."

Beast continues stalking me until I back up against the railing. Pressing his body up against mine, he runs his nose up my neck as he inhales my scent. Mouth close to my ear, he growls again and now I'm breathless.

I gaze into his blue eyes. My voice full of desire. "Ravage me, my beast."

"As you wish."

In a matter of seconds it seems, I am divested of all my clothes. Strong hands grip my ass and he lifts me up so that I'm sitting on the railing. While I know what he's going to do next, my heart is still hammering in my ears as I lick my lips in anticipation. With one flick of his tongue, I'm practically gone in a world of pure ecstasy.

Oh fuck!

The animal is out of its cage and ready to play as he goes to work on my body. All I can do is cry out as he does exactly what I asked him to. My hands fist into his hair as I hold on for dear life while screaming his name as I come.

I've barely recovered from my first climax and am panting for more when he slams into me with a roar. Surrendering to him completely, I wrap my limbs around his body and hang on for dear life as the monument disappears and he takes me straight to heaven.

Chapter Fifty-Eight

Right here, right now, I am nothing but blissfully happy. It's amazing how quickly things can turn around in your life. I have everything. A partner who cares for me and has my back. We have enough food, water and fuel to make it to our destination. Hell, I even have tampons.

We're heading up Highway 491, closing in on our destination. Beast has told me all he can about where we are going. He's shown me the exact location on the map and that the number on the map is the door code for getting into the bunker. Additionally, he's explained that it's camouflaged and told me how to find it. He's even given me code words should we meet some of his family. At the speed we are traveling, he figures we should be there tomorrow.

When the truck starts to slow, I pay attention to the road ahead. Indian casino. More importantly, a travel center. Might have some useful supplies. With the way the world is now, you can never have enough. Clearly Beast agrees, bringing Truck to a stop and parking across the highway.

"Grab your guns, and let's go shopping," he tells me seriously.

I smile at him. "Mmmmmm, I love shopping. And these days, I've got the best credit card."

Pulling out a crowbar, I show it to him. Beast lets loose with a low, deep laugh before getting out of the vehicle. I slip on my tactical vest and then grab the dual P-90 rig instead of getting the Tavor. Since we're going into a building, the ninety's will be a better choice in close quarters. Of course, fifty rounds per magazine doesn't hurt either.

Once Beast is ready, we move out across the highway, staying low. So far we haven't seen any signs of life, but we haven't gotten this far by being stupid. Beast once told me to always assume that you are walking into an ambush. Never let your guard down and have a plan to kill everyone you meet. The more flexible you are, the greater your chances of surviving a deadly encounter.

As we cross onto the grounds for the travel center, there is still no sign of movement. The place appears to be completely deserted. In some ways that doesn't surprise me. Looking at the map, we are damn near in the middle of nowhere. Cortez is probably at least ten to twenty miles further north and there is nothing else.

Closing in on the travel center, I get a strange, itchy feeling that something is wrong. It's so quiet that our soft footfalls on the dirt strewn asphalt sound like breaking glass. The feeling that I'm being watched creeps into my gut, but I sure as hell don't see anyone as we finally reach the entry way. I glance at Beast and he has a look of concerned wariness as well. Good. We are in agreement then. Something's hinky.

The doors are safety glass and most of them are cracked or shattered. One large pane lies on the floor, a wrecked mess. Some of the glass crunches under our boots as we sweep into the storefront, looking for hostiles.

I'm surprised to see that there are clothes hanging on racks and items still sitting on the various shelves laid out across the floor space. It seems so untouched I almost expect to see customers come walking in at any moment. A hint of movement catches my eye and I focus on a man coming at the far entrance, weapon in hand.

"Tango," I yell, right before adjusting my aim and firing.

The P-90 bucks in my grasp as I keep it held tightly to me. The trio of rounds rip through the safety glass and splatter my target. And that's when all hell breaks loose. A hail of bullets zip around us as we quickly make our way to the cashier's desk in the center of the floor. We both take hits to our trauma plates as we move, making us stumble.

Fuck! Where are these guys coming from?

There are at least two dozen bandits, all gunning for us as they melt out of the woodwork. Bullets rip through the air, through clothes and shelving as we trade fire at each other. Wood, glass and other debris fly like shrapnel through the gun smoke haze as I take down two more targets.

For the first time in a long time, I'm really, truly frightened. Not as much for me, but for Beast. I can hardly think. I so do not want anything to happen to him. Summoning up all the anger I can, I push the fear away and keep cycling my weapon until it clicks.

"Reloading!"

I drop down behind the counter and switch magazines, then rack the action to load the first round. Rising back up, I start shooting again, ignoring the two rounds that hit my vest and the one that grazes my right arm. When I catch sight of the weasel-looking man I thought I'd killed in Phoenix, Kane's man, limping in and firing a pistol, I abruptly understand what's happening.

Fuck you, asshole! Fuck ME for leaving you alive. An oversight I intend to rectify now...

Resting my red-dot sight on him, I pull the trigger. All three rounds rip through him, center mass, and blood splatters against the wall behind him. My mind races as I try to figure out how we are going to get out of this mess, wondering how the fuck these guys found us, let alone traveled so far to hunt us down. The only people who knew we were going to Colorado were the people in Globe. I spot another one of Kane's raiders, this one wearing a green checked shirt, exactly like the Mayor of Globe had. Exactly.

I let out a shriek and send the fucker to hell.

Suddenly, I feel something wet splash against the back of my head right before Beast slams into my back. His hand grabs my vest and drags me down into cover as we both collapse onto the floor and the shooting stops. Heart filled with dread, I turn to look at him. In despair, I see that a bullet has ripped right through his neck.

Frantically I'm trying to stop the bleeding. "No, no, no! Don't you die on me!"

Fuck, there's so much blood.

Beast coughs, some blood spitting up. "It's… okay. You… saved me. I… save… you. Fair trade."

"But I can't go on without you," I cry, shaking my head furiously.

"Have… to," he tells me through gritted teeth. "Don't… let them… take you. Go on… for me."

I choke back a sob, tears falling down my cheeks as he caresses my face softly. Even dying, he's thinking of me and I can't stop the tears. I cup his hand in mine and return the gesture with my other hand as an ever widening pool of blood forms under him.

"Tu es… tres belle... mon ange," he whispers harshly.

Reaching further up, he slips his hand into my hair and pulls me to him, bringing my lips to his in one last, fiery passionate kiss that assuages my pain temporarily. I feel the sweet pain as his hand fists into my hair until he breathes his very last breath into my lungs. Then his hand slackens and falls way.

When I look into his eyes, he's gone. I raise my head to the heavens and scream in a combination of rage and pain at the death of my love. Then I break down and lay my face into his chest and sob.

A voice, sick and twisted, calls out. "Awwww, did you lose your boyfriend, little girl? Not to worry. My name's Kane, honey, and I'll be your lover now. Until I tire of having you in my harem, of course."

I hear a number of other men snigger as a fiery rage starts to build in my chest. It was in this moment I realized how easy it was for my Beast to shed his humanity, to embrace that primal side. It's simple, really. This man was the one true love of my life, and he's been callously ripped away by these assholes. Now is the time to get some killing done! It's time for them to learn that for every cause there is an effect.

What happens next is a blur. With a roar, I come up out of cover with both P-90's in hand and spin. Both guns blaze away and I briefly recognize a few shocked faces right before they are replaced with a spray of red mist. Some don't even have their weapons up. They thought I was defeated, that I was broken, that they had won. They were wrong! And now they are paying in pain, in blood, with their lives.

As both guns run dry, I catch sight of their leader hiding behind the shelves in the food and drink area. He's the only asshole left alive. The slide is back on his pistol, telling me he's dry. Dropping the guns, I pull Beast's short sword from its sheath and stalk my prey.

I hear his gasping breaths, brought on by a combination of fear and exertion. The sound of him trying to insert a fresh mag into his pistol is obvious. The hunter has become the hunted, and like most bullies, he has no stomach for a real fight. He fumbles it, drops the mag, picks it up and tries again. I smile wickedly as I move up in a low crouch, getting close to the corner.

The bastard has no clue he's already dead. He finally swings around, gun raised toward were I was. That's when I spring the trap. From my low crouch, I thrust up and the sword rips into his gut, blood gushing out and spilling everywhere as he cries out in pain, the pistol falling from his hand. Looking down, he sees the woman who delivers his death this day.

Big hands wrap around my throat. "Fucking bitch!"

"That's Ms. Bitch to you, asshole."

I twist the blade and he lets go of my throat and shrieks in agony. It's the sweetest music to ever grace my ears. With all the strength I can muster, I jerk the blade up and into his heart before ripping it out. He falls to the ground, eyes wide in horror and very dead.

Chapter Fifty-Nine

When I come to my senses, I realize there are a large number of dead bodies littering the floor of the bullet-ridden travel center. Slowly, with a growing sense of horrified sorrow and dread, I stumble back to where Beast fell.

The sight of him there, so much smaller somehow with his life gone, the tears that haven't really stopped, renew their vigor. I fall, uncaring, to the hard tile floor heedless of the pain in my body, and cry into his chest once more.

I lose time. I don't know how long I sob into his lifeless body, hopeless and broken, but it's dark when I finally come back to myself. I feel drained of everything, a walking corpse of a woman, but I can't bear to see him like this. I need to get him away from the ugliness of this evil place.

With Herculean effort, I struggle to drag his body out from behind the counter, past the majority of dead. I heave and strain, yelling in frustration as I only manage a few feet before collapsing. He's just too heavy and there are too many obstacles. I am too weak, tired, and brokenhearted to go on.

Dropping to my knees, I cradle his head in my lap and cry once more. I consider eating a bullet, and lying here with him for the rest of eternity. I have the pistol in my mouth when I recall he died wanting me to go on, to live.

"WHY???" I shriek in despair. "Why must I go on without you, my love? I can't. I can't do it. I can't do it without you." I weep in desolation, but there are no tears left, only pain.

So here I am, dead bodies all around me, only one of which matters. I have tried, but he is simply too large and heavy for me to drag out through this fucking obstacle course. Something inside is telling me to go on, for him.

Spying a large Native American rug, I cover him with it to give him some of the respect he has shown to me. Some of the symbols remind me of the tattoos on his arms and chest, and it feels right somehow. Catching my breath, I bend down and kiss my Beast softly one last time. His cold lips do not respond and I know I cannot stay, but I hate to leave. I feel torn in half.

Grabbing my guns, his sword and sobbing uncontrollably, I stagger out of the building, not really paying attention. If someone shot me right now, I wouldn't care. In fact, I might just welcome it. Apparently, I'm too good at my job, as no one greets me when I exit the building into the faint light of dawn. Lurching across the highway, still only half-conscious of what I am doing, I unlock Truck, dump everything in and then? I simply drive away.

I vaguely remember drinking some water, remembering his lips were the last to touch this vessel and have to pull over to have another crying jag. I long to just go back and lie down beside my mate, but he told me to go on, so go on I will.

I'm so numb inside that the road becomes a blur as I drive through miles of countryside, deserted towns and mountain passes. When day turns to night, I still don't stop. Turning on the headlights, I continue on without a single thought to my safety until I finally become too tired to continue.

Now I sit in front of a campfire, in a somewhat secluded campsite. Not that I really care anymore. With Beast gone, I just don't know what to do. I gaze down at the pistol in my hand and yet again it looks like the answer to all my pain and grief. I don't think I will resist this time.

I'm startled when a familiar arm settles around my shoulders. I look up to see Beast, concern etched plainly of his face. I can't find any words and just bury my face into his chest and start crying. While holding me tightly to him, he runs and hand through my hair and croons softly.

"Hey, it's all right," he murmurs softly.

Anger spikes in me and I disagree. Loudly. "No! It's NOT alright. You're dead!"

"Well, yeah," he replies with a slight smile. "Still, not the end of the world. Besides, you need to go on. Don't make my sacrifice a poor one. Go on for me—for us. Live a happy life. Don't become a wrecked and bitter shell like I was."

That makes me cry even harder. Here he is, dead, and he's still thinking of me. How am I supposed to go on without this amazingly beautiful soul? How can he expect me to be happy when I will never find his like again? His shoes are far too big to fill.

"It's so hard," I finally choke out. "I couldn't even carry your body out."

"That's all right. I don't need it anymore."

I choke back a laugh and thump him on the chest. "That's not funny."

"No, it's not. But it is true."

Two fingers lift my chin up, bringing my eyes to his. Those amazingly blue eyes that I loved to get lost in. Softly he brushes my tears from my cheek with the back of his hand.

"You need to promise me you'll go on. That you'll be happy at some point. We had our time."

"It wasn't enough!"

"It never is, beautiful. But what time we had was glorious, and I'm thankful for it. You should be too."

I just don't know what to say in return. His words make me both happy and tortured, all at the same time. Part of me is still far too numb with grief to be able to provide a rebuttal. I just nod silently while sniffling.

"That's my girl," he states proudly. "Leave in the morning and head straight for the bunker. Don't stop. Winter is coming, but at least there you will be safe and warm."

I nod somberly. "All right."

"Do good things, my lady. Make me proud."

His voice is a whisper right before his lips touch mine. In desperation, I crush my body into his. Holding him tightly, I hope beyond hope that somehow, some way, I can cheat Death and keep Beast here with me as our kiss deepens.

And then I wake with a gasp and search frantically for him, only to find that he's not there. Unbearable pain lances through me as I break into sobs once more. It takes me a few minutes to regain my composure. The sun is close to poking up over the horizon as a new day begins, while smoke curls up from the spent fire. Off in the distance there is a storm brewing.

Somehow I force myself to move and pack my gear, tossing it into Truck so I can move out. Winter is coming, I need to get moving. I step up and rest my weary head against the truck door. When my hot breath washes over the window, I catch a hint of a pattern, of writing on the glass. Taking a deep breath, my exhale washes onto the window and what I see makes my heart stop.

"I love you, my precious Chloe. Do good things, my lady."

Choking back a sob, I damn near collapse onto the seat as tears water my eyes. My Beast was here, I know he was. With that thought, a surge of strength washes over me and I shakily smile at the window.

"I love you too, my Beast," I say aloud, hoping that he can hear me. "I will make you proud, I promise."

Starting up Truck, I pull out of the campsite and get back on the road. Checking the map, I think that I should be able to make the bunker long before evening. With grim determination, I pay attention to the road as I drive through the Colorado mountains toward my destination.

Hours go by, and it's probably a good thing that I don't encounter anyone on my way to the bunker. While I'm a little stronger, there's a still a hole in my chest that saps my will to live. A few bullets ping off Truck's armor as I finally drive through the town of Gunnison and keep heading north, but I'm in no mood to play.

The bunker is situated a good three to four hundred meters west of Route 135, between Gunnison and Crested Butte. Hidden in a stand of trees, it takes me some time to find a path that I can navigate. Thank God that Truck is four wheel drive. The ground is muddy and soft and it takes effort to pick my way through the trees. Once I do, I quickly go to work tossing a camouflaged tarp over the vehicle and anchoring it as a cold wind

251

is kicking up. I backtrack to the road to make sure the tire tracks are not too obvious, and do what I can to erase the marks of my presence here.

To the southeast ominous, dark clouds loom over the mountains not far away. While I'm no expert, I think I might have an hour, possibly two before that nasty looking storm hits. Quickly I search for the concealed entrance, trying to remember his instructions through a cloud of grief. A little further to the west, I hear the music of the river that runs past the bunker area.

Finally, after at least an hour of searching, I find it! Lifting up a dirt covered slab of plywood, I find a steel door recessed in the ground. I tap in the code and I hear a lock click open. With a grunt, I lift the hatch up and head down the shadowy stairwell with my pistol at the ready.

Chapter Sixty

The short flight of stairs leads to another door, once again with a keypad. A small red light blazes underneath it. He didn't tell me about a second keypad. What if the code is different? Tapping in the code again, I'm relieved when the light turns green and the lock clicks open. As soon as I open the door, LED lights flicker on to reveal a living room, bedroom combination bunker and I already I feel a little warmer.

The wind is kicking up, telling me I don't have a lot of time before the storm arrives. I'd rather not deal with the rain, hail or snow that is coming. Running back up the stairs, I start grabbing the gear from Truck and hauling it down into the bunker. It all gets dropped into a pile on the floor. I can sort it later. I'm almost done when snowflakes start failing in the biting wind. My fingers are numb despite the exercise, and my cheeks wind-burned.

With everything unloaded, I lock up Truck and pat it softly on the hood. "You stay safe, okay? Keep my message from Beast protected for me."

Running down the stairs, I close the outer hatch and lock it. Then I enter the bunker and close that door as well. Safe in the steel and concrete confines of my new home, I relax and start to take a look around.

The first "layer" of the bunker is designed to make someone think that it's all there is. It has everything you'd expect. A small living room, beds. kitchen, bathroom, storage, and even its own generator and air pump. It takes me a while to discover the two shelving units that hide security doors leading deeper in.

"Hello," I call out as I walk in. "Is anyone here?"

I'm hoping that some of his family actually made it here. I'd like to know more about the man who saved me and ensnared my heart. So far no one calls back and everything seems untouched, unlived in.

As I explore, I discover the bunker is four complete homes. Each has its own, independent facilities, though they all rely on the one kitchen; a huge family kitchen for feeding everyone at once. I feel very small and alone in this huge space with only me inside it, and that intensifies my grief.

The last home in the back makes me lose my resolve as I walk into the master bedroom, complete with a king sized bed, adorned with dark red. satin sheets. This was the surprise he had in store for me. I laugh for a moment, thinking about how he would have smiled as he led me in here, that wicked, lustful smile I love.

Then I drop to my knees at the foot of the bed and break into heavy sobs, wishing that Beast was here with me. The pain is too much. It's hard to breathe. Collapsing into a fetal position, safe in the home Beast thought to take me to, to protect me and care for me. I let go of my stoicism and cry and cry. Part of me still wants to die so that this unbearable pain can end.

But in my heart, I know he's with his lost wife and daughter, and I will never be with him again. The bitter taste of jealousy is not one I like and it is not like me, but I wasn't through with him. I still need him, and he's gone, and I'm alone. After a long time, my exhaustion takes over, darkness descends, and I fall asleep.

I wake with a start, my mind in a fog as I look around, trying to remember where I am. The slide of satin under my cheek reminds me. The bunker, right. Only one of the lights is on, providing just enough illumination for me to see by. As soon as I stand up, they all come on and my eyes blink furiously to adjust. My eyes ache anyway from the hours of tears and there is a lump in my throat that will not go away. A lance of pain rips through me when I look at the king sized bed. Tearing my gaze away, I flee the room and explore some more in an effort to make myself busy.

The next three weeks, I fall into a routine of cry, sleep, barely eat, cry, sleep, and so on. Each night I'm plagued with bad dreams, usually Beast dying in my arms and I wake up screaming. I tried venturing out one day only to find the entrance packed with snow. The muffled sound of a howling wind told me winter was raging, so I crept back inside.

I find ways to keep myself busy. In that three weeks I've taken a complete inventory of everything. I've got almost all the weapons stowed in the bunker's armory; save a shotgun, SKS and two handguns. I keep those in the first bunker so I have them easily on-hand. But also to help with the illusion that the forward section is the only section. I also keep the Beretta 93 on me at all times.

I've discovered books tucked away everywhere. Some are survival-type manuals, but others are novels, classics and such. There's also a surprising number of torrid romance paperbacks. Inside the cover of each of those is the name "Katherine" or "Miss Katherine Barry." I don't know how, but I am sure these once belonged to Beast's mother. It warms me to hold something that once belonged to his family, and I love that she liked romance novels.

I also found a cache of children's books. Many of those books had "Katie" scrawled inside, and I had to wonder if they belonged to Beast's daughter, or his mother's. It makes me sad, and I put them away.

What I have really wanted, of course, is just one surviving photo of my Beast. I search for days and find no photographs at all. It is disheartening, but I eventually force myself to let go of that obsession. I have to steel myself with the realization that I will never be granted the privilege of seeing his face. Of course, the notion sets me off again and that is a very bad day.

Most days, when I've exhausted the chores I've given myself for that day, I sit in the security room and numbly watch the monitors. I will Beast to come walking through the door. Of course he doesn't, and once again I cry myself to sleep, but not on the satin sheets. I've put those in the closet. I can't bear to sleep on them anymore.

Into week five, I wake up one morning and dash to the bathroom, barely making it before I throw up into the toilet. It's nothing but bile and I have to fight back the dry heaves. Once I'm done, I rock back while on my knees and take a deep, shaking breath.

What the fuck was that?

If I had the flu, I'd be coughing or something, right? Did I eat something bad? But then an idea hits me and a feeling of dread rushes through my veins.

Scrambling to my feet, I run to the infirmary and pillage the drawers. I know I saw some pregnancy test kits when I did my inventory. Third drawer down, I find one and then rush to the nearest bathroom. Sitting down, I pee carefully onto the stick and then watch it intently. Minus means no, plus means yes. I get a big pink plus. Fuck me.

Actually, that's what got you into this mess, Chloe.

I hang my head in despair. And then I laugh hysterically. A baby is wonderful! A baby with Beast is amazing, incredible, fantastic, a miracle! But he left me. And all of the sudden I want to hate him for doing this to me. Not for knocking me up, no, but for leaving me alone, God, *us* alone, without him to help guide and watch over us.

FUCK!

Launching myself off the toilet, I run into the bedroom, snatching the keys off the night stand. Then I grab a winter coat from the closet and my rifle before rushing to the front door. I need something to keep me going, and I don't care how cold it is outside.

With some effort, I'm able to push the hatch up with all the snow that was on top of it. I pop out of the hole with the Tavor at the ready. The land is covered in white, and the cold air is brisk, even in the afternoon. Naked trees stand like silent guardians all about me. I don't see anyone as I glass over the area with my scope. Truck looks like one big hill of snow.

Instead of trying to brush the snow off and remove the tarp, I work my way under instead. Unlocking poor Truck, I squeeze into the driver's side and sit down. I really should turn the poor boy over. It's so cold I don't know if he will. Slipping the key into the ignition, I click it over just enough to get power and start the warming process.

While that happens, I look at the driver's side window and breathe my hot breath across it. The letters appear like they were just drawn today and my eyes get wet. Wiping the tears away, I read it again.

"I love you, my precious Chloe. Do good things, my lady."

"I'm trying," I choke out through irregular sobs. "But Beast, I'm pregnant. I know, I know, I wasn't expecting this either, but I am. And I'm not mad at you, exactly... Aw hell, I am mad at you for leaving me in this state with no one to help me get through this."

And then I'm lost again, crying fiercely as the tears just don't want to stop falling. Why I'm talking to him is beyond me, he's not here. He'll never be here.

It takes a long time to compose myself again. Finally, I am able to try to start Truck up. I'm rewarded by his throaty growl and smile. I pat the dashboard like he's my trusty steed, pleased that he's working.

"Good boy."

After letting him run for a few minutes, I shut him down and then slip back out and look around. I still don't see anyone across the stark, white landscape. Certainly doesn't seem like there is anyone remotely nearby, which is the point, I guess. Locking Truck up, I sigh and head back inside the bunker and lock everything up for the night. I don't know what I thought I was going to do outside, but I feel like I'm finally coming out of my funk.

That evening I make myself eat a decent meal as I plan out what I'm going to do. Making an excursion to Gunnison seems like a good idea. Someone was shooting at me, so perhaps it's time to find out who. Mentally making a note of what all I will need, slowly the Angel of Death tries to come back to life.

Chapter Sixty-One

My Beast did not screw around when it came to preparing for survival. While I thought he had a good selection of guns when I met him, it is nothing compared to the armory at the bunker. I could outfit a small army.

More than three dozen handguns, three dozen assault rifles, a dozen bolt action rifles, eight shotguns and six sniper rifles. That was before I added what he had in Truck to the list. On top of that are scores of magazines and at least ten thousand rounds of each caliber. As if that isn't enough, I found some explosives. Low grade stuff called Tannerite. To top it all off like a cherry on top of the entire armory sundae is a station for reloading. That means I can make my own ammo, reusing my brass. There's even books on how to do that, and supplies.

Then there is all the knowledge. Between all four houses, are stacks and shelves of books on every subject pertinent to survival. Even the seed bank has books about farming, the various types of crops planned and how to rotate them. I have found school books for every age, history, engineering, so many things I would never have thought of, including libraries on military training—all kinds of training.

After much deliberation, I load up with the SVD and attach his oil filter suppressor. I don't know how long it will work, but I haven't trained enough with anything else. Then I decide on the P-90s and my Beretta for backup. Instead of my combat knife, I take Beast's short sword. I need to feel like he's with me, still fighting at my side. Don't mock. It's what's working right now.

Fortunately, he also took Colorado winters into consideration. I found a few sets of full, military surplus arctic wear, including a snow camo ghillie suit. I pile all of this into Truck, along with two days of MREs and water. I leave for Gunnison while I still have daylight.

I spend some time worrying about hiding my back trail. How to do this in the nice clean snow field eludes me, so I make do by traveling parallel to the road for a while before leaving the area. It's not a perfect idea, but at least it's not a straight line to my shelter. Besides, I figure the blowing wind will do much to hide what tracks I do leave.

Truck is anything but quiet, so I pull off the road a good couple of miles before the outskirts of town and hide my monstrous steed in amongst some trees and low hills. By the time I get him hidden, it's almost sundown. Posting up at the crest of a hill, I glass over the town, looking for any signs of human habitation.

I've almost lost the good light when I spot movement. I focus and find a guard walking a patrol on a roof. The building appears to be a hospital and is at least a thousand meters from my position. So far I haven't seen anyone else though. If they are bandits, they might be all that's left in Gunnison, so they're concentrated in one location. I need to get in closer and see what they're up to.

Snow is thick on the streets and brush, weeds and grasses have started taking the town back. I've noticed in my travels that Mother Nature is exceedingly good at that. The nice thing is that all the snow and overgrowth will make my insertion easier. With a grim smile, I slip down the hill and work my way around and into the town.

Many of the buildings are in poor shape. Some have collapsed roofs from too much snow, while others look wrecked by other means. I am almost caught when I hear a door open and dive behind a snow-covered hedge. I hear the voices of two men, voices indistinct. Then I hear a cough, and a rattle of metal. Easing my way through the hedge, I get a glimpse of who is making the noise. The two men are leading four hooded and chained young women—two of them are practically girls—woefully underdressed for the weather. The men are laughing in an all-too-familiar lecherous way as the door closes behind them. I set my teeth and continue cautiously through the snow.

Moving slowly and carefully, I pick my way through the snowy town to a better, more protected view of hospital. I'm maybe a hundred meters away when I post up inside the remains of an old, single-story apartment building in the shape of a "C." Part of the corner of the wall is missing, giving me good line of sight.

Remembering what Beast taught me, I find a good spot of darkness and set up behind an old couch. Focusing on the hospital, I note fires burning in steel drums placed near one entrance. Two men are standing guard, if it can be called that. They seem quite relaxed standing there, trying to stay warm while they shoot the shit. Slowly I lay the rifle over the back of the ruined couch and take aim, waiting for the right moment.

Being a good sniper requires the patience of a saint.

Beast's words come back to me and I practically hear his voice. I force myself to push those memories away and focus. I can't have a breakdown right here, right now. I have a job to do and a promise to keep. If I have a meltdown and am noticed, I won't be safe as my Beast wanted me to be. We won't be safe, I remind myself, and tell my pea-sized baby I will take good care of her. Dropping the scope's crosshairs on my first volunteer, I wait for the perfect shot.

That opportunity comes when one of them turns and walks away after having some sort of a disagreement. They now have their backs to each other, each at a separate barrel. With a smile, I aim—and fire.

Perfection is the definition of my shot. Thanks to the subsonic rounds that were at the bunker, the rifle report sounds like a BB gun. The bullet strikes the man right in the skull and his brains splatter against the wall. I've got time to aim on the second target because he's cold and slow to react. My second bullet hits center mass and I think it's a heart shot, because he drops and doesn't move. I give myself an internal *squee*. Beast would be proud of me. But I'm working. *Focus.*

Looking to the roof, I search for the guard up top to see if he has been alerted in any way. I don't catch sight of him anywhere near my edge, so it looks like I'm clear. Now I wait.

At least ten minutes pass before he finally shows up near the edge and starts walking along. Taking aim, I wait for a good shot. I'm not even remotely skilled at shooting a moving target, so I hope he'll stop. Something catches his attention and he halts, looking across the roof at something I can't see.

Maybe a bird or something?

I don't take time to ask why, aim right for his chest and fire. The rifle bucks against me as he goes down in a dark spray of blood. Then I wait and strain to hear any hint of an alarm. Nothing. All is quiet. I realize that I am holding my breath and exhale.

Shedding my ghillie suit and pack, I leave the SVD hidden under the couch. It's just too big a weapon for inside a building. I ready my P-90s and then move towards the entrance quietly, looking for any sign of hostiles.

Once I make it to the door, I check the two and make sure they're dead. One man has a hunting shotgun, the other a revolver. The pistol goes to the small of my back after I check to make sure the cylinder is loaded. The dead men don't have any extra ammo. That means they might be running low. If true, that might make them hesitate to waste ammo against a lone woman. I like my odds. When I slip into the building, the Angel of Death firmly takes hold.

The sound of a woman's scream and crying becomes evident once I get inside. I'm immediately spotted by a couple men lounging in what was once the waiting room, which appears to have been turned into raider central. They are up and moving for their weapons when I gun them down, sending their souls straight to Hell.

My stealth is ruined when one of the men gets a shot off. *Fuck!* I slip into the deepest, darkest shadow I can find and wait for whoever shows up. One thing is for sure, the screaming stops. It's replaced by a man, shouting angrily.

"What the fuck is going on?"

Sounds like he's somewhere on the second floor, in the same direction as the screams. All in due time. Right now I focus on the men piling out from various locations and converging on my latest two kills.

I am absolutely stunned by the level of their stupidity. Seven men run up and start staring at the two dead bodies, all clumped together. They aren't looking around like they should be, providing cover, nothing. Instead they seem to think these two killed each other in a fight.

Are you fucking kidding me?

Okay then, if you insist. Taking aim, I switch to semi-auto and open fire. I cycle the weapon as fast as I can, and all seven men go down in a cacophony of yells and screams. As I gun them down, I can't help but laugh as they drop.

Idiots!

Quickly and quietly, I move up the stairs. Stopping briefly, I take a moment to swap a fresh mag in as I get close to the landing for the second floor. I don't know how many more assholes there are, and having to change mags during a firefight is a moment in which you can easily be killed.

The smell in here is awful, nauseating. A mingled stench of body odor along with human waste. Worse, it makes me want to throw up, and now is most certainly not the time for that. I fight it back, taking in a deep breath before finally continuing.

"I said, what's going on!?"

I'm betting that's their leader shouting his fool head off. He's just as stupid as the rest of his crew. God, suddenly I find myself missing the University Raiders. I've been reduced to hunting morons, and there really isn't much sport in that. Oh well. Bad guys are bad guys. Shaking my head, I move up to the door where the shouting came from.

As I post up at the door, I have to fight back memories of Beast. I don't have him to watch my back and help sweep a room. I'm all alone on this one and need to be more on my game than ever before. The trauma plate may protect my chest, but a bullet to the head will still kill me. I steel myself, quit procrastinating, and burst through the door.

Chapter Sixty-Two

Moving through the door, I find myself in an office that probably belonged to a doctor or administrator in its former life. Someone important, since it is a spacious room and has an expensive desk in the center. On one side of the fancy desk is a mattress, one edge against the wall. A bunch of candles burn in the room, providing the only illumination and casting lots of dark shadows.

A rough-looking man stands behind the desk, holding a pistol to the head of a naked woman. It's hard to make his age, not that I give a fuck. He's a little portly and has a balding head that does not hold much hair left on it.

Oh god. Tell me that's not a comb over?

The woman is blonde, and I imagine she looks about what I looked like when Beast saved me. Hair is stringy and greasy, framing a face that's too thin. She might once have had a nicely filled-out body, but it's clear they barely feed her. The scene is so familiar that rage starts to build in my chest.

"Who the fuck are you?"

I level a cold, hard stare at him. While I want to put a bullet in his head instead of talking to him, part of me hesitates. For the second time in my life I am stuck in a hostage situation. In the last one, the woman held at gunpoint almost got killed.

"I'm your death," I spit venomously. "Drop your gun, and I might let you live. Otherwise, I will kill you."

There is fear in his eyes, but it doesn't last long before he summons up some fool's courage. Pressing the gun against her head, he nods toward her, reminding me that he has a hostage, and therefore the advantage.

"Try and kill me and she dies! Put your weapon down."

Fuck!

Perhaps I can get him to let his guard down. I really don't want to put her life at risk if it can be helped. Holding one hand out, I slowly lower my weapon and show him the other hand. I can't stand the smug smile he gives me.

"Good girl. Debbie, quiet her down some."

I realize too late that I've walked right into a fucking trap. In the shadows under the desk, I just pick out the twin barrels of a shotgun right before a bright flash lights up the entire room.

The impact of the shot hits my chest. Between that and shock, I feel like I'm lifted off my feet. In reality, I just stagger back and hit the railing which drives the air from my lungs. Slumping down onto the floor, I wince in pain while trying to breathe. My vest caught the bulk of the blast, but my left arm stings something fierce.

When I lift my head, I see Debbie climb out from under the desk with a crude, sawed-off shotgun. Both the gang leader and that bitch are laughing as the slave is thrown callously to the floor. The two are confident. They think they've neutralized me. Probably don't realize that I'm wearing armor. The blonde locks eyes with me and I see the fear in hers, a hopeless fear I know all too well.

"Good shot, Debbie!"

"Thank you, baby." Debbie is cracking open the shotgun and reloading. "A chest full of rock salt should keep her down for a good ten minutes."

I hear Beast's voice in my head. *Ignore the pain. Otherwise you'll end up back where I found you. Is that what you want?*

They kiss and that's my time to move. Pushing through the pain, I draw my Beretta 93 and take a quick aim. It's already set to burst fire, and I grit my teeth as I force my left arm up and flip down the forward grip. The fire flaring up in my arm brings tears to my eyes as I pull the trigger.

Three, then six, then nine, then twelve rounds rip through Debbie and her beau. They scream in outrage and agony as the bullets hammer them backwards, blood splattering against the wall until they hit it themselves. Both have utterly shocked expressions as they slide to a heap on the floor, dead or dying.

Taking a deep breath, I rest my head against the railing and try to control the pain. The blonde slave scrambles up to me, eyes now full of concern instead of fear. Already she's looking me over and checking my wounds.

"Are you okay?"

I nod slowly. "Yeah. Vest stopped most of it. Is there anyone else I need to worry about?"

She scampers to the railing and looks over, taking count. "There's three missing."

"Oh good," I say with a smile. "That means I got them all. By the way, my name is Chloe."

She pauses for a moment as if she's forgotten social norms. Finally, haltingly, she says, "I'm Liz."

"Good to meet you, Liz."

With a groan, I push myself up off the floor and my new friend helps me. Once I'm back onto my feet, I holster my pistol and raise my P-90 back up. Just in case. Then I look at Liz with the same kind of seriousness that Beast showed me.

"Liz, we need to move. If they have any clothes in there, get dressed. You've got five minutes."

Hard to tell if she's scared of me or just in shock. Could be a little of both. As I wait for her, I try to remember what emotions I was going through when Beast rescued me. Feels like a lifetime ago and I finally give up when Liz comes out of the office with a wide mix of men's and women's clothes.

"I'm ready."

Inspecting her, I then shake my head. "No you're not. Go get their weapons. Make sure to grab any ammo they have."

Nodding almost frantically, Liz runs back in and isn't long before coming back out. It's almost comical as she tries to juggle a shotgun, a pistol, five shells and two magazines. Letting go of my weapon, I take the sawed-off from her and the shells, setting them on the floor. Then I take the pistol mags and put one in each pocket of her baggy pants.

"Have you ever used a gun before?"

"N-not really."

Liz is looking a little green. Could be from the sight of blood, then again it could be adrenaline wearing off from the emotional roller-coaster ride she's just been on. Still, if she's going to be sick, now's the time.

"If you need to throw up, please do it over the railing."

Eyes go wide, and I imagine she is wondering if I can read her mind. I want to laugh, but I hold it back. That would be a little rude, and I think this poor woman has already been through enough right now.

"No, I think..." And she runs to the railing and throws up.

I hold her hair out of the way until she is finally done. When she stands up and catches her breath, I hand her my canteen. I get a grateful nod and smile and I'm impressed when she pours the water into her mouth without letting it touch her lips. She rinses and spits a few times, then swallows some water gratefully and hands it back.

"Thank you," she exclaims with an exhale.

"You're welcome." Putting my canteen away, I continue. "This is a handgun. Semi-auto. Every time you pull the trigger, the slide kicks back and loads the next round. This is your number one safety." I point at my trigger finger. "You don't put your finger on the trigger until you are ready to shoot. Understood?"

"Yes ma'am."

"Good," I reply. "You slide the magazine in like this, pull the slide back and let it go. You are now ready to shoot. When you are empty, the slide locks back. You push this button, take the empty magazine out and put a fresh one in. Then push this lever with your thumb and the slide will kick forward and you're ready to shoot again. Got it?"

"Um. Y-yes ma'am."

The lounge and office is starting to stink, but I survive it long enough to find a bag that I can stuff the gear of the dead gang members into. Just because I have a bunker full of supplies doesn't mean I leave anything useful behind.

"Now, you have to lead me to where the others are being kept."

Liz nods, gulps, and skitters from dark shadow to dark shadow all along the hall, until we get to a room with an old-fashioned padlock on it. She looks worried, and tells me the key is on the body of one of the dead men in the lobby. I shake my head and pull out the crowbar.

Once the lock is removed, we sort out the others—a woman and her four teenage daughters. In the end, we leave them to their own devices. They don't want much to do with me, but I share some of the weapons and ammo I took from their tormentors. While they thank me, they make it clear they have a home to return to in town. In turn, I make it clear that I am no threat to them, and, in fact, want to keep this area safe and free of bandits. I suggest I might eventually be in a position to trade food and services one day.

The woman, Patricia, nods slowly in agreement. "We have food we didn't tell those bastards about. We've only been kept here for a few days. I think my boy got away, so we need to go find out."

I give her a nod. She squares her shoulders, looks me in the eye, and tries a tentative smile. "Thank you, Chloe. But we'll be fine. You keep in touch, you hear?"

Giving them one more nod, I let them go their own way. Then I turn to Liz. "All right. We're going to move out. You follow me and do exactly what I do. Don't shoot unless I tell you to."

Liz nods, squaring her shoulders with a light of determination in her eyes. We move out, heading back towards the entrance. As we walk carefully, my mind is spinning with questions I don't know the answers to.

Chapter Sixty-Three

Now here I am; bruised, battered, but with someone that needs to get to safety. What am I supposed to do? I don't really want to take her to the bunker, but I don't have anywhere else to go. I feel cornered, and I don't like the feeling. I recall the way Beast reacted when he found me and I demanded to be taken with him. I sigh and pass a hand over my mouth. Guilt seeps into the cracks and I sigh again. Damn it.

"Liz, where did you live before these people captured you?"

We are standing in the entry to the hospital, watching the sun begin to light the sky. It is a clear morning, though cold. I don't relish going out there. She doesn't speak at first. There's a haunted stare at the question, and I squeeze her shoulder lightly to encourage her.

"I, I moved here from Santa Fe right before the Collapse. I got a job as a bartender. It's easy work, you know?" I nod and she goes on. "Anyway, the owner had apartments above it, said I could live up there free if I worked for just tips, and it seemed like a really good deal."

We've started walking now, and I lead her toward the old apartments because I want to get the stuff I left behind, under the couch. So far the area is deathly quiet, almost too quiet. My paranoia steps up a notch as my new companion continues.

"It's actually right down the street from here." Liz laughs bitterly. "Bastard was a voyeur. He had cameras hidden in all the rooms, and he recorded it all. Bathroom, shower, changing clothes, taking someone home, all of it. Son of a bitch made money on all the waitresses and bartenders by not only having us work for free, but by selling the recordings online. A bunch of us were going to sue him, we'd talked to an attorney in town. Of course, that's about the time the economy collapsed. God, it was awful. I mean, we worked for tips. We didn't have a lot. All of us pooled our resources and had enough food to last maybe a week."

Liz begins crying. "We had to, you know, do whatever we could to get food. It wasn't pretty. And when we decided to get out, try to find a way on our own, well, you saw what happened next. I was the only one left out of the original five girls."

By now we've reached the building I've been leading us to, and I stop, giving her a brief hug. She clings to me and I hope I'm helping and not hurting by making her talk about this. She wipes her tears and smiles tremulously.

"Shit, that's the most I've talked to anyone in over a year. I didn't know I how much I needed a sympathetic ear." Tears spring into her eyes again and she dashes them away angrily. "Sorry, I can't seem to stop crying."

"Honey, I've been there, honest-to-god, I have. And it gets better, I promise."

Looking around, I tuck her into a corner of the building and tell her to wait for a moment while I go get my stuff. She huddles there and nods tightly. I am back quickly and she looks so relieved, I think she's going to cry.

"Do you have anything at your old apartment you want?"

Liz looks surprised and her face turns thoughtful. "Maybe. Can we... ?"

Giving her a reassuring nod, she leads the way back down the street, past the hospital again, and toward the center of town. Snow has piled up in ways that would never have been allowed in the old world. We manage to slog through it toward the main drag and find the building.

The entire walk, she's silent. So am I, but that's because I'm focused. I've got the SVD in hand and looking for hostiles as she leads me. I find myself increasingly uncomfortable moving in the daylight. There are no shadows to hide in, the way Beast taught me.

Liz stops when the destination comes into sight and just stares for a long moment. Then she turns back to me, terror and panic written on her face.

"I can't."

"It's okay. You don't have to. Take a breath, relax."

The only reply I get is a frantic nod.

Slinging the rifle, I have hold of both of her shoulders and she is trembling. "Does someone still live here? Is that the problem?"

"No, no. It's... I can't explain it. If I go back, I feel like it's going to suck me back in, you know?"

"In that case, we are definitely going up there." Her eyes widen at my words and she begins to back away as I continue. "You are not going to be trapped up there. You have the power now."

I point at the pistol, forgotten at her belt. "Come on. You can do this."

At the thought, her eyes well up and she freezes, unable to move further. I feel for her. She's gone through some of what I did. But difficult or not, she needs to face her demons.

Turning from her, I start walking toward the building. Liz lets out a squeak behind me that I can only interpret as panic. She doesn't want me to leave her behind, but does she want to stick with me enough to go face her old life? I finally hear her steps in the snow quickly catching up to me.

"Don't leave me," she gasps. "Please."

"I'm not leaving you, Liz, but this is something that you should do." I stop for a moment. "Look, I'm not going to force you. But will you trust me?"

Wide eyes are pinned to mine, and she finally nods, terrified. I start forward again and this time she is beside me. Progress.

The building is run-down. I can see why it has been abandoned. It looks like water has seeped in downstairs, but the stairway to the upper level seems sturdy enough. Liz looks like she really doesn't want to do this, but glances at me and then follows me up the stairs. There are windows at each end of the dusty hall, motes dancing in the silence.

"Which one was yours?" I whisper out of habit.

Liz silently points to the door with the number four hanging on it at a crazy angle. We walk toward it, and I can practically feel her terror, so I reach out and take her hand. She clutches it, and I'm glad I made the effort.

It's not locked. I reach out and take the knob in my hand and turn it. P90 at the ready. The door creaks as it swings open, and more dust swirls in the morning sun. Liz lets out a breath as she peeks into the room.

It is a very small studio apartment with a tiny bathroom and a kitchenette with a hot-plate, a microwave and a mini-fridge. The bed is a single, with messed up sheets. There is a tiny table attached to the wall with only two chairs. Liz lets go of my hand and takes a step inside.

"It's just the same. Just the way I left it." She whispers and then spins to look at me. "What was I so afraid of?"

Without waiting for an answer, she walks across the room and opens a built-in drawer inside the small closet. Pulling out some clothing, she digs deep, then squeals as she pulls out an unopened box of tampons. She holds it to her like a treasure and I swear, more tears are spilling from her eyes.

Of course I laugh. "Those things are worth their weight in gold."

She laughs too, "Right! You have no idea."

"Yes, I do. I almost died fighting a raider over a box."

We both laugh, and she digs some more and finds another box. This time I squeal. Then I remember my delicate condition and the smile fades.

"What? What's wrong?" Liz's smile is gone now too.

"Nothing, I'm fine. It's okay. Thank god you thought to hide a few boxes."

"There might be more. The other girls and me all hid things we didn't want to run out of, but it didn't matter much to them. When they got pregnant, well..."

"Yeah, that's... that's just what those assholes do." We share a seriously pissed off look.

"Anyway, my clothes, I want my clothes, not this stuff."

She goes to take off the scavenged clothing she's wearing, but then pauses, looking up at me. It doesn't matter at that moment that we are both women, that I've seen her naked, that I rescued her. She needs privacy.

So I tell her I am going to go search the other rooms for supplies while she changes, and her relief, though quickly hidden, is palpable. All told, we have a good load of non-perishable items to take back to the bunker.

267

Yes, I've finally decided I need to take her home. It's not like that, I swear. She needs a place to be safe, and the bunker is that place. Before we leave town, I make a few stops at other places, notably a pharmacy. I'm hoping to find some prenatal vitamins and iron tablets.

To my surprise, I find all I can manage in this trip. I wanted to see if I could find diapers, too, but I imagine they were among the first things to go, back when everything was going wrong. I do find someone's old cloth diapers in a laundromat, for which I am eternally grateful. We snag one of the rolling laundry carts to help us carry all of our goodies back to where I parked Truck.

My new friend hasn't questioned anything I'm doing. It's like she's relieved to just follow, even though I could be living in a van down by the river. All the same, when we reach Truck, she sighs with relief as I unlock the doors. I pull a tarp out of the back seat and trundle the laundry-cart to the back of the truck. Wrapping the tarp around the cart, I tie it tightly with a rope I pull from the back of the truck. Dropping the tailgate, Liz helps me tip the cart on its side and push it into the back.

Once that is done, I dust off my hands and turn to Liz. "I'm going to take you to my home. I don't have anyone else right now, and I'm going to need a hand in the near future, and it looks like you're it."

I know she noticed the kinds of items I had been picking up while we scavenged. It doesn't take a rocket scientist to realize what my condition is and why I'll need help.

Liz nods and appears happy, which kind of surprises me. Of course, when Beast rescued me, well, I didn't know what kind of man he really was. I was still afraid. It is different with Liz, I rationalize, because I am another woman. Still, she had been held captive by a man and a woman. How can she just trust me so blindly? It kind of bothers me, but I push the thought out. I don't have a choice anyway. I am going to need help soon enough.

We climb into truck and Liz is quite happy ensconced in the passenger seat, warming up with the heater on full blast. Again, I am struck by how easily she has accepted whatever I want her to do. It is a relief, but also, a little aggravating. But she is nice enough, and seems to be pretty good company. Even though my heart is aching for my Beast, I try to feel happy about it.

Chapter Sixty-Four

It's slow work going getting Liz up to speed, and I'm struggling to keep my patience as my pregnancy progresses. Bless her heart, though. Throughout my berating, yelling and cursing, she continues to learn and get better. I sometimes wonder if Beast's silence was better. He might have had a point. At least he didn't yell at me.

On the other hand, she doesn't seem to have the same zeal to learn that I did. I have to convince her to stick with it sometimes. She simply does not have that dark drive to kill those who hurt her. She seems mostly content that the bad men are dead, regardless of the tales I tell of bad men everywhere. It's my insistence that keeps her learning, not any real desire of hers. And one thing I've learned is that she really wants to please me. It's sweet, and I'll take it because I need a partner and she's all I've got right now.

My first trimester is filled with nausea in the mornings, and ravenous hunger the rest of the time. I develop an extreme dislike to bacon, ham, anything smoked or cured. It makes me sick, and I crave anything with salt in it. What I wouldn't give for a bag of onion and sour cream potato chips. You have no idea.

My second trimester begins a few weeks after I rescued Liz, and is actually kind of awesome! I have new energy, and feel kind of unstoppable. It's fine except for the emotional roller coaster I seem to go through over every little thing.

It is impossible to understand what it's like to be pregnant until it happens to you. For a woman of action like me, it's… well, let's say it's complicated. My center of gravity is shifting, and it makes me feel clumsy. I am still fit, but my growing belly becomes an obstacle to most activities. And though Beast thought of so many things, turns out maternity clothing is not one of them. I can't even wear a tactical vest. Running has morphed into a kind of jogging waddle. I am still light on my feet, but laugh and I will kill you.

Through it all, I'm kind of thankful that Liz is here. I don't know that I could have ever gotten through the pregnancy by myself. Fortunately, she had a sister she helped through hers, and that experience has come in handy. I found a few books on pregnancy, labor and delivery in Beast's library. Those have helped as well.

Once I am well into the third trimester, it is more difficult for me to go out on excursions. I have to pee every ten minutes anyway, so there I am, stuck padding around the bunker like a trapped animal. To make matters worse, my nightmares have returned with a vengeance.

Maybe it's the hormones, but the nightmares that had slowly become less frequent came back just as bad, if not worse than they ever were. Most times it is Beast being killed and dying in my arms. Every time I wake up screaming and crying, torn in two with grief and loss.

Liz had been sleeping in the same bed, at first because of her own fears, but then mostly to help look after me. She consoles me when I wake up from a bad dream. I do the same for her, and I know exactly what she dreams because, thanks to a fucked up world, PTSD is commonplace.

I'm into the eighth month of my pregnancy (I think), and busily putting together a nursery, when my water breaks. I stand there staring as the puddle soaks my slippers, and I don't recognize the quavering voice that calls for Liz. The contractions start hard and fierce and never let up. I know I am supposed to breathe and let my body do the work, but I am a fighter, god damn it! It's hard to stop and relax when my body feels like it's trying to pull itself apart.

I'm walking as much as I can, as the books say, to help progress the labor. After four hours, I get a sudden, intense urge to, well, not to be indelicate, but to poop. I tell Liz, because we both know this is the final stage and the baby is coming. Not an hour later, I am holding my tiny daughter, and I can't believe this perfect little being belongs to me.

I name her Leona Katherine, after both my mother and Beast's. It seemed fitting, and I hope that wherever he is he knows and it gives him some solace. I also hope that she has a better future than Beast's other daughter had.

I had contemplated naming her Katherine after Beast's other daughter and his mother, but that didn't feel quite right. Then I remembered my own mother's name, Leona, and it just sang out to my soul. I knew my daughter would need the strength of the strong women before her. And a warmth and lovely vision of a blue-eyed lion being caressed by a goddess-like figure convinces me I'm either crazy or onto something.

My daughter's eyes are so blue, I see my Beast looking back at me whenever I look at her. Leah—we've taken to calling her Leah for short— fusses, and looks at me so querulously. I am grateful Liz knows something about breastfeeding, too, because formula is going to be impossible.

"I guess at this point I'm rambling a little, huh?"

Liz scratches my back lightly, smiling warmly at me. "Of course not. I'm glad you finally told me. It goes a long way towards explaining why you never really open up. I'm so sorry for what you've been through."

"We've all been through the wringer," I state sadly.

"But because of Beast, that's why you've never been interested in any relationship since?"

"Pretty much. My Beast was my whole life, and the pain of him dying killed that life. Now I have Leona and a new life with the two of you."

Of course, I know what she's getting at. I fear Liz has idolized me too much. I see the way she looks at me and if I could, I would love her back, she's a good woman. But the affection I feel for her cannot even begin to touch the depth of my love for my Beast. I hope that I can find happiness, though, so I try not to count anything out.

I just can't be entirely truthful with Liz. Don't get me wrong, she's become something of a rock for me, just as I have for her. I can't hurt her, telling her my feelings for him are still so alive. Hopelessly sure, but never gone. Memories of Beast and our brief time together haven't lessened. He's still in my dreams, and never far from my thoughts. No matter what I've tried to do, I can't forget him. Hell, I sleep in his bed, miss him every night, and every now and then I touch the satin sheets I hid away, sadly wishing he was still with me.

I care about her, but I haven't told Liz I love her. I can't. Though I do feel love for her, I am not in love with her. I know she would take it the way she wants to take it, and that would be a lie. Yet, I feel I hurt her by not loving her the way she wants me to. All I can do is simply try to be happy, and hope that love will come, for her sake if not for mine.

Besides, I just can't bring myself to think about being with another man. Any man who seems interested or even looks at me suggestively, gives me an unhappy, nauseated feeling. Clearly Beast was the only exception. And Liz is no different. Our shared moment has thrust us together.

Gazing at Liz, she smiles sadly at me. I think deep down she knows, but doesn't want to admit it. Hope is all she has, *I* am all she has, and I really hate to push her away for no good reason. I made a promise to be happy, and in some ways Liz does make me happy. At the very least, she helps me live.

"Honestly, Liz, I am as happy as I can be. I have you, Leah, this wonderful shelter." I continue softly. "I know it's not the same, it never can be, but he wanted me to be happy. So I'm going to try as hard as I can. All I know is, our relationship is good, better than many I've seen in the old world. So no more worries, okay?"

"Do you think that will ever change?"

There's worry in that question. I can't answer her because I don't know. So I caress her face before giving her a passionate kiss. It takes both our breath away until we finally come back up for air. Now she's happy again, more at ease and I smile. Making someone else happy is almost as good as being happy oneself.

"There isn't any other man that can live up to his standard. I don't think there ever will be. He was one in a million."

"You're such a hopeless romantic."

"Hell yes," I exclaim. "And there's nothing hopeless about it. Romance and love are two of the most important parts of being human."

Liz laughs and I take the moment to give her a playful smack on the ass. Oh, the look of excitement that shows up in her eyes when I do that. There is a little ache in my heart, wishing for a moment to hear that growl of his, and I smile wickedly to cover my grief.

"C'mon. Let's get in some private time," I smile lasciviously. "Besides, we need to burn off the stress of that last excursion before Leah wakes up from her nap."

Liz laughs at me. "So much for romantic."

"You know you love it."

The compound has grown in the months I've been here. We now control everything from a mile south of the bunker, all the way to Crested Butte. We've even been able to get a couple of the lifts to work and set up lookouts at the top of the mountain. We have eyes watching for trouble 24/7, and some of those eyes are mothers and fathers. That makes me much more comfortable leaving my daughter with a babysitter occasionally.

There are twenty-nine people living at the compound area, and another fifteen in the town of Crested Butte. Thanks to all the books I have, we've started setting up a number of fortifications and defensive walls. We have built homes from what materials we have or have been able to scavenge. We've also found some RVs and prefab homes and moved them into the area.

I don't let many into the bunker, except as an emergency measure. I use it as a command center, and I admit I feel a little jealous of it, keeping this part of Beast for myself. I try to be more open, but I don't think I've healed enough yet.

Thanks to a large amount of good glass and Plexiglas we've able to scavenge, we also have a number of sunken greenhouses, allowing us to grow some things almost all year round. We also have livestock, and having chickens means we are able to have an omelets for breakfast whenever we want.

I may have lost my Beast, but he is still with me in more ways than one. Leah is growing so damn fast. She's such a beautiful child and brings me so much joy. More importantly, she has her father's eyes, and somehow that takes some of my pain away. I just hope he's somewhere watching over us. I hope he's happy and at peace. God knows he deserves it.

Epilogue

Eight months earlier.

An almost unnatural silence hangs over the Ute Mountain Travel Center as the sun is high in the sky. Birds stop chirping. The song of the crickets ends abruptly. Even the breeze dies down to the point where there's hardly any air movement.

From the shadows of a broken wall, a lizard darts out and along the broken asphalt. Stopping, it looks around, as if trying to figure out why everything has calmed.

The sound of footsteps crunching on gravel and debris shatters the silence like breaking glass. The lizard darts back to safety as a woman heads for the entrance.

Dressed in a fine white gown of gossamer fabric, she strides confidently toward the building, almost as if she were gliding. A lack of sleeves displays muscular arms with tanned, brown skin. Clasping her slim waist is a silver belt studded with lapis lazuli. The only weapon is a dagger hanging from her belt, with a gleaming copper hilt.

Running ahead of her are two huge lions, easily the size of ponies. Entering the building, they leap from body to body, sniffing at each of them in turn. Once they find the bandit is dead, they move on to the next as they escort the woman through the entrance.

A large number of dead, decomposing bodies still litter the store. Flies buzz, scavenger animals flee or hide at the presence of the two large predators. The combination of blood, dead bodies and human waste has created a sickening fog, redolent of death. Yet it doesn't seem to affect the woman at all.

With slow and deliberate care, she walks around dead bodies. At each one she stops and regards them for a minute or so before moving on to the next. A pattern forms as she moves in a rough outward circle that spirals in towards the center of the store where The Beast still lays dead.

As the woman approaches the body at the center of the chaos, the Native-American rug lifts from atop of Beast and floats away. The woman frowns slightly as she bends down and gives his peaceful face a soft caress. With her touch, the wound on his neck disappears, becoming a faded white scar. Bending down, she brings her rose colored lips to his ear and whispers something in a long-dead language. Then she pulls back and smiles.

"Come back to me, Beast. I yet have need of your rage in this world."

All at once, The Beast draws in a deep, shuddering breath, as if he'd been underwater for too long. His back arches off the floor and he convulses, hands reaching out and grasping at the air. Gritting his teeth, he rasps as if in unimaginable pain. The woman kneels there, waiting patiently until he finally relaxes and his eyes snap open.

I sit up with a gasp, wanting to cry myself as Leah's wail wrenches me into reality. With a groan, I start to climb out of the bed to check on my daughter. But I can't get this last dream out of my mind. I am shaken and alert, terrified and grieving all over again. I replay the dream in my mind as I go to Leah and let her grip my finger with her angry hand.

What was that? It seemed so real.

"Shhhhh," I croon softly. "It's okay. Mommy's here, sweet girl."

I pick up my daughter, cradle her in my arms, and rock her gently. She stops crying almost instantly. When I smile at her, she smiles brightly back and her twinkling eyes make me think of him. A bittersweet pain lingers in my chest, in that void that's been there since I lost him. An empty space I don't think will ever be filled.

Leah starts crying again, pulling me into the here and now, and I sing softly to calm her. I hear Liz come up behind me and lean in as she rubs my back lightly while looking at my baby. We smile at each other as my daughter calms.

"She okay?"

"I think so," I whisper.

"Awwww," Liz speaks softly. "Look at her. She's falling back to sleep already."

Rocking Leona lovingly, I step towards the crib that Liz and I scavenged from an old mattress store. Laying my beautiful daughter down gently on the bed, I keep contact by patting her back. She fidgets a little but quickly settles into sleep. Carefully, Liz and I sneak back to bed and lie down.

Before I know it, my blonde-haired beauty is snuggling into the crook of my arm, her head on my chest. Kissing the top of her head lightly, I stare up at the ceiling and can't stop thinking about that dream. After a while, I finally fall back to sleep, wishing for the impossible to happen.